# THE
# CHILD'S
# ELEPHANT

www.**davidficklingbooks**.co.uk

# THE
# CHILD'S
# ELEPHANT

## Rachel Campbell~Johnston

David Fickling Books

THE CHILD'S ELEPHANT
A DAVID FICKLING BOOK 978 0 857 56076 6

Published in Great Britain by David Fickling Books,
a division of Random House Children's Publishers UK
A Random House Group Company

This edition published 2013

1 3 5 7 9 10 8 6 4 2

The Random House Group Limited supports the Forest Stewardship Council®
(FSC®), the leading international forest-certification organisation. Our books carrying
the FSC label are printed on FSC®-certified paper. FSC is the only forest-certification
scheme supported by the leading environmental organisations, including Greenpeace.
Our paper procurement policy can be found at www.randomhouse.co.uk/environment.

Set in New Baskerville 12/15pt

DAVID FICKLING BOOKS
31 Beaumont Street, Oxford, OX1 2NP

www.**randomhousechildrens**.co.uk
www.**totallyrandombooks**.co.uk
www.**randomhouse**.co.uk

Addresses for companies within The Random House Group Limited can be found at:
www.randomhouse.co.uk/offices.htm

THE RANDOM HOUSE GROUP Limited Reg. No. 954009

A CIP catalogue record for this book is available from the British Library.

Printed and bound in Great Britain by Clays Ltd, St Ives plc

*For Katya, and in memory of Bob Foulerton*

PART ONE

## CHAPTER ONE

The sound of the rifle shot rang through the air. For a few moments it seemed as if the whole world had stopped. The cicadas fell silent, a bush rat dived for its burrow, the cattle paused in their chewing and looked upwards with wide empty stares; and Bat, the lone herd-boy who up till then had been dreaming, swishing at bushes with a long whippy branch, let the switch fall and dropped suddenly down on his haunches. His head was quite hidden by the tall, yellow grass.

He felt the slow, rolling shudder through the soles of his feet. It rumbled his bones like the beat of the big tribal drum. Something that mattered had just happened out there on the savannah. He could feel it: something momentous that he didn't want to know about and yet knew at the same time he would have to find out. But not now, he thought, as he ducked even lower in the grasses. He let his breath leak through fingers clamped hard to his mouth. A lizard clung spellbound to a stalk right beside him. He gazed into the rapt gold-ringed bead of its eye. It stared back, unblinking, as if it had been stunned.

It seemed like for ever before the last fading echoes were finally quieted, before the waiting cicadas picked up their old song and the lizard, as if some bewitchment had suddenly been broken, darted off with a whisk of its skinny brown tail. In the shade of the thorn trees, the cattle returned to their grazing. They pulled at the grasses with long, curling tongues. But Bat, still as a sandgrouse that keeps low in its cover, hugged his arms round his knees and stayed down where he was.

He listened. Somewhere not so very far away he could hear people talking. The sound drifted like wood-smoke upon a slack wind: murmuring voices . . . then a clatter of laughter . . . the silence that followed it . . . then a sudden angry shout . . . then nothing again . . . then the bark of an order. The air carried the fragments in faint tattered snippets. They sent flurries of nerves stirring across his bare flesh.

Who was it? He could feel his pulse racing. His heart jumped in his throat. Every shift of the breeze could have been someone approaching; every glint of the light could have been a stranger's glance. Was someone even now stealing up upon him? Unable to bear the uncertainty, he rose to his feet.

Nothing looked very different. The cattle were peaceable; a new calf was suckling; the scrublands that stretched all about him looked quite undisturbed. It was funny how hiding played tricks with your imagination. He shouldn't have allowed himself to get so scared, he thought. He was seven after all: far too old to be behaving like some panicky chicken.

Ducking his head low, Bat set off through the grasses. Their tall, feathered fronds brushed as high as his chest. His eyes darted warily as he slipped through the thorn bushes. When the branch of one snagged him he didn't cry out. He just paused for a moment and watched the blood trickling. It dried almost immediately in the afternoon heat.

After a while, he began to see traces; he started noticing places where the scrub had been squashed. Branches were broken and bushes were flattened. He slowed up his pace as he crested a ridge. The down-slope was stony. He would have to be careful not to trip. Flitting between boulders, half running, half scrambling, he arrived at a river-bed that had all but run dry. A basking snake slipped from a smooth sun-baked stone. Bat skirted the spot and it was then, in a patch of damp sand where the last buried moisture still lingered, that he spotted the footprint which brought him suddenly up short. It was huge! His heart thumped. It was truly gigantic, he thought, as big as the biggest circle that he could have made if stretching out both arms as wide as he was able he had then brought them round and tried to brush fingertips.

Bat swallowed. He'd already come too far . . . far further than he'd first meant to . . . much further than anyone would have told him was safe. He cast a quick backwards glance. He could no longer see his cattle. The dry riverbed glittered and flashed in the heat. On the far bank was a thicket. Something had crashed straight through it. A bush was splattered with red. Perhaps it was a hibiscus, the boy found himself hoping; but he didn't need to look a second time to know that it was not: it was blood.

He scuttled for the cover of some rocks ahead. Beyond, he could now see a vast shadowy shape. From where he was crouching, it loomed high as a mountain. It blocked out the horizon. It blocked out, for a moment, all the thoughts in his head. But then, with a jolt, the full truth broke upon him. This mountainous form was a dead elephant.

Hands pressed to the rock face, Bat struggled to steady his breathing. His heart was racing so hard it was outrunning his head. Who? How? Why?

A figure emerged from beyond the great carcass. Bat swallowed the cry that almost burst from his lips. It was a man . . . a bare-chested man . . . with dark skin. . . so dark that it shone almost purple . . . and he was tall, Bat noticed, particularly tall . . . he must have stood as high as a stem of grown maize. And now he was moving. Bat could no longer see him. Was he coming closer? Dropping down even lower, the boy peeped through another gap.

There were two other people, both standing a little further off. A rifle was slung round the back of the nearest; the other was supporting what Bat realised with a shudder could only have been an elephant's tusk.

Poachers! These were poachers! The boy turned dizzy with fright.

4

He had to get away! But how? He glanced frantically about. The dark man was squatting. Bat scarcely dared breathe as he watched him. He was fiddling with something on the ground at his feet; but when he glanced up, eyes scanning the horizon, Bat saw for the first time the tribal scars that branded him. They ran straight across his brow: three lines like a frown cut deep into his forehead. Bat flinched from the menace embedded in that face.

Wiping his palms on a pair of dusty green trousers, the man half rose and, putting one booted foot forward, gave a sudden hard tug. A chainsaw snarled into life. For a second it snatched all the silence from the air. Then it sputtered and stopped. There was a moment of stunned hush. The man cursed. His cry rang round the stones of the dried riverbed.

Terrified, Bat tried to squeeze himself in even tighter underneath the boulder. He reached up for a hand-hold. A loose stone was dislodged. It rolled down the slope with a sudden loud clatter.

'Stop! What's that?'

'What?'

'That sound.'

'Nothing.'

'Yes, it was something. There's someone there . . . someone watching.'

The speaker grabbed at the rifle slung over his shoulder. The man propping the elephant tusk jumped quickly aside. His load slipped from its shoulder and hit the ground with a thud. A swarm of flies rose in a cloud of black buzzing. They bumped about like the thoughts that dashed round in Bat's head.

'Leave it. It's nothing.' The command grated like metal.

But the man with the gun remained unconvinced. Raising his rifle, he began to move outwards. He was heading directly to where the boy was now crouching.

'I heard someone.'

'Who?'

'Could be a ranger.'

'What are the chances of a ranger being here?'

Bat's heart thumped so wildly he was sure they would hear it. Through a chink in the rocks he saw a blood-spattered face. Every step brought it closer. He listened to the slow crunch of boots.

Should he run now, he wondered? Should he make a dash? He glanced at the riverbank down which he had stumbled. There was no way he would make it. He tried to pretend he was stone. A fly crawled over his lips. He didn't so much as twitch: if he did he was dead.

The footsteps came nearer. A shadow slipped past the rock. The man was so close, Bat could smell his sour sweat. Somewhere in the bush a francolin was singing. It's clacketing call was so very familiar . . . and this would be the very last time that he ever heard it, the boy thought.

'Who's that?'

The man with the rifle swivelled. A vehicle was approaching. A sudden silence fell as the poachers all strained to see.

'I told you we'd come too far!' Bat heard one of them

crying. 'We're too close to the village. Anyone could have seen us.'

'No one has seen us.' The tall one remained calm. 'Look! It's only the jeep.'

In the distance, a Land Rover was bouncing towards them, kicking up billowing clouds of red dust.

'Still, I don't like it here,' one of the men was grumbling. 'It's time to get out!'

'Get out?' It was the driver of the still-running vehicle who was now shouting.

'There was a noise!' the man answered. 'Anyone could be watching. They could be right over there behind one of those rocks.' He nodded towards the boulders beyond which Bat was hiding.

The driver slid out of the jeep. He was wearing a pair of dark glasses. The boy couldn't tell where his eyes were looking. His gaze swept over the very spot in which Bat was now crouching. For one heart-pounding second, he thought it was going to stop. But then the man turned back. 'For God's sake! No one's going until the job's been done.'

The next thing Bat knew, two figures were scrambling onto the elephant's corpse. A third fetched the chainsaw. This time it ripped into life at first tug and, snarling, lunged forward, ferocious as a chained dog. Bat heard the long rising whine as it finally bit. Its blade spewed bloodied flecks. Surely they would leave soon, he prayed, as he clutched at the rock face. Surely they would go when they had the second tusk. The machine choked and stopped.

One of the men dropped, half climbing, half tumbling,

down the slope of the animal and was lost from view. Bat heard him grunting as he shouldered the weight of the tusk. An argument broke out but Bat couldn't tell about what. Then the booty was loaded into the back of the jeep. It fell with a *thunk* that made the suspension rock. The chainsaw clattered in behind. Then the tailgate was slammed. The idling engine revved up. Bat could hear the gears grinding as the jeep ploughed off.

Little by little, the silence washed back in its wake. But it was only after the first of the rock hyraxes had begun to creep from their crevices that Bat felt that at last for him too it might be safe. He scanned the horizon for a glimpse of the Land Rover but it was by now out of view. Clouds of red dust were re-settling. The hyraxes grunted and then, seeing him rising, edged back bottom-first into their holes again.

The boy slipped through the boulders. There, right before him, loomed the dead animal. It rose like a mountain from a lake of purplish blood. Flies stumbled drunkenly about on its surface. They sunk into deep sticky pools and drowned. And for a long while Bat could do nothing but stand and stare numbly. He felt as if his whole mind had been swept away by force. He gazed at the baobab, a vast solitary mourner.

Soon the vultures would come. The first pair had already settled. They were shuffling impatiently in its silvery branches and Bat could see several more circling greedily above. As soon as he had gone, they would glide down to feast.

A marabou stork paced to and fro at a distance, its pink gizzard swinging, its black shoulders hunched.

The boy rushed at it angrily, flapping his arms. 'Shoo! Shoo!' he shouted. 'Get back! Go away!' It fluttered onto a fallen branch and rattled its bill. A jackal yipped in alarm and slunk a little further off.

Bat did not pursue it. What would have been the good? It was already too late. Taking one last slow look, he turned and set his step homewards. The sadness was so deep that it made his bones ache. Above him, in the depthless blue spaces of an African afternoon, he noticed an eagle. It inscribed its great circles upon the sky's emptiness.

'Only the eagles know everything in this country,' his grandmother had told him.

The bird gave a thin scream. It sounded more like a wail.

## CHAPTER TWO

The next morning, Bat drove his cattle out of the village to graze. By the time the sun was touching the tops of the acacias he was already well on his way: a small, lithe figure with a light, easy gait jumping through the undergrowth and leaping over branches, chivvying his cows outwards with whistles and high piping calls. In one hand he clutched his steel-bladed panga. He used it to cut the forage that he would later bring home. His other hand he kept free to flap and wave at the cattle or to hitch at the waistband of his pair of too-big brown shorts. A small sisal satchel with some lunch in was slung over one shoulder, along with a length of rope. A gourd to scoop water bumped against his hip. But, although he did own a pair of twisted hide sandals, his feet, as so often, were bare. He preferred it because he could run faster like that.

Sometimes, on his way along the paths that led out to the pastures, his cattle would stray onto somebody's crop. They would snatch greedy mouthfuls of maize leaves and uproot millet stalks. If the owner was there, they would yell out and scold them; but if they were not, Bat was likely to pinch something too: a small plump banana or perhaps a ripe avocado. He would eat it later once he was out of sight, his black eyes sparkling with pleasure through their fringe of thick lashes; a big gap-toothed smile brightening his small round face.

The cows moved ahead of him, their pace gradually slowing until he caught up with them when, with a burst of new energy, they trotted briskly on. They wove this way and that, their gaunt hipbones jutting, their long curving horns borne aloft like great crowns on their heads and, although now in the dry season their spines poked up like ridges, after the rains when the grasses swiped their bellies, they would soon grow sleek and fat. Then their hides would shine like polished wood.

Bat had eight cows in his herd, eleven if you counted the trio of still suckling youngsters that jostled along, nudging at their mothers' flanks. But he wouldn't have told you that if you had enquired. When anyone asked him how many cattle he looked after, he would just smile and say: 'As many as I looked after yesterday'. And yet he knew each of the animals as well as if they were part of his own family: he knew their names and their characters, their habits and their moods, their strong points and their failings, their preferences and dislikes. He knew that Kayo was inquisitive and could easily get into trouble; that Leko was a daydreamer with a tendency to lag; that Toco always slouched, head low and back sagging, unlike Tara, her chestnut twin who stood upright and foursquare with her muzzle stretched out. He knew that the pale freckled Anecanec had a scar under her belly from the time when, as a heifer, she had met a bush pig; and when he found watercress, he would always call Bwaro because she, more than any of them, relished its damp bitterness; but he knew that black Mutu would also slip in beside her because, wherever the restless Bwaro chose idly to wander, Mutu would slide along like a shadow at her side.

But Bat's favourite cow was the silvery Kila with her deep curved horns and her dark violet eyes. They had been born on the same day and had grown up together. Bat couldn't remember a time when she had not been there by his side and often, down by the water, they would lean contentedly together, the boy's arm draped companionably across the cow's sun-warmed back, gazing dreamily outwards as if lost in some land of shared memory. The water that dripped from the cow's lifted muzzle would fall through the air in sparkling droplets of light.

The boy was proud of his herd. Cattle are like their owners, his grandmother always told him: thin, wretched beasts had thin, wretched handlers; listless creatures belonged to those without direction to their lives; dishonest men owned the sort of sly animals that would steal from the cattle that stood right beside them; and ill-tempered cows would lash out because they themselves had been beaten by someone too ill-tempered to be trusted to bring them up. But Bat's animals were all good-natured and lively and strong. He had inherited his grandmother's eye, the villagers said; he had that inborn ability to detect hidden traits, to know when a calf would blossom into maturity, to tell whether a puny animal would eventually flourish and fatten or if it would only further sicken and fail. They would always back his judgement when they wanted to buy.

The cows trusted Bat too, and now, though all morning they had wanted to move on, to follow the course of the river like they usually did, they remained with him instead on the grasslands that lay nearer the village. Bat did not want to stray too far that day. He didn't want to risk running into the gang of men with guns again.

His grandmother had tried to reassure him. 'Poachers are terrible people,' she had said. 'They will betray their own tribesmen just for the money. They will kill anyone who crosses them rather than risk being caught. You were brave to try to face them; but you were stupid too,' she had scolded. 'If you ever come across them again, just run. Run as fast as you can and don't stop even to think. But there's no need to worry now. Those poachers will long since have left the savannah. They'll have gone to the city in search of a buyer of ivory and people like that don't belong to these parts.'

But still Bat was edgy. As he squatted in the shade of a spreading acacia, his eyes flicked about nervously, constantly watching. It was almost noon. The sun was rising to its sweltering heights and the cattle were dozing, heads lowered and tails swinging. Every now and then a breeze stirred through the branches, sending a shower of golden flowers tumbling onto their backs. The cows blinked their long lashes and breathed out with great lazy blows. Not a care in the world troubled them. But still Bat couldn't rest.

He jumped to his feet the moment he spotted a far distant figure. It wasn't a villager, even though this was the way girls occasionally came to draw water, because the girls always travelled in chattering gaggles; you would hear the noise of their laughter wafting over the grasses long before you saw the tops of the water pots that they carried on their heads. With a single big leap and a short burst of scrabbling, Bat swung himself up into the boughs of the tree. He flattened himself against a branch. All his fears of the previous day were flooding back. His lips started fizzing. He bit them so hard that he tasted his own blood.

But it was only a girl who was coming after all. He recognized her from some way off by the bounce of her gait. The enormous clay water jar that she carried almost dwarfed her and yet still she stepped out as if crossing the first springy grass of the rains. It was Amuka, the solitary stranger who had only recently come to live in the village. Her mother was sick, he'd been told, and her father lived in the city, and as she had no one at home any more to look after her, she had been sent here instead to stay with an aunt. Bat had heard the woman moaning away to his grandmother. 'It's just another mouth to feed,' she had complained. 'As if I haven't got five already; and they're all eating like locusts. What would I be wanting another daughter for?'

That had been less than a moon ago, but Bat had seen the girl often enough about the village since. He had watched her bending over her hoe as she planted cassava, halving the longer stalks with a single slice of her knife, stamping with a heel as she pressed down the dry earth; but she had never returned his gaze. She had never called out a greeting like the other girls did. And the time she had caught him staring as he had yawned his way through a village meeting, she had just stared straight back at him with her usual fierce scowl. That, he presumed, was how she had earned her name.

Everyone in Bat's tribe had two names: the one they were given at birth by their parents and the tribal nickname that they later earned. The second would be chosen because it described them, and it would often be the one by which they were from then on known. Hers was Amuka. It meant ferocious creature. At first, when he'd heard it, Bat had been surprised. She had looked so graceful. She was slim as a sesame pod and, while the rest of the village girls had their hair cropped short as his or else tugged up and knotted into tight little spikes, she had long shiny braids that swung to and fro as she walked. Her black eyes were fringed with long fluttering lashes that fell onto the cheekbones of an oval face. But when she looked up you would see their whites flashing and you would soon understand how she had come to be called what she was. If anyone crossed her she would fly into a fury. She was like a mongoose, the villagers laughed, slender and sinuous and sweet enough to look at, but as soon as you meddled, she would bristle and attack. Like a mongoose, they said, her claws were never retracted, and so Bat, who by nature preferred avoidance to encounter, had tended to stay clear of her.

He didn't want to get scratched – and especially not by a girl.

But now he was curious. Why did Amuka prefer to fetch water alone? The other girls in the village always went in a group. And why did she come now when the sun was still hot? And to this spot when there was another pool much nearer? There must be some reason. Perhaps she had a secret that nobody else knew. From his treetop vantage point, the boy watched her. But though he noticed her pausing as she spotted the cattle, she didn't see him as he lay there spying down through the leaves.

For a while, Muka just stood gazing out over the river. Apart from a broad channel that looped down the middle, it was almost dry. She looked at the ducks as they dabbled in the mud at the edges, at the flamingos on the far bank as they dozed with necks bent. Then, stooping, she picked up a handful of pebbles and, one by one, skimmed them across the surface of a pool. Most of them disappeared in a few splashy plops; but a couple, Bat noticed with some admiration, hopped right across to land skittering on the far side. He wanted to scramble down, to see if he could throw better, but by the time he had decided that this was what he should do, she had sat down again – not like a girl with her legs stretched straight out in front of her, but squatting like a boy on her haunches, her hands cupping her chin. She was humming softly to herself. Was she missing her family? Bat wondered. The boy began to get bored. He was relieved when Muka eventually got back to her feet. Hauling her big clay pot down the banks of the river, she let it fill before hoisting it from the ground to her shoulder, and then from her shoulder onto her head. Adjusting it carefully, she began her slow homeward walk. Bat was disappointed. Was that all that was going to happen? If so, then it certainly hadn't been worth the wait. Plucking an acacia pod, he playfully hurled it. It landed right where he had meant it: right before her feet.

Amuka froze instantly, watchful as a mongoose when it first senses danger and, standing on its hind-legs, starts to utter its shrill growl. If she had been a mongoose, Bat thought, the neat little ears on either side of her skull would have pricked and her hair-braids would have bristled; and forgetting completely that she still hadn't seen him, he laughed out loud. The sound made the girl jump. Her water jar toppled. All its contents spilled. Bat scrambled down from his tree. He was going to apologize; he was going to make sure that her pot hadn't cracked; but the girl didn't wait to find out what he intended. Springing at him in fury, she knocked him flat on his back.

Now Bat was enraged. He leaped to his feet in a rapid counter-assault. Arms flailing, eyes flashing, he lashed out, temper boiling. The girl was ready and seized him in a head-to-head lock. Shoulder to shoulder they tussled in a fierce riverbank scuffle, clawing and heaving and kicking and shoving until suddenly, pushed backwards and losing his footing, Bat found himself sliding. The situation was desperate, he realized, as he felt his grip slipping: he was about to lose to a girl in a fight. He made a last grab at Muka. It didn't stop him from falling; but at least he pulled her down too.

They landed with a splash in a stagnant pool. The water was filthy: slimy with bird-droppings and stinking of rotten fish. For a moment the pair of them sat there, completely stunned. Then Bat, wiping the gloop in a handful from his face, looked up and saw to his amazement that Muka was smiling. He flung the mud at her in impotent fury. She hurled a handful back. He retaliated. His aim had always been good. He could explode a ripe melon from twenty paces with his catapult. The shot landed smack in the middle of her forehead. But instead of howling as he had fully expected, she let out a peal of open-mouthed laughter. It poured from her like the new rains pouring over a rock. She reached for her own load of slopping ammunition and, even as she drew back her arm for the chuck, Bat could feel his own laughter starting to wriggle about inside him. It broke out in a great gap-toothed grin on his face.

A few moments later, they were both plastered head to toe in flung goo. Their shouts rang out around the rocks, sending the ducks bustling and unbalancing a fishing stork. Even a flock of flamingos came eventually to the conclusion that the time had at last come when it might be more prudent to take flight. They rose from the water in a honking pink cloud. The children laughed all the louder and flapped their arms about.

They were completely exhausted by the time they had calmed down and started to try and clean themselves. The water poured from their skin in thickly muddied runnels. 'We'll smell like old fish for weeks now,' said Muka as she scrubbed. Bat giggled and nodded, but inside he was hoping that their friendship might last even longer. He still wanted to beat her at making stones walk on water.

'Are you hungry?' he asked when they had finally finished washing. He knew that she would be: even after the harvest her aunt's grain store was never more than half full. Muka nodded as she wrung out the folds of her wrap. In Bat's little satchel were two roasted maize cobs. 'Here! Take one of these,' he called, and soon they were sitting side by side, backs propped against a tree-trunk, silently eating their way through his lunch. Bat gnawed his from the side. One big front tooth had recently fallen out and, though the new one behind it was already emerging, the thin wavy edges pushing through the pink gum, it still had a long way to go. Muka nibbled in neat little lines down the cob. Curious, Kila came ambling over. She stared at the intruder and picked her nose with her tongue.

'My mother used to roast maize for me,' said Muka eventually, wiping her mouth and handing the husk to the cow.

Kila crunched at it meditatively. But Bat just sat puzzled. Why was that so remarkable? Surely everyone everywhere roasted maize cobs.

'I don't know where my mother is now,' Muka said. Her voice was so low it was barely more than a whisper and, half turning her head, she gazed at the cow as if it was the animal and not the boy whom she was now addressing. 'She was sick,' she murmured, 'and the villagers drove her away. "Why should we feed you," they said, "since you are going to die? You do not feed a ghost."

19

So one day my mother just got up and left. She told me she had to while she could still walk. She was going to look for my father, she said, and I couldn't go with her. She just handed me over like a bundle of washing to a neighbour. She asked her to take me to the home of my aunt. And that's what the woman did. I was handed over . . . again . . . and I've been here ever since.'

She paused for a moment. Bat wondered if she was crying. He stole a quick slantwise look but, although Muka's lips trembled, her eyes remained quite dry. 'Auntie thinks that my mother will come back and fetch me,' she whispered, 'but I don't suppose she ever will. I don't even think she's alive any more.'

'What about your father?'

Muka just shrugged. 'I don't know. I don't know him.'

A long silence hung between them. When Muka eventually turned she saw that it was Bat who was crying. The tears were spilling from the rims of his eyes, hanging in sparkles at the end of his lashes, rolling in big shiny drops down his cheeks. Seeing her looking, he hastily wiped them away.

'I don't know my father either,' he said and, stretching out a hand, he reached over for Kila, letting his fingers ripple down the loose folds of her neck.

'Do you know where he is?'

Bat shook his head. 'But I know that he's dead.' His mind darted back to the scene of yesterday's slaughter, to the great swollen carcass and the clambering people; to the clouds of black flies and the hacked-apart face. For a moment he thought he was going to retch. 'My

20

father was killed by poachers,' he said. 'It was before I was born. He was a ranger, you see. He worked with elephants, and although he had often been warned of the danger, he still went out on the savannah, and it was there that he was shot. My grandmother says he died for the animals that he most loved.'

Bat gulped, trying to get rid of the lump that was rising in his throat. 'People told my grandmother she was lucky,' he said hoarsely. 'They said that my father had died a warrior's death; that it was better to be killed out in the bush, to lose your life hunting or fighting, than to die on your mat like a weak old man. But she didn't think she was lucky at all. "I know luck when I see it," she told me. "It's when a swarm of locusts flies over your crop without settling, or a delicious ripe mango drops straight into your lap. It's not when someone turns up at your home to tell you that you have just lost your only son." They never brought my father back. They couldn't find him; so he couldn't be buried outside his hut like he ought to have been. He had no family beside him to watch over his grave or throw sand on his body or plant a tree where he lay.'

'But didn't your grandmother do the ceremonies?' asked Muka. 'Didn't she say the prayers that bring the soul back?'

Bat nodded. 'She did. She performed all the ceremonies but her prayers were never answered. She never feels his spirit brushing by her in the hut. She never looks up and senses him just standing there watching. And now she says it's all over. He'll never return.'

'And your mother? Where's your mother?'

21

'She died too. It was only a few days after I was born. Her blood ran dry. That's what the villagers whisper; but my grandmother told me it was not her blood but her soul that could not drink. She missed her husband, my father, so much. Death is a scar that never heals: that's what my grandmother thinks.'

Bat's face brightened a little. 'It was my grandmother who brought me up . . . in the city at first. She worked for the white people with sky-coloured eyes.' He gave a slight smile. 'It was the white people who gave me my nickname, you know. My mother had called me Nakisisa. It means "born of the shadows". But the white people just started calling me Bat. Bats are born of the shadows, they said. And somehow the name stuck.'

'Because it suits you,' Muka said. She had seen him out with his cattle, weaving through the dusk as he brought his cows in, zigzagging this way and that way across the open spaces, skimming the savannah like a bat skims the night.

The boy nodded. 'That's what my grandmother thinks. She says I suit a world as wide as the sky. That's why she stopped working in the city and brought me back here. I was still only tiny when she bundled me up in a cloth, knotted me round her shoulders and carried me home to our village.' Knuckling his fist, Bat leaned forward and rubbed fondly at Kila's broad brow. 'I was fed on the same milk as this cow,' he told Muka. 'She was born on the same day as me and so we shared her mother's milk.'

Kila shifted and kicked at a fly on her underbelly,

then, stretching out her neck, she gave his arm a rough lick. She liked the taste of the salt; but it made both children laugh.

'I've got to go!' Muka jumped up suddenly. She hitched at the waistband of her crumpled blue wrap. 'I've already been too long and Auntie will be waiting.' She pulled a face. 'She'll be grumbling away by the time I get back.'

Bat clambered up too. Hastily they returned to the river, where Bat helped the girl fill her water jar and hoist it on to her head. Then he stood and watched her as she walked away, one crooked arm raised to support the balancing container, the other hanging loosely. Her hips swayed lightly from side to side.

'See you later,' Bat called when she was a short way off.

She half turned and, with her free hand, gave a shy little wave. 'I'll come back and find you,' she cried.

Bat smiled. He hoped that she would. He was still smiling to himself as he turned to check on his cattle. She had had a secret after all, he thought, and that was the secret of her real self.

## CHAPTER THREE

That afternoon, Bat led the cows a little further down the river where the grasses were longer and thick bushes gave shade. He lay down beneath one to shelter. The day was still very hot and he must have fallen asleep because the next thing he knew he was waking, head throbbing, tongue thick. The sun had moved on, pulling with it the shadows that had covered him like a cooling blanket. Jumping hurriedly up, he looked about for his animals. For a few worried seconds he thought they had strayed, until he spotted them shining amid a patch of far scrub. He squinted into the light. They were anxious; he could see them shifting about restlessly, hear the low rumble of Toco as she called out for her calf.

Grabbing his panga, Bat walked swiftly towards them. Something was moving. He tensed. A shadow slid secretively under a bush. He froze, still as a duiker surprised on a forest path. Every nerve in his body was trilling. And then, just as suddenly, he relaxed again. It was a skulking hyena, hunting a spurfowl or a perhaps a ground hare . . . nothing larger than a jackal, or it would be with its pack; but even so, Toco's calf would still have been tempting. Breaking into a run, Bat sprinted towards it, flailing his arms and uttering loud whoops. The hyena tucked in its tufted tail and loped off. Hitching up his too-big shorts, Bat raced in pursuit, bounding so rapidly through the rough scrub that he didn't see the little creature crouched low among the bushes until he nearly tripped right over it. He stumbled to an abrupt halt and looked down.

A tiny elephant lay at his feet. Bat stared in astonishment. It couldn't have been much more than a couple of weeks in age. Its ears were still folded about it like the leaves of a cabbage; its back was still sprinkled with russet-coloured hairs; and it was thin, he now noticed . . . far too thin. Its spine stuck out in knobbles and its skin looked all crumpled. The dust filled its loose folds.

Bending, Bat reached out one slow gentle hand. The little creature tried to stand, pushing up with its forelegs, its trunk waving about; but it failed and flopped back bewildered, its eyelids opening and closing as its flanks rose and sank. It nuzzled at Bat with its long fumbling nose.

He backed away slowly and the baby elephant tried again to rise, managing to follow him for a few staggering steps before once more collapsing. Bat knelt down beside it. Its trunk fiddled weakly in the palm of his hand. Where was its mother? It would die without her, he thought. He could already see the blue mist in its wide baby stare. And then, with a sickening thump, he remembered the dead elephant. Was that how the poachers had managed to single out so mighty a creature? Had she been lagging behind to protect her newborn?

Bat would have known what to do with the orphaned calf of one of his cattle. He could coax even the sickliest to suck milk from a bucket by letting them latch on to two of his fingers. But they had little blunt muzzles that could reach into a pail. A creature with a trunk would not learn to drink that way; and this tiny animal must be thirsty, he thought. He was parched himself. It must be so terribly thirsty. It had probably been wandering all night alone on the savannah. It was a miracle that it wasn't already dead. Bat ran to fetch his calabash and, filling it with water, he held it out tentatively. The elephant ignored it. Bat tried opening its mouth, curling its trunk back over its head so that the damp, pink triangle of its under-lip was exposed. He poured the water in; but most of it dribbled straight back out again.

Kila wandered over. She snuffled at the baby with her damp, breathy nose; shunting it gently with the tips of her horns. The little animal shifted, its trunk drifting uncertainly in the direction of her udder. It could smell her sweet milk, but still it couldn't drink.

Bat emptied the last of his water over the little animal's ears. At least that would cool it. Then, hunkering down by the cow, he filled his calabash with milk. He tried to pour that down the baby's throat next. The pink tongue wriggled as it tasted the warmth. Bat tried again:

it wasn't very successful, but the boy kept on going, tiny bit by tiny bit, until all of the milk had either been swallowed or spilled.

He didn't notice how quickly the afternoon was passing and the sun was already very low in the sky when, hearing a faint cry in the distance, he looked up and saw his new friend Amuka. So she had kept her promise! He had hoped so much that she would; and now, scrambling to his feet, he bounded towards her.

'Come! Come and see! Come quickly!' he shouted. He grabbed her by the wrist, gabbling out his story of the poachers as he pulled her into a run. 'And they killed the mother . . . and there's a baby . . . I've found a baby,' he gasped, the tale tumbling out in broken snatches between big puffs of breath. She would know what to do, he was hoping. Between them they might be able to come up with a plan.

He watched Muka's eyes widening in wonderment as, dropping to her knees, she stretched out one hesitant hand for the creature as though to check for herself that his story had really been true. No, she was not imagining it. Pity for the tiny animal welled up in her heart. They couldn't just leave it. They had to find a way to help.

'If we don't take it home, the hyenas will be back for it,' she murmured. 'Somehow, between us, we have to help it to walk.' She glanced about for a moment as if searching for the answer. 'Perhaps it will follow the cows,' she suggested. Bat nodded, and leaping to his feet he ran swiftly through the grasses, sounding the low whistles that would set his herd trotting, bunching closer together as they started for the track.

Then, joining forces, he and Muka started trying to get the elephant to stand. Muka, using all her strength, shoved it from behind, while Bat got underneath it and pushed upwards as hard as he could. It staggered onto its wobbly feet and stood there for a few moments, swaying gently, before, step by tottering step, it set off in the direction of the cows. The two children walked on either side like props while Muka hummed softly to encourage it along. She had heard mother elephants singing to their young like that, she said.

The village was not far but it took a long while to get there, and the baby collapsed several times on the way. It got stuck on small roots and amid thickets of spear grass. Where a branch had fallen it stumbled and had to be pushed. At one point it stepped on its trunk and tripped over. And the children began to feel scared when they heard the low moan of a lion. It was dangerous, Bat knew, to stay late on the savannah. They glanced at each other, worried frowns in their eyes. But the going got easier once they had reached the track, and when they passed a muddy waterhole, still damp from the rainy season, they stopped to dig down and find a bowlful of water that they poured in cooling runnels over the little animal's back.

Night had almost fallen when finally they reached the shambas, the little thorn-fenced gardens where the villagers grew their crops. Now Bat was kept busy hurling clods at the cows that, without someone to chivvy them constantly, would stray off the path in the hopes of stealing a bite. From there the track threaded its way through the village, the little groups of huts scattered all about it like the beads of a necklace whose string has been snapped. Bat's home was right on the fringes, and he and Muka branched off towards it.

The cattle barged forward to get into their pen and Bat ran to the gate to count them in: not with his fingers but by remembering each individual and checking to see that she was safely back. The calves were separated off into an enclosure that they shared, reluctantly, with a trio of shaggy-haired goats.

Bat's grandmother stooped as she came out of a doorway. The lintel was not high enough for a grown person to walk upright. Pausing amid the profusion of yellow and blue flowers that had been planted in old tins and nailed up, she squinted across her yard to where the two children stood. Her eyes were not good. She was growing old. Threads of grey silvered her short unplaited hair so that it looked as if she had just brushed a hanging cobweb, but her skin had the glow of a sheet of burnished copper and she was wearing an old cotton wrap the same colour as the sun as it dips below the horizon. The sun was that soft orange now, and Bat knew he was late. He was supposed to get home before the guinea fowl had gone to roost. Their clattering squawks were his dinner bell.

'Bat! Where have you been?' His grandmother put her hands on her hips. 'Do you grow your ears for decoration?' Worry had made her cross. 'I heard a lion, and how often have I told—' Suddenly, she stopped. She had just seen the elephant. She stared at the creature that tottered before her, its trunk bobbing up and down like a piece of elastic. For one long moment she just stood there, her mouth open but silent. Her voice was a questioning whisper when at last she spoke. 'Abili?'

The swallows that nested under the thatch swooped in and out of the doorway that framed her, catching the first flying insects of the night.

'That little creature is too young to live,' she snapped. 'It's too young to survive without its mother's milk.' And then suddenly she softened. She could hold out no longer against a growing hope. 'But we will see what we can do about it,' she said as she turned away into the hut. 'Abili?' she whispered again as she stirred up the embers of her cook-fire. It was the name of Bat's father. She turned to look at the boy as he hesitated in the doorway. A pan of milk slowly warmed. 'You are just like your father,' she murmured, 'more and more every day . . . and now the elephants have come for you too.'

# CHAPTER FOUR

'Throw your heart out in front of you and run to catch it.' That's what Bat's grandmother always said. And now she hurled her own forward in the hope that she could somehow outrun it. The tiny elephant was weak. It would die if they could not feed it. It needed milk. But the little that she had prepared for it the previous night had all been wasted. The animal had refused to swallow.

All night, curled on her sleeping mat, Bat's grand-mother had pondered the problem. Now she had a plan. 'I think I can come up with something,' she told the boy as he hovered anxiously about her, 'but not if you don't get out of my way. You are like a pestering bee.'

Taking the gallon can that she used for carrying milk to the market, Bat's grandmother cut a hole in the plastic cap. Through this she pushed a teat that she fashioned from the inner tube of a car tyre. The screw top, when jammed down and twisted, held it tightly in place.

Bat hugged her tight. He knew that she had been saving that inner tube for some time. She had been planning to make a sofa: to nail the bouncy strips of rubber criss-cross over a frame. 'Then, when I come home exhausted after a day at the market, I can lie here in state,' she would tell Bat and the pair of them would break into laughter at the prospect, even though Bat still wasn't sure what a sofa actually was.

But when they tried to insert the makeshift teat into the baby elephant's mouth it started to fight them with a surprising strength; thrashing about wildly, even when Bat sat on top of it. He would have given up if his grandmother had not had another plan.

Each village homestead was made up of a cluster of traditional mud and thatch shelters: a kitchen, a grain store, a hut where the men and the older boys slept and another separate structure for the women and the little boys and the girls. But the men's hut in Bat's compound had for many years been used only for storage. He had not yet reached the age when he would be expected to sleep apart.

'The elephant can make her home there for the time being,' Bat's grandmother now said and, having thrown out a tangle of drying firewood and swept the floor vigorously, she set about fastening a sackcloth blanket to the rafters. It sagged down from the ceiling in a low hanging swag. 'This will feel to the baby like a mother's belly,' she explained, observing her handiwork with some satisfaction. 'It can shelter underneath and imagine it's safe.'

Shoving the bewildered animal in through the door, the pair returned to the struggle of trying to persuade it to drink. For a while it kept fighting the strange rubber protrusion. And then suddenly, almost by accident, it got the hang of what to do. Fastening its under-lip tight to the teat, it started to suck. And once it had started it did not stop. Soon the contents of the gallon can had been all but drained. Bat's grandmother had added a small gourd of goats' milk to the mix. It had natural sugars in it, she explained, that could make a child rest more deeply. Slowly the baby's eyes closed. It was blissfully sleepy. It collapsed in a huddle beneath the hanging sackcloth. It looked just like a bag of maize, Bat thought and, folding up his thin legs, he leaned against it and fell back to sleep himself.

When he awoke, he found his grandmother watching him quietly from the doorway. He recognized her look. He remembered it from when he was tiny, when, exhausted by playing, he would lie drowsing in her lap while she fiddled with his curls and brushed the flies from his lips. Then he had dozed off and dreamed, knowing that when he awoke again, the first thing he would see would be her eyes staring deep into his.

Bat's grandmother was kind and loving, but her concern for her grandson also made her strict. She would set him a task and then spit in the dust. 'I want to see it completed before that dries,' she would tell him and the boy would have to hasten if he wanted to avoid a scolding, although only too often he would get distracted along the way, spotting a lizard and pausing to try and catch it or making a detour to follow a snake-track in the dust. 'You can't go on relying on an old woman for ever,' she would tell him. 'I don't want you turning into one of those idlers who feed their families on millet porridge while they feast in the market on plates of stewed goat.' That was why, even though men weren't expected to, Bat's grandmother had made the boy learn to cook. He knew how to fry plantains until they turned black and gooey and make matooke with goat meat and a gritty groundnut sauce.

'No time for lazing! There's work to be done,' his grandmother now snapped as, briefly turning, she squinted off towards the fields. For a moment she followed the slight figure which was winding away through the crops. If it had been her grandson, she would have been able to hear his high calls as he chivvied the cattle that trotted ahead of him, but it was not. It was one of the village boys, Bim, and Bim had been born mute. The only sound he had ever been able to utter was a hoarse animal bellow: a roar so harsh and which burst so roughly from his throat that even he seemed alarmed by it. His eyes would widen with fear as it broke from his lips.

Bat's grandmother turned back. 'While you were sleeping I sent Bim out with the cattle,' she explained. 'I think he can be trusted. He's watchful and gentle and that's what the cows need. And so, for today at least, you can stay home. But that doesn't mean you can lie about and do nothing. When you aren't busy looking after that little baby, there are plenty of other jobs to be done. There's wood to be gathered and grass to be cut.' She smiled. 'And that girl Amuka has been fluttering about like a weaver bird. Maybe her aunt hasn't given her enough to do . . . in which case perhaps she can help you instead. And then when you've finished I've got another important job.'

Bat divided the afternoon between doing his chores, helping Muka with hers, and attending to the baby elephant, which never came out all day from under its swag of old sacking, except when they forced it to so that they could wash it. Elephants needed to keep cool, Bat's grandmother said. Their own mothers bathed them, dousing them with water and scrubbing them with their trunks. The baby liked the wetness. It spread out its ears and let the liquid run behind them. They were a delicate pink at the back. And in the heat of the afternoon, the two children sat beside it, using their rush sleeping mats to fan it while the guinea fowl dashed in and out and picked ticks from the folds in its hide.

Later, when Bim had returned with the cattle and Muka had left at the summons of her irritable aunt, Bat followed his grandmother out to their fields. Together they selected four flat stones, so big that it took Bat four journeys to fetch them back. 'What's that for?' one of the village boys had called out as he passed. Bat, his arms stretched and straining, gave the shadow of a shrug. He didn't know either, but he did know when it was better not to ask.

He placed them all as his grandmother instructed on a patch of carefully swept ground at the back of their kitchen hut. One was set at each corner of a rectangle. Then they sat down together: the woman with her legs stretched straight out in front of her, her dark shiny old hands loosely clasped in her lap; the boy with his arms hugged around folded knees. He tapped his toes lightly. He was waiting to find out what this was all about.

'These stones mark the spot where your father Abili would have been buried had his body been brought back to us,' his grandmother eventually said. That was all. She didn't speak another word, but Bat could see the memories as they flitted across her lined face. They scuttled like beetles from a carcass that you stir with your foot. He let his chin drop to his chest. Strange feelings were pushing around deep inside him; but he couldn't have found words for them, even if he had wanted to. One by one, he just locked them away in his heart.

The sun slowly sank. The guinea fowl flapped cackling to their roosts in the mango and the goat pen fell quiet; at last they finally rose. Bat's grandmother folded the boy to her for a moment. 'To lose a child,' she said, 'is something that can end one's world. You can never get back to how it was before. The stars go out. The birds fall silent. The moon disappears. But I have you, my grandson, and you help me to start again even though I am old.' Laying his head against her, Bat breathed in the familiar dry wood-smoke smell of her skin. Then the pair moved apart.

'And you can ask your new friend Amuka to eat with us tonight,' his grandmother added. 'Her aunt won't mind. She always says she has too many mouths to feed.' Bat grinned and took off at an eager run.

The three of them, Amuka, Bat and Bat's grandmother, sat late round the fire that night, dipping pieces of millet bread into a stew of salted meat. It was tough and they chewed in weary silence. The smoke filled the room. It drooped like a net hanging down from the thatch. Afterwards Muka made tea like her mother had long ago taught her, measuring the leaves out into her palm, adding spice for extra flavour and then covering the pot. They sipped it in silence, watching the embers of the fire slowly fading, listening to the calls of the owls as they swept through the night. Tiny secretive rustlings came from the thatch. Occasionally a bat swooped in from the darkness, scudding round in a circle before returning back out. A long gleaming millipede flowed up Muka's foot. She didn't move. It poured itself slowly back down the other side.

'You mustn't hope for too much,' said Bat's grand-mother at last. 'That baby is probably too young to survive; and even if it does, a hard job lies ahead. You will have always to be with it, to feed it and teach it and then, in the end, you will have to let it go.'

The two children both jerked their heads up at once, eyes searching her face from beneath a pair of confused frowns. 'Why?' asked Bat. 'I don't want to. Why do we have to let it go?'

The moths around the last flames cast dancing shadows on the walls.

'Can't it stay with us always?' Bat pleaded. 'I promise I'll look after it. And when it's big I'll just take it out with the cows. And Muka will help, won't you?' He turned to the girl. She was nodding so hard that her braids were set swinging.

Bat looked back to his grandmother. He could feel his chin wobbling but he tried to control it.

'You must understand *now*,' said his grandmother, '*now*, right from the very beginning, that an elephant is not tame. It hears ancient wild voices singing in its soul, voices as old as the rocks against which they ring. You can't alter its spirit. You can't make it a pet. If that little animal does live, you will have to learn to love it, to love it so much that one day you will gladly let it go. You must bring it up knowing that it will leave you one day. Do you think you are ready to do that?' she asked.

Both the children looked away. Bat gnawed stubbornly at his knuckles. Muka fiddled with the end of a plait, rolling it back and forth, back and forth between her fingertips. The wordlessness hung in the room like a veil.

'Then sleep on it,' said the old woman.

Rising, she trimmed the wick of a small kerosene lantern and handed it to Muka. 'We'll see you in the morning,' she murmured, laying a hand upon the girl's head.

Then Bat took his sleeping mat, blanket and the flattened banana stem that he used as a pillow and, leaving his grandmother's sleeping hut for the first time ever, laid down his bed by the side of the baby elephant.

## CHAPTER FIVE

The village of Jambula was named after the tree that stood in its middle. It had been there long before the little round houses with their rough mud walls and their matete thatch roofs had first started to gather. The tree bore high, unreachable fruit. But once a year the fruit would ripen and fall in a thick plum-coloured carpet, turning tongues purple with its bitter-sweet taste.

Life in the village had the same mixed flavour. In the dry season, the sun would bite into your skin like a dog with a quarrel. Colours would fade; leaves wrinkle and drop. The cattle grew thin and the scorpions sidled from crannies. If you accidentally trod on one, the pain made you cry out. Then your neck would swell; your tongue would feel as rough as a piece of old wood. You wouldn't be able to taste food for weeks.

The rains in their turn could be equally fierce,

pelting down with a force that would rip crops to shreds. Huts filled with water and armies of hopping frogs, and though the women, bent double over their palm-frond brooms, would do constant battle, no amount of sweeping could ever ward them off. Mosquitoes arrived in clouds. Drawing back your lips, you had to breathe through your teeth if you didn't want to choke.

But there were long in-between times when Jambula felt like a good place to live. In one direction the savannah rolled towards a wide-looping river that twice a year over-spilled to make a lush fertile marsh. In the other a track led away to the forest. From there, the trees started to clamber up the foot-slopes of an escarpment. They got almost halfway before they finally gave up, leaving the cliff face, a wall of sheer rock, to glow pink in the light of the sun as it set.

On the grasslands there were sand grouse and spur-fowl and plover and, if you were lucky, horned topi to hunt. There were baobab trees for building and wild cane for sweetness, elephant grass for forage and acacias for fuel. From the woodlands came duiker and honey and date palms, medicines and paw-paw and fat little bush pigs. Mangoes and bananas grew thick in the shambas, giving shade to the groundnut and sorghum, the maize and cassava crops. And for anything else, for salt or kerosene or lengths of cloth for a wrap, there was always the market. If you kept a good pace, it was only the first part of a morning away along the track.

This was the village to which the baby elephant had come to live and now, on the second morning, the village chief was planning to make his official visit. Even

41

as the first rays of the sun were filtering down through the thatch, the women were blowing on the ashes of their cook-fires and gossiping about the newcomer that had arrived in their midst. By the time Bat had milked his cows, an impatient crowd was gathering, whispering and grinning around the elephant's hut. Hordes of little children jumped about in excitement, darting and peeping like swarms of spring hares.

An elephant would bring them good luck, the villagers were saying. This animal was the emblem of their tribe. It was a creature with intelligence, resilience and might. They waited for old Kaaka, the wise woman, to turn up, shuffling along the grassy path with her walking stick. They wanted to hear what she would pronounce. She paused under the mango tree that sheltered Bat's homestead, casting its hazy shadows over the clean-swept earth. Its leaves trembled despite the lack of wind, and one of them, wafting gently down from the branches, landed at her feet. She bent creakily over. 'It means we have a visitor who comes from far away and, like this leaf, has no intention of returning,' she said.

The village chief, who always wore his spectacles even though they had no glass in them, was the next to come forward. He was wearing an old pair of gumboots on his feet but, to show that he was visiting in his official capacity, he was also sporting his ceremonial spear. A pipe poked out of the corner of his mouth. Held in place by his last two remaining teeth, it puffed vigorous clouds of smoke. Now he removed it with a flourish. 'Unity is strength,' he declared. 'That is the motto of our people. And that too is the motto of the elephant herd.' Pulling his drape up under his armpits, he crossed his arms in front of his chest. He was proud of his standing. 'Since the days of our furthest ancestors, our people and the elephant have walked together. Now this little baby has been brought to our village as a sign of old friendship. We will call her Meya because it is the name that we give to those we most love.'

Meya soon became part of everyday village life. She would be at Bat's side from first thing in the morning, when the boy splashed his face in a calabash of water, to last thing at night, when he cleaned his teeth with a strand of matete grass. She came to feel as familiar to him as his brown shorts and green T-shirt and, since like most of the villagers he only ever had one set of clothes at a time, this meant that she felt like a part of him.

Bat ate cassava-flour biscuits for breakfast. They filled the stomach, said his grandmother, so that he wouldn't feel hungry all day. Then he gave Meya a feed of warm milk before, slinging the gallon can around his shoulders with a length of twisted sisal, the pair followed behind the cattle as they ambled off to graze. At first, Meya stumbled on the hard ruts of the track in the dry season and skidded in the slippery mud of the rains. She had to be helped along. But as she grew older, as the long reddish hairs on her back were replaced by black bristles and her crumpled ears unfolded and fanned out from her head, she got more confident; and as she grew more confident she became also more playful. She dashed at the guinea fowl as they darted across the compound,

Art lesson:
Watercolour of the Mango
Tree?

or butted at the cattle with her broad forehead, and though, in the beginning, Bat worried that they might turn and jab her, they seemed to understand that it was only a game. The young calves frolicked and scampered and kicked up their heels as they ran from her and Bat's favourite cow Kila allowed her to twine her trunk around her tail.

At first, Meya needed to be fed frequently; she seemed constantly hungry. But as the moons waxed and waned, she learned to suck properly, lifting her trunk and curling it back over her head. She started to lose her crumpled appearance. Her small gourd-like body was soon quilted with fat. 'Soon you must teach her to find her own food,' said Bat's grandmother. 'We can't give her all our milk for ever. I haven't got any spare for the market place.' It was true. Where normally on her way down the track that led into town the big can on her head would be almost full, now there was nothing left over. She would carry a blanket of baked vanilla cakes or ripe jackfruit instead, and there would be no fresh-caught Nile perch to grill with a handful of red tomatoes when she came home. Dipping his matooke into a gristly stew of goat's neck, Bat would chew disconsolately. Then, to make matters worse, the lamp would be snuffed out. Without the sale of milk, his grandmother explained, kerosene had to be saved for when it was most needed; there was no longer money to spare to buy more. Yes, Meya would have to learn to forage for herself, Bat thought.

But learning to find her own food meant learning to use her trunk and Meya seemed to treat hers like an unruly rubber toy. It wasn't that she didn't try it out constantly. From the very beginning it was always exploring: sniffing and poking and pulling and stroking, prodding and twiddling and twining about. Whatever Bat was doing, it would seem to find a way in: jogging his elbow when he was trying to pour water, nudging his back when he wanted to sleep, sending his piles of cut cattle fodder scattering, knocking his lantern out of his grip. Sometimes Bat grew exasperated. 'Why did you do that, you clumsy clot?' he would shout. And the little animal would look sheepish. Sidling over, she would push herself up against him until he finally relented and scratched her behind the ears. Then she would smile and lift up her head so that he could also reach her chin, where she was sprouting a little whiskery beard. But, however much Meya practised, her trunk remained a source of problems. Sometimes she stepped on it and stumbled and tripped; sometimes it got stuck in a big clumpy knot; and often, snuffling about, she breathed

47

up a great whoosh of dust which would madden her with its tickling and she would writhe it and wave it and slap it violently about.

Once, shambling off to investigate an indignant mongoose, Meya had got her trunk trapped in a tree hollow. Her squeals brought Muka running in from the fields, hotly pursued by a furious puffing aunt who, when she finally caught up, stood legs akimbo, bent almost double as she fought to catch her breath, while Muka, who had only just succeeded in extricating the stuck elephant, backed on her hands and knees, bottom first, from the piece of hollowed-out wood. Scrambling quickly to her feet, she dusted down her wrap. She looked sullen. She suspected she was in for a scolding and indeed she was right.

'That's it. I've had enough,' her aunt managed between puffs. 'Do you hear me? I've had enough.' She glowered meaningfully at the girl. 'One moment you are working and then the next you have gone. You have dashed off who knows where . . . and I won't put up with it! Do you hear me: I won't put up with it!' And as if repetition weren't enough to emphasize her point, she slapped hard down on her thigh. 'You are completely unbiddable,' she bawled, mopping hopelessly at the sweat that had sprung to her brow. Her lips, fat as bananas, were quivering with fury. Her eyes shone with impotent rage.

For a moment Muka held her gaze and they stood there locked in head-to-head combat. Then the girl let her eyes drop. If she had actually apologized, it would have felt like a rare capitulation; but she didn't, and the silence that rose between them grew rapidly into its own kind of contest.

The auntie's hand was just rising to deliver a great slap when Bat's grandmother appeared. 'What's the matter? What brings you here, Mama Brenda?' she enquired politely. 'Can I offer you water? You look so very hot.' She gave a quick wave of her wrist to Muka who, already ducking in readiness to receive the blow, dashed off.

'What's the matter?' replied the woman with a great exasperated sigh. 'That girl is the matter. As if five aren't already a handful, I'm expected to make room in my house and my heart for one more. And what can I do with her? She's like a wild animal. As soon as you aren't watching her, she's running away. Who can blame her mother for getting rid of her?' she wailed. 'What can be done with a girl like that?'

Muka, returning at that moment with a calabash of water, scooped from the clay pot inside the kitchen hut, approached with the bowl and, eyes respectfully lowered, handed it to her aunt, who merely gave a great huff. The water was cool and clear. It refreshed her. 'What would *you* do with her?' she asked Bat's grandmother at last when the bowl had been drained.

'What would I do with her?' Bat's grandmother paused and thought for a moment. 'I would give her a home. Would you like that, Mama Brenda? Would you like it if she came to live with me? You have five girls already and I have none.' She didn't so much as glance at Muka. 'Bat is growing now. He sleeps with the elephant in his own boy's hut. So your niece Amuka can come to stay with me. I will feed her. I think we can find enough to spare.'

Muka's face sparkled bright as a bush-full of fireflies. Beyond downcast lashes, her black eyes were aglitter with hope. For a moment the three stood there, the silence electric between them. Muka could feel it like the static of an approaching storm.

'Well . . . hmmm . . .' Her aunt hesitated. 'That is good of you,' she ventured. She was starting to wonder if there was some hidden catch. 'Yes. If she could live with you . . . until her mother comes to fetch her . . . just until then . . . then yes . . . if you were able . . . it's just that I . . .'

'I have plenty of room,' Bat's grandmother reassured her. 'And I will try to bring her up as well as you have done.'

The aunt nodded and smiled, fatly satisfied by the praise.

'Well, that's all fixed then,' said Bat's grandmother, taking the calabash. She turned to Muka. The girl's face was wreathed with smiles. 'Now go back to the fields,' she instructed her sternly. 'Go and work with your cousins. Your auntie needs help with the hoeing. She doesn't want to see any more slacking today.' Muka sprinted off as fast as she could, the soles of her feet flashing pink in the dust.

But that evening, she and Bat could barely contain their excitement.

'How long will it be?' he kept asking his grandmother. 'How long will it be before Muka comes to live with us? She could even stay tonight. We have a spare blanket.'

'The sooner the better,' grinned the wriggling girl. 'Then no more of this . . .' Jumping to her feet, she walked right up to Bat and, planting her hands on her hips, started yakking as loud as she could. She was imitating her aunt when her temper was lost.

'She always does that,' cried the giggling Bat. 'She stands right in front of you and yells. Even though you're right in front of her . . . she yells right in your face.'

'Enough!' scolded his grandmother. 'Show some respect. Every tree has its own anthill.' Everyone has their own problems was what she meant. 'Mama Brenda has to struggle to hold her family together. She and her girls have little enough as it is. And it is not right to mock them. Remember that she took you in, Amuka,' she admonished. 'She might have complained, but she never rejected you. And if she works you hard it's because she has to. Her family can get by, but there is no room for slack.'

Muka hung her head. She felt ashamed. Would Bat's grandmother not want her now? She sat down meekly again.

'I will work you hard too,' said Bat's grandmother. 'And I will still want you to go and help your cousins. You still have a lot of learning to do.'

The elephant also had a lot of learning ahead of her. Right now, how to suck water remained the great mystery. Meya preferred to kneel by the river and scoop it up with her mouth, and this worried Bat. The crocodiles listened for the noise of an animal lapping. They sneaked up and launched their surprise attacks. He was relieved when one day she at long last got the knack; suddenly discovering that she had drawn up a nose-full of liquid, she trumpeted joyfully in her amazed delight, spraying it all back out again in a blast of rainbows. She had to make dozens more experiments before she mastered the art. Sometimes she sucked up sand from the riverbed too. Then, mad with the itching, she would writhe her trunk into clots until finally she worked out how best she could scratch it, holding it down with one forefoot and rolling it gently back and forth.

Little by little, she became adept. 'An elephant's trunk

is an amazing thing,' Bat's grandmother said. 'It can feel the tiniest shapes and the subtlest textures. It can test minute changes in temperature and tell the precise bearing of a scent on the wind. But you have to be careful. It is strong enough also to snap an acacia. It can smash the bones of a lioness with one swipe.'

By the time the short rains came, swathing the savannah in wild flowers and filling the air with fresh scents, Meya was learning to forage. At first, she would twirl her trunk round and round a solitary grass stalk, eventually securing it only, once more, to let it drop; then, having spent twice as long again in her efforts to retrieve it, she would seem to forget why she had originally wanted it and pitch it pointlessly over her head. But soon she worked out how to choose one tussock at a time, how to grasp at it firmly before giving a strong forward kick that would sheer through its fibres as efficiently as a panga swipe. Then she would pop it, free of earth, into her mouth.

Sometimes Bat would sneak her bananas from the shamba. He would bring her sweet potatoes and guava fruits. He would show her acacia pods and give her bunches of sweet dates. Meya guzzled the hard bitter fruit of gardenia bushes and, popping them in, two or three at a time, she would get the next couple ready with her trunk while she chewed; but she never touched the long yellow pods of the fever trees or the black and red beads of the trichelia bush, and she avoided the dangling beans of the sausage tree if she could.

As Meya grew bigger, she grew bolder. While Bat watched the cattle, she would go off exploring: pushing at termite mounds to see if they would topple, probing the burrows of the bush hyrax, shaking high branches and setting the weaver birds chattering as their nests swung to and fro, scattering leaves and loose twigs. Once she disturbed a porcupine. It rattled its quills and lumbered off with the inquisitive elephant in pursuit. When Meya returned squealing, Bat had to extract several needles from the tender skin of her trunk and afterwards she had stood there sucking at it disconsolately, like a tired human baby sucking at its thumb.

One day she followed a spur fowl that was dragging its wing, pretending to be wounded so as to lure the clumsy intruder away from its nest. When it thought it had gone far enough, it whirred miraculously off. Only then did Meya look round to discover that she didn't know where she was. That was how Bat learned her distinctive 'I'm lost' call: a sound that, beginning with a low throaty rumble, cranked up louder and louder to end in a panicky scream.

Elephants talk all the time, the children found out. Each different trumpet blast, they gradually discovered, each bellow, groan or snort, had its meaning; and slowly they learned them. 'It's like learning our letters,' said Muka who, every evening, sat down at Bat's side while his grandmother, pulling out the tattered old book which she kept in a tin chest to protect it from termites, ran a long bony finger along the lines of words.

The children learned to distinguish Meya's deep 'let's go' rumble from the lighter 'I'm here'; the scream of excitement from the scream of distress, the mock playful trumpet from the urgent 'come at once' call. And they discovered that, if they tried, they too could talk. Licking his lips, Bat pressed them together and blew with all his might and the elephant would respond with high-squealing excitement, racing in circles, trunk curled tight under chin, returning back-end first with a funny high-tailed shuffle, the whites of her eyes showing as she watched him from over her flank. But when she was frightened and started squeaking like a dry branch in the wind, Bat would come running to offer her comfort, humming a sound that seemed to rise from the very depths of his heart.

Towards the end of the afternoon, when Muka had finished her last village chores, she would go out to fetch water and meet Bat and Meya by the river. The cattle would browse while the children waded out, splashing each other and sometimes ducking right under until their dark skin was gleaming and Muka's braids dripped. Their happiness would shine like the air: Bat's laughter breaking around him like airlocks bursting open in his ears while Muka's higher peals rang out, chinking against the rocks, bright as the jumbling cadences of a twittering sunbird. Meya would join in, squeezing the tips of her trunk together so that the water sprayed like a fountain. She would do it again and again, waggling her head from side to side in never-tiring delight.

The hippos, which paddled half submerged in the shallows, would monitor her warily with little pouched eyes. Meya liked to visit their wallows. Flopping down on her side, she would wriggle about until she was completely plastered, before heaving herself over onto the other flank. It was only much later that she learned to be more dignified, to fling mud in dollops that landed with luscious wet slaps on her skin.

After bathing, they liked to play on the banks. Sometimes the children would hide, dodging behind termite mounds and waiting for Meya's squeal. Sometimes they would play throw and catch. But they had to be careful: where they chucked a stick, Meya would fling a whole branch, and once a wildebeest bone had landed right on Bat's head and left a bump on his temple that, when he touched it, had felt almost the size of a speckled plover egg.

When Meya was at her most boisterous, when she went on the rampage and beat up the bushes and charged through the pampas as if on the attack, the children learned to jump smartly out of her way; but when she was gentler they would join in her games, one of them leaping away through the grasses with Meya lumbering after until the other dashed suddenly in at a tangent and set her galloping off on another tack. She would get so excited that she raced around in circles, trumpeting shrilly with her trunk held aloft. And when she felt particularly silly, she would lollop and flop, waggling her ears and wriggling her trunk.

## CHAPTER SIX

The village boys liked to wrestle in the evenings. While their sisters fanned cook-fires and their mothers rinsed rice, they locked arms together and shuffled round in slow circles, each waiting for a chance to wrong-foot the other, to trip him and hurl him on his back in the dust. Often the matches ended in a real fight. Women stormed from their huts, hands wet and knives waving, to pull their squabbling offspring back home by the ears. But the girls peeped eagerly out of their doorways, finding any excuse to run over and find out what was happening, and when the tussles between the elder boys had finally produced their victor, he was sure of coy smiles as he strutted home to eat.

Meya soon learned to enjoy this evening sport and the village children, gathering excitedly under the jambula tree, were delighted to find in her a new opponent. Arm wrapped about trunk, boy and beast shoved shoulder to shoulder, the former heaving away until his calf muscles ached, the latter planting herself, a solid unbudgeable force, until she grew bored and, with slow easy strength, shunted her wriggling antagonist back across the marker line that had been drawn in the dirt. And among the loud cheers that rose after each bout, none would be louder or more excitable than Bat's. He would dart forward to congratulate the little elephant, scratching her vigorously behind her ears. 'No one can match her.' He would grin as proudly as if it was he who had just stripped off his T-shirt and fought.

'Lobo might have,' one of the older boys piped up one evening.

The others, who enjoyed few things more than an argument over tactics, over feints, throws and stances, grips, lunges and headlocks, quickly picked up the challenge. They loved to recall the great moments of such now near-legendary fighters as the Cat, who had never once let his back touch the ground; or Weasel who, however tight the spot he was trapped in, had always managed somehow to wriggle his way out. Lobo, when he had lived in the village, had been known as the Hog for the sheer power of his head-on frontal pushing; for his trick of ramming straight into his opponent, sometimes so hard that you could hear skulls crack. Locked forehead to forehead, the two combatants would tussle until Lobo found some way of delivering his brutal trademark swipe: a killer sideways blow that sliced assailants from their feet. Failing that, he would bite. 'Everything is fair in war,' he would say and, fixing his bludgeoned and often bleeding loser with his slitted stare, he would utter the deep *whooomph* sound of a warning warthog.

Now, a few of the older boys nodded: 'Lobo might have,' they agreed.

'He wouldn't have been tall enough,' one of them ventured.

'But that made him better,' another argued back. 'Nothing could knock Lobo off those thick legs.'

'And he was heavy. I would have got him once if I'd been able to lift him. I'd got my shoulder right—'

'But you didn't.'

'I nearly did.'

'I was there! You had no chance.'

'Remember the day he broke Okeny's finger?' interrupted another and, as if even the thought of it still had the power to hurt, he sucked air through his teeth and started flapping a loose hand about.

'And the time he bit Komakech?'

Bat shifted uncomfortably. He was younger than Lobo and, like all the other little ones, had learned to be wary, to try to keep out of his way. He glanced across at Bim. He looked agitated too, and though he didn't say anything, Bat could tell by the way his eyes flickered that he would have liked to if he could.

'That bite got infected,' Komakech cried out excitedly. 'My mother said it was poisonous as the bite of a market-place dog.'

Several boys giggled. But Bim got up and crept towards Bat, squeezing in beside him where he squatted, one in a line of boys on a log. Only Bat saw the shiver that moved across his face. It was like a breath of wind stirring across a pool of still water: just the tiniest motion – but if someone can't speak, other things become more eloquent and this slightest of tremors left Bat feeling disturbed.

No wonder then that he felt his heartbeat start fluttering when, a few months later, sitting under a tamarind cracking one of its pods, he spotted a far-off figure coming along the track, plodding doggedly on in the direction of the village. It was Lobo. Bat knew it at once. He didn't need to see the dark face with its small deep-set eyes or the scar on his neck from a long ago viper-bite to recognize him. He could tell at once by the short thickset figure, the heavy straddle of the walk. He let the bean that he was about to pop into his mouth fall.

Lobo had left the village more than three years ago. He had gone to live in town and no one had heard more than the odd rumour since. So what was he doing now coming back to Jambula? What did he want? The afternoon sun was striking hard as a hammer, but the boy felt a sudden chill running down his spine; like when an evil spirit brushes by you in the forest, he thought.

'Who's Lobo?' Muka asked carelessly when Bat told her later by the river. She was busy scraping the mud from Meya's toenails and she didn't sound very interested.

'He's the son of the medicine woman,' said Bat. That got her attention. Everyone knew the medicine woman but few ever visited her dilapidated hut where it stood in its weed-fringed dirt patch at the very edges of the village; so far off, some insisted that it wasn't even a part of Jambula. Foul-smelling smoke would rise up from its cook-fires. Even to breathe it was dangerous, people whispered. They seldom braved the dark interior with its tangles of roots and its bits of dried animals, its charms stoppered in bottles and its baskets of snakes. To do so was to risk running foul of a temper that was quick as a striking cobra, and many a village child had taken a hard crack from the medicine woman's stick.

'When Lobo was little, you would hear his cries ringing out even from under the jambula,' Bat told Muka. 'And sometimes you would see his mother chasing him, raining blows and black curses. The bruises would come up in big lumps. But when he got older, all she could do was scream at him. You would hear her howling like a jackal at night, but Lobo would just laugh. Sometimes he would show us the scar on his neck. He got it from a gaboon viper. It escaped from a basket in the medicine woman's hut. "See this," he would say. "Her bark is no worse than this viper's bite and I survived that."'

Muka looked up from where she was kneeling by Meya. 'But who would have married the medicine woman?' she asked in astonishment. 'Who would have wanted to live with her in that hut? I didn't know she'd had children.'

'He isn't her real son,' Bat explained. 'She just brought him up. She found him living on scraps in the market and brought him back. Nobody knows who his real mother is. Some say that she came from the land across the mountains, others that she's in prison and will never be let out, and others that she's dead; but once I heard a market woman tell my grandmother that she knew someone who had met Lobo's real mother, that she was still living and had replaced him with more sons.'

'Do you think that's true?'

Bat shrugged. 'Lobo used to tell us that he had a father who lived in the city. He used to tell us that one day his dad would come to fetch him and that he would drive here in a motor car.'

Muka's eyes widened. 'Did Lobo make that up?'

Bat shrugged again. 'Don't know . . . but we always pretended to believe it; he would have leaped on you in a fury if he had seen you shake your head. He would have sat down on top of you and pushed your face into the dust. Lobo is scary. One moment he is smiling and joking and laughing, and the next, for no reason, he is flying into a rage. "Staying near the termite hill turns the antelope brown." That's what my grandmother thinks. She says that since roughness is all he has ever known, it's the only way he now knows how to be.'

'Oh well . . .' cried Muka, dropping the subject and jumping to her feet. She gave the back end of the elephant a hard, playful shove. 'Let's play catch,' she called.

But Bat wasn't in the mood. 'Anecanec has a cut on her hind leg. I've got to wash it now.'

'Why are you being so dull today?' Muka kept taunting as they walked home together. 'It's boring! Why are you being like this?' But Bat refused to be shifted from his sombre brooding. Whenever Muka asked him he would just hitch up his shorts and shrug.

He spent much longer than usual in the cattle pen, milking. It always calmed him to squat there, his forehead pressed into warm flanks, listening to the slow purling of milk into a calabash. By the time he had finished, two village boys had been delegated to go and fetch him. 'Come and fight! Come and fight!' they were crying, dancing eagerly about him. 'We're fighting under the jambula. Come and bring your elephant.'

Reluctantly, Bat was persuaded to follow them. He picked his way along the paths that wound around each compound, the two little boys still hopping about him, tugging at his T-shirt and pulling at his hand when he lagged. Meya, who loved wrestling, shambled hastily along behind him, barging into his back when she wanted to break into a trot. Then even he had to smile a bit.

Hastily, he scanned the crowd that had gathered under the jambula tree. No sign of Lobo. That was good. He was beginning to brighten.

Meya took her place. She was eager to get started. Impatiently she swung her trunk back and forth.

'What a squit of an elephant!'

The sneer curled up from the back of the crowd. Bat felt his smile dissolve. It was Lobo . . . he had come, just as Bat had feared he would, and now he was elbowing his way roughly forwards. He pushed behind Bim. The little boy was blocking his path.

'You!' Lobo cried, narrowing his eyes. 'I had forgotten about you!' Bim tried to skip aside before Lobo could grab him, but his way was blocked by the crowd and, pushed backwards, he landed instead on Lobo's foot. Twisting his head, he looked upwards with large frightened eyes. 'Look what you've done now!' Lobo shouted.

'You've put dust on my shoes.' He grabbed the child by the shoulders, spun him round and shook. A bellow of fear erupted from the boy's throat. The surrounding watchers shrank back.

'What was that?' taunted Lobo. He cupped a hand to his ear. A few laughs broke out. 'Has someone trapped a little bush pig?'

The laughs broke out again.

Bat looked away. Muka, he noticed, was loitering on the fringes. He glanced back at Bim, whose mouth was still open, like a tear ripped in a face down which the tears were beginning to spill. Tugging free of Lobo's grasp, Bim dashed unhappily away.

'The little bush pig has escaped. Well, it was too scrawny to eat!' jeered the bully, inspecting his footwear. His shoes were new and made of leather. No one else in the village owned a pair as good as that. He rubbed them back to a shine against his trouser leg. Then with a slow swagger he came to the front of the circle.

'So, this is your elephant, is it?' he asked. 'What a puny creature!' With a snort of derision, he started to unbutton his shirt. Folding it carefully, he handed it to an onlooker. He may not have grown any taller but he looked even stronger, Bat thought. His chest was broad as a man's. He started to limber up, flexing thick arms to display bulging muscles. He tilted his chin upwards. Bat spotted the old snake-bite scar: two dark shiny knots at the base of his neck.

'The Hog is ready!' he called as he kicked off his shoes.

The village boys fell back. The eldest of Muka's

cousins came hurrying over to look, crossing the compound with a funny wriggle-trip walk.

'Come to cheer me?' asked Lobo. His smile brought out a pair of boyish dimples on his cheek, but it never reached his eyes, which were small and so deep set that, when he frowned, they disappeared into the furrows like a pair of pebbles flung into the mud. Muka's cousin clamped her hand to her mouth and broke out in shy giggles. Her mother was probably even at that moment bawling for her, but she didn't care. She wandered round and round: 'Like a hen looking for a place to drop her egg,' whispered one of the boys near to Bat.

Then Fat Rosa arrived, her three little daughters jostling along in her wake. And a short while later old Kaaka came hobbling in with her stick. Even Bitek the fisherman, the only person in the village who had never appeared interested in the elephant, paused as he made his way home with his nets. Marula, who had been named after the plum because she had no legs and sat all day as if dropped onto the hard-packed earth outside her hut, leaned back on her hands and, raising her face skywards, called out to her sons, 'I can't see. Come and help me. Come and carry me across.'

Lobo's eyes swept the crowd. Two of Marula's boys were already there. 'Go and help your mother,' he ordered. He had always had a trick, Bat remembered, of being obsequious to his elders. He could adapt himself like a chameleon according to the company. But what colour was the chameleon before it first started changing? Bat wondered, as Marula was hoisted upon her sons' shoulders. Striding forward, they planted her like a yam on the ground near the front.

Lobo strolled over to where the elephant waited. Bat felt tight as twined cord. He wished that this wrestling match wasn't happening.

'Worried, are you, Bat?' Lobo flexed his muscles nonchalantly as if he was already growing bored. The smell of cooking wafted over with the drifting wood-smoke. 'Mmm! Smells good,' he taunted. 'Perhaps you should go back and help your old grandma. Cook like a woman if you can't take a man's fight.' And then, spotting Muka moving in a little closer, he glanced up and gave her his most winning smile. 'Who's that?' he said; but Bat didn't answer and Muka just scowled.

Lobo shrugged. 'Come on then, you excuse for an elephant!' Squaring up to the little animal, he braced his legs. His fists were tightly clenched. Meya did look rather small: her back was barely as high as Lobo's waist. But she wrapped her trunk trustfully around his strong arms.

Lobo pinched its soft tip. The elephant gave a confused little squeal. 'Crying already? Before you've even lost!' Lobo rubbed her patronizingly on the head. Then, rolling his shoulders, he fell silent and leaned in for the match.

A pair of drummers who, for too long now, had been awaiting the moment, drew their instruments to them and struck up a fast beat. Their hands flickered and darted across the taut skins. The two combatants started to shove, one against the other, just testing at first, the elephant pushing forward, quietly implacable,

66

while Lobo shunted, head down and arms locked into place. Soon he was straining so hard that his shoulder muscles sprang into knots. The gathered children cheered as they watched his nostrils flaring, the beads of sweat breaking upon his furrowed brow. The tendons in his legs were stretched almost to breaking point. He grunted and heaved. His feet slipped in the dust. 'Meya will win in the end,' a little boy burst out. Lobo flashed him a furious slantwise look. The veins in his neck were swollen: they strained like tugged cords. Bat was praying so fervently that Muka could see his lips moving. The contest seemed to him endless. The drums throbbed. Their rhythms rolled outwards in long reverberating waves. The air was alive with their pulse and his nerves jittered to the tune.

'Come on, Meya!' piped a voice.

The little elephant jerked as if startled and gave a rough shove, sending her opponent staggering backwards, arms flailing. Lobo almost lost his footing. Meya backed off, ears flapping.

'That's cheating,' cried Lobo. 'That shout put me off,' and he glared at the little boy who had suddenly called out. 'Pathetic creature,' he muttered to Meya, who was now eyeing him warily from the far side of the compound, swaying her foot and shuffling uncertainly about. 'You're not even a proper elephant. Not even worth shooting. You don't have any tusks.' He spat in the dust.

Meya lifted her head; then, coiling her trunk, she spread her ears and charged. The crowd gasped. Fat Rosa's hands flew to her wide-agape mouth. The drummers halted in mid-beat. Someone uttered a loud shriek. The ground shuddered and, inside Bat's head, the whole world turned wavy. Was this just a threat? Or was she going to smash into the boy?

At the last possible moment the elephant skidded to a halt even as Lobo, who until then had stood frozen, crashed panic-stricken into the surrounding crowd. Meya bellowed. It was the first time Bat had ever seen her so angry. It was the first time he had ever heard that enraged call. Seizing a branch of firewood, the elephant smashed it to smithereens in front of the crowd.

For a few long moments the watchers remained rooted and gaping. Then, slowly, little by little, they began to mutter and whisper and shift nervously about. Lobo looked awkward. Clasping both hands at the back of his neck, he sucked in a huge clump of air. He rolled his broad shoulders and wiped the sweat from his face. And then he stepped forward again. His mouth had been pulled into an unexpected smile. Crossing the compound, he stretched out a hand to Meya, but the elephant, swivelling round rapidly, lashed out a back foot. Lobo was sent sprawling. He fell backwards and landed on his bottom in the dust.

The whole crowd dissolved into giggles. Muka's cousin clutched her hand to her mouth and let out a series of sharp yelps. The lady with no legs threw her head back and shrilled, and Fat Rosa doubled over, guffawing and gasping so violently that tears streamed down her cheeks and her whole body shook. Even Bitek the fisherman broke into a grin. Muka's laughter bubbled up like water as it breaks over rocks. It was the first time many villagers had ever heard its sparkling ring. Lobo was mortified that he was its cause. Picking himself up, he retrieved his shirt and shoes and stalked stiffly away. A dusty red patch marked each buttock from when he had fallen. A little boy pointed and cried out. One last time, the gathered crowd broke into loud guffaws.

Only Bat didn't join them. Meya's temper had worried him. She was bewildered and confused now and he couldn't soothe her. She trotted to and fro, her head high, her spine humped. What was wrong with her? He was frightened. It was as if some connection between them had been broken. She wouldn't listen to his voice.

Slowly, he and Muka persuaded her back to their hut, stroking her gently and humming to calm her. They scraped the cracked mud from her skin and plucked out a few ticks. The guinea fowl dashed with sharp eyes to peck up the plump treats. Gradually the little elephant began to relax, her eyes growing tranquil under their long curling lashes, her trunk slowly stretching until she brushed the ground with its tip. Bat ran his fingers through the little sprouting beard on her under-lip, and it was then that he discovered it: a deep, jagged tear in the flesh. Meya jerked her head back as he touched it, and Bat, quickly withdrawing the hand that had hurt her, spread it out palm upwards before him and stared. The tips of his fingers were wet with blood.

He understood in a flash. In his mind's eye he saw Lobo squaring up with clenched fists. He must have had something hidden in his hands . . . something sharp . . . like a stone . . . or a bit of metal perhaps.

He had jabbed it as hard as he could into Meya, in the place where her skin was most tender, where her nerves were most sharp. As Bat touched the wound gently, the little elephant shook her head. The memory troubled her. Her ears flapped like stiff blankets being shaken of dust.

The boy sprang to his feet and stormed from the hut. He was trembling with rage. He was going to thrash that big cheat, he was going to beat him until he cried like a baby, he was going to make him regret that he had ever come back, he was going to force him to apologize in front of the whole village . . . he was going to . . . he was going to . . . his fury broke out in great impotent sobs as he walked round and round, kicking anything he could. He thumped at a wall. The blood burst from his knuckles, but he didn't care; his heart was boiling inside him.

Bat didn't notice his grandmother until he had almost walked into her. She reached out a hand for him but he jerked himself away. 'Muka told me,' she said gently. 'She's just told me what happened. And no, it's not fair. But don't go after the boy. Don't turn him into an enemy.'

'But why?' shouted Bat. 'Why did he have to hurt her? She's only a baby. Who would hurt a baby? Who would break its trust?' And suddenly, everything felt far too much for him. His grandmother drew him towards her and held him until all the rage was cried out of him. Only then did his body finally fall slack.

## CHAPTER SEVEN

Every fifth day was market day. The villagers counted the time passing on their fingers; when they got to the thumb they knew that it had come round again. Rising in the darkness, they left before daybreak, chattering in low voices as they set off down the track, clutching trussed chickens or piglets or big speckled pumpkins, with buckets or baskets or enormous wrapped bundles carefully balanced on top of their heads.

A few weeks after the wrestling match, Muka, with a blanket of groundnuts from the shamba, was among the first to be leaving for the market place. Even at her swift pace, it took the whole of the first part of the morning to walk there, and only those who arrived early could ask for the best price. Before the long shadows were starting to shrink, she had sold half her heap to the usual morning shoppers and the rest to the lady who made stew at the lorry drivers' stop. For the rest of the day she was now free to do as she liked.

Muka loved this time of liberty. She wandered up and down the lines of traders, looking at the mounds of stacked kola nuts and embankments of bananas, pyramids of green oranges and gourds of goats' milk, at the clay pots and old clothing, the coloured blankets and tin buckets, the packets of spaghetti and parcels of salt. She watched the women as they haggled and bargained and tried to hold to their prices, scowling and puffing and pulling at their under-lips, spitting in the dirt when a deal had finally been done.

In the street leading away from the square, Muka paused to look at the wood-carvers assembling their miniature armies; at the cobblers with rows of bright tin-tacks clamped between their lips; at the tailors whose needles streamed ant-trails of stitches or the braiders who plaited corn-rows and starbursts of spikes. Walkers passed, bent almost double under huge bales of cotton. Men pedalled bicycles with their wives perched on the back. Dogs skulked along gutters, goats blundered about bleating and stray chickens dashed excitedly wherever they spotted a tasty scrap. The bus that came in from the east would send them all scattering. A clutter of shrieking children dangled off its back.

At the far end of the street was a clearing where the kapok tree stood. It was there that the butcher strung up his carcasses, wielding his cleaver amid clouds of buzzing flies, wrapping sloppy purple livers in banana-leaf bundles and scolding the buzzards as they made off with giblets in their beaks. But Muka, as always, headed straight on past it towards the shadowy corner where the witch doctor sat, his little square of black cloth laid out neatly in front of him. On it a grisly jumble of medicines was arrayed: phials of bright powders and flasks of dark potions, snake heads floating in alcohol and tangles of healing roots. Sometimes he would pull out the goat's foot that stoppered a bottle, offering some passer a gustatory sniff.

The witch doctor could tell fortunes by throwing chicken bones in a calabash. He could find the future in splashes of blood on the dust. But what he predicted was often not good. It was better to stay away from such things, people muttered, although, when push came to shove, when a baby cried with colic or an uncle got into debt, when rats raided the grain stores or a nursing mother had no milk, there were always ready customers for his magical remedies, and when old Kaaka had fallen so ill that the spirits had come for her, she had been dragged back from their clutches by a flask of rock-python fat.

Now the witch doctor called out to Muka as she lingered. 'Give me one of your plaits,' he croaked. The decaying stumps of his teeth were bared in a smile. 'I can weave it with gizzards and a rat skull,' he persuaded. 'It will make the boys crave you more than the sweetness of a newly cut piece of cane.'

'I don't want them to,' Muka snapped, stepping briskly away, and, clasping her arms round her chest, she walked hastily off. She was heading, as she always did, up the hill into that part of the town where the shops were more than just blankets thrown down on the ground. Walking between buildings made of bricks and breeze-blocks, of sheets of rusted metal and cross-nailed struts of wood, she made her way towards the shack of the man who sold electrical goods. She was fascinated by this place. Easing her way into the group of gathered children, she stood and stared entranced into a row of little boxes full of light. There were pictures inside them; they shifted and flickered like the shadows of moths, and she gazed at them, mesmerized by each changing fragment. They all seemed so different. She struggled to work out how they might all come together, but there were always more gaps in the puzzle than pieces that could be made to fit.

Muka was about to leave when she heard someone calling her from inside a doorway. She turned but couldn't see who it was: the day was so bright and the interior so black. All she could make out was shapes among shadows. She stepped closer, and suddenly Lobo dashed out. 'Come and meet my friend,' he cried, grabbing her round the wrist.

'This is Amuka,' he called, as he tugged her into a bar. 'She's the prettiest girl in Jambula.'

A man swivelled round slowly in his chair to inspect her. Even though he was inside, he still wore a peaked cap. It was pulled low on his forehead so that half his face was hidden, and his sunshades had mirrors instead of smoked glass in their lenses. She couldn't see past them to tell what he was thinking as he looked. He took a puff on a cigarette that had been bought ready-made rather than rolled.

'Want one?' he offered, holding out the packet.

She was silent.

He shrugged. 'A drink for the young lady,' he called to a man behind the bar. A waiter returned a moment later with a bottle of orange liquid. Tiny bubbles were blinking and bursting at the top.

Muka didn't move to take it. She watched herself scowl in the mirror of his glasses. She was wary of this stranger. His skin had a sharp oily tang that made her nose wrinkle. It gleamed almost purple in the gloomy light.

'It's nice,' encouraged Lobo. 'Take a sip,' and picking up the bottle, he thrust it towards her.

She shied away.

'Muka and I are alike: we neither of us really belong to the village,' explained Lobo.

The man nodded. 'So you like the town?' he asked, reaching for an empty chair and dragging it across. He motioned to Muka to sit down. She ignored him, but he didn't seem to notice. 'I expect the market seems exciting to a lively girl like you. You are far too pretty for dull village life.'

'Or a boring old elephant,' Lobo added.

'Elephant?' The man's voice rose in quick enquiry.

Muka sensed the sudden fine-tuning of his attention. She turned instinctively to go. Quick as a snake, the man darted. A hand encircled her wrist. 'Don't leave just yet,' he persuaded; but though his mouth was smiling, there was no mistaking the tenacity of his grip. 'Tell me about this elephant.'

Muka hung her head and remained stubbornly mute but Lobo, despite a passing frown of puzzlement,

75

was now sprawling splay-legged, looking pleased with himself. He took a long slug at the bottle from the table in front of him, then, smacking his lips in satisfaction, said: 'There's this boy in the village with an elephant. He's had it for ages.'

'How long?'

Lobo shrugged. 'I don't know. I only saw it a few weeks ago.'

The man looked at Muka.

Still she didn't speak.

The man gave her wrist a sharp rousing shake.

'She's nearly three,' the girl mumbled.

'A three-year-old elephant . . . and where did you get it?'

Muka shifted uncomfortably. 'My friend found her,' she murmured.

But Lobo was eager to go on with the story again. 'Its mother was shot by poachers,' he said, 'and so the villagers reared it.' He smiled, a single boyish dimple popping into each cheek. 'And the boy's learned to speak elephant, so the villagers say.'

'Speak elephant?' From behind his mirrored glasses, the man was scanning Muka's face.

Shrinking, she cast her eyes quickly around the shack. Another man was slumped in the corner, head down on the table, while his drinking companion, legs stretched out in front of him, leaned a cheek on one hand and stared emptily out through the open door. Outside, a man wobbled by on a bicycle. A child bowled the rim of a car wheel along with a stick. The waiter, arms folded, stared impassively from behind his wooden counter. A hard-shelled beetle dashed itself hopelessly, again and again, against a dusty strip light. This is not a good place to be, thought the girl. She could feel her anxiety pulling like a hot wire through her blood, tweaking at secret fears.

'Just sit down,' Lobo was saying, tipping his head back to take another pull at his bottle. For the first time, she noticed the scars on his neck: two shiny nubs at the base of his throat.

'I've got to go now,' she mumbled. 'I've got stuff to do.'

'Let us persuade you?' A smile slid from the man as he at last loosened his grip.

Muka gave a sharp tug and, shaking her head, slipped rapidly away. She could feel their eyes following her as she pushed between two tables. A clatter of laughter broke out behind her – as if she had barged into something and it had fallen and broken, she thought. She felt as if something inside her had also been dislodged. She hurried away down the street, the tassels of her wrap whipping fretfully at her ankles, her nerves rattling like palm leaves when a sudden breeze picks up. She didn't look back.

Walking briskly on, she found herself winding through the small tin-roofed shanties. The rank odour of rubbish steamed in the hot afternoon. Ditches brewed foul smells. The alleys were strewn with broken glass and discarded plastic, with fish heads and eggshells and the green crowns of pineapples, with thrown-away tins and sliced-off chickens' feet. A hog snivelled in the muck, its eyes closed as if meditating. For a moment Muka thought of the village women, bent double every morning, as they swept round their huts with little palm-frond brooms. By the time they had finished, not a maize husk or mango stone littered the stamped earth. It helped keep the pests away from the home. But here in the shanties, the flies gathered in thick buzzing clusters. They rose in zigzagging clouds at the approach of her shadow and then dropped back down again like black scabs as she passed.

At the end of the street, she could see the rough grass-lands beginning. The transition was so abrupt. One moment you were standing amid a maze of cluttered buildings, the next you were in the rolling savannah. It stretched unbroken to the furthest horizon, interrupted by nothing but acacias and great termite citadels and, somewhere in the far haze, a tree with flowers so red that it looked, through the shimmer, as if it was aflame. What had one world to do with the other? she wondered. It was a bit like watching the television sets. She could not see how the different bits of life could ever quite meet.

Muka took no more pleasure in the market that day. Finding a cluster of women in the square, she sat down in the feathery shade of a spreading mvule. The women had finished their work and now they were relaxing. They were peeling oranges and talk-ing, drawing gossip like honey sucked from flowers by bees. Normally, their chatter would have washed over Muka. She would have only half listened to their tales of bad husbands and good children, of trouble-some neighbours or beneficent uncles, of the crops they were growing and the prices they would fetch. But of late, she had started to grow more attentive. Rumours were rife of a strange rebel army. There were gangs of fierce children living up in the hills. They seldom came down to the plains, it was whispered, but when they did they stole chickens and cut the maize from the shambas, they raided the tool stores and slaughtered the goats.

'They will burn down your hut if you utter so much as a squawk,' one woman now said.

'Or worse,' nodded another.

'In the village next to mine,' a lady whom Muka had never seen before was now saying, 'a boy has disappeared . . . a youngest son. He went out with the goats, just as normal . . . and then *pouf* ' – she puckered her lips and blew at the air – 'he was gone . . . just vanished . . . nothing seen of him since; not of him or his animals. His family has searched . . . but not a single trace found.'

'A lion?' someone suggested.

The lady shook her head firmly.

'Abducted?' another ventured.

The storyteller nodded solemnly. 'They say so.'

'By the rebels?'

She nodded again.

'Tssk . . . the child army,' a round-eyed mother murmured, clutching her nursing baby a little tighter to her breast.

'They are coming closer,' her neighbour warned. 'And they say that there's nothing the government can do about it. The bush is too wide and the cover too thick. They send out their soldiers and they fall into ambushes; so now they just sit in their camps instead and smoke.'

She shrugged. 'I don't blame them. I wouldn't want to be cut up into pieces by a panga.'

'And so . . . what? . . . the child army should just be allowed to run wild . . . to go anywhere it likes?'

'They already do,' said the woman who sold eggs. 'The stories are terrible if you travel further east. There the rebels have taken over whole towns. Their commanders sit in the market squares, laughing and drinking, their guns hanging on straps over the backs of their chairs. And out in the bush the villages are empty. No one dares stay any more. They go to live in the camps that the government has set up for them. Their stomachs are empty while the rebels feast on their crops.' She paused to shift herself into a more comfortable position, but nobody else began speaking. Everyone wanted to hear what more this woman had found out. 'Life in the camps is dreadful,' she continued. 'More people than you can name are all crowded onto one tiny spot. They hand out food but it's not enough for a family. You send your daughters for water and they have to queue all day long just for one gallon can. But who would dare leave?' She spread her hands helplessly. 'If you go, you just run into the rebel army. And what then? If you are young and strong they abduct you and force you to join them; if you are old and weak you are lucky to escape with your life.'

'No one will take my children,' Fat Rosa declared stoutly. She seldom went anywhere without her daughters at her side. In the village they joked that all three could fit inside her broad shadow. But there was nothing funny about what the egg-lady was telling her now.

'That's what you think. It's what they all think,' she

said. 'But you have no choice. One moment you are working out in the shamba, the next the child soldiers are in your compound. They are running like rats around the village . . . and they are just as ferocious. They will slaughter your laying hens and take all your seed grain, strip your crops of their harvest and steal your knives from the thatch. In a village called Jwato,' the woman went on, 'they rounded everyone up at the point of a gun. Even the chief's youngest son, who had seen them and run to hide by the river, was found in the rushes and dragged back. Everyone was gathered into the central compound. They were weeping and begging; but the soldiers just laughed. Mothers had to stand and let their children be chosen. That's what you must do if you value your life. And even if you don't, it's no good. They will shoot you . . . or worse . . .' she added with a significant look. 'And your children will still be abducted just the same.

'In Jwato,' she continued, 'all the strong boys and girls were separated out. Those that clung to their parents were beaten with millet pestles. One had his arm broken. And then, laden with burdens of whatever food had been ransacked, they were marched off into the bush. None of them, as far as I know, has ever come back.'

Muka listened, appalled. She could feel the sweat creeping in runnels through her scalp; it ran down the sides of her face and the back of her neck but she kept her mouth firmly shut. If Bat's grandmother had been there, she suspected, she wouldn't even have been allowed to listen. The old lady would have dreamed up an errand for her to do. Better keep it a secret, the girl decided; better not to discuss what she had just heard. In the corner of the market place, a huge dark bird was wrestling with a creature that it had pinned under its claws. It was a rat: one of the impudent rodents that scuttled through the shanties, sitting up on their hind legs to examine those who passed. The bird tugged at the fur with its beak, exposing raw flesh beneath.

As they set off for home, Muka was unnaturally silent; but the worries were simmering away in her head and she hadn't gone far before they finally boiled over.

'What would happen if the child soldiers came our way?' she asked Bat's grandmother.

A dark frown flitted across the old woman's face. She too had heard the rumours. 'The rebels are a long way from here,' she eventually said. 'They live right up in the mountains. The government soldiers will stop them from coming as far as us. But if they should reach these parts . . .' She paused. She did not know what to say.

'If they do?' prompted Muka.

'If they do we will have to think . . .' She let the sentence drop. 'What does that say?' she asked, changing the subject abruptly and pointing to a sign that had been painted on a tin sheet and propped up beside the road.

Muka squinted and began slowly to spell the letters out. 'It says: *Beware of invisible cows!*' she said.

Bat's grandmother chuckled, but Muka, who would normally have broken into peals of laughter, could force only the faintest smile. Her mind was elsewhere. What if the child army did come as far as Jambula? What if, even now, they were creeping out from their hills?

What would she do if, one day, she looked up and found one of them watching her? Should she run, or give up? And what if they found Bat? He wandered so far with his cattle. He might stray into their territories, and then he would be taken. Someone should warn him; he should be made aware.

'Would you mind if I left you now . . . if I went on a bit quicker?' she asked.

Bat's grandmother smiled. 'No, you run ahead and find him,' she said, reading the girl's thoughts. Bat had got into the habit of waiting to meet them on their way home and all three would walk back together, sharing whatever treats had been bought in the market if there had been enough milk to sell: chicken wings grilled over a charcoal brazier, perhaps; or a comb of dripping honey still stuck with black bees; a paper bag filled with plump, crisply fried caterpillars; or grasshoppers seasoned with pepper so spicy that water streamed out of your eyes as you ate. Bat loved the mixed sweet and tangy taste of the last.

'Run along then,' encouraged Bat's grandmother. 'I'll follow slowly. I'm feeling a bit weary. So off you go.' She watched the soles of the girl's feet flashing away through the dust. Then, frowning, she paused to re-adjust the wrap around her waist. She was growing slower. She had started to notice it. Her bones often ached . . . far more than they used to. She would have liked to have bought a bit of camphor oil in the market. It helped when she rubbed it onto her hip. Or perhaps she might have got a poultice from the lady who traded with the pygmies in the jungle. They had compresses made from the bark of rare trees. But, nowadays, she thought with a slow inward sigh, by the time she had paid for kerosene, tea and salt, there wasn't much left to spare. The elephant was still not yet weaned. She was still drinking too much of their precious cows' milk.

Bat's grandmother shifted the weight of her bundle to try to ease the pain. She had found herself doing that a lot of late. But she was still limping pronouncedly when Fat Rosa caught up with her, a cage of pigeons balanced precariously on top of her head. Everybody enjoyed the company of this jolly woman. Her big half-moon smile split her face when she laughed. 'I hope these birds didn't come from that rogue Lacan Jonathan,' she giggled as she fell into step with the old woman. 'Remember how he would sell and re-sell the same pigeons again and again. Each time someone bought them, they would come flying back home to him as soon as the unwary buyer let them loose; then the next week he would take them to market and sell them all over again.' The two friends laughed. 'Until that lady from the shanties took them,' remembered Bat's grandmother, 'and finally wrung their necks.'

Muka, meanwhile, her worries whirling faster and faster around her head, barely broke from her run until, coming around a corner, she spotted Bat – and there, just beyond him, the familiar bulk of Meya. They were hanging about expectantly just where they always did. She smiled as she at last slowed. It was the running that had done it. It whipped up your thoughts. She lifted her arm and gave a light-hearted wave.

Usually, in the lazy heat of the late afternoon, while

the drowsy cows were chewing the cud, Meya would be taking a dust bath, blowing great sighing clouds over her belly and back. It kept the biting insects away. Then she too would doze. But she would always be the first to know that Muka was coming. Her rumbles of greeting would roll through the air.

But today she was silent. A faint lick of worry flickered up in Muka's stomach again. Then she saw another figure hunkered down beside them. There was someone else there. That would explain it. But who? Muka wondered. She strained to see. With a jolt she realized that this stranger was Lobo. What was he doing there? It had been quite a while ago that she had left him drinking. She had assumed that he would stay in town. But now here he was. He had returned home ahead of her. And how had he got there so fast anyway? A bulky black bicycle thrown down under the tree soon explained it.

'I'm going to be the first person ever to ride an African elephant,' Lobo cried eagerly as he saw her approaching and, jumping up from the root on which he had been squatting, he swaggered towards her. Muka just scowled.

Lobo returned to his perch and examined his foot. A jigger had lodged itself in the tip of his toe. With a frown of concentration, he set about extracting it, piercing the blister with the point of a thorn. He impaled the curled parasite and then, carefully removing it, flicked it playfully at Bat. The boy brushed it away. He looked sullen and miserable, Muka thought.

An amulet hung round Lobo's neck, she noticed. She

hadn't remembered him wearing it in the bar. It looked like the skull of a rodent and it was all knotted up with some long wiry hairs. He must have bought it from the witch doctor, she thought, remembering how only that morning he had tried to sell her just such an amulet. Lobo, brought up by the medicine woman, probably believed in the magic of spells. She wondered if he had bought it in the hope that he could make people like him. Perhaps he had heard what the villagers muttered behind his back.

Lobo interrupted her reverie. 'Why pedal an old bicycle when you could ride an elephant?' he cried, aiming a kick at the black machine he had brought.

He was drunk, Muka realized. She could smell the sourness on his breath. The acrid smoke of the bar still clung to his skin.

'Imagine if that animal could be turned into something useful . . .' Lobo mused, casting a look of derision at Meya, 'if it didn't just hang around idly like some pointless pet.'

Meya slapped her ears indolently against her neck. Clouds of flies danced in the currents of stirred air.

'It would be great, wouldn't it?' the boy persisted, determined to provoke some sort of response. 'Then your grandmother wouldn't have to slip-stump along all higgledy-piggledly,' he cried. 'Like this!' and, jumping up, he began imitating the old woman's limp. He laughed. Bat clenched his fists but still he said nothing. Muka looked stubbornly down. She was willing the bully just to go away.

'Hey, you! What's your point?' The frustrated Lobo

now turned his attention to the elephant. Meya watched him warily through the fringe of her lashes. Reaching down for a bit of dirt, she slung it over her back. It was a threat, the children knew. The elephant was uncertain. She didn't understand what this boy wanted either.

'She makes us happy,' Bat ventured. 'That's point enough.'

'You're just a coward! You're too frightened to ride her.' Lobo's voice had turned nasty now. His eyes glittered with malice. 'Well, I'm going to prove that your great elephant is just a tame farm animal.'

'Don't,' warned Bat. 'She won't let you.'

'You mean you've never dared try!'

'She won't like it,' Bat said.

But Lobo stood up and, swaying slightly, took a step towards Meya. Her trunk twitched. He was testing her patience. Her forefoot swung to and fro as she tossed her head.

'Come on, you puny she-elephant,' mocked Lobo. 'You're not a wild beast any more. You're just a little kid's pet.' And suddenly, with a leap, he was on the animal's back.

Meya whirled round with a squeal and dashed straight for the trunk of an acacia, and before any of them could even tell what was happening, the startled Lobo was lying spread-eagled on his back, his shirt ripped, his elbow bleeding, his cheek badly scratched. It had all happened in the blink of an eye. For a few moments he just lay there with a look of dazed confusion, rubbing at the shoulder that had taken the brunt of his fall. Then, swearing, he started to struggle back to his feet. Meya turned, her eyes gleaming, and picking up a bolus from a pile of fresh dung, she hurled it as hard as she could straight at her tormentor. It hit him squarely in the middle of his chest.

Just at that moment, Fat Rosa and Bat's grandmother came into view. From afar, they had seen the whole thing and now they were both doubled over with laughter, chuckling and wheezing and wiping helplessly at their streaming tears. 'The white ant does not eat beyond the river,' Bat's grandmother cackled. Even this famously daring little creature, she meant, did not venture into territories that it did not know.

Lobo's face was twisted as a puff adder's as it prepares to strike. His eyes almost vanished into the thick furrows of his frown. Rising to his feet, he stalked unsteadily off and picked up his bicycle. He was weaving from side to side as he pedalled away down the track.

'He's so mean. He deserved it!' Bat shouted. His face glittered with anger as he tried to soothe the startled elephant.

'He deserved it!' echoed Muka. 'I wish Meya had hurt him; I wish she'd hurt him *much* more.'

But Bat's grandmother, after listening to the enraged children as they blurted out the whole story, only shook her old head. 'Lobo can't help it. Just remember that. He has no one to guide him. You are both embedded in the village like a tooth in a jaw. But he has been pulled out. That has hurt him and made him angry. He doesn't know to whom he belongs. When he grows older he will finally discover, and then I expect you will begin to see a change.'

## CHAPTER EIGHT

Lobo left the village whenever he wished, stayed away as long as he liked and returned when it pleased him. 'I am my own man,' he would say. But whenever he did choose to come back to Jambula, Bat from now on did his best to avoid him. He was pretty sure that the older boy would be contemplating revenge. Lobo had been made to look ridiculous in public. Even now he would be planning a way to get his own back. And what would Bat be able to do about it? The question kept troubling him.

Bat was not one of that little gang which liked to trip along at Lobo's heels. The smaller boys were impressed by him. He was the best wrestler; he had new clothes and a bicycle; no one bothered to scold him or order him about. They had bare dusty feet and a list of daily duties, and wherever they went in the village there was always an adult to tell them what to do. They would glance up enviously from their chores when they saw Lobo swaggering by, lounging about indolently with his hands in his pockets or trundling down the pathways on his new black bike. When Lobo requested something, they would run immediately to fetch it, shinning up trees to pick the ripest mango or running down to the shambas to get a maize cob. Then Lobo rewarded them for their obedience. He would mete out the sweets that he brought back from town and let them take sips from his bottles of beer or palm wine. Once little Gwok had returned home, his head reeling, and everyone had known it was Lobo who must have given him too much to drink, although even the next morning when the boy was sick as a dog, his brain throbbing so hard that it felt as if his skull would crack, he had refused to tell anyone where he had got the alcohol.

'Those little boys don't really like him. They're just frightened; he's a bully,' said Muka, and Bat had agreed, but still, when he thought about the child who had cheered for the elephant in the wrestling match, he would feel a nervous fluttering deep in his gut. Lobo had ambushed that boy on his way back from the shambas and given him a beating that had sent him howling for his hut. 'That'll teach you that I always win in the end,' he had said, and now, whenever the child came anywhere near him, hovering timidly at the edges of his circle, hoping to be allowed back to play with the gang, Lobo would reach down and pick up an imaginary stone, the way people do when they want to frighten a dog. He would pretend to fling it and then jeer when he saw how he flinched; but on the day the boy hadn't ducked and just stood there and faced him, he had flung a real stone and then laughed when the blood ran down his head. 'Go home and whine to your mother,' he had mocked.

The boy hadn't dared. What good would it have done? Lobo wasn't scared of the elders or their scolding. The medicine woman had long ago lost all control. 'I would beat her back if she lifted a hand to me, and she knows it,' he told listeners whose own mothers thought nothing of cuffing them and sending them squealing about their chores.

After Lobo's fall from Meya, Bat took to leaving with her and the cows as early in the morning as possible and only coming back again as late as was still safe. But when almost a moon had passed, he began to think that perhaps the older boy had forgotten. He had been drunk after all. And anyway he had asked for it.

'He probably knows it was his fault,' Muka suggested. 'If he hadn't climbed on her back, Meya would never have hurt him, and if he hadn't fallen, Fat Rosa would not have laughed.'

'It was only a tumble, after all,' Bat agreed. 'And he's used to a few bruises. When he was a child, the medicine woman made sure of that.'

And so the days passed and eventually Bat forgot until, one evening, just as he was locking up the cattle, separating the bleating calves from their mothers for the night, one of Marula's sons came dashing to find him. 'Lobo says that he rode the elephant!' he panted excitedly. 'He says that he climbed on her back . . . that

91

she squealed like a pig . . . but that he rode her and she couldn't stop him . . . he says that he's the only man in Africa ever to have ridden an elephant.' The breathless outburst ran suddenly to a halt and the boy looked up at Bat questioningly, as if his opinion now hung in the balance, as if he couldn't decide whether he wanted the boast to be true or not.

Bat's fingers were trembling as he fastened the gates. For a few long moments he tried to hold his feelings back, and then, like a pot of milk left too long on the fire, they all boiled over, spitting and steaming and bubbling up froth. 'He's a liar!' he flared. 'He's a stinking bully and a liar and he knows it. He never rode Meya! No one can ride her! Meya is wild. She can't be ridden like a pet. Go and ask my grandmother or Fat Rosa . . . they'll tell you. They saw what happened – they saw Lobo sprawled on his backside like a flipped-over toad.' Flinging a look of black-eyed fury at the youngster, he ran off.

'Have you heard what Lobo's been saying?' he demanded as, dashing into the cook-hut, he confronted his grandmother. 'He's saying that he rode Meya. He's claiming that he rode her like some tired old mule. How can you feel sorry for him? Just because his mother left him . . . she probably dumped him because he was so horrible . . . she probably knew what a lying bully he was.' Bat paced around the hut, fists curled and eyes flashing, frustrated as a genet cat trapped in the cage of an overturned basket. 'Next time I'm really going to get him,' he fumed. 'I don't care if he's bigger than me. I'm more furious than him.'

92

'A lion which roars does not catch an animal,' said Bat's grandmother calmly. 'Don't make an enemy of him over this either. Just let it blow over. You know it's not true. And, deep down, all the little ones know that too. They'll discover it soon enough.'

Slowly, notch by tiny notch, Bat's temper subsided. But still he was too agitated to eat properly that night. As he picked at his rice, fresh memories kept flaring. Muka would see them as they swept for a moment across his face. His jaw muscles would bunch as he ground his teeth hard together and he would strike his cupped palm with the knuckles of a curled fist.

But after a while the whole incident, like most of the boyish feuds in the village, blew over. Life settled down.

'No hard feelings,' said Lobo, strolling over one morning. Bat was warming himself in the early sun on a log. A clutch of newly hatched chickens dashed about peeping and Meya was pestering impatiently for her first feed. Her little pearly milk tusks had recently dropped out, revealing a new permanent pair sprouting beneath. Bat was trying to wean her but still she expected as much milk as she wished.

Lobo held out a mango for Meya. 'No hard feelings!' he repeated.

Normally Meya would have popped the fruit straight in her mouth, ground it appreciatively to a juicy pulp; but now she wouldn't take it. She shook her head and flicked her trunk.

'Aha!' cried Marula as she adjusted the swathed mass of her calico headcloth. 'The elephant doesn't trust you.'

'You don't trust me?' cajoled Lobo, looking the animal in the eye. 'Oh well, you give it then.' He handed the mango to Bat. If the sun had been up just a tiny bit higher he would have seen that Lobo's smile was in fact no smile at all.

Bat held out the rich-smelling globe to his elephant who, reaching out tentatively with her trunk, twirled the fruit round and round for a while before placing it carefully in her mouth. She chewed slowly, as if she was thinking about something, and then suddenly she spat it out. A long, rusty nail lay amid the fibrous orange flesh.

'Aha – the elephant is too smart for you!' cried the legless Marula, and clapped her hands with delight.

Bat stepped rapidly forward, his feelings of anger, relief and pride at the animal's cleverness all confusing his face. The nail was sharp in his hand as he bent to retrieve it. He would have hurled it at Lobo, but Bitek, the fisherman, was passing at that moment, his nets slung over his back. He too had seen what had happened and now he shook his head.

'Don't mess with an elephant, son,' he warned, turning to Lobo. 'They have powers far greater than you can understand.'

The older boy shrugged. 'It was only a joke,' he muttered, pushing out a laugh.

'Joke or no joke, it wasn't funny,' the fisherman said. 'Come here and I'll tell you a story.'

The two boys looked at each other sullenly.

'Sit down!'

Reluctantly, they sat.

'When I was a young man,' began Bitek, 'I fell in with a bad gang in town, just like you.' He fixed Lobo with a stern look. The boy, who until then had been casting his eyes about, ostentatiously bored, stopped fidgeting now and looked down at his feet.

'We used to go out and hunt bush meat,' Bitek continued. 'We killed anything . . . wild pigs, monkeys, gazelle if we could . . . and sold them in town. And one day we shot a cow elephant. We didn't even notice, or much care, whether she was with young. We just killed her. It was a terrible thing.' It was clear that the memory still pained the teller of this story. Bat looked up and saw that the man's whole face flinched. 'Her massive legs buckled, her great body trembled and stiffened, and she crashed to the ground, her calf crushed beneath her,' said Bitek. 'And I felt dreadful, as if everything inside me had suddenly been shaken out. I had to go and sit down in the shade of a tree. I told the others I felt sick. I didn't want them to think that I was a coward. I was a young man then, and strong, and I didn't want to lose face. And this thing would pass soon and I would forget it. But what I had done was worse . . . far worse . . . than even I thought.' He twisted and turned his hands as he spoke, as if trying to untangle some net that still trapped him. 'I began to feel awful. The whole world was turning dark. For two days I did nothing but sit in the hunters' camp. And I was still there when someone brought me the news. My wife and my children and my brother's eldest son had all died in an accident. A boat had capsized on the river and rolled over on top of them. And it had happened at the very moment

I killed the elephant. And that's why I know about the strength of these animals,' said Bitek. 'They have powers that are greater than we can ever tap into. Never mess with them.'

He leaned towards Lobo and put a hand on his shoulder. 'It was a long time ago; and after that I laid down my gun. I came here to live with my brother in Jambula. I taught myself to fish. It's a better way of earning a living and I am contented. But still I can never go back. And when I see that little elephant' – he nodded at Meya – 'I sense that she knows my story. That's why I never touch her. Elephants never forget, even if they forgive.'

Lobo was silent. His brow was knitting deep furrows and the fisherman, patting his head gently, eventually moved off. Only then did the boy rise again. He shook his head quickly. 'It was only a joke,' he muttered, and straightening his rumpled shirt, he sauntered off.

But then, a few days later, Meya started to behave in a very strange way. Normally, when night fell, she would go into the hut which she and Bat shared, shambling in hastily as if ready for bed. But this time she refused, standing outside, refusing to budge, however hard the boy pulled her; however determinedly he shoved. He even tried prodding her with a pointed stick.

'Women can be difficult for no reason,' Bat's grandmother laughed. 'Leave her be for a while.' And she moved to slip past the stubborn elephant. She needed a clay jar that was kept inside. Meya rushed at her with a squeal, knocking her flat with her trunk. Bat stared, appalled. He dashed over to his grandmother.

'I'm quite all right,' she said, brushing herself down. But she wasn't. She was shocked. Bat could feel her shaking. Meya just watched. Her rolling eyes showed their whites. Bat's grandmother set off calmly for the hut again.

Screaming, Meya rushed towards her. She barged her roughly aside and made a dash for the doorway; then, backing in bottom first, she stood like a guard. Her rumble was low and threatening as thunder. She flared out her ears and flicked her trunk back and forth. She looked dangerous. The fear flooded Bat's head. What had made her behave like this? Was it all Lobo's fault? Or did this just happen when an elephant grew up? He had heard about a man in another village who had cared for an orphaned lion cub. For months it had played like a kitten, rolling about in his hut, letting him tickle its butterfly-spotted belly and purring with pleasure as he ruffled its throat. But then, almost from one day to the next, it had changed. 'It was as if its true spirit had suddenly possessed it,' he would tell any listeners. 'Its eyes would turn hard and fierce. And it wouldn't recognize anyone . . . only the call of its wild instinct.'

Bat walked cautiously towards his elephant, holding his hand out and humming; but Meya didn't reach out to touch him like she usually did. She shifted about uncertainly, swaying and shuffling.

Suddenly, she squealed and backed into the hut. Bat ran to the door. Meya was crashing about wildly inside. He could see her spinning and stamping, rousing clouds of red dust. It took a few moments for his eyes to adjust, for him to see the snake thrashing about in the gloom. It was a mamba. He could tell by its gun-metal gleam. Writhing, it lashed out. Its black mouth was agape; but its spine had been smashed by Meya's foot.

Bat stared. It felt as if a cold hand was groping at his heart. That snake would have killed his grandmother. He stood frozen, sounds washing around him, giddy as a man who looks over the plummeting drop of a cliff. Slowly, he turned. The old woman was now limping towards him. Her lips were moving but he couldn't hear the words. They fell like the first drops of rain that just bounce off the skin. Only after a while did they begin to sink in, seeping gradually down into the very depths of his being.

'Your little elephant knew that snake was there,' his grandmother was saying. 'It must have dropped from the roof thatch. It must have been looking for a way out of the hut, just as I was trying to find my way in. And your little elephant knew it. She did her best to protect me. Meya saved my life,' she said.

Bat turned and ran to his elephant and flung his arms about her neck. His eyes were running with tears. If he hadn't been crying so much he might have paused and spotted the two fierce pinpricks that marked her back foot.

## CHAPTER NINE

Meya was sick the next day. She hung about listlessly, her once gleaming eyes dull. She fiddled absent-mindedly with dried leaves in the dust. She couldn't even be tempted with a sweet banana. Normally the first whiff of one opening would have brought her running; now, even a stick of sugar cane was turned down. When she moved, she walked gingerly on her soft pads. Bat bent down to look. The sole of her hind foot, its criss-cross pattern of fissures as distinctive as a human handprint, was puffed up and swollen. He felt with his fingers around the rims of her nails, and it was only then that he came across the puncture wounds.

Soon the whole village was gathered. They all understood the danger of snakes; and the mamba was notoriously fierce. When one dropped, as occasionally they would, with a thud from the thatch to land hissing furiously on the floor of a hut, the inhabitants would scatter. No one could sleep until it had been dispatched. Of all the poisonous serpents that slid through the bush, this was the most feared. Every villager knew of someone who'd been bitten, who had felt that first tingling at the ends of their toes and known from then on that they had not long to live. Crowding round the hut, they looked anxiously at Bat.

Little mute Bim was the first to come forward, his bright eyes brimming with worry. Waving his hands about, he made signs to say that he could take the cattle out to the pastures so that Bat could stay home with his elephant.

'And we'll cut forage and collect firewood,' volunteered the spokesman for a shuffling gang of youngsters, and all of them dashed off for their pangas, eager to help.

Fat Rosa sent two of her girls with palm leaves to use as fans, and later that morning, Bitek the fisherman also passed by, hesitantly approaching with a blanket full of yellow pods. It was the first time he had ever come near the elephant.

'She won't eat them,' Bat told him as he unwrapped his bundle. 'She doesn't like sausage fruit.'

'She will now,' said Bitek quietly. 'She will understand that they are an antidote.'

He was right. Picking one up with her trunk, Meya placed it tentatively in her mouth and began listlessly to chew.

Meanwhile, Bat's grandmother was dispatching Muka to the town to get herbs. 'The woman who trades with the pygmies will know what to do,' she said. 'You will find where she lives if you go to the kapok tree and ask.'

Muka had never run as hard or as long as she did that day. She was like a panicking creature trying to outpace its own shadow; but she could not escape the relentless pursuit of her thoughts. What if she couldn't get the medicine in time? What if the woman who sold herbs was away? Would Meya understand why she had suddenly left her? Would Bat manage without her? What if Meya died? She would not even have said goodbye to the little elephant. The unanswered questions rose up like spectres to taunt her. The breath broke from her lungs in hot bursts. Her throat burned. Sweat poured down her dusty skin but she never stopped until she at last saw the shanties, their tin roofs glittering like water in the light.

Muka returned to the village that afternoon clutching a bottle of oil and a handful of leaves. They were to be boiled up with maize flour and packed into the wound, she told Bat's grandmother; then a piece of damp sacking had to be made into a tight bandage. That was their only hope, the market seller had said, of drawing the snake poison out.

The next day Meya moaned continually. Her ears hung slack. The flies crawled through the fluids that leaked from her eyes but she didn't even bother to blink. A chain of children ran back and forth with clay pots to the river, bringing water to cool her. It poured down her back, sliding in runnels over ears and flanks. Still Meya seemed no better. She was painfully weak. By the evening, her head was hanging and her breathing was stertorous. She went to sleep on her belly. Bat had never before seen her lie and sleep like that.

He and Muka sat up the whole night beside her: whispering softly and humming and begging her to remember all the good times that together they had shared, pleading and pleading with her to make a struggle, to do all she could to try to get well. 'Remember the time when you were tiny and first discovered a spurfowl,' Bat reminded her.

'And the day you first learned to suck water with your trunk,' Muka said.

'And when you stole Fat Rosa's flip-flop,' Bat prompted, almost smiling.

'And how much you love pineapple,' encouraged Muka.

The children slept only in brief snatches that night. While the moon sailed like a boat through the infinite blackness and faint winds ruffled the seed heads of the savannah's dried grass, they crouched in the hut, stroking the creature they loved, talking to her gently so that even when her eyes were closing, still she would know they were always there. 'We are your family,' they told her. 'Don't leave us now,' they begged. They brushed the flies from her face like a mother brushes them from her baby. Softly they stroked her rough hide, tracing its wrinkles and furrows with their fingers as a pair of lost wanderers might trace the lines on a map. It was as if they wanted to find a way back to a place they had once known. Muka crooned softly and picked the ticks from the folds of Meya's skin, and from time to time, Bat rested his head against her heart. It beat like distant thunder from those clouds that gather but won't bring the rain when you need it most.

In the morning, Meya was barely moving. The thump of the pestles as they pounded cassava was pulsing through the village. *Thud-ah; thud-ah; thud-ah,* they sang. Meya, who would normally have been up much earlier, shambling mischievously about the compound, tugging at the roof thatch until Bat's grandmother came chasing, was now stretched out, flanks heaving, on the floor of her hut. Every now and then she would struggle to stand, putting out her forelegs and pushing, but before she had managed to haul herself even halfway she would topple and fall, panting, her sides rising and sinking, her trunk slack in the dust. She would surely die if she stayed that way too long, thought Bat. Like a cow, she was too heavy an animal to sleep on its flanks. The village men came with thick sisal ropes and, passing them under Meya's belly, threw the ends over the rafters and hauled her upright. The wood groaned and the whole structure shook, but the makeshift sling held and all day the elephant dangled. Her eyes were fading away into the smoke of her dreams.

Village life came to a stop. Everyone gathered round her shelter. Even Lobo arrived. Bat watched as one of the little boys showed him the mamba that still lay in mangled grey loops in the grass. Another boy poked at it with a stick. The blowflies had laid their eggs in the caverns of its mouth. But no one dared touch it. Even its grey armour was supposed to be poisonous. Lobo picked it up bravely and brandished it at the watchers.

They scattered like chaff when a stray breeze blows. Then he hurled the dead body away into the bush.

'Is the elephant going to die?' he asked Bat's grandmother.

'No, she is strong,' the old woman replied. 'But suffering is worse for an animal because it can't understand what is happening. It just knows it's in pain and that it must endure.'

'Can I see her?' Lobo asked, starting suddenly forwards.

Bat's grandmother put out an arm to prevent him. 'Leave the beast now,' she said.

'But I want to—'

'Leave her!' she interrupted, and this time she sounded fierce.

Lobo threw up his hands. 'I only wanted to help.'

'Right now, you can best help by leaving,' Bat's grandmother said. She moved over to her grandson and laid a hand on his head, but he didn't respond. To him, the whole world had the melting edges of a dream. He was desperate. He could barely hear the sound of Meya's breath any more.

As the third night fell, Bat and Muka were still keeping their vigil. They listened to the low mournful call of the owls, the *pee-oo-wee* of a nightjar as it swept the blackness for insects, the *scritch-scratch* of squirrels as they scuffled through the thatch; and somewhere far off they could hear a pack of hyenas. There was something horribly intimate about their howling that night. It was as if they could smell death approaching, floating towards them on the breezes of the night.

In the early hours of the morning, the pair fell at last into a fitful slumber. When Muka awoke, dawn had come. Her stirring roused Bat. For a moment he lay there, eyes closed, contentedly drowsing, until, like a reflection re-forming on disturbed water, the memories slowly began to coalesce. Outside he could hear the first cockerels crowing, the stock pigeons cooing from the fringing trees, the clatter of a tin can in somebody's kitchen, the first thud of a pestle as the cassava-pounding began. But he wouldn't open his eyes. He couldn't bear to wake up to a world from which Meya was gone. He couldn't bear to confront that moment when he would have to look loss in the face. He thought of the iguanas that sunned themselves by the river. They shone like a heap of precious gems; but if you killed one, as the boys sometimes did with their slingshots, even in the few steps that it took to reach the dead animal, it had turned to stone. Once the flame was put out, the ancient glittering creatures were no more than drab lumps of chill flesh.

Something crawled like a caterpillar across Bat's cheek. He reached out, instinctively. It was warm and rough. He folded a palm round it. It was the tip of Meya's trunk. Hardly daring to hope, he peeped through the fringe of his lashes. A deep amber eye met his disbelieving look. For a second he lay there stunned. It was as if a great stone had been lifted from a dam. All the blocked feelings gushed back into his body. Rising to his knees, the boy flung his thin arms tightly around the elephant's neck.

Meya came out of her hut that morning. She weakly accepted a bunch of sweet dates, then a handful of

acacia pods, and a couple of oranges, a whole sheaf of cut grass and a calabash of milk. Everyone in the village had something to bring her, and she would have eaten the lot if Bat's grandmother had not scolded her, telling her that if she didn't stop she would get stomach ache.

At noon, she returned to her hut to rest, but she wouldn't lie down to sleep. She paced about restlessly, probing at millet sacks and sniffing at maize bundles, running her trunk along the tops of the rafters and poking it into the crannies of the walls. 'Do you think she's checking for snakes?' wondered Bat.

'Maybe,' said Muka.

They both continued to watch.

Suddenly, the elephant discovered what she appeared to be seeking. She picked up a piece of string and flung it from the door. Curious, Bat walked across to examine it. 'What do you suppose this is?' he asked. A knotted string dangled from his fingertips.

Muka squinted; then snatched at it rapidly. What she found brought a gasp of shock to her throat. It was an amulet. And she knew where she had seen it. She recognized the rat's skull that gleamed in its dark knotted nest.

'It's Lobo's! It belongs to him. I know. I remember it. I remember him wearing it on market day. But what's it doing in our hut?' The words had barely risen to her lips when she stopped. She met Bat's silent gaze.

The unvoiced questions flew back and forth between them. Could it have been Lobo who had left the snake? Was it one of the serpents that his mother kept? They remembered the creature in its flailing anger. Was that

Lobo's revenge? Was it he who had put it there? Muka looked at her friend, his hair standing in uncombed spikes round his head, his cheeks smeared with the dust through which tears had left their tracks.

Suddenly, Bat could contain himself no longer. Something had snapped inside him and this time nothing would stop him. Folding the amulet into his fist, he ran off without a backward glance. Every muscle in his body was tightly knotted. Every nerve was on fire. His grandmother watched him from her doorway. She could see his fury and this time she didn't try to call him back.

But when Bat reached the broken-down hut at the edge of the village, he found only the old medicine woman sitting mumbling by the door. 'Lobo left for town again . . . only this morning,' she told him. 'He pedalled off on his bicycle a few hours ago.'

Bat stood a few moments, blinking. He felt as dazed and confused as if he had just run into a wall, and then abruptly, without another word, he wheeled about and stalked off. He was thumping his fist into a half-curled palm again and again as he strode stiffly homewards.

'If he ever comes back again . . . If he ever dares to return . . .' he muttered, finishing every broken sentence with the hard smack of knuckles against flesh.

## CHAPTER TEN

The whole village loved Meya. They called out their greetings when she got up in the morning. They waved an evening welcome when she came lumbering home from the pastures with Bat. 'She has fallen like a coconut amongst us,' the headman liked to say as he stood and perused her through the thick frames of his spectacles, puffing away at his pipe until the smoke made her snort.

'Meya was sent to forgive me,' said Bitek the fisher-man who, ever since he had done his bit to cure her from the snake-bite, felt no need to try and avoid her any more. Instead of taking circuitous routes round the village, he strode right up to her hut bearing gifts from his shamba. Meya liked pineapples best. Placing them whole in her mouth, she crushed them with her huge grinding molars, releasing a great ecstatic gush

109

of juice. Fat Rosa stroked her and let her steal kola nuts from her pockets; old Kaaka raised a hand in blessing whenever she crossed her path; the young boys ran laughing and skipping beside her, and even the tiny nursing babies started giggling, their round faces breaking into wide gummy smiles as they reached out splayed hands to grab at her gently probing trunk. Little mute Bim crouched in her cooling shadow while Bat taught him to whistle. He loved the high bird-like noise that he learned to make; it was so far from his bellow. His eyes shone as he listened, head cocked to one side.

Meya learned to be useful. She grubbed up stubborn tree roots from ground cleared for planting; she shook down unreachable mangoes from the trees. Too big for wrestling now, she joined in village games of football, proving the best goalkeeper that any of them had ever had. Her loud trumpets warned villagers that a genet cat was stalking and she was the bane of the insouciant brown rats. She hated small things that scampered and, hurling a stone with the accuracy of a boy with a sling-shot, she struck the raiding rodents dead with one blow. It delighted the villagers. These creatures robbed their grain stores and ransacked their root crops.

But Meya caused problems too: she walked off with washing bowls and knocked over clothes lines and punctured the plastic jerry cans with which she tried to play. She bashed down woven fences and jabbed holes in thatch roofs. Bunches of bananas were hung on the sides of the houses so that the baboon spiders which lurked in them could clamber out when they liked, but when Meya was passing and thought no one was looking, she would snatch the whole cluster and devour it as fast as she could.

Once she strayed into a sugar-cane plot and, mad with excitement at discovering so much sweetness, she trampled and broke every stem in the crop; and another time, shambling over to visit Marula, she snagged the folds of her turban on her now sprouting tusks; then, startled, galloped off, a long strip of bright calico unwinding like a streamer behind her. By the time Marula's eldest son had been summoned to retrieve it, it had been ripped into tatters and trampled into the dust.

The final straw came on the day Bat left the elephant quietly browsing while he followed Muka and his grandmother to the shamba to work. The wet season was approaching, and they had not yet heaped up the little mounds in which they would do their planting. These humped rows were important. When the rains came sluicing in thick sheets from the sky, the water would run off their surfaces instead of carrying the soil away in thick red rivulets. All morning, the three workers bent over their hoes, and the sun had already risen high in the sky when, glancing upwards, they noticed that Meya had drifted off.

Just at that moment they heard the sound of uproar in the village. There was a clattering of pots and a succession of loud screams. Muka and Bat shot a single glance at each other and dashed off, leaping bushes and jumping thorn hedges as they raced to get back. But by the time they arrived it was already too late: Meya was hastening across the compound, back arched and ears flapping, and a trail of destruction lay in her wake.

The little elephant had been hungry and, creeping into the cook-hut where Bat's grandmother kept food in a battered old tin trunk, she had decided to help herself. Upending the box and stamping until the clasp had flown open, she had waited for all the good things that she could smell inside to come tumbling out. The noise had disturbed a neighbour who, flying over to see what was the cause of the clatter, had startled the guilty animal which, swivelling in panic, had bashed over the cooking pots and broken a stool. Then Meya had made a sudden dash for the door.

She was almost five years old now. Her back was high as Bat's shoulder. She was too tall to fit easily through an entrance way and her sides were too wide. Creeping in carefully she could just about manage, but at full pace she caused havoc. Barging the lintel post, she had broken it. The wall had crumbled, the rafters been dislodged; the thatch had come tumbling down in a heap. The cook-hut lay in ruins, and Meya was standing in the far corner of the compound, eyeing them anxiously, the piece of brightly coloured plastic that had once carefully wrapped some tasty market purchase dangling like a piece of torn ribbon from her mouth.

'An elephant isn't a pet,' the headman told the children the next day as they sat with Bat's grandmother around a makeshift cooking-fire. 'She can't have a home in the village for ever. You do understand that eventually she will have to go.'

Bat's grandmother nodded. 'It's time to wean her completely. Meya must learn how to live on her own. If she was wild her mother would have a new calf by now.

She would no longer be nursing. She would have to be able to take care of herself.'

'Elephants have vast ranges,' Bitek the fisherman told Bat the next day as they sat amid scattered debris, plaiting thatch grass to make a new roof. 'They travel right up over the escarpment,' he said, nodding in the direction of the great wall of rock that formed their northern horizon. 'They know secret paths that run over it. Sometimes a family will be away for years. By the time a wild elephant has reached Meya's age, it will have travelled miles and miles, visiting every corner of its tribal lands. It will have learned where the grasses are richest and in which season; it will know all the trees and when they bear fruit; it will have wandered the length of the river to find the lush sedges and been up to the forest to discover the figs. It will be able to look at a line of blue hills and know from their shape precisely where it is now and where it needs to go next. Meya must be able to do all this if you want her to survive as a wild animal. She needs to move outwards if you want her to live a true elephant life.'

Bat sat on the earth. It still felt warm, even though the shadows were lengthening across the yard. He pushed his palms down. When he raised them again he could see the red patterns that the ground had pressed into them. It was because he was young, strong and healthy, he thought. He had plenty of blood. But his grandmother didn't. Her palms were silvery pale. They felt dry and scaly. Her fingers were gnarly as a twist of dug root and the pain in her hip was growing worse with each passing moon. She had taken to using a thorn stick as she walked. She wouldn't be able to go on working for ever and, when she couldn't any longer, then Bat would have to be there to help her. He wouldn't have time to waste with his little elephant.

'But what can we do about Meya?' he whispered worriedly to Muka a little later. 'We can't just send her away.' He jumped to his feet and began pacing anxiously like he did when his mind was beginning to race. 'I am not going to leave her. I don't care what the chief says. I know she still needs us. We can't just push her out.'

'She would be so lonely,' agreed Muka. 'She needs us for company. Even if we tried to get rid of her she would only come back home. So let's just tell them that, shall we? Let's just tell them that she wouldn't leave us, even if we wanted her to. That's the answer. Isn't it, Bat? Don't you agree that that's what we should say?' She glanced up at the boy, expecting to find him in complete agreement, but Bat had dropped back down onto his haunches, his head clutched in his fists.

In the end it was Bitek who was sent to persuade them. 'Of course you can't just push her out; and no one would even want that,' he said gently. 'The whole village loves your little animal. But look how big she has grown.' He nodded across at a nearby acacia. A ladder of notches climbed up its trunk. Every few moons, Bat had cut in a new one to record the height of his growing elephant but, as they climbed up the tree-trunk, one on top of the other, they seemed to be scaling the tree faster than a pair of monkey paws. Bitek turned back and nodded at the debris around him as if to emphasize his point, and then he smiled. 'And you, Bat, you may be growing faster than a yam tendril in the rainy season, but already you have to stand on tiptoe if you want to scratch her along the ridge of her spine. How much longer do you think you can look after her like she needs to be cared for? She must have the company of her own kind now. She's no longer a baby. She needs to find a family into which she can fit.'

Bat stared at him obstinately. 'But we're her family! If she needs a family why can't she just stay with us?' He turned to Muka. But the girl didn't answer. Her under-lip was quivering. She folded her face in her hands. She understood what it meant to live among the wrong people. As a little child, sent away by her mother, she had sometimes felt so lonely that her whole body had ached. And then Bat's grandmother had come along and she had found a home. The whole world had been different once she had found the right place. Would Meya feel the same? she wondered. Did she long for other elephants? Would she yearn all her life to find her real home?

'The time has come to introduce Meya to the wild elephants,' Bitek said softly. 'And that's what I have come to tell you about. It will be dangerous. But if you are careful and can get them to trust you, you will have a chance and, more importantly' – he cast a hard look at the children – 'you will be giving a chance to Meya too.'

Bat refused to meet his eyes. He felt a slow sinking in the pit of his stomach. He loved the little creature. He could not bear to lose her. His whole world would feel empty without her great shambling bulk. He could hardly remember the days when she had not been alongside him. She had formed the backdrop to almost half his life. How could he part with her? He stretched out his hands as if trying to catch the last of the sunlight, but the shadows were already stretching across the compound.

'What are elephant families like?' he heard Muka whisper.

'Elephants move in families of females,' explained Bitek. 'Each has a powerful matriarch to protect it, a leader who can be trusted to know what is right, to know where to feed, when to rest, how to find the best wallow. The bulls only come along when it's time for breeding. The rest of the time they hang about on the fringes, daydreaming and feeding and getting into fights – a bit like the village boys when they haven't got enough work to do,' he added with a smile at Bat. 'You will understand how it works when you have watched them for a bit.'

Muka smiled weakly but the boy refused to look.

'And I promise you, Bat,' continued Bitek, ignoring the fact that the boy refused stubbornly to so much as glance up, 'when you have seen how the elephants live you won't regret your decision. If elephants ruled this land instead of men, our world would be happier; it would be kinder and gentler. There would be less quarrelling and lying, less fighting and cheating. We would live in a land of love and respect. And besides,' he muttered darkly, 'how do we know right now what might happen? There are rumours. What if we had to flee? What if we suddenly found that we had to leave Jambula. Then what would happen to Meya?'

For the first time Bat jerked his head up. Muka had told him the stories from the market. A wave of uncertainty swept over him. It fluttered like a shadow as the night wind brushes by. He swallowed.

'Will the wild elephants accept her?' His voice was faint and small.

'It will be difficult,' Bitek answered. 'It will take all your skill. But there are tricks. I can teach you.

'Look,' he said, pulling a small square of cloth from his pocket and, stepping lightly across a fallen rafter to the ruined cook-fire, he scooped up a palm-full of ashes. 'You creep up on a herd by tying a handful of these up like this.' He knotted the corners of the material. 'When you think you are close, scatter a few of them onto the breeze. That will tell you which way it's blowing. You must always be sure to remain upwind. Otherwise they will smell you. They might even attack. And not many people can stand up to the onslaught of an elephant. This hut certainly didn't.' He laughed, looking at the wreckage that was strewn around the compound.

Neither of the children laughed back. Nothing seemed funny to them right now.

Bitek pulled his face straight. 'Little by little you will have to introduce her. You will have to take it step by tiny step. Nobody is expecting you to banish Meya from the village. It will take a long time, and only when the moment is right will she finally choose to go.'

Bat's grandmother came looking for them. She had not got her stick; but stepping over the fallen rafter of the building that for so long had sheltered her, she looked suddenly frail. She walked stiffly, placing one

117

slim foot in front of the other and, as she approached, Bat noticed, as if for the first time, how grey the hair had become on her close-cropped head, how bony her shoulders, how knotted the hands that now hitched at the waistband of her wrap. *Water does not flow back to the source*, he thought. That was what she always said. She would only get older. She would never be young again.

'We have talked,' she said to the children. 'We have made a plan. Muka, you from now on will look after the cattle. You will care for them in the same way that Bat now does. And Bat, you will go out with the elephant. You will lead her back to the herds to which she belongs. You will lead her back gently until she finds her right place. You say that you love her. Then the time has come to show it. The time has come to show that you can love her enough to leave her, to let her find her own life.'

Bat looked up. He felt as if he was trapped in an airlock. He didn't know what to say. Thoughts scurried wildly back and forth across his head. Every now and then he made a frantic dive to grasp one; but it was like diving at a brood of newly hatched quail. They darted from him and scattered, and when finally he managed to clutch one, he found that he had killed it. It lay limp and still in his mind as if it was dead.

Meya ambled over. He gazed at her lovingly. She blinked her eyes slowly. She was penitent after all the damage she had caused but she also knew that there was an orange in his pocket. She could smell it and she was wondering if he was going to let her have it. She reached out hopefully with her trunk. Bat smiled wanly and retrieved the hidden fruit. He watched her as she stood there chewing it contemplatively. Meya watched him back. She seemed to be aware that something serious was up.

'Will she forget me?' Bat whispered.

The elephant stared at him with a strange fixity. It was as if their thoughts were colliding, he thought, mingling like the light and dark of the gathering dusk.

'She will never forget you,' said Bitek.

Bat gazed into the depths of her russet-brown eyes. He could hear his heart pounding; the blood singing in his ears. He could see his tiny reflection, stilled like a speck in her long slow gaze. It was like a fly trapped in amber.

'She will always hold you in her heart and her head.'

## CHAPTER ELEVEN

During the dry season the wild elephants spent most of their time in the cool of the forests and, though you might sometimes glimpse them browsing at the fringes, upon your approach they would melt away. But when the rains came and, as if by magic, the river over-spilled into swamps, they were easier to find. They came down to the marshes to feed in the morning, churning the mud into deep, sloppy wallows and leaving huge foot-prints on the sandbanks.

Sometimes, when the wind was blowing up from the river, the elephants would pass right by you if you stood quite still, shambling along one by one, the cows slowly flapping their huge tattered ears as they ambled; their young trotting eagerly along behind. Occasionally there would be a great bull elephant among them, a vast mountain of muscle with a huge bony head and an immense sweep of tusks. His breath would blow thick as a thundercloud. Then it was best to step away as quickly as possible. Even the ill-tempered buffalo would shuffle out of his path.

The months of the long rains was everyone's favourite time of year. Fresh green grass sprouted, all the blossoms burst open, the breeze filled with butterflies and sweet flowery scents. Mothers sang songs to their babies on the way to the shambas. The children scampered through pastures, intoxicated as bees. The goats jumped about amid the rocky boulders, and the cattle, growing frisky and sleek on so much rich grazing, would headbutt each other and kick up their heels with loud snorts.

Meya was light-hearted the first day Bat left his cows in the care of Muka and set off to search for the wild elephants. She barged through the bushes and clambered onto anthills and made little mock rushes at an indignant sand grouse. They were going to the river; but not to the places where the villagers went to bathe and draw water. They were heading further downstream.

Keeping pace with the islands of water hyacinths which floated, buoyed up by their tangles of rubbery roots, they followed the course of the swollen brown flow until they reached a place where it gradually widened, sweeping swift and shallow over a sandy bed. Bat paused under a tamarind. The elephants came to this spot. He could tell by the footprints in the soft earth. He picked out the sharper, more clearly defined patterns of those left by the younger animals before singling out one that he thought must have belonged to the matriarch.

Its ridges were smoother, its heel more worn . . . and it was so big. He gasped inwardly as he bent to measure it as Bitek had taught him. The size of an elephant can be estimated by its footprint, the fisherman had told him. Twice the circumference of the pad is the height of the animal at its shoulder. The creature that had made this must have been truly enormous.

Untying a knotted rag, Bat shook out a sprinkle of ash. The wind was perfect. This was where he would wait. He leaned back to rest. The sound of the insects was like a wind in his ears. Where did they all come from? he wondered dreamily as he watched them, darting and hovering and swooping and crawling, millions of tiny creatures with sheeny bright shells and gauze wings that glittered like splinters of pure light. They just appeared out of nowhere at the end of the dry season. It was as if they had fallen with the rains, he thought.

Suddenly, Meya paused in her grazing. She had heard something. Bat couldn't tell what. He waited, pulse fluttering. A short while later he thought he heard something too: a slow, steady, sluffing of softly padded feet. His eyes darted around him. His breath caught in his throat. A long file of elephants was arriving, the cows in an orderly column, their calves keeping close in obedient formation, scurrying a little faster every now and then to keep up. They were making their way towards the riverbank.

Only when they had almost reached the water did the little ones break rank, squealing and splashing as they plunged into the river, tumbling and squirting as they scrambled about, disturbing the storks and sending the ducks scattering, while the calmer matrons, wading into the shallows, dipped their long trunks and sucked slowly and drank. Meya was spellbound. She stood still as a rock.

Then the wind ruffled through the grasses and changed course, carrying the scent of the watchers in the wild elephants' direction. The effect was immediate. The whole herd moved off at once, the matrons surging like great ships through the flow of the river, the waters rushing and foaming about their baggy knees, while the little ones dashed after them, backs arched and chins high. They glanced over their shoulders and showed the whites of their eyes.

As soon as they were safely on the far bank they wheeled round in unison as if at some silent order. Ears flared and a row of trunks lifted. They waved above the line of massive heads, sampling the unfamiliar smell that was drifting towards them; letting the air out again with a soft low whoosh. Then one beast emerged. She must be the matriarch, Bat thought; and his heart swelled with pride that perhaps one day Meya would look like that. She was magnificent: tall, with great hollow cheekbones and long deeply curved tusks. They were pointing straight at him as she advanced in his direction, step by slow step. Shaking her head from side to side, she clapped her huge ears like thunder and kicked at the water in a movement which he recognized all too well as a threat. A loud shrilling trumpet reverberated through the air. Bat tensed, his blood pumping, every nerve-end singing, every tendon strung taut as he froze, suspended in the stillness of that split-second moment that lies between utter fixity and the first thrust of flight. If she charged now, his chances of escape were slender; but if he stayed she could crush him as easily as a crouching sand grouse. Just as the balance finally tipped in his brain; just as, pushing up with his knuckles, he steeled himself for the sprint, she flipped her trunk forward and wheeled slowly round, the currents eddying about her, and, wading out of the river, the water streaming from her flanks, barged her way back into the watching herd.

When, a short while later, she returned once more to the river, he again got ready to run, but this time he was not panicking. Calmly, he watched her. There was something in her manner that made him think that she meant no harm. Perhaps it was the way she was moving, he thought: like an old village woman who feels she has not been accorded befitting dignity; like his grandmother when he helped himself from the calabash before her, or old Kaaka the time that a guava fruit had dropped on her head. There was a haughty self-consciousness to her gait. She headed stiffly towards him, the waters churning about her, and the whole herd of elephants followed splashing in her wake. They walked right past his tamarind without even pausing, ambling away, their great sagging bottoms swaying, their outlines gradually blurring and fading and eventually disappearing as they melted back into the hot dusty shimmer from which they had first come. Their slow padding steps made barely a sound. And neither did Meya: the young elephant just stood there and stared, transfixed.

After that, Bat would return to the same spot every morning. Normally, at this time of year, he would have been hard at work with the threshing. The millet was cut. The yard had been spread with cow dung. It had baked smooth and hard. And usually it would have been Bat who was driving a pair of horned cattle, flicking his switch to keep them moving in circles, trampling out the grains for his grandmother to collect. But now, leaving the village as the first smoke from the cook-fires streaked the damp morning, he headed straight out instead into the flaring pinkness of dawn.

Often he arrived at the swamps before the wild elephants. Then he just sat dreaming while Meya grazed, as peaceable a part of the African landscape as the high-stepping ibis that waded through shallows or the spoon-bills that sliced the deep pools with slow sweeps. Only the fish eagle remained annoyed by his alien presence. It would take off from the branches with a fluting call of alarm. The wild elephants soon learned not to pay it any heed.

Little by little, as the days passed, they seemed to grow used to Meya. The first time they reached out to her, the boy squeezed his eyes tight, too frightened to look. His hands, clutched hard round his kneecaps, were trembling. But soon they began to greet her as naturally as he would have greeted a visitor to his village. They wandered towards her with deep belly rumbles, sniffing her all over and putting their trunks in her mouth. They let her feed by their sides, plucking and twirling and munching and swallowing, while the ox-peckers perched on their backs and hissed.

Bat learned to recognize each member of the herd individually. It was a bit like learning the alphabet with his grandmother, he thought. Just like he had worked out the shapes of the letters, he came to tell the elephants apart by the shapes of their ears: some big and some small; some stiff and some floppy; some ragged round the edges, full of holes, tears and notches; others smooth and clean-edged. Their tusks were different too: they could curve outwards or inwards, be asymmetrical or crossed. One of the cows had broken hers: only a gnarled stub remained; and the old matriarch's right tusk was much blunter than her left. She probably used that side, explained Bitek when Bat described it, for digging up roots and over the long years it had got worn away. Slowly, just as individual letters come together to make words, Bat came to recognize each elephant as clearly as he knew his own cattle; he could tell them, even from afar, by their postures and attitudes, by the way they moved or the company they kept. And then, as words in their turn come together to create meanings, he learned to read their separate characters, to realize that each member of that elephant herd was as distinct in its own way as the people who lived in his village.

It wasn't long before Meya began to play with the youngsters. As they charged in mock fury, their tusks clonked together. They wheeled, skipped and scrambled about the riverbanks or engaged in long wrestling matches, pushing and shoving like the village boys did. And then, when from time to time the elephants vanished, sometimes not returning for several days, Meya would be sad and restless. She would trumpet down the river and gaze anxiously about. It made the boy anxious too. What if this time the elephants don't come back? he would fret.

'Don't worry,' said Bitek when he met him on one of his searches. The fisherman was untangling the nets he had spread on a fallen trunk. 'The elephants will only have found a ripe fig tree or a marsh of lush grass a little further upriver. Look at the colour of their skins and you'll find out where they've been. White means a forest wallow; ochre a mud pool among the acacias; and dirty grey is probably from the river a bit further south.'

Bat looked and learned. He found out, just as Bitek had told him, where the herd had been. He read the signs that they left in the mud or dust; understood how to tell which way they were heading, what they were doing, how many had passed and how long ago. He discovered which springs they favoured. Some were so tiny that only one animal could drink at once, but these had minerals, explained Bitek, and so the elephants were prepared to line up and wait.

Soon Bat discovered that he could sense where the herd was. It was not just the vibrating rumbles that alerted him, or the sound of thorns brushing against rough hides. He would know they were coming even before their arrival. If they were absent, the landscape had a peculiar emptiness; if they were there, it was pervaded by a strange trembling life. He would feel it like a singing in the marrow of his bones.

'Don't be deceived,' Bitek warned him. 'Elephants are dangerous. They might look perfectly peaceful, but deep down they are wild. You must beware; especially of the bulls when they are in musth. When you see dark liquids leaking from the corners of their eyes, they are ready to mate and then nothing will stop them. They will kill you without a thought if you cross their path.'

Bat nodded. He had seen the huge footprints of these creatures in the dust. He knew for himself how vast they could grow. He had heard their great rumbles. They set the air quivering. They rattled his body right down to the bones. He would lie still and stay hidden at the sound of their approach. But often he would feel sad as he crouched in his nest of grasses or ducked his head down behind some stony outcrop. Why couldn't he walk among the elephants like Meya? Surely they could understand that he meant no harm. Surely they would sense how much he loved them. And then he would wonder again if Meya would always remember him, and all the qualms he felt whenever he contemplated losing her would return. Why did Meya have to go anyway? He knew how to look after her. Why shouldn't she stay with him? Couldn't he care for her just as well as any herd of elephants?

But then came the day when Meya found herself in trouble. Everything had seemed so perfectly ordinary that afternoon. The hoopoes were calling from their woody hollows; the weaver birds twittered as they built their dangling nests, and in the far distance he could see a herd of zebra grazing. They looked as brightly polished as little wooden toys.

Just at that moment, he heard Meya calling. When he had last looked, she had been browsing in the swamps by the river but now, turning, he saw that she'd sunk through a crust of mud. As he ran towards her, she tried to heave herself out, but the more she struggled, the deeper into the mire she was dragged. She panicked and bellowed, but there was nothing she could do. She floundered and rolled, but she remained firmly embedded. The air was alive with her terrified squeals.

Bat was desperate. She was stuck. He tried pulling her trunk but it only made her squeal louder. He tried pushing her from behind but he was nearly trapped himself. And how could he hope to shift so heavy a bulk anyway? He was frantic. His heart was thudding so hard that his eyeballs almost shook. Who would help him? Should he run back to the village and find someone with a rope? Or should he stay behind and try to calm her? But what about the crocodiles? What if they came to get her? Or if a lion was lurking? Frenzied images chased through his brain. He started to run. But he was a long way from home. His breath broke from his throat in shallow burning gasps. His fear tasted bitter at the back of his tongue. And Meya cried out ever more desperately as she saw him disappearing. She thought he was leaving her. His heart pounded louder and louder as the sound of her terror faded slowly away. He imagined her lying there in forsaken silence. 'I'll be back, I'll be back!' he promised as he took each panting step.

Approaching the village, he found Muka out with the cattle. His heart leaped with frantic hope. She would have a rope; not a very long one, it was only for the cattle, but it would have to do . . . it was all they had. Within moments the two children were racing back, side by side, their lungs bursting as they leaped through the long grasses, round trees, over rocks, not speaking, not daring to think what would happen if their plan didn't work. But as they came to the spot where Meya had been left struggling, the pair of them pulled up to a sudden astonished halt.

The elephants had heard Meya's terrified calls. They too had come running to help and, as the two children watched, they were gathering anxiously around her. The matriarch stepped forward. Edging her tusks beneath the trapped animal, she started to lever like a man with a pivot trying to move a great boulder. Rocking slowly back and forth, she gradually worked Meya loose until, all at once, with a resounding smack, she was out. Two other females reached out with their trunks, tugging her towards them until, step by laboured step, she was floundering free of the mud. The herd gathered around her, rumbling as she stood there amid them, frightened and grateful and covered from trunk to tail in sludge.

The sense of relief washed over Bat in great waves; but a painful new realization was dawning upon him too. He reached out for Muka's hand. She took it without looking. Her eyes were bright with wonder. But, even as they stood there, caught up in this moment of miraculous witness, they both felt the same loss welling up in their hearts. However much they loved Meya, they had not managed to save her; they had not been able to care for her in the way the wild elephants could. Bat felt something change at some deep level inside them. He knew from that moment that Meya would have to go.

That night, as the young elephant drowsed under the mango, the wild herd came looking for her. Bat could hear them moving about in the scrub near the village, cracking through the bushes, backs brushing low boughs. He could not sleep. What if they broke through the thorn hedges around the shambas? What if they wandered right into the village, raiding the grain stores and pushing over the huts? They could break any barrier if they wanted to badly enough. They would flatten wooden fences and stroll through cattle enclosures. New-laid roads, Bitek said, would be ploughed up with their tusks. They had even learned how to get through electrified cordons, the fisherman had told him, by throwing branches to short-circuit them and then just shoving past.

Bat got up from his mat and stood amid the dense buzzing darkness. The herd was so close he could hear their low growling, the scratch of their hides as they jostled and shifted; their thick breathy sighs exhaled upon the night. Meya was their kin and they had come to claim her. She had awoken and was answering them, flapping her ears and shuffling, lifting her trunk as she smelled them on the drifting night air.

Bat's ears strained the blackness. The blood sang in his head. The wild elephants had stopped. They were coming no closer. They stayed at the brink of their mysterious borderlines . . . but they were just waiting, the boy thought; waiting for Meya to cross those unfenced boundaries between the world of the village and the wild's vast expanses; and he knew in his heart that she was already on the edges. She was hovering upon the fringes. She was already half in that land in which a human could never have a true part.

## CHAPTER TWELVE

The first night Meya spent with the herd, Bat was distraught. For more than five years, the elephant had been his most constant companion. 'What if they leave her behind? What if they lose her?' he fretted. 'What if she's calling for me and I can't hear?' Straining his ears, he listened out in the darkness. Nothing but the shrill of the cicadas, the boom of the frogs came back.

Bitek tried to reassure him. 'They'll look after her,' he soothed. 'They'll only have taken her up to the forests. They'll be teaching her how to follow their paths. If she was going for ever she would have said goodbye to you properly. It won't be too long before she comes back.' But Bat couldn't settle. The next morning he set off for the forest himself, scrambling through the creepers that covered the boulders which had tumbled in ancient times from the escarpment's great cliff. He climbed

132

further and further through thick spiky branches. The bird song collided with the cackle of monkeys. A troupe of baboons swung by, babies clinging to their backs. They ambled easily through thickets that tore his skin to shreds. A grizzled old male paused and bared his fangs; then, barking, he loped off to catch up with the rest. They vanished into the undergrowth but, when Bat tried to follow them, the wild sisal speared him. Swarms of vicious black tsetse flies alighted and bit. The itching lumps maddened him. He scratched and scratched.

Bat sat down. Big tears of missing welled up in his eyes. It was hopeless, he thought. A butterfly settled on his shoulder; wide as the span of his outspread hand. He watched its red and blue wings slowly opening and closing, its tongue curling and uncurling as it tasted the salt of his sweat. Normally Bat would have smiled at a creature so beautiful; but now he stared drearily. It fluttered away. Rising to his feet, he turned, dejected, and followed his tracks home.

Several days later Meya returned. Bat was in the middle of splitting the firewood so that his grandmother could start cooking when, pausing for a moment to wipe at his brow, he saw something approaching down the track: a grey apparition shambling slowly towards him through the gathering darkness. The panga dropped slack at his side. For a few long moments he waited, suspended without breathing upon a swell of rising hope, before suddenly, recognizing that this was reality, he landed back in the world with a thump. A gasp of sheer happiness was jolted from his lips. He felt light as air. It was as if some great load that for days he had been carrying had all at once been lifted. His panga dropped with a clatter as he ran forward.

Meya was back; she was well; she had come to no harm. He wanted to throw his arms round her, to tuck himself in beside her and hug her as tight as he could, but instead as he ran closer he found himself slowing to a halt. It was as if he was seeing her suddenly through fresh eyes. She was massive. He could hardly imagine that the creature which now rose above him so tall and broad-shouldered and magnificent and strong had once been no more than a tiny crumpled heap in the grass. The last light of the evening gleamed upon her great tusks. And he could feel her new wildness, an invisible barrier around her. She seemed possessed of a strange power that he had never before felt.

Bat thought of old Kaaka who could talk to the spirits. When you met her most days she was just like any other villager, scolding and chattering as she went about her work. Sometimes she would come and sit with his grandmother, squatting in the shade of the mango, swapping stories. Her face would dissolve into laughter when something amused her, all its wrinkles and creases drawn suddenly inwards as if at the tug of some single secret string. But when she was working her magic, calling the souls of lost people to answer her questions, her lined face would simplify into a mask of great strength. She would grow distant and strange. No one would have dared to touch her at those mysterious moments. She was moving through worlds in which ordinary life had no part.

Bat gazed up at Meya and felt suddenly abashed. But

even as he hesitated uncertainly before her, waiting for her permission before taking another step, she reached out her trunk and twined it gently about him and, drawn slowly inwards, the boy felt himself relaxing as he was pressed into the crinkled underside of her throat. He gave a deep sigh of contentment. It felt so very familiar. He filled up his nostrils with her rich musky smell.

From then on Bat knew that he could no longer hold Meya; that, although he had reared her, she was a truly wild creature. And now it was he who, for the first time, determined that she should finally go. He would refuse her food when she came to the village, turning his back and ignoring her when her trunk crept towards him, searching his pockets for the treats that she hoped he had hidden. He would slip quietly away once she had met up with the herd and, when she looked back to find him, he would already have left. Later, when he returned to check up on her and she came running to meet him, he would pat her only briefly before pushing her off. Meya was confused; she would look at him quizzically, shaking her head and blinking reproachfully before eventually lumbering back to her companions' side. Then she would turn to face him, her eyes never leaving him as she watched him walk off. Often, Bat faltered. Occasionally, unable to bear it, he would have to turn back. He would run towards her and fling his arms round her. But little by little he learned to harden his heart. 'The links in the chain must be broken one by one,' Bitek said. 'Like a jackal that crosses the water so that nothing can track it, you must break the trail that leads your elephant back to Jambula. If she is to survive, she must learn that men are not to be trusted. She must look for her safety to the herd alone.'

As the seasons passed, Meya began to stay out longer and longer and her visits to the village became increasingly brief. When she was not there, Bat yearned for her. He would think back to the days when he had curled up beside her, the thump of her heart like the beat of a drum in his blood, and then he would stare into the cook-fire, his calabash of food untouched.

Muka would try to distract him, telling him stories of what the cattle had done, of how Kayo had trapped her foot in a bush-hyrax burrow or Kila's new calf had found a kitten to play with, and she would watch Bat smile as he remembered his own days with the cattle, while the boy's grandmother, in her turn, kept watch on Muka's face. She would see from the way the girl lifted her head, clenching her jaw muscles to stop her mouth trembling, that she too was missing the young elephant. Sometimes the tears would film over her eyes. The girl would blink them away before they rolled down her cheeks, but not before Bat's grandmother had taken notice. 'I think tomorrow you need not go out with the cattle,' she would say. 'I'll send Bim instead so that you two can go elephant-tracking. It's always better to journey with a companion,' she told them. 'You never know when you might need someone to remove a grass seed from your eye.' And Muka's eyes would brighten and a smile would flash over her face.

Muka loved nothing more than those days when she and Bat wandered together, their hearts humming with excitement as they spotted the elephants surging their way through the savannah's wide spaces, silent as ghosts as they steamrollered along.

It was on one of those days, after one of the now rare occasions when Meya would return to the village, that the two children set off together with the elephant at their side. It was bright, though a few clouds were still chasing across the sky. Bat gazed across the open plains. The grass fled like water in the strong wind and in the distance he could see a herd of wildebeest, their horns and high shoulders poking out from the scrub. There must have been about twenty of them, he thought as he squinted: a sure sign that the dry season would soon begin. As pastures grew sparser, the nomads began to gather. Soon they would begin the migration which carried them across the continent. Soon the damp earth would be nothing but dust.

They had been walking and browsing and ambling all morning, hoping to meet up with the other elephants, but by the time the sun had dropped more than half-way down the heavens, they still had not found a trace of the wild herd. They were on the point of giving up and going back when Meya suddenly paused and lifted her trunk. She had sensed them. The children stood quiet and alert. Bat could sense their presence too. It was a feeling far inside him, a strange visceral stirring: like the sound of a song before it reaches the tongue.

Meya was moving now. They followed her forward, ducking through a thicket of thorn bushes, climbing a low rise and skidding down a slope that led towards a riverbed. But still they saw nothing. And then Bat, who was just ahead of Muka, found himself drawing to a sudden stunned halt. He put a hand on the girl's arm to restrain her. There, on the far side of the water, was a great baobab. It towered over the scrub like a gaunt sentinel.

The boy recognized it. He didn't know how; but he had been here before. His thoughts scooted about like a flock of scared chickens. What was alarming him? His flapping mind confused him. And then, like a child in the fowl pen trying to catch a bird for dinner, he got a firm grip on the memory: there he was . . . many years back . . . a little boy of just seven . . . crouching on the far bank . . . just behind that big boulder. Bat blinked and shook his head. He wanted to dislodge the picture, but it was too late. The past was flooding over him. He was huddled amidst it, small and so frightened that even now he could feel himself starting to shake. He was staring giddily up at a dead elephant. The carcass loomed above him, filling his whole horizon. He was watching a gang of poachers . . . they were scrambling up onto the great bloated corpse . . . they were clambering around like beetles . . . the blood whined in his ears like the engine of a chainsaw. The memory flooded his senses. It stickied his breathing and clung to the back of his throat. Muka could feel him trembling as his fingertips gripped her. He was beginning to hurt her; but she did not cry out. She glanced at him, confused. And then she felt his hold loosen as he returned to the present. He stared stricken at Meya as she waded into the shallow river. For a moment his mouth opened as if he wanted to call her; but no sound came out. Instead, stepping forward as determinedly as if he was going finally to confront some hidden fear, he started to follow her. Muka hitched up her wrap and slid into his wake. The waters were already shrinking; they barely reached up to their knees. It wouldn't be long before this bed had run dry.

Clambering up the far bank, the children slipped between two boulders and then stopped. Muka was gazing, eyes shining, as she spotted the wild herd browsing a short way beyond them; but Bat seemed barely to notice them. His stare was glassy and fixed, as if what lay before him was only a surface reflection and what he was searching for lay in the depths below. This was the very scene of that long ago slaughter. This was the place where Meya's mother had been shot. Bat had never returned since. He could not even have remembered how to find it. So why had the elephants come there? he wondered. Why were they leading Meya to this terrible spot?

He searched the ground for some clue. Only a few bones remained, bleached and broken and strewn about the dry grasses; and now, even as he watched, the elephants were slowly moving towards them. Their silence was unsettling. The only sound in that lonely gravesite was the sigh of their breath. Softly, they reached out the probing tips of their trunks. He watched one of them pick up a bone, turn it over and examine it, stroke it softly and then gently lay it back down again. He saw the matriarch reversing slowly towards another great rain-smoothed fragment, nudging it delicately with a hind foot. It was a movement Bat recognized. That was how a mother elephant would have woken a sleeping baby from the herd. So why was the matriarch doing it now? Was she trying to rouse the lost memories? Was she awakening the secrets that slept in that bit of bone? Bat watched as the elephants hovered and circled and sighed and came back again and reached out and stroked.

Meya, beside him, waited transfixed. It was some time before she too approached. She reached out with the tip of her trunk for the skull. Grass had long since grown through the empty eye-sockets. The teeth had come loose and lay scattered about. Lowering her head, she sniffed at one gently. With a delicate precision she turned over a detached jawbone. She stroked its long curve with a wandering trunk; then she let her touch stray across the slope of the skull, probing its cracks and its knobbles and cavities, picking a loose stone from the place where an eye had once looked. She tried to dislodge it from the clambering grasses; first with a gentle push and then by a harder shunt. She seemed to be searching for something, Bat thought; for some hidden meaning that these fragments held.

He had often seen her pass the remains of other dead animals, the leathery cases of buffalo picked clean by scavengers, the strewn bones of antelope that wild dogs had brought down, and once even a giraffe that had fallen, legs stretched as if still running, neck slack as the stem of a wilted flower. But she had never paused to investigate. She had simply walked by. So why did she now stand for so long at this gravesite? It could only be, Bat thought, because she understood what had happened. The other elephants had led her there so that she could know the truth. They wanted her to share in their moment of mourning, in their memories of the days when her mother had been part of their herd, of the long years when she had wandered the savannah at their side. They wanted Meya to know how deeply she belonged to them.

Bat felt something huge and mysterious welling up inside him. He was in the presence of a force far beyond that which he could explain. He glanced at Muka, but she didn't look back. She just stood there, eyes lowered in respect. And Bat remembered the stories of Bitek the fisherman. 'Elephants have powers far greater than you can understand,' he had said.

Meya returned home to the village with the children that evening again, but though they walked in her shadow, she felt a long way off. They wandered homewards, lost in the world of their thoughts.

Neither of the children was alert as they should have been at that hour on the empty plain. They didn't notice the shadows lengthening as the sun sank towards the horizon, nor the fact that the antelope which liked to graze upon the woodland fringes had long ago left for the greater safety of the grasslands beyond. They didn't see the lioness slinking low-bellied through the undergrowth, stealing towards them, her ears flat to her skull. But Meya did. She jerked up her head; her whole body tense. With a bellow of anger, she broke into a spanking trot.

The children, jolted out of their daydreaming, clutched at each other, confused. They didn't know what was happening. Their eyes darted about. And then, with

141

a half-stifled scream, Muka pointed. Bat's heart jumped a beat. The lioness was rising. Any moment now she would be launched in a swift grappling rush. Her claws, sharp as meat-hooks, would be dragging them downwards. There would be nothing they could do. But, even as the boy sprang instinctively before Muka, the elephant bore down on the crouching animal. It twisted and leaped sideways. Slewing around in a cloud of red dust, Meya pursued. Ears flared and trunk lifted, she screamed her mad rage. The lioness slunk away with furious growls. Still Meya did not stop.

She bore down on the big cat like a creature possessed. If she had caught it, she would have crushed it; she would have picked up its body and smashed it with one blow. The lioness, with a last enraged lash of its tail, turned and bolted. It did not stop running until it was long out of sight, but it was even longer before the terrified children could steady their legs enough to continue their homeward walk.

'Meya drove a lion away,' Bat told his grandmother, as he swallowed the last bit of sesame paste from his supper and put the calabash back down. He was trying to sound calm as he told her the story, but his hands gripped his knee-bones, and one of his feet jittered nervously against the floor. His grandmother glanced across at Muka. She was crouched in a huddle of angles, her big eyes still glittering with remembered fear. Both children knew that they had been foolhardy; they had been warned again and again of the dangers on the savannah at dusk. They knew they had had a narrow escape. If it had not been for Meya, the lions would, even now, have been snarling and snapping around their dead bodies, cuffing at each other as they fought for the choicest bits.

For a long while Bat's grandmother remained silent. She examined her hands. She had been pulling ground-nuts all day but, with the soil now drying, the plants were hard to uproot. Her palms were blistered and raw. From time to time she looked up at the children and shook her head. The fire flickered, sending their shadows leaping about the mud walls. They rocked and wavered, wildly exaggerating every gesture. The big white moths fluttered perilously close to the flames.

'You must be careful,' she said at last. 'How many times have I told you that?' She searched their faces for answers, but neither of them would look up to meet her eye. 'Well, I want this to be the last time,' she declared, rising slowly to her feet. 'Both of you, go to bed now and think about that while I go outside and thank the gods . . . and that elephant . . . that you have been brought home to me.' She made her way towards the door of the hut, but just before she ducked under the lintel she turned one last time. 'You must always be watchful,' she said solemnly, fixing her stare upon each child in turn. 'It is not just the lions you must fear on the savannah these days.'

## CHAPTER THIRTEEN

Life in Jambula returned to normal for a while, its rhythms as steady as the rise and fall of a pestle, its routines as settled as the melody of a song; but in this undisturbed soil the rumours were still growing. Gossip was brought home by women from the market, stories were carried across the plains by the herders of goats, and now, even from this side of the town, there came troubling tales. Voices had been heard out on the savannah. A cow had been stolen from a nomad by night. A child had vanished. No one knew how or where. Families were beginning to leave their villages in the evenings, to carry their mats out into the bush to sleep; and a few with relations who lived in the south were talking of packing up and travelling, crossing the plains with their children and possessions. They were planning to stay away until the danger passed.

Soon, even in Jambula, people began to grow nervous. Rumours whipped like wildfire across the savannah. Fears, sharp as burned grass stalks, were left behind in their wake. Villagers would look over their shoulders if they heard footsteps approaching. A rustling in the trees, a shadow flickering over grasses, a cry of an animal in the darkness, could all make them jump. An abandoned bicycle was discovered by one of Marula's sons a short way from the river. He didn't go near it but dashed immediately for home. Bitek the fisherman saw strange lights in the bush.

The headman was worried. He had left for a visit to a fellow chieftain and, on the way, been passed by a pack of wild dogs. 'They cantered right by me,' he said, 'looking neither right nor left . . . travelling so fast . . . as if with some fixed purpose . . . and so close I could see the white tufts of their tails.

'These dogs are an omen,' he declared. 'They are carrion eaters. They arrive with a war.' And he puffed at his pipe, even though its bowl was empty. He had run out of tobacco quite some time ago, but his wife no longer felt safe making the walk into the market. She was frightened of being ambushed upon the path.

A twelve-year-old boy from a village not far off had been snatched. 'He and his mother were on their way to town to sell eggs,' said Mama Brenda, who had heard the story first-hand from a friend, 'when two strangers suddenly leaped out in front of them and trapped them with sticks which they held to their throats. One was a boy but he looked more like a wild animal. He had long matted hair and he smelled sour as a goat. The other was a girl,' Mama Brenda told her listeners, 'but she had no gentleness. When the mother looked into her eyes and implored her, she saw that they were completely cold. Her little boy was sobbing. "If you cry any more, we will kill you!" the rebel girl said. And she meant it. So his mother just turned away. She turned her back on her son so that he would not see her, so that he would not shout for her and be killed. And then she just walked away. She had to. She had to leave him to save him. And he has not been seen since.'

'Who are these rebels? What do they want?' Bat asked his grandmother that evening.

But the old woman had no answer. 'Nobody is quite sure,' was all she could say. 'Their leader lives wild in the forests and no one can catch him so no one knows why he's fighting or what he hopes to get. But his army is said to be growing every day. You must be careful, Bat.' She paused and looked in turn at the two children who squatted by the cook-fire. 'This is a violent country,' she said. 'On the map, it is shaped like the holster of a pistol. That's what the white people I used to work for would say; and one day, they said, the firing will begin. You must be alert, both of you. You must always be watching . . . and don't go too far into the forests,' she warned Bat.

But now that the boy had learned his way into the mountains, he loved them. During the heat of the dry season, there was no greater pleasure than to pad his way cautiously along the elephant trail. The forest felt secret and shadowy. Its rich sappy smells filled his lungs and refreshed him. Its paths, trampled to softness by the passing of hundreds of thick-soled elephant feet, were so easy to walk on. He would watch the colobus monkeys grooming in the high branches, the bush pigs grubbing for roots in the dark crumbly loam. He would listen to the cuckoo as it sang from its hiding place in the bushes. It felt like he was hiding at the heart of the world.

And yet, where once the sound of a buffalo browsing in the thickets would have spelled his greatest danger, now the snort of a forest hog could make him freeze in his tracks; and one day, when an eagle had come crashing through the canopies, talons outstretched for some clasping potto, he had fled so fast that by the time he had stopped running he had looked all around him and not been able to recognize where he was. He started imagining eyes watching him from amid the striped shadow. They belonged to fierce children with glittering eyes and guns.

One afternoon, returning home, he saw a person ahead of him and his chest grew so tight that he could hardly breathe, but it was only the honey-gatherer strolling down the pathway, puffing at his fat roll of smouldering leaves. The smoke calmed the insects as he raided their store-houses. Too dopey to sting him, they just crawled helplessly about. A block of comb in his hands dripped its sweet golden syrup and he broke off a piece and gave it to Bat.

The boy's nerves calmed a little when the short rains arrived in November and the elephants returned to the savannah to feed. Like the antelope, he felt safer out there in the open. On the plains he could spot danger from much further off. But then came the day when he stumbled across a set of strange footprints. He followed the tread of heavy boots through the dust. He knew that they could not have been left by one of the villagers because the villagers wore only sandals if they were not barefoot. He cast his eyes watchfully over the disturbed ground. A car had passed down the track.

Bat ran back to the village expecting to find strangers, only to find that Lobo had returned unexpectedly that afternoon. It was the first time he had been back for months.

Lobo was sixteen years old now. He had learned to walk with a confident swagger that made him look like a man. But his hands gave him away. They were too big for his body and he could never decide what to do with them. As he sauntered about they were constantly shifting, now beside him, now behind him, now stuffed deep in his pockets, now touching the moustache which he was constantly hoping would thicken. He would sit there stroking it meditatively with the crook of a forefinger; but what he was thinking the villagers could only guess at.

'He does not fit,' they whispered, 'not with himself, nor with the rest of our community.' They were beginning to distrust him. They did not trust the way he disappeared for months, vanishing like the smoke from the medicine woman's fire, leaving only his memory, a dark smell on the air. Nor did they like the way, just when they were beginning to believe that he had left for ever, he would arrive back unexpectedly, with no word of warning.

Every time he returned he would boast some shiny new possession: a pair of sunglasses balancing on the bridge of the broad, flat nose that he had broken in a fight; a watch with a strap made from metal that stretched out when he pulled it; a radio that for two days he had carried about everywhere until finally, on the fourth evening, its batteries had run out.

'Where does he get it all from?' the villagers wondered. 'Who does he work for? How does he earn so much?' The elders would eye him suspiciously. They were no longer persuaded by his shows of politeness.

'He is like a chameleon plucked from a tin roof,' said Marula. 'Flung into the foliage, it can't change colour fast enough. He has the look of a town boy when he comes to Jambula. He doesn't belong.' And she warned her own sons not to mix with him. Muka's cousin no longer put a wriggle into her walk when she passed him, and where once she would have loitered listening shyly to his stories, letting out half-stifled 'eeehs' and 'aaahs' of delight, now she hurried on by whenever she saw him. Her mother would have scolded her if she had not.

Even the little boys who had once buzzed like bees about him became more hesitant. 'Don't wrestle with him. You only get hurt by the Hog,' they told one another. 'Remember the time he broke Okeny's finger,' they would remind each other. 'And the time he bit Komakech.' Stories that, in the past, had been recounted like the feats of a hero were now harboured as evidence against the boy.

But Lobo seemed unconcerned. Nothing worried him. 'Could be anyone.' He shrugged, when he heard about the mysterious tyre tracks that Bat had seen out on the savannah. 'Or more likely no one.' He laughed. He dismissed all the rumours of the mysterious child army. He didn't seem to mind travelling alone down the track. He'd brought a hunk of raw bush-meat for the medicine woman for supper. The smell of roasting flesh drifted through the village that night.

'Come and eat with us,' Lobo invited Muka as he stepped onto the pathway in front of her, waylaying her on her evening walk home from the river. 'Come and eat with us. The meat is good and you can sit by our fire and tell us everything that's been happening; you can tell us all the stories of your elephant.' A smile dimpled his cheeks, and for a few moments Muka found herself wavering. Was he trying to show her that he had turned a new leaf? The villagers had set their hearts so firmly against him. But maybe they misjudged him?

She looked at him standing there, his hands dangling awkwardly. If he was rough, it was because roughness was all that he had known. That's what Bat's grand-mother had told her. So shouldn't he now be given a fresh chance?

She remembered her own awkwardness when she had first arrived in Jambula, dumped like an unwanted package in the home of her aunt. She remembered the loneliness, stuck like a stone at the bottom of her heart. It had made her spit like a wildcat at anyone who approached her.

'Come,' Lobo coaxed. His hands moved to his pockets as if to prove he was harmless. She could see the eagerness brightening his eye. 'Come. Tell me about your elephant. Is it true about the wild herd?'

Why did he want to know? Muka searched his face but found no answer. She let her eyes drop. Something shiny was dangling from a string round his neck. She remembered the amulet they had found in the grain store. With a hard little shake of her head, she dodged him and ran on.

'There's plenty of food,' she heard Lobo calling behind her. But she was already gone. Bat's grandmother would be waiting, frying green bananas in the hut. Food was getting scarcer these days, now that people were too frightened to go to market, but when the plantains had turned dark and gooey they would be good all mixed up with cassava flour.

Lobo perched on a log and ate alone that evening, the rich gamey juices dribbling down his chin. He held out scraps to the village boys who peeped from a distance; but even the hungriest just shook his head.

## CHAPTER FOURTEEN

Bat knew that this day was going to be different, from the moment he woke. All night, the wild elephants had been growling and moaning in the grasslands outside the village. It was as if they were unsettled, excited by something. He rose yawning from his mat and went out of the hut.

The sun streamed through the wood-smoke of the newly stirred fires. There they were. He could see them as he squinted against the low morning light: gathered in a group among a cluster of low acacias . . . and there was Meya too, standing alone and a little nearer, hovering fretfully between the furthermost perimeters of the village and the open expanses that belonged to the wild herd. Bat could tell from the way she was moving that something was troubling her. She was shuffling about, shifting anxiously to and fro.

'I'm going to see what she wants,' he called out to his grandmother.

'Wash your face first,' she cried.

The water from the earthenware pot in the cook-hut was cool. He cupped his hands and splashed. The droplets that clung to the tips of his eyelashes sparkled with rainbows as, grabbing his panga, he dashed off, leaping the bushes that bordered the compound rather than bothering to run round to the gap.

Bat's grandmother smiled. Clutching her stick with her shiny old hands, she watched the boy go, following the paths that wound between gardens then, reaching the edges, zigzagging away across wide open spaces, growing smaller and smaller until he had all but disappeared.

Meya was nearly seven years old now. She had reached her full size. Tall and strong, she must have stood more than nine feet high at the shoulder. Her long curving tusks swept upwards in a great gleaming arc and her ears, shaped like the continent over which her species roamed, were not ragged but smooth and clean-edged. When she spread them out she looked like a thundercloud in full sail.

The herd began to shamble away slowly as they saw the boy approach. They were used to him by now; they knew he would not harm them and they were happy to let him tag peaceably along; but only Meya would allow him to walk up and touch her, only Meya would twine her trunk around his tall, whipcord frame, let him scratch at the coarse hairs that sprouted from her under-lip and then, lazily blinking, lower her great head so that he could scratch behind her ears also.

The short rains were over, the grass had been grazed right down to the nub, but the herd spent most of the morning quietly browsing on high foliage while Bat sat not too far away and waited and watched. He allowed himself to be lulled into a false sense of peace. Perhaps he had misread the signs; perhaps nothing out of the ordinary was going to happen. The youngsters were playing, barging and squirming like a basket full of puppies, clambering the slopes of their recumbent mothers, only, when they had finally straddled the bony spinal ridge, to slide back down the far side and land in a mess of sprawled limbs. Twice, the youngest of the babies came running in Bat's direction, getting as close as it dared before skidding to a halt. Then, brought to its haunches like a begging dog, it would trumpet its shrill treble as hard as it could before tearing excitedly back to its group. The game delighted Meya. She got down on her knees and started tusking the ground through sheer excess of pleasure, as if remembering the days when she too had played like that. But when one of the racing babies slipped and got stuck, sprawled on its belly, its four legs splayed out, she was the first of the herd to hasten over to help it, to lever it carefully back up with her tusks, offering it comfort by rubbing its back before prodding it gently away to return to its mother.

Bat stayed with the elephants most of the day. He drowsed as they dusted themselves with great puffs of dirt. The ox-peckers hissed as they snacked on fat warble flies. A vast cloud of starlings gathered over the savannah, wheeling and diving in mysterious unison. A pair of giraffe wandered across the horizon, their heads swaying like flowers that have caught a slight breeze. A lonely old bull buffalo came down to drink. Only when it had finished did it finally notice Bat. Startled, it gave vent to a loud huffing snort. A long drool of slobber swung from its black snout as, with head held aloft, it trotted stiffly away.

By late afternoon, the elephants too were thinking of leaving. It was time to move back to the thicker bush. The matriarch rumbled her low 'let's go' call. The cows stirred sleeping babies with a nudging hind foot. Only Meya seemed uncertain. Swaying from side to side and swinging her foreleg, she looked back and forth between the boy and the herd. She was confused, Bat knew. But why, when of late she had not slept in the village at all?

His musings were broken by the arrival of Muka. She always came out to meet him when her day's work was done, when Bat's grandmother, finally heeding her growing impatience, would give the nod of her head which meant that she could at last go. Momentarily distracted, Meya wandered over to greet her. The girl reached out a hand and rubbed at Meya's rough hide.

The sun was beginning to fall in the sky. The matriarch rumbled again and, lifting her trunk, looked directly at Meya. The other elephants gathered and began to shuffle off. A low growling like thunder reverberated around the group. Meya rumbled back, but still she was hesitant. The children were holding her with their

wistful looks. Now they knew in their bones that something out of the ordinary was happening; they could feel it like the prickle of static that precedes a storm.

'They are leaving,' Bat whispered. But he could say no more. Even if tears had not been choking his voice, he could not have found words for the feelings that now welled up inside him. His little elephant, his beautiful Meya, the creature who had walked alongside him for half of his life, had finally reached her moment of unbreakable decision. She was making the choice between him and her wild herd.

Bat looked at the matriarch. She looked back, tall and commanding, from the fringes of the troupe that for so many years she had led. How could he compete? How could he promise the safety that this great animal offered? How could he offer the freedom that the wild herd knew? The thought of Meya leaving was like a knife in his heart; but he knew at that moment that they must finally part. It was what, from the very beginning, had been supposed to happen. The tears brimmed in his eyes. But he was sure now, at last, that he loved Meya so much that he was prepared, gladly, to let her finally go.

'You get along with them, girl,' he whispered and, stepping out into the open where all the other elephants could see him, he pushed her. 'Go on, Meya,' he called out. 'You can go now!'

The elephant stretched out her trunk and laid it upon his shoulder. Thick wafts of hot breath fell upon the boy's cheek. He stared into the depths of her soft russet eyes. Slowly they closed. It was as if she was trying to remember this moment, to lock an image of his face inside her mind for ever. He stroked her gently. Then he kissed her and let his hand drop.

Muka now moved towards the elephant. The animal encircled her slender waist with her trunk. Muka spoke not a word, but she could not hide the feeling that swelled up from within her, shaking her thin shoulders and trembling her lips. She put out her arms and wrapped them around Meya. A powerful flush of remembering swept like a wind through her head, bearing upon it all the memories of the moments she had spent with this beast. They swirled up together as she leaned forward on tiptoe and planted a slow farewell kiss and then, tensing, as if her fragile body could no longer take so much strain, she pulled away and stepped back.

The matriarch turned to them and uttered another deep growling rumble. For a moment Meya remained motionless, as if she had not heard. Then she blinked and shook her head rapidly. It was as if a rush mat had been beaten. A thick cloud of dust billowed over the children. They crinkled their eyes and began to cough. Wiping their faces, they spat granules from their mouths. The spell had been broken. Muka began to giggle. Bat's face spread in a grin. Soon the sound of their laughter was ringing out across the savannah. Meya eyed them wryly and waggled her head.

The children were still smiling, though now through the first spilling tears, as they stood hand in hand and watched the elephants leave. The sun was sinking towards the horizon. Its pink light flared out across the vast open spaces, fanning upwards like wildfire into the African sky. An eagle soared to its roost on the furthest horizon. The escarpment turned carmine and then pink and then mauve. Then the shadows began slowly to seep out across the grasslands, swallowing colours and blurring distinctions, expanding and swelling and finally flooding the world.

A huge moon came up. The trees shone silver-grey. The night wind blew softly down from the cliff face. In the far distance the children could still see a line of dark forms swaying slowly though the blackness. They looked almost like phantoms. The moonlight shimmered upon them. It sparkled and glinted as it caught their tusks. Meya was among the elephants, they knew, but however hard they strained their eyes they could not single her out. She was part of the group. She had rejoined her wild herd.

PART TWO

## CHAPTER FIFTEEN

Bat returned to the way of life he had known before Meya. All through the short dry season he went out with the cattle. The herd had expanded. It was the calves of the calves of his first cows that he was now caring for, spotting in them the traits of their familiar forebears, discovering that Kayo's offspring were all just as inquisitive as she was and so all just as liable to get into trouble; that the speckled heifer which came from Leko's sturdy line was, like her, a daydreamer and hence last in the file. Though several of his original cows had now gone, Kila had always been kept. She shambled along, though increasingly stiffly, Bat noticed, her curving horns balanced like some cumbersome crown on her head. But she still threw a single sound calf every year and, though her silvery hide was now cross-scarred with scratch-marks and worn bare in patches,

Bat still loved to stand at her side and stroke her, finding solace in all the memories that they by now shared. He would still lean against her as they looked out over the water, and run his long fingers down her rippling neck-flaps.

Together Bat and his cattle roamed the savannah, drifting from marshy riverbanks to forested foot-slopes but, although he was constantly scanning the horizon and hoping, his heart skipping a beat at a rustle in the bushes, his breath stilled in his throat by the sight of a far distant rock, he never caught so much as a glimpse of the elephants and gradually, as the moons waxed and waned, his expectations subsided and the slow peaceful shifting of his cattle browsing the undergrowth ceased so often to stir up the fretful memories.

'Don't worry,' Bitek the fisherman tried to reassure him. 'It's quite normal for elephants to leave like that. They'll be high in the forests where no one can find them. They'll be following paths to feeding places that even you don't know. But before you know it, they'll be back.'

Still, Bat couldn't help feeling anxious. The forests were no longer safe. Only a few days earlier, the charcoal burner had turned up in Jambula. His camp had been robbed, he said. Everything had been taken: hunting knife, water bag, rice sacks and stock of salted meat. He had had to return. 'Not that I would have wanted to stay out,' he added. 'There are bad people travelling through the trees nowadays.'

The villagers had given him green bananas and maize meal and Bitek had contributed a few strips of dried fish. But there wasn't much food to spare. Times were hard in Jambula: even Fat Rosa was beginning to shrink. The exuberant rolls no longer bulged from her waistband and her round face had new angles. Only when she puffed out her cheeks, her eyes squeezed with laughter, did she look like she used to, and that wasn't so often now: there was less to laugh about.

One evening, Bat found himself watching his grandmother as she prepared the supper. Her cheeks were losing their burnished copper glow. Her skin had grown dry and shiny. It was thin as the paper in the books with which she had taught him to read. When she lifted a heavy cooking pot, he noticed how nearly she let it slip. Her fingers were buckling. They curled like the claws of the lizards that clung to the thatch.

Once she would have worked all morning in the shamba, pausing only occasionally to wipe the sweat from her brow, but now she breathed heavily as she bent over her hoe. She had to stop frequently. She always walked with her stick. She was wearing out, Bat thought, and suddenly all the feelings he had for her boiled up inside him and he flung his arms round her and squeezed her as tight as he could.

'I love you,' he told her, as he breathed in the smell of the wood-smoke that always clung about her.

'If you love me, stop squeezing my old bones so that I can stay alive a bit longer,' she laughed.

Bat was fourteen now. He had grown tall and strong. He had a proud bony face with high cheek-bones, a wide nose and full, clear-cut lips. His eyes were bright as the freshest leaf on a twig. 'He burns like a new flame,' Bitek said to Bat's grandmother. 'He's like a thorn tree in flower: it becomes the focus of the entire landscape.'

'You are a man,' the village chief told him. 'Up until now, your grandmother has always looked after you; now the time has come for you to look after her. You are the head of the house.'

From then on, Bat's grandmother found that she no longer had to chivvy him. She no longer had to spit in the dust when she set him a task. He would always have done it before the wet patch had dried. Nothing gratified him more than to be sent for to help with some manly duty, with the splitting of firewood or the lifting of some maize sack, and although, when it was one of the small boys who delivered the message, he liked to raise his eyebrows and grumble, 'What now?' even they could tell that in truth he was only pretending, that he was proud to have become the man whom the women had to ask. He seldom had to be told what to do twice any more.

Outside the village, he and Muka cleared a new plot for planting. He sliced through the dry brush with fast, efficient strokes, making sure that he covered more ground than the girl did, and, although at the end of the morning his shoulder muscles were aching, he went on to help her collect the firewood, cutting it into short lengths which she then piled up in a stack. Even the repair of the huts in the compound, a job that in the past would always have been done by Bat's grandmother, was now left for the two children. Mixing mud up with cow dung, Bat smeared the wet plaster over walls and floors before leaving the sun to bake it, while Muka, with quick fingers, knotted grass stalks to mend holes in the thatch.

When the long rains came, there would be planting for the pair of them to do. The first puffs of cloud were already drifting over the escarpment. They were the messengers. It would not be many days now, they thought as they squinted. But, where once the villagers would have awaited the arrival with chattering expectation, this year the mood was strangely subdued. The headman no longer stood in his gumboots, surveying the scene around him with quiet satisfaction. He no longer folded his arms contentedly over his barrel chest. The musical voices that had once gossiped and argued around cook-fires in the evening were muted. The bright printed cloths that the women wrapped round their waists were tattered. But no one went to buy new ones. The market was not safe. 'The rebels will attack in broad daylight,' people said. Even Marula wore a faded old turban. Her pink and blue plaid that had once been so jarring had now been washed so many times that its colours were muted. 'You can barely distinguish it from the dust,' she said as she sat beside her doorway. 'People will start tripping over me soon.' And when Fat Rosa sat down beside her, her plump thighs no longer splayed like a pair of wallowing hippos. Her family hadn't had enough to eat for some while.

Bat's grandmother decided to kill one of their cows. She never liked doing this. 'Without cattle you are naked,' she always said. 'But Mutu is old and her hind legs are weak. We can't afford to keep anything out of compassion any more.'

Bat could not bear to be there when Bim's father came with a knife to dispatch the beast, to scoop out the entrails and strip the glossy black hide from her muscles. But at least the whole village had eaten well that night. Marula hadn't even waited for her sons to carry her over to the feast. Scooting down the path on the palms of her hands, she had arrived in Bat's compound and dropped herself down in eager anticipation. Fat Rosa puffed out her cheeks and smiled like she hadn't smiled for months. Even the medicine woman crept out to join them, a huddle of angles and sharp teeth at the fringe of the gathering, while the village children stared with eyes that looked too large for their faces.

Afterwards they had all lingered for far longer than had become usual by the fire, the men belching contentedly and spitting in the dust, the women chattering softly as they brushed the mosquitoes from their drowsy youngsters. The headman put his empty pipe in his mouth and sucked and blew meditatively, surveying them all through his empty spectacle frames while toothless old Kaaka, whom everyone now said looked set to live for ever, sucked and sucked at each lump of meat until it was soft enough to mash.

Bat was light-hearted the next day as he followed the cattle. He and Muka had been working so hard in the shamba of late that the cows had all but entirely been entrusted to the care of mute Bim. The whistle with which Bat had taught him to speak to the elephant worked well for the cattle, and they would come trotting at the sound of his chirruping call. But that day, Bat went out in the morning, like he had so often done and Muka met him in the evening, as she had always liked to do. Now, perched side by side on a stone, they watched the sun as it lowered itself towards the horizon, bathing the tops of the acacias with its shining, and splashing great swatches of pink onto the escarpment wall.

Suddenly, Bat tensed. He had heard a movement in the scrub. 'Shhh, there's something there.'

Muka froze.

They strained their ears: but nothing.

A porcupine shambled off through the brush.

Muka laughed. 'It was only him!'

Still, porcupines were night foragers: it was time to get home. Bat bundled up his pile of cut grass and, collecting his panga, called to the scattered cattle. They lifted their heads and lowed. Muka heaved a huge knot of firewood onto her head and the pair set off. The backs of the cows gleamed in the fading light. A soft brown duiker, disturbed from its hiding place, skipped delicately away on its dancer's light feet. A mourning dove uttered its soft growling call. It sounded so peaceful. And it felt to the children, as they wandered home together, as if everything would always stay that way.

But suddenly, in the time it takes for a bird to flit from one branch to the next, the whole world changed. Nothing would be the same any more.

## CHAPTER SIXTEEN

An arm locked round Bat's waist. He let out a shout.
A hand clamped his mouth. He kicked as hard as he
could. A knee was brought up into the small of his
back. He gasped and doubled over. Someone dragged
him back upright. Who was it? He couldn't see them
and yet they were right there behind him, one crooked
arm round his neck crushing down on his windpipe,
the other pressing a rough hand hard down on his lips.
He could feel their breath bursting in hot pants on his
cheek. He struggled for air. His own lungs were explod-
ing. His heels scuffled helplessly. He could get no grip
in the dust. The whole world was blearing. A vast sea of
blackness was drowning his head.

He heard a scream. Muka! Her cry cut right through
him. It sliced through the darkness and awoke every
nerve to new fear. For a moment he froze. Then fresh

energy surged through him, flooding his body with a wave of wild fury. Biting down as hard he could, he sank his teeth into the flesh of the hand that was holding him. Someone gave a sharp gasp. It might have been him. Lashing out with his nails, he ripped himself free and ran, racing as fast as he could through the twilight, knees skimming the bushes as he zigzagged for cover. The blood tasted bitter as iron in his mouth. The cattle were scattering, veering and kicking about him. He twisted like a bat through the shadows and escaped.

Where was Muka? He ducked down and listened but his heart was drumming so hard he could hear nothing else. His eyes scanned the grasslands but the sun, dipping at that moment below the rocky horizon, suddenly let the night loose. Darkness stampeded across the sky.

Looping back the way he had come, Bat stole through the brush. He could hear his cattle, confused and frightened, trotting about calling for each other and for their scattered calves. Bat felt as bewildered as they did. He wanted to cry out. 'Muka!' he wanted to shout. 'Muka! Where are you?' But he knew that he had to be wary if he wanted to help her. Step by slow prowling step, he crept on.

Suddenly, not so far from him, an engine started up. He thought he heard scuffles and a low muffled cry. Was that Muka? It must be. They must have caught her. They must be trying to take her away. Once they had left, thought Bat, he would never be able to find her. He had to act now if he wanted to save her.

He had no plan in his head as he dashed blindly in the direction of the sound. Hard ruts of earth bruised the soles of his feet. He was on the track. A glare of light struck him as he raced straight down the middle. The roar of the engine throbbed louder and louder. He was dazzled. He flung up an arm to protect his face. The lights were almost upon him. He could see nothing but their burning ferocity.

A cow, lost in the commotion, stepped straight out in front of him. There was a sickening thud and, even as he stared horrified, arms were circling about him. The grip that held him was strong as a waterfall. He could see the silvery flank of the fallen animal heaving up and down before him. A back leg looked broken. A jag of pale bone glistened amid the dark blood. A single dark eye gazed up into the night. Bat could hear the low groaning. It was Kila – Kila, his favourite . . . the cow he had grown up with, who had wandered beside him for as long as he could remember . . . It was Kila, the cow he would never have killed. Something gave way inside him. It was as if the string of a tightened bow had just snapped. He fell limp. By the light of the headlamps, he met Kila's dying gaze. It was the soft purple colour of a jacaranda's petals. He watched her eye as it filmed and then flickered and closed.

Bat was thrown to the ground. The fall jarred his shoulder and bruised his thin ribs. A wedge of rough cloth was shoved into his mouth. It cut into the corners of his lips. His arms were yanked behind his back. Then a rope was flung around him and tugged until his elbows almost touched. He tried to move: it hurt so badly that he almost screamed aloud. Knots bit into his wrists. Then his ankles were bound and he was left lying

172

among the grasses. Were they going to abandon him? Were they going to leave him to be eaten by wild beasts? Three shadowy figures stood upright. One wiped his brow while another wandered off. A knife was drawn. Bat could see the wink of its blade. They were going to kill him. The fear scudded through his brain. He was about to die.

'Shut it up,' a voice ordered.

One of the figures stepped over to the cow. The knife was for Kila. He heard steel ripping flesh and then the groaning stopped. The blade flashed in the headlights as the carcass was rapidly butchered. Bat smelled the stench of the guts as they slopped onto the dirt, and into his mind came a picture of Kila ambling off in the morning towards the savannah, his baby elephant shambling slowly behind her, the tip of its trunk curled comfortingly around her tail. The image passed through his head like a reflection that slides across water. It was a picture from another time, another place, another world.

Bat could feel his mind slowing. It was as if everything had stopped moving. His arms were pulled back so tightly that he could hardly breathe without hurting. He tried to turn over, but it only made it worse. Needles seemed to be jabbing where his joints should have rolled and for a while his mind vanished. He didn't know where it went.

The next thing Bat knew, he was being hurled into the back of a jeep. The pain jagged through his shoulder; it burst in sharp flashes against the backs of his eyes, but the cloth in his mouth soaked up the sound of his shouts. He could taste the fear at the back of his throat and for a moment he was terrified that he was going to choke. Panic surged through his veins, bursting his arteries and leaking into his guts. He gasped frantically for air, but tasted only gasoline. It burned his lips. He felt his whole stomach heave.

A torch-beam was flung quickly around the interior and, in the brief flash of light, Bat saw Muka lying motionless in a corner, her wrap rucked up around her, her eyes closed in a face that was flung back on its neck. Was she dead? Her legs and arms, like his, were bound; and she too was gagged. The rough knots were biting into the soft flesh of her nape. That must mean she was living. Otherwise why would they tie her? But then why had they captured them? What did they want with them? The questions raced back and forth.

Bat gave up trying to catch them. Something heavy was flung into the jeep beside him. It landed with a thud. He felt a warm dampness seeping into his shirt. The boy shuddered. There was another soft *thunk*. It was Kila, he thought. They had carved her up into chunks. Then the door slammed. The darkness was complete. The engine roared into life. He could feel it juddering in every muscle of his body. The side of his head rattled against a ridged metal floor. And then for a while he felt nothing any more.

When Bat came round again, with a nod so sharp that it felt as if his neck would crack, he realized that he was travelling, but he had no idea for how long. It was still dark. The cords round his wrists cut into his flesh and made him want to cry out. Dust clogged his breathing, but when he tried to suck air through his gag, nothing came. He pulled at the thin strand of air that was filtering in through his nostrils. Only this one faltering thread linked him to his own life. It could break any moment.

He tried to stretch out his fingers, to see if he could touch Muka; but all he could feel was his own fumbling grasp. His hands seemed strange and fleshy, as if they didn't belong to him. Something crawled across his scalp but he didn't know what. And then the jeep bumped over a ridge and, hitting his head, he lost consciousness again.

He thought he must have passed in and out of blackness several times. Everything was muddled. A thirst raged in his throat. Sometimes he tried to remember a tune to sing. He thought it would lure his spirit into calm. But no song ever came. He heard only his heart pounding. He expected to die. Clenching his tied fists, he tried to steady his breathing. Like a man who, hand over hand, inches across a swaying rope bridge, he refused to look down and stare into the abyss. He could not afford to start sobbing. He could not afford to let go of the thin line of his breath. Where were they going? he wondered. But the question just drifted. And after a while he discovered that peculiar feeling of safety that arises from knowing that the worst that could happen is already taking place.

Once, the jeep stopped. The engine was cut. He could hear the noises of the African night, rising and falling and swarming giddily about. He tried to pick out the individual voices . . . the shrill of cicadas . . . the *tok tok* of the nightjar . . . the *skreak* of a bat . . . but they all got mixed up. They were melted down by his brain. He could hear people speaking, but he couldn't tell what they were saying. The tailgate opened. He saw the tip of a cigarette glowing like the eye of a crocodile in the night. The cow's meat was pulled out. The door slammed again . . . then laughter and snatches of conversation . . . then a pause that lasted for what might have been minutes but could equally well have gone on for several hours.

When the door opened again, a hand shoved him. They were checking that he was still there and alive, he supposed. He writhed against the knots, but the shooting pains in his arms soon made him give up. A hard smell of alcohol mixed with the fumes of diesel and cigarette smoke. Then the tailgate was slammed and locked. He felt the hot uproar of the engine through the metal. Once more, they were off.

They were still driving as the day dawned. Light filtered in through the hood of the jeep which Bat could now see had been made from bent branches with a sheet of brown tarpaulin stretched over the top. He wasn't facing Muka, but he could feel her behind him. They had been thrown together by the vehicle's jolts. And she was still alive: he could tell from her warmth.

And then they were climbing a steep slope, the jeep bouncing and sliding, its gears grinding laboriously. The side of Bat's head hurt so much each time it banged against metal that for a while he tried to stiffen his neck. It only made the pain worse. And then they were back on the flat. Clouds of dust filled the jeep, puffing up through the floor. Bat struggled to breathe. The heat was now growing. Every fibre in his body felt as if it was on fire. The blood in his veins was starting to simmer. His tongue was parched. The thirst was terrible. It throbbed through his mind, driving all but this one desperate craving from his head.

At one point they crossed a river. The swishing of water was cruel as a torture. Thoughts of its freshness flowed and splashed through his brain. The torment was so terrible he wanted to scream. He tugged at the knots that bound him but he couldn't loosen them. Only his mind could float free of this trap. It drifted away into the land of his dreams and he imagined for a moment that he was among the elephants, following the slow herd of huge swaying creatures, marching unstoppably across vast open spaces, set free to wander across an entire continent.

There was another halt. A voice called out. Bat strained his ears for the answer but it came in a tongue that he didn't understand. Voices drew closer. Footsteps scuffed about and he heard the harsh scrape of laughter. Again, he smelled alcohol and cigarette smoke. Another vehicle was approaching. It sounded like a lorry. Perhaps the driver would help. Surely he would do something if he found two children tied up? Drawing in all the breath he could muster, Bat let his lungs swell, and prepared to give a great shout. But the sound broke like a puffball of spores in his cheeks. All that could be heard of the hoped-for explosion was a faint sighing whimper. Soon the big rolling wheels were rumbling slowly off.

And then they were travelling uphill again. It was

cooler now; but Bat's thirst was so dreadful that he thought it would kill him. Branches slapped the tarpaulin. Thorns squealed as they scraped against metal sides. The vehicle laboured slowly on, sometimes lurching through potholes, occasionally bumping over what felt like a fallen log. Bat's head smashed onto metal again and again.

When they next came to a stop, the boy had given up hope. He just lay there. At least he wouldn't be hit against the floor for a while. Maybe he could even sleep for a bit. He was so horribly tired. He longed now for unconsciousness, but the tailgate was opening and the next thing he knew he was being dragged out.

There was a moment of stabbing brightness when he couldn't see anything. The pain of blood returning bolted through his cramped limbs. The soaring trunks of forest trees were reeling all about him, and then he was looking into a pair of red eyes. They were set in the middle of a round dark face, with cheeks so full that it looked as if their muscles were clenched. Though the short, thick mouth in the middle wasn't saying anything, Bat seemed for a moment to hear the words that it spoke in his head. 'I could kill you if I liked,' it was saying, 'and nothing would come of it. I will kill you whenever I like, and nothing will happen at all.' Bat had never seen an expression like that before. He tried to confront it, fear giving him courage, but though his eyes didn't move, his body was swaying. He couldn't find his balance on his tightly bound feet.

A gun was slung over the man's shoulder. *Yes, he is going to kill me*, Bat thought. He felt suddenly calm. He thought of his father. It was funny that he was going to die just like him . . . shot by strangers who didn't know him but would end his life anyway. He tried to clench his fists behind his back, but his fingers were too swollen. He would be brave for the moment. He felt the back of his head growing hot. That was where the bullet was going to go in.

'Don't worry . . . he isn't going to kill you. We don't want you to die . . . not yet. You'll be no use to us dead.' The voice that spoke sounded horribly familiar. Bat was sure that he recognized the jeer of the man who was now standing behind him, unknotting his gag, dragging it from his mouth. Bat's numbed face slewed round at the wrench. He inhaled through a throat that was so clogged with dust that even the thin stream of air made him choke. He longed to swallow but no moisture came. His lips hung in a gape.

'Lobo?' he mouthed, but it was no more than a whisper. His tongue was too dry to twist itself round the letters.

'Sergeant Lobo to you,' the voice said, and suddenly, there was the boy, standing right in front of him, a wide grin on his face. His deep-set eyes narrowed to slits as he drew on the stub of a cigarette. 'Quite a haul,' he announced. 'Like a caracal: two plovers with one pounce!'

He glanced over to the jeep from which a man was now hauling Muka. The look in her eyes was half fear, half fury as she fought to stay upright. Lobo stepped closer to her and ran a hand down her cheek. He would never have dared touch her like that back in the village;

but she didn't flinch. Her face was bruised, Bat noticed, and dried blood clotted her temples. One of her eyes was half closing. Her braids were tangled and dusty and her crumpled blue wrap was stained a dark rusty purple. Bat hoped it was blood from the butchered cow.

'Leave her!' barked the man with red eyes. 'Get on with your work!'

The boy shrugged and, walking off, began hacking at trees with his panga, dragging back branches to throw over the jeep. They were trying to hide it. Bat wondered why. Might people be looking for him and Muka? Might help have already been sent?

The man with the bloodshot eyes drew a knife from a sheath and sliced carelessly through the ropes that bound Bat's legs. The blade drew blood. Bat gasped. But he couldn't have cried out for help even if he had tried to; even if there had been anyone about to hear. His mouth was too dry.

'Now walk,' he commanded, 'and don't even think about escaping. If you so much as breathe without my permission, you are dead.' Prodding Bat in the back with the stock of his rifle, he set him stumbling across the clearing. The pain of the blood rushing back into his numbed limbs was excruciating and it was hard not to trip with his hands still tied; but ahead of him, a third person – he looked no more than a child, Bat now noticed – was already leading the way down a narrow forest track.

The path seemed endless to Bat. He wondered how Muka was managing. He could hear the smack and swish of the bushes as she stumbled behind him, and Lobo's casual whistling as he sauntered along at the back. What was the boy doing here? Bat was too bewildered to think much about it. In fact, oddly, he realized, he almost welcomed his presence. At least he and Muka were not quite among strangers.

Thorns tore at Bat's clothing; insects clung to his skin; branches slapped him across the face. His feet were so swollen that every step hurt him. Sometimes he was forced to scramble over a fallen tree-trunk. The sun slammed down through the hole that had been ripped in the high canopy. Dense thickets of new plants clambered for the light.

After a while they reached a pool of water. Pushed to their knees, he and Muka were allowed to drink. They lapped like animals in a drought, neither looking at the other as they quenched their first searing thirst; but with water inside them, they began to recover a little. They flashed one another a quick reassuring glance as, dragged once more to their feet, they were set roughly back on their path again.

## CHAPTER SEVENTEEN

Almost at a step, the two children passed from the gloom of the trees to the glare of the sun. They were at the edge of a small forest clearing. For a moment they stood blinking, half blinded by the light.

A few huts were scattered about the fringes where the overhang of the trees would have all but hidden them even from an eagle flying above. They looked makeshift, Bat thought, cobbled together from hacked branches and pieces of corrugated metal and bits of old sacking. A fire smouldered unattended just in front of him. Rusting tins, scraps of plastic, bones that had been smashed open and sucked of their marrow, and gnawed maize husks lay littered about it. Nobody had swept the trampled red dust. There was nobody to do so, he thought. And then he saw a young boy, standing alone at the far side of the clearing holding a gun that looked almost as tall as he did. He was leaning against the door of one of the shelters, a low circular construction with no windows and a flat corrugated-iron roof. And it was towards this shack that Bat, pulled away from Muka with a barely stifled cry of panic, was suddenly pushed.

A door scraped open and he was shoved inside. At first he could see nothing. He stood swaying and befuddled while someone fumbled at the ropes around his wrists. The blood gushing in his veins hurt so much that he wanted to run about, but the door was dragged shut behind him. All was darkness, except for those pinprick spots where the sun, streaming down through nail holes in the roof, inserted shafts of pure brightness like shining wires through the black. He heard branches being propped against the entrance.

Bat was too exhausted and frightened to know what to do next. He just stood there while slowly his eyes adjusted to the gloom. And it was only then that he realized, with a start, that there was someone else with him. A boy was huddled in the corner. His thin legs were drawn up to his shoulder-blades and his hands clung about them, but his head was dropped down so that Bat couldn't see his face. 'Who are you?' Bat whispered. But the boy didn't answer. Bat looked at the cuts on his close-shaven scalp. Then, slumping down miserably against a wall opposite, he sat and waited. He didn't know for what.

A while later, the door opened and the child with the gun came in. He was clearly Bat's guard. But now his weapon was slung by its strap over his left shoulder and in his hands he was carrying two plastic bowls instead.

One contained water, the other food. It was just a millet flour paste but the boy in the corner scuttled over, took a fistful and, retreating, started gulping it down as if he was starving. Bat only drank. The boy eyed him warily as a hyena that shares the kill of a lion.

'Take it,' said Bat, pushing the rest of the food over. 'Take it if you're hungry.'

The boy scuttled over again and then back to his corner. He had a strange crab-like shuffle. He crammed the paste into his mouth before Bat could change his mind.

Bat studied him. He was wearing nothing but a pair of ragged green shorts and he was thin: so thin that his shoulder-blades stuck out in knobbles and his ribcage protruded like a basket's wicker struts. A pair of heavy black boots made his feet look far too big. His legs were like the bits of charred bone that you find when you clean the ash from a cook-fire. There was no flesh on them. But when Bat looked again he could see that they were corded with muscle. It was impossible to tell what colour his skin really was. Layer after layer, the dirt had baked onto his body. But it was not this dead blackness that made Bat shrink: it was the darkness in his eyes. They were completely blank.

Time passed. Bat must have slept because the next thing he knew it was night. The moonlight shone down through the chinks in the roof. Outside in the forest, insects chirped, sawed and hacked. Bat heard the gobbling whoops of a troupe of mangabey monkeys crashing through the leaves as some predator roused them. He imagined the babies clutched tight to their mothers' shaggy backs. He felt a terrible loneliness. He had never slept beside a stranger. There had always been Meya or his grandmother or Muka. The worst thing about loneliness, Bat thought, was that it left too much space to think.

Where was Muka? he wondered. Was she hurt? Was she as frightened as him? The questions crowded about him, closing in like a quagmire. They were sucking him down. He was helpless to resist. His thoughts drifted to that day when Meya had sunk in the swamp. How desperate he had felt! He clamped his hands to his ears as her squeals rang down the tunnels of memory, rising more and more frantically as he ran further away. He had not wanted to forsake her, he thought, as he tried to stifle the sound of them. But there had been nothing else at the time he could do.

The wild elephants had saved Meya. But who would come for him? Who would come for him and Muka? His grandmother didn't even know where he was. What was she doing now? he wondered. She would be hopelessly searching, he thought, shouting their names out across the savannah, eyes glued to the ground as she cast about for their tracks. She would have found the scattered cattle; perhaps even the very spot where Kila had been slaughtered. She would have seen the trail of the jeep vanishing into the dust. She would have guessed what had happened.

In his mind's eye he saw her sitting alone by her cook-fire. Who would look after her without him there to help? Or had his kidnappers gone on to the village? Was it even now laid waste: huts burned to the ground, shambas trampled and raided? Had there been something more that these people had wanted?

His whole body flinched as he remembered once more the moment of the ambush. Why hadn't he been watching? Why had he been such a fool? It was his fault that Muka had been taken. He should have looked out for her, not led her into a trap. He hoped that she wouldn't fight. She could be so ferocious. He prayed that they wouldn't hurt her. He prayed that she wouldn't struggle and lash out.

Before he had even begun to try and answer one question, another was rising. He tried to stop them from coming, but they kept piling up, an impossible muddle that towered higher and higher and then toppled and fell crashing down through his head. In a shaft of moonlight, he saw a chameleon. It watched him, eyes swivelling in their baggy sockets. Old Kaaka said it was bad luck to disturb one of these lizards. Their colours, as they changed, were the spirits of the ancestors passing over. Bat reached out and picked it up gently. He found solace in the feel of its dry fingers plucking at his flesh. The questions whined in his head, like the mosquitoes around him. They bit at his thoughts. There was no point brushing them away. They would always come back. Where was Muka? What was his grandmother doing? Who were these people? When would he know what was going to happen to him?

*

Dawn broke. Every bone in Bat's body ached. He was tired and hungry and he was also very cold. He must be high in the mountains, he thought. Bundling his legs up into his arms, he shivered. Outside he could hear people stirring. Voices were speaking. There must have been several people. An order was barked. Someone turned on a radio and tinny music floated out.

Bat looked at the boy opposite him. He was awake, though it was quite hard to tell if he had ever been asleep. He was staring blank-eyed at the wall. He looked even younger than Bat had at first guessed. He couldn't be more than ten years old. And yet already he seemed completely broken. He still didn't speak; and even if he had done, Bat wasn't sure that he would understand anyway. There were so many languages spoken in his country: more than fifty, his grandmother had told him; and besides, Bat didn't even know if he was in his own country any more.

'My name is Gulu,' the boy suddenly said. It was a shock to Bat: not just to hear him talking, but speaking with the familiar glittery sounds of Bat's own tongue.

'My name's Nakisisa,' he answered. 'But everybody calls me Bat. I come from Jambula. Do you know where we are now?'

The boy shook his head.

'Don't you know?'

The boy shrugged as if it didn't much matter.

'But who are these people?' Bat asked.

'These people?'

'Yes, who are these people who have put us in this hut?'

'You don't know?'

Bat shook his head.

'They're the army,' said the boy. 'You are in the army now.'

'Yes, you're in the army now.' A voice made Bat jump. He turned. Lobo had dragged the door open. Now he towered above the two boys, his broad shape blocking the abrupt flood of light. 'You are in the army now and I am your officer.' He grinned. 'From now on you do as I say.'

He didn't explain further, only, taking a step forward, he prodded Bat to his feet with the stock of a rifle. Then, pushing the muzzle into the small of his back, he shoved him out of the hut.

Bat glanced, bewildered, about the forest clearing. The trees rose up on all sides. They looked impenetrable as a wall. But he could see several other children now, gathered in groups around the edges. A few turned to look. Some of them could not have been more than seven or eight years old. They were as small as the little boys who peeped and played in his village, their eyes dancing with mischief, their noses running with snot, and yet these children seemed more like adults already. Most of them had close-shaven heads, though a few of the taller ones had matted dreadlocks. Some had boots, some didn't; one wore a dented tin helmet and several had strips of green cloth knotted around their brows; but all of them looked ragged and tattered and hungry as they turned to examine him with indifferent faces, as if all curiosity had long ago been blunted, all expectation long since fallen flat.

Bat's gaze swept rapidly across them. He was searching for Muka. She must be among them. Narrowing his eyes, he squinted against the light, but before he had even had time to search half the faces, the muzzle of the gun prodded him onwards again. It jagged him just below the rib cage where the body is most unprotected. He stumbled and bit his tongue as he cried out. The sound as he swallowed it tasted sour as blood.

Crossing the compound at a half-trot, he reached a shelter made of palm fronds that had been set up on the far side. There, a man sat on a grimy plastic chair. His back was turned to them, his thick legs sprawled to either side of him as he leaned back and listened to the radio that Bat had heard from his hut. It was playing a tinny dance tune.

The man swivelled slowly. Bat recognized the dark bulging face with its slow bloodshot gaze. He dropped his frightened eyes and found himself looking at a pair of black leather boots. An empty bottle lay between them. The man had been drinking. His trousers were stained and he smelled like a hyena. He reached forward, using the blade of a knife to lift the boy's chin. Bat trembled so hard he could feel his lips shaking.

'Look! He's scared as a soaked monkey,' he heard Lobo jeer.

The man didn't answer. He had a crocodile's

stare. He smiled, but there was no emotion in his face.

'So, you are the boy who knows about elephants?'

Bat nodded dumbly.

'Good. Then we've got work for you.'

Bat was bewildered. Was that what they wanted him for? Had they brought him all this way to look after an elephant? He looked around as if half expecting to see one, searching the clearing for that familiar grey shape.

'Do exactly as you're told and you'll be fine,' the man assured him, unpeeling the cellophane from a packet of cigarettes. He took one and placed it thoughtfully between his lips. He spun the wheel of a lighter. A flame sprang into life.

'But if you don't do what I tell you, then—' He made a swiping movement across his throat. It was the movement a butcher makes when he kills a goat, its last bleat pouring out on a flood of dark blood. Bat's stomach cramped as a wave of fear swept over him. A plume of cigarette smoke was puffed into the air. He could feel his head growing giddy. He tried to steady himself by fixing his eyes on some small detail, but they couldn't seem to focus until he noticed the scratches that raked the man's forearms.

'Where's Muka?' he blurted.

'Muka?' The man looked faintly surprised.

'He means the girl we brought with him,' explained Lobo.

The man gave a slow smile. 'You mean the wildcat?' he said, glancing wryly at his scratches.

'Let's just say we've tamed her.' He laughed. 'Now

take him back.' The last order was addressed to Lobo.

'Back to the hut?'

The man nodded. 'Yes . . . for a bit. Until he's learned that this is his new home,' he said. 'Until he's learned to be obedient. And I don't want him even so much as seeing that girl,' he added in an undertone. 'I don't want them running off and dying. Not when we've gone to such trouble for the elephant boy.'

At that moment a fight broke out amid a group at the far side of the camp. Fierce as spitting genets, two children wrestled in the dust, grappling and pawing and biting and screaming. The man rose to his feet with a thunderous look.

'Lock him in!' he barked over his shoulder at Lobo. Then he cast a last glance at Bat. The eyes burned like red lamps. 'And don't even think about escaping because we won't waste a bullet on you. We will find you out in the bush. We will make you wish you had never left us. You will die wriggling and squealing like a half-bled pig.'

Bat was thrown back in the gloom of his hut. What now? The time stretched endlessly ahead of him. *At least I know Muka is alive,* he supposed. *And while she's alive there's still hope . . . still some hope of escape . . . I'll find her . . . and then we'll . . .* His ideas petered out. He strained his ears. He needed to orientate himself, find out what was happening. But all he could hear was the thump of his heart in his head. He tried to imagine that he was back in his village, that the drumbeat of his blood was the sound of the girls pounding cassava in the mornings. *Thud-ah . . . thud-ah . . . thud-ah.* He longed with every fibre of his being to be back where he belonged.

'I'm in the army now,' he whispered, as if testing the idea out.

'Yes, we're in the army,' murmured Gulu from the far side of the hut. 'And it would be better to be dead.'

The words echoed around Bat's head the next morning when the door was suddenly flung open and two children stormed in. Seizing Gulu, they dragged him from the hut. Bat was left all alone. Outside he could hear talking, sometimes even laughing. He could smell the smoke of the fire. They were cooking. He thought he could smell roasting meat. He ran his hands around the mud walls as if seeking some opening; but he knew it was useless before he even began. He pressed an eye to the door and through a crack saw the guard still standing. It was hard to tell from behind if it was the same boy as before. He shifted his weight and changed his gun to another hand. And then, almost as if sensing that someone was spying on him, the guard turned abruptly and slammed its hard butt against the tin door. The noise rattled round the clearing. 'Back,' he growled, 'or you'll be getting the same as your new friend.' Bat shrank back into the darkness and slumped hopelessly down on the floor. He could hear a faint commotion somewhere on the far side of the camp. There were thumps, cries and curses. He hoped that it had nothing to do with Gulu.

But it did.

That afternoon they brought the boy back, hurling

him down, a broken straggle of limbs in the dust. He made not a sound now; not even a groan. Had they killed him? Bat inched his way hesitantly through the half-darkness. He was almost too scared to find out. Stretching out a hand, he touched Gulu's shoulder. There was no response, but the skin was still warm, and when Bat leaned his head closer, he could just hear the rasp of breath between teeth. What had happened? Should he rouse him? He tried to look into the boy's half-hidden face. He put out a hand again, intending to shake him, but then let it drop. Rouse him for what? To remind him that he was a prisoner? Why let that reality intrude on his dreaming? At least in unconsciousness he might find some sort of escape.

Bat crept away. Curled up on the ground, he lay watching the dust motes that danced in the light as it streamed through the holes in the roof. He watched as they faded away into the black. He listened to the sounds of the camp subsiding until only the cicadas trilled their endless night song. He was cold now, but he had no blanket. He huddled himself, shivering up in his arms. He had never felt so lonely. The night had never felt so endless. Despite the chill that leaked through the bones deep inside him, hot rashes of sweat broke out, burning on his skin. It seemed like for ever until at last he fell asleep.

'Where am I?' he whispered the next morning when he woke to the sound of the door scraping. But it was only a tiny boy bringing a calabash. It was water mixed with millet flour again. Bat carried it over to Gulu where he lay curled up, his head to the wall. The boy had been so hungry, but now he didn't respond.

'Take some; it's food,' urged Bat and, cradling the back of the boy's head in his palm, he held the bowl up to him. The boy turned and, gasping, Bat let the bowl drop. Where there had once been a face, there was now only a swollen mess of flesh. Blood caked Gulu's brow, his lips and his cheeks; a front tooth was broken and his arm was scored with deep cuts.

Bat edged away, appalled. What had happened? How could he now help? His grandmother would have made a bitter herb poultice to bring down the swelling; she would have boiled up hyena dung with the bark of a fever tree. That would have scalded and cleaned the deep wounds; but all Bat could do was dip a corner of his shirt into the bowl of drinking water and with that try to dab away the worst of the grit. The boy moaned and flinched. Bat wasn't sure if he was doing much good but he kept on going anyway. Somehow it soothed him to think he might be helping. He remembered the time he had sat with his elephant when she was sick. 'Suffering is worse for an animal because it can't understand what is happening.' That's what his grandmother had said. Bat gazed into the face of the boy lying beside him. It didn't feel any different. All he knew was that he was in pain and that he had to endure it. Bat kept on dabbing, as tenderly as he was able, only stopping when he noticed that the boy was once more closing his eyes. Then he sat and watched over him. Gulu's boots had been taken; not that he could ever have put them onto his feet. They were too swollen. It looked to Bat as he stared, his brain flinching from the thought, as if their bones had been smashed.

For two days Gulu lay, barely moving. Bat remained by his side. Sometimes he stroked his head gently; sometimes he hummed softly like Muka had taught him, singing the songs that they had sung to their elephant; and sometimes he just waited in silence, staring at the light as it streamed through holes in the ceiling, or gazing out into an impenetrable black. The sounds of the camp outside seemed to fade further and further as the solitude inside the hut slowly thickened. Bat could almost feel the emptiness that surrounded him. It was like the brushing of dewdrops, breaking cold on his skin.

Once a day the door opened and food and water was brought in by the guard. He seemed less like a child, Bat thought, than some diminutive adult: he looked so resigned. He never spoke; he never even so much as met Bat's watching eye. He just laid down the bowls and went.

Left alone, Bat ate his share and drank some of the water before trying to help Gulu take what was his. Parting Gulu's swollen lips, he placed the rough paste into his mouth with a finger; then he held up his head while he swallowed and winced. Sometimes Bat saw the tears dribbling down Gulu's bruised cheeks. Their salty fluids soaked into his wounded flesh.

The days passed. Bat lost count of how many. He retreated further and further into the world in his head. He lived inside his dreams. Sometimes he fell asleep and imagined that he was sitting with his grandmother, sipping bowls of spiced tea. The cook-fire was smoking. It brought tears to his eyes. When he awoke he had to wipe them from his cheeks. He was hungry. He dreamed of his grandmother's cooking. She was preparing the stew that she always cooked for special occasions, for his birthday, or the last day of threshing, or the time when he and Muka had finished reading their first ever book. He watched her taking malakwan leaves from a basket. He saw her cutting ripe tomatoes into a pot. She added the fermented hide of a hippopotamus and mixed in a handful of groundnuts to form a thick soup. They were just about to start eating – when Bat suddenly woke, his stomach growling with hunger. The pain gnawed at his belly. He was hungry . . . so hungry.

He imagined the honeycomb that came from the forest, dripping from his fingers, whole bees stuck in its gloop. Smoke from the camp fires drifted into the hut. He yearned for the familiar wood-fire smell of his grand-mother. Where was she? Where was Muka? When would he see her? He thought of the way they used to wander, so carefree, drifting the grasslands with their elephant. He wished he could go back to that untroubled world. He yearned for Meya's touch, for the feel of her trunk slipping over his shoulder, probing his pockets for a hidden piece of fruit or snatching at his herd-switch in the hopes of a game. He wished he could breathe in her thick musky smell . . . just one last time, he thought . . . that would have comforted him. Even the memory made him feel a bit less alone. But she had left with her herd and now, when she came back, she would find he had gone . . . gone without even telling her. She would think he had forgotten her and would never again return.

Clutching his arms round his stomach, Bat rocked to and fro, as if trying to soothe the feelings that now welled up within him. But it was no good. Memory after memory burst open inside him, blooming for a moment before wilting and dying. For the first time since he had been caught Bat felt utterly without hope. He put his hands to his head and sobbed like a child.

He didn't notice Gulu moving until the boy was already halfway across the hut. He was crawling on hands and knees because he couldn't stand. The hard dirt of the floor dug into his palms. He put his arm gently round Bat and finding his fingers, he squeezed them. 'Don't cry,' he said. 'Don't let yourself cry. You have to stay strong to survive in this place.'

A rising sob shook Bat's shoulders as he remembered the rumours that the women in the market place had whispered: the tales of fierce gangs of children who raided the shambas, who burned down the villages and slaughtered livestock. He remembered the stories of boys who had vanished without trace. He swallowed. 'Are they going to make me fight?'

Gulu nodded.

'But what for?'

'I don't know.' Gulu shrugged. 'No one does. You just do as they say. Every day is the same. It's just another day in which to kill or be killed. Eventually you get used to it. Everyone does.'

'But we could escape!' cried Bat. A flicker of hope lit his face. There must be a way. He would slip free and run like a lizard that finds the hole in a fist. But Gulu just gazed at him with his blank stare.

'I tried. That's why they beat me. I tried to escape. I don't even know if I meant to. But a little while ago they sent me out into the forest to set traps and suddenly, without even thinking, I found I was running. I was running and running as if my legs couldn't stop. I didn't know where I was going, but when at last I pulled up I didn't recognize anything, and so for days I just drifted. I ate berries and grubs. I always know how to find food in the forests,' Gulu declared flatly. 'I have lived with the army since I was just eight. I've learned how to find nuts and mushrooms and fruit and wild yams; to get water where there isn't any by cutting a bamboo cane; to catch fish by making a little pronged spear. I know that plants with umbrella-shaped leaves are poisonous, that if something tastes soapy to spit it out quick. But what I didn't know was where to go next. And after a long time . . . I don't know how much later . . . I just tracked my way back round in a circle again. I came back to the army because I had nowhere else to run. I told them that I had got lost. But still they threw me in here and they beat me. They beat me and beat me,' he said as he stared at his mangled foot. 'They would have killed me if they hadn't thought that I was still useful. They would have killed me,' he repeated. 'And I don't think I'd have cared.'

'But I could help you,' urged Bat. 'You, me and Muka . . . we could get back to our villages.'

Gulu just dropped his head. 'I can never go back,' he said. 'It's too late.' Then, wearied by so much talking, he lay down on the hard earth to rest. Bat curled up beside him and watched him closing his eyes. His breathing slowly steadied and soon Gulu was sleeping, twitching and flinching in a troubled slumber. Every now and then a half-cry choked in his throat. Where did he go in his dreams? Bat wondered as he lay there. For hour after hour he lay wakeful beside him. His mind ached like a broken bone.

## CHAPTER EIGHTEEN

The days and nights passed. Time bleared and slid. And then, early one morning, while the boys were still sleeping, the door was suddenly flung open and Lobo stamped in. 'No more lazing about now, elephant boy.' He chuckled. 'It's time we toughened you up.'

Gulu scuffled quickly away on his bottom, squatting watchfully against the farthest wall. 'And you!' Lobo scowled. 'You are being put on woodcutting duties. There's a pile of branches in the compound. You don't need your feet to work with an axe.'

'Can't I help him?' asked Bat. 'I'm not sure he can manage.'

'More likely he can help you.' Lobo laughed. 'He can tell you how not to end up like that. Look at him! That's what happens to people who get *lost*. If he learns to walk again, we'll keep him. He's useful. He knows how to mend engines. If he doesn't . . . well, he knows what happens to soldiers who can't fight. Military life begins now. Here, put these on.' He threw Bat shorts and a shirt, then turned on his heel and went out.

'Dead men's clothes,' Gulu whispered as Bat held them up. 'They come from the people the army has killed.'

Bat, who for so long had been wishing he could wash his blood-stained shirt, shuddered as he changed. The shorts were too big and he had to roll the waist-band up.

'Hurry up!' Lobo shouted as Bat finally stumbled out. His legs felt strangely weak. Lobo pushed him into a blundering run. On the far side of the compound another boy was waiting and Bat was forced down into a squat in front of him. He froze still as his curls were shaved with the blade of a knife. A group of other children were being herded into the middle of the compound. There must have been about twelve of them, he thought, counting them with the same rapidity as he could count cattle. All were wearing the same hotch-potch of ill-fitting garments as he was; all were looking as worried and bewildered as he felt.

His eyes darted around them. Was Muka among them? He had to look twice before he finally recognized her. He had never seen her wear anything but a printed wrap. Now she was dressed in a T-shirt and trousers like a boy. Her braids were all gone. She was shorn down to the scalp and she was thinner, much thinner, than when he had last seen her. A blue shirt hung in straight folds from her angular shoulders and a pair of brown trousers had been belted with string. But she flashed him a look that meant she was managing and he felt an answering wave of relief. He longed to run towards her, to ask her what had been happening, to find out where she had been, what she had found out, but even as he began to edge hesitantly towards her, the man with the bloodshot eyes strode across to the group.

'Line up!' Lobo bawled.

The children jostled about confusedly as he forced them into some sort of file.

'I'm your commander,' the man told them. His eyes crawled down the line, drilling into each of the frightened little faces in turn. 'From now on you will know me only by that name. From now on what I tell you will immediately be done. My second-in-command here' – he pointed to Lobo – 'will make sure of that. Now fall in!'

And so the military training began: a programme of exercise and hardship and discipline so relentless that it drove every thought except that of their next breath from the children's brains. They had to run and keep running until every muscle screamed for rest; to lie and keep lying until the ants trailed over their skin; to squat and stay squatting until every sinew was groaning; to obey orders as instinctively as they would have swatted a fly.

The sun blazed down on Bat's newly shaven scalp as he marched on the spot, up and down, up and down, until the sweat streamed from his face, neck and back and the insects that blundered against him got stuck. He felt thirsty and giddy and sick. But there was no respite.

'You must act as one person,' the commander yelled.

If the children flagged, they were beaten. If they fell behind, they were beaten. If they failed to act fast enough on an order, they were beaten. Sometimes it was the commander or Lobo who exacted the penalty, striking the elbows, knees or ankles with a stick. But it was worse when it was another child who was chosen to do the beating; when a soldier was forced to turn on his or her fellow sufferer.

If they didn't strike hard enough, they would get a beating themselves. Bat dreaded the moment when he would be ordered to hurt Muka. What would he do on the day when her spirit flared up? Would he be able to punish her? His mind winced from the thought. Could your spirit break like a bone? he wondered. He suspected that Lobo also was waiting to find that out. Sometimes he would see his eyes flickering between him and Muka, narrowing cannily as he waited and watched.

Days passed into nights; but Bat, who now slept in a line of boys under a palm shelter, was almost too weary to notice the difference between them. 'The army is like a machine,' the commander would tell them. 'You are parts of a whole. If one of you doesn't function, the whole mechanism will fail.' At the bark of an order they had to be up and ready, forgetting tiredness and hunger as they were drilled back and forth until each was so alert to the movements of the one standing beside him that the merest tensing of a muscle was enough to elicit a response. Over and over they went through their routines until after a while, Bat came almost not to mind it. At least it helped to distract him; at least he felt too exhausted to do anything other than what he was told.

He came to prefer the marching to the times when the commander would have them dragged from their sleep in the middle of the night. Then they would be made to stand in a line, still as the statues on a wood-carver's stall, while flying things whined around their faces and bit. The commander, planted straddle-legged before them for what started to feel like for ever, would talk. On and on he would go. Sometimes his voice was rough edged and menacing, sometimes it softened and sounded almost cajoling in the dark.

'Our job is a serious one,' he told them. 'We are not like those government soldiers who fight for whoever pays them. We are here for the people. We have the gods on our side. We kill those who deserve it. The gods want it. It's for the good of this nation. We are fighting against unfairness. We are fighting for peace.'

The words drummed into his brain like a tribal beat in the blood, until sometimes Bat found himself almost believing they were true.

'We are here to protect you. We are your family. We will fight alongside you when the rest have gone,' the commander assured them.

'Sometimes I think that he cares,' Bat whispered to Gulu one evening as they crouched together on the out-ermost fringes of the fire. A tree hyrax was roasting and they had been drawn to the flames by the rich drift of its smell. But they dared go no closer. The child leaders, the ones with the long matted dreadlocks who had been in the army so long that they now commanded their own squads of child soldiers, were the only ones who were allowed to get up close to the warmth, to take the choice morsels as soon as they were ready.

'Don't believe him,' muttered Gulu. 'You can't trust anyone here . . . not even yourself.'

As if to prove it, at that moment, a fight broke out. It was between two of the leaders who by now Bat recognized. One they called the Thief because, it was said, he could purloin pretty much anything. The other was nicknamed the Goat because he disliked getting wet. He wore a camouflage jacket with long sleeves and a wide grubby collar from which his sinewy neck poked. He looked like a child who had put on his father's clothes, Bat thought. But there was nothing childlike about his outburst.

'I'll kill you! I'll cut you up into pieces. I'll slice off your lips,' he screamed, leaping in fury at the Thief, who had just taken the last morsel of bush meat from its spit. The watchers scattered like clouds of tiny fish in a stream. A knife flashed through the firelight. The Goat made a grab and, securing his prize, drove his snarling rival back off with the blade. He gnawed on his gristly morsel as he watched the loser retreat, eyes glowing, sullen as a beaten hyena.

'And they are friends,' whispered Gulu. 'Friends are dangerous things to have in this camp. You can't trust.'

'But I trust you,' Bat murmured.

'Don't,' Gulu snapped. 'Friendships only bring trouble. Your allegiance is to the army. And the commander is always on the watch.'

'But Muka?' Bat faltered. 'I will always trust Muka.'

'Then guard your secret,' Gulu hissed. 'You will only be forced to betray her. There are informers among the children. They are starving. They will sell you for the price of a chicken leg.'

Bat believed him. He had seen the older soldiers snatching food from the fists of the youngest. They would sit grinning and eating while the little ones tried not to sob.

'We have to pretend not to like each other,' he whispered to Muka three days later, drawing her into the shadows beyond the ring of firelight. Behind them, at the fringes of the forest, he could see one of the sentinels who were always left on guard watching them, but he had to take this opportunity to speak. They could so seldom be together outside training times. Where he and Gulu slept among boys huddled under a palm-leaf shelter, Muka was kept always on the girls' side of the camp.

'We have to pretend that each of us is angry with the other,' Bat urged Muka; 'that each blames the other for having been caught. We can't afford for them to talk of us in the same breath.'

'But what about Lobo?' the girl replied. Her question was almost a whimper. 'If he thinks that you hate me . . .' Her voice straggled off, but Bat knew what she meant. He had seen the way that Lobo strutted when he knew she was watching, the way he constantly monitored through narrowed eyelids. He knew why her lips now quivered. He watched her struggle for self-possession.

'It's so hard,' she faltered. 'I don't know if I can manage without you. You don't know what it's like. There was one girl I spoke to in my first days here,' she whispered, 'who had been snatched from her village with her sister. The little one was only eight but she was forced to march all day with a huge sack of flour on her head; to walk and to walk until shc was too tired to go any further, until she was wailing so much that one of the child leaders flew into a rage. "If you're so tired, let's give you a rest," he said and he struck her on the head with the handle of his panga. She fell to the ground and never got up. And now her sister who was with me has gone too. She left the camp with the commander. I don't know why. All I saw were the tears shining on her face as she left. And then I was glad, so glad, to know that I still had you with me,' Muka whispered, 'and though I tried to wish that you hadn't been captured, that you hadn't run back to find me, I was so glad that you had. At least together, I thought, we could find a way to escape. But how can we do that if we can't speak to each other, how can we do that . . .' Her voice broke into a sob. The sudden sense of abandonment was overwhelming her, bringing the girl who had been so strong to a breaking point.

Bat watched the feelings that flickered across her shadowy face. He could read them almost as clearly as if she had spoken aloud and, unable to bear it, he reached out.

But Muka, steeling herself, jumped up and, stepping rapidly backwards, turned on her heel.

'Muka!' Bat cried. Two other children turned at the noise. But all they saw was the girl stalking stiffly away and Bat, his hand still half lifted, following her with his eyes. Lobo glided over. He too was now studying them, his eyes thin as slits. Bat let his hand drop and just stared into the night.

That was the last time he and Muka would let anyone see any contact between them, he thought. And though often in the days that followed they would exchange secret glances, they were warily alert whenever anyone was watching. They stalked stiffly about each other as a pair of village dogs. At first, tired and hungry, the loneliness tormented them; but it was strange, Bat realized one morning as he stole a slantwise look at his friend: the feigned distance was starting to make them feel all the more close.

# CHAPTER NINETEEN

One day the children were all given weapons. Anything served: hoes, sharpened stakes, knives, pangas or spears. They were made to lie on their bellies and crawl forward with their elbows until an order was given. Then they had to run onward as fast as they could and attack a banana palm that drooped faintly at the fringes of the camp.

'Imagine that tree is your enemy,' the commander barked. 'Imagine that it's coming to get you. If you don't kill it now it will kill you . . . or far worse.'

The children stabbed, sliced and pierced. If they didn't look fierce enough, the commander sent them back.

'Is that how you would kill your enemy?' he bellowed. 'That's pathetic. Let me show you how it's done.' And unslinging his rifle, he uttered a bloodcurdling shriek and leaped forward. 'The neck! The stomach! The heart!' he screamed. A bayonet blade flashed as it flew in and out. The veins in his neck swelled, tight as the cords around a tugging cow. His sweat broke out in beads. 'I would slaughter it before it slaughtered me,' he panted as he wiped his weapon clean with a torn banana leaf. 'Remember you are in the army now. You are the sworn enemy of the government soldiers, of the people who give them shelter, of the villagers who won't join you; of everyone but your fellow fighter at your side.'

The children lunged at the palm, this time with a renewed vigour. If they didn't please the commander, they wouldn't be allowed to eat. They would have to stand at the side and watch while the others were fed, their bellies growling as the hunger gnawed deeper into their guts.

A few days later they were all handed guns. Bat had never held one before. His hand trembled. The commander glowered at the group. 'It seems that you all have two things in common,' he sneered. 'You are afraid to look a man in the eye and you are afraid to hold a weapon. Your hands are shaking as if that gun was held to your head. Well, it soon will be,' he snapped, 'if you don't learn fast.' He paced up and down the line, searching their faces with his bloodshot eyes. His cheek muscles bulged. 'This gun' – he held it high above his head – 'will soon belong to you. So you better not be scared of it. It will soon be your best friend. You will look a man straight in the eye and you won't tremble. You will pull the trigger and laugh. Our salvation lies here where our ancestors have always known they must seek it: it lies in the barrel of a gun.'

'Ignore the safety catch,' the commander told the children; 'it will only slow you down.' He showed them how to raise their new weapons, to wedge the butt hard and shove their cheeks against the stock. Two of the little ones weren't strong enough to support it. They had to lie it down on a piece of wood. Bat gripped the barrel tight with his left hand and, with his right fore-finger on the trigger, squinted down the gun's length. Things looked impossibly small as he lined up the sight. A row of bottles had been set out at the far side of the clearing. Bat squeezed. The kick hurt his thin shoulder. Everything felt a long way away. Everything felt distant – even his own thoughts. It was as if he was looking at himself down the barrel of a rifle. He felt as brittle as the bottles which leaped upwards before falling, tum-bling to the ground in a glitter of shards. That night, he couldn't sleep. His ears rang with the gunshot. The smell of cordite stained his breath. He could taste it whenever he tried to swallow. It was the taste of his new life. It was the taste of death.

It was chilly at night when the sun went down and the children all slept in a line on thin scraps of plastic, the thirty-two boys on one side of the camp, the seven girls on the other. At night they would often scream out in their dreams. They would wake sweating and shaking, with racing fears and wild eyes.

Bat shared a blanket with Gulu. The boy had almost recovered, though he had lost a front tooth and, despite all his best attempts to disguise it, he now walked with a limp. The tiny child who had brought them food when they were shut in the hut slept on his other side. He was called La, Bat now knew, but it was not the boy himself who had told him. He never spoke. 'Not because he can't,' Gulu told Bat, 'but because he doesn't want to. Only the commander can draw a sound from his lips. Kindness is useless; only fear now works.'

But sometimes, late at night, Bat would hear La whispering to a bushbaby that he kept in his pocket. It came out at twilight and sat on his hand, swivelling its head and cuffing the backs of its ears. When the patrol swept their bodies at night with the beam of a torch, its eyes would glow orange as embers in the light. Then Bat would fall asleep dreaming of the days when he had lain alongside his elephant. He would imagine the sound of her heartbeat, like the far-off rolling of thunder, as strong and as powerful as the heartbeat of the world.

During the day, the camp was mostly empty. Only the trainees and a couple of sentinels stayed behind, loitering in the shade at the fringe of the trees, waving their guns about as casually as a herd boy waves his switch. Bat wasn't sure if they were there to keep the rebel soldiers in or the government soldiers out. He suspected the former. Sometimes he caught them staring at him, as if they knew what he was thinking; knew that every time his eyes strayed towards the fringes of the compound he was wondering whether he could escape, whether he could find his way home through that wilderness of trees. The guards would tense and lay their hands on the stocks of their guns.

Only the trained child soldiers were trusted to go looking for food. 'They lay traps,' Gulu explained to Bat as they lay under their blanket one night. 'They dig pits for the bush pigs to stumble into and set snares for hyrax and squirrels. They prise the porcupines out of their holes. It's easier to get them once they've lumbered down their burrows because then their spines can't stand up. But even out in the open they'll risk their sharp quills. Porcupine meat is the fattest in the jungle, and when they come back they will fight over who has the feet.'

The soldiers in training were never given such tender morsels. Grown thin on a diet of millet porridge, they had to hunt lizards and grasshoppers instead. When the gristly stews were prepared, they dipped their handfuls of goo eagerly into its gravy. They didn't care if their fingers got burned. They were too hungry to mind about that.

One day Lobo killed a chimpanzee with a slingshot. Its flesh was dark and rich and the smell of it roasting drew the children into a circle of glittering eyes.

'Here, it's for you,' Lobo beckoned, and held out a steaming hunk to Muka. His cheeks dimpled with a smile. 'Take it,' he said, reaching out cautiously, as if he was reaching to a stray dog that might bite. He saw the girl hesitate. 'You only have to ask me if you want anything,' he encouraged. 'We are from the same village. I'll always help you.'

Muka vacillated for a moment. Her stomach was churning with hunger. She let her eyes drop. The lopped-off hand of the chimpanzee was lying, cupped like the palm of a pleading market beggar, in the dust. Her face flinched as she backed off.

Lobo shrugged. 'One day you'll be glad I am so patient,' he muttered, and stalked stiffly away with an over-confident swagger, cuffing a small boy across the ear as he passed. His eyes vanished into the thick furrows of his frown, but later he was laughing as he and the commander returned to the fire and, squatting beside it, ate the liver and heart smoking-hot. The children stared round-eyed with yearning as they chewed.

The only time the children ate well was when the older soldiers had returned from a raid. They would be away for days, and all the while the trainees would wait, longing for them to come back with corn cobs and pumpkins and the carcasses of slaughtered goats; with sticks of sugar cane which they sucked down to dry fibre and the biscuits which they tore at, scattering wrappers across the clearing. Once, the raiders even brought back a thin dun cow. For a while it had stood there, tethered short in the compound, gazing with mild interest at the alien forest; and then it had been shot. Bat thought of his own cattle as he watched it crumpling to its knees. He let their names reel through his head in a list: Kayo and Leko; Toco and Tara; freckled Anecanec and the restless Bwaro. For a moment it steadied him; but then he remembered the silvery Kila and the memory was no longer a comfort to him.

The child leaders squabbled and yapped, ferocious as wild dogs, as they dashed to cut up the carcass. Bat was scared of them. Their skins were marked like a map of all they had gone through. The Goat had great welts on his arm from the swipe of a panga that, in a battle with a villager, he had tried to fend off. The Thief had a hard, puckered burr in the skin of his back where a government bullet had entered his flesh. But the worst scars, Bat thought, were the invisible ones. When he looked into the eyes of these child leaders, he would see that they were dead. And yet it was they – they who bore the brands of the army not just on their bodies but inside their heads – who ruled the camp.

In the evenings, stripped to the waist, the leaders liked to play football: jostling and trampling and stirring up clouds of dust, they would scuffle over a plastic bag stuffed with sacking, barging and tussling and kicking until it was no more than a tattered scrap; then the members of the victorious team would swagger about, ammunition rolled around their waists. 'We are kings,' Bat heard the Thief crow. 'No one can defeat us. We are kings and we're going to take over this land.' And he burst into laughter. It was not like the laughter that Bat remembered from his village. It was fierce and staccato as the firing of a gun.

'It's witchcraft that gives him his strength,' Gulu explained the next day as he and Bat crouched together in the evening, cleaning their guns. They were old and rusty and their mechanisms jammed easily. 'He has met the Diviner, who founded this army. And he has bush magic. The Diviner can change shape when he likes, become a leopard or a dog. He can pick a rock from the ground and it will sparkle like a storm of lightning. The government forces can't catch him because he knows when they are coming. Like a spider, he sees the fist falling and always scuttles off.'

Gulu twisted the butt stock from the barrel of

his rifle, and set to work cleaning a rusted bolt with a rag.

'Once an ambush was laid for him on the far bank of a river,' he went on. 'It was in the very place that he had been about to cross, but somehow he sensed it and, fording further downstream, he doubled round in a loop and attacked his ambushers from behind. "We will kill the crocodile that waits in the water," he said. The current of the river ran red that day.'

'Were you there?' asked Bat.

But Gulu didn't answer. He was absorbed in adjusting a metal spring. All his stories were told as if he had just been watching, reporting on something in which he had no part. It was almost as if he stood outside himself, Bat thought; as if he was watching his own actions like some appalled witness. He never spoke of the feelings that made him screw up his face and scream in the night, that left his eyes so dark and blank when he woke.

'When the Diviner speaks,' Gulu eventually continued, snapping the rifle's clip-latch back into place, 'his voice echoes all around you. It's as if it is rising up out of the air. It swirls all around you and gets inside your head.' He looked critically at the gun, which he had now almost reassembled, and screwed the barrel a little tighter into the chamber end. 'You too will meet him one day. He meets all his soldiers. He will come for you one day; one day when he's sure that you've finally become his, and he will sprinkle you with water that has the power to ward off bullets and tell you that no one who is true to him can ever be harmed again.'

Bat shivered as he glanced across the camp at a

gang of child leaders. They wore trousers and grubby canvas shoes that had come from the market, and the Goat even sported a watch on his wrist. A few were dancing to the music on the commander's radio, their dreadlocks whipping around their necks. The rest squatted by the fire, gambling and passing a bottle of maize spirit between them. The giddy smell of dagga mingled with the wood-smoke.

Gulu followed Bat's gaze. 'Dagga is a strong drug,' he warned him. 'It's dangerous. It can make you do anything. And you won't even mind doing it because it somehow makes you feel as if everything that's happening is happening somewhere else. And for a while that seems good,' he told him. 'You can forget for a bit. Forget what you've seen . . .' His voice trailed off as, turning, he looked outwards into the night, as if he could see something, as if there were pictures out there in the blackness. 'And forget what you've done,' he added quietly as he finally turned back.

The eyes of the two boys met. And for a moment Bat thought he saw a fresh life flickering up in that blankness. He saw the sorrow that made this child cry out at night. He saw the pain of the memories unlocked from his head. He reached out an arm and slid it around his shoulders. But Gulu's thin back hardened, resisting his touch. He shook his head rapidly as though trying to dislodge something from it. 'But dagga only works for a bit,' he murmured. 'The memories always come back . . . they always come back . . . and then they are even worse.' And picking up his rifle, he rose swiftly to his feet and went.

Bat was left alone. It was true, he thought sadly. All the soldiers were troubled. He had noticed how shaken they would be on their return from a raid. Then, even the most fearsome might sometimes be spotted withdrawing into the shadows, watchful as a spider whose web has been shaken, stroking his gun as tenderly as a little girl strokes her painted wooden doll, as if it was the only thing in the entire world he could trust. Once, he had even seen the Goat squatting alone on a stump, his head dropped in his hands as he rocked back and forth, back and forth. He had gone on for hours, as if his whole being was tuned to the swing of a soldier's march.

And then suddenly, a few days later, the boy they called Bonyo because he was like a locust went mad. He jumped up from the fire where he had been smoking dagga and staggered about waving his gun over his head. 'I killed the last owner of this,' he cried. 'He deserved it. He had done too much damage with it . . . and since then I've used it to do some damage myself.' Then all at once he began shooting, firing all over the place, round after round singing across the compound, rattling the tin huts and ripping through the forest foliage. The air smelled of cordite. The camp was blue with smoke. Most children ducked; hurling themselves flat on the ground, their hands over their heads. A few reached for their weapons. Lobo fled.

The commander stormed over in a rage. 'What the hell do you think you are doing?' he thundered. 'Do you think we have bullets to waste?' He sent the boy reeling to the ground with a ferocious blow of his arm. The blood poured from his head.

The commander turned away and spat. Then he swept his slow stare across the now rising children.

'Ammunition costs money,' he said. His tone had grown frighteningly calm. And then, to Bat's terror, it was his face that was singled out of the crowd.

'But you are going to help us with that, aren't you, elephant boy?'

# CHAPTER TWENTY

The following morning, as dawn was breaking, a detachment of soldiers was assembled: a mixture of seasoned fighters with a handful of youngsters. As usual, nothing was explained, but then, so much that Bat saw didn't make any sense to him that he sometimes wondered if he had completely stopped wondering. It was so much easier just to do what you were told, he mused. And then, with a jump, he heard his name called.

A few moments later he was part of a squad. He was leaving the camp. He glanced back instinctively to search for Muka, but the girl hadn't been picked as part of his group. Gulu was behind him and he saw him turning. He gave a hard warning frown. 'This is a raiding party,' he hissed.

The child soldiers set off through the forest, twisting their way along a slender trail, twining through creeper-draped thickets, winding between trunks before eventually arriving at the top of a steep and treacherous slope. Bat checked up on Gulu as the land sheered away. He was flinching at each step. The bones in his foot had not mended properly. But even where the drop was sharpest, he never cried out. The silence was absolute. Anyone who broke it would be beaten. Even to send a stone skittering would have earned a punishment. The children stole through the shadows like prowling beasts.

For three days they walked, sleeping out among the trees, making their beds in shallow scoops in the leaves. Then, on the evening of the fourth day, the Goat, the squad leader, suddenly raised a clenched fist. It was the order to stop. The forest cover had ended. An expanse of flat scrub lay ahead. They would wait here until darkness fell. Some of the children lay down to doze in the thickets; others, more restless, skulked noiselessly about. Bat hunched down in the undergrowth. He blinked at the sweat that was blurring his vision. His heartbeat was fluttering. The whole world felt alien. Instead of the freedom he had so long dreamed of, he felt only frightened by the open spaces ahead. He no longer belonged to them, he thought. He was no longer a villager. He was one of their enemies. He was one of the wild soldiers the bush people most feared. He had become a stranger . . . even to himself.

As dusk approached, the squad of children stole out. They zigzagged, ducking low through the scrub, as they had been taught: each on his own and yet each keeping watch on the figure alongside him, linked as closely together as if tied by a rope. It was a long while before they finally reached fields that had been cultivated and even then they were bare. All the crops had been stripped. The ground was hard. It should have been planted by now, Bat thought. The rains should have been falling on emerald maize shoots. Instead dead weeds straggled over untilled dust. The dry grass crackled underfoot as the children stole on. They were following the Goat who, clad in a pair of green trousers with a heavy belt of bullets slung around the waist and a bandana tied about his brow, spoke to them only through the signals of his fist. He couldn't have been more than fourteen, Bat thought; not much older than he was, but he would have thought nothing of surviving alone in the bush. 'With a gun in my hands, I can get anything I want,' he had once boasted, using its hard wooden butt to crush a lizard for soup.

They reached a village. Bat couldn't tell where he was. He couldn't tell anything except that he was terrified. What if there were people? What if they tried to shoot him? The palms of his hands felt clammy. Perhaps someone would kill him without realizing that he had never wanted to join this army. But then, wasn't that what had happened to all the children? he thought. They had all been abducted. None of them had gone into the army from choice.

The village was deserted. The raiders poured in like the swarms of soldier ants that would stream in from the forest, stripping every tree, every bush in their path. Bat remembered a time in his own village when these creatures had once passed implacably through, sending the villagers racing in panic for the river, crying out for lost children and grabbing tethered goats. Every surface had boiled with shiny black specks. The shambas had been stripped, the grain stores devoured. Even the fresh thatch on the roofs had been eaten. The army of ants had left nothing behind it and, when the villagers had finally returned and Bat had gone back to search for his broody hen, he had found her just where he had left her, trapped under a basket, a skeleton squatting upon a clutch of eggs.

The soldiers lit flickering torches to give themselves light. The huts were abandoned, but possessions had been left behind: there were knives, tins and pots in the cook-huts, maize in the stores and blankets on the mats. Roosting poultry shuffled anxiously in the boughs of the trees. Bat stood there uncertainly.

His companions were already rampaging about. They broke down the thatch in search of hidden possessions, found dried fish and kola nuts, a tin can of honey and a gourd of goat's milk. A girl discovered a bottle of medicine and gulped it down at one draught. A boy's grin gleamed in the torchlight as he carried a pumpkin. But Bat just stood there and stared. He wondered if, even now, the inhabitants were hiding and watching, hearts thumping, the fathers clutching their pangas, the mothers clamping their palms over trembling children's mouths.

'This was my uncle's village,' a young soldier informed him. He was munching at two corn cobs, one gripped in each fist, taking a mouthful out of each in turn.

Bat's eyes widened. 'Does he know you're a soldier?' he stuttered.

The boy shrugged. 'Perhaps . . . every family gives soldiers . . . but I don't suppose mine know if I'm dead or alive.' He grinned. 'This is my family now,' he said and, jerking his chin back at the gun which dangled over his shoulder, he crammed in the next mouthful of yellow corn.

Bat slipped into an empty hut and stood there. He didn't know what to do. His mind was humming inside him. 'Our heads may be small, but they are as full of memories as a hive of wild bees.' The words of his grandmother rose up through his thoughts, and even now, even amid all the alarm and confusion, the pictures came flooding back to him to remind him of who he was.

He thought of Jambula's shaded huts and its trees; of the passers-by who, when offered a calabash of cool water, would say how much they envied its peaceful spot. He imagined his cattle browsing in the long grass by the river, the herds of wild animals that speckled the plains, the elephants drifting through their forested tunnels. He saw his grandmother squatting wide-kneed over the cook-fire, throwing handfuls of peppers into hissing clay pots . . .

'What the hell are you doing?' A voice made him jump. A face scowled at him furiously. A brandished torch was held aloft. 'Scram!' the Goat barked as he touched his firebrand to the thatch. A tongue of flame flickered upwards; the dry grass crackled and caught.

Bat dashed from the hut. All the soldiers were gathering. The smoke of burning houses was swirling around them. Their eyes glittered in the light. At a cry from their leader the raiding horde made off. The flames that leaped from the roofs seemed to be waving their farewell. They licked the night sky with their hot yellow tongues.

A row of flapping chickens had been slung upside down on a pole. Two of the youngest soldiers carried it between them; the rest laboured along under sacks of maize and rice. They returned far more slowly than they had come but still dawn was only just breaking as they slipped back into the trees.

Stopping after a while at a forest pool, they rested. The water was slimy. It felt almost viscous to the touch. If the rains didn't come soon, it would dry up completely, Bat thought. He watched two of the soldiers who were now sitting beside it. They were girls. He had seen one of them earlier, prowling through the darkness, her filthy face ferocious, eyes drilling into the black; but now she was unfolding a cloth that she had stolen and tucked away like a trophy into her belt. It was a woman's wrap. A pattern of red and green flowers burst open as she shook it. The biggest and brightest were in the middle, but they were not as bright as the smile which suddenly broke upon her face. For a moment she looked like a child again.

'It's not too late,' Bat whispered to Gulu, who was sitting beside him. 'It's never too late. We just have to find a way . . . a way to get back.' But his friend didn't answer. He didn't even seem to hear. He just stared into the distance. He looked dazed as a beetle, Bat thought, which, scorched by a lamp, tumbles onto the ground and lies there, too hurt to recover. And then they were shouldering their burdens again and setting off.

Gulu struggled under the weight. Bat lagged to help him. They were falling behind. 'We have to keep up,' Gulu muttered. 'We have to keep going. If we don't we will get lost.'

'We must think of a way,' urged Bat. It was so hard in the camp to find time to talk safely. 'We have to think of a plan,' he hissed. 'We have to find a way for you, me and Muka . . .'

The boy just shook his head between gasps, and struggled to catch up.

'We'll help you,' Bat urged, pressing hard on his heels. He had to get through to him. 'Muka and I . . . we can help you.'

Gulu still didn't answer. The sweat was dripping from his brow. It was running into his eyes and blinding him. He blinked rapidly, over and over. The muscles on his thin bony limbs were bulging, his sinews stretched taut. The smell of dagga drifted back along the column. The Goat and Bonyo the locust boy were smoking to keep their strength up. They hadn't noticed how far back the two boys were now lagging.

'Why not now?' The thought leaped into Bat's head. He felt the surge of his heartbeat. Why not run now? He could make it. He and Gulu could make it. He stopped in his tracks. But what about Muka? His heart scudded in his chest. Could he leave Muka? He could come back and get her later. He could bring help. A picture of the girl suddenly rose up in his mind. He saw her as she stood there, tall and skinny, in the middle of the camp.

Unbidden tears were shining in her huge black eyes; but she refused to acknowledge them, refused to cover her face. She would never compromise. Bat winced from the thought. It was unbearable to him to think of her suffering. He could never leave her. He would not go without her. He hurried to catch up with the still struggling Gulu.

'We can't give up hope,' he whispered as he pressed closer to him. He was trying to reassure himself as much as to persuade the boy. 'Once you've given up there's nothing left,' he murmured, 'and when there's nothing left . . . well, then you just die.'

'We'll just die anyway,' Gulu answered.

Suddenly, Bat stopped once again in his tracks. There was something there. His eyes scanned the forest; there was nothing to be seen. But he wasn't mistaken. He could feel it. There were elephants. He could sense them. It was like a singing in the air. The memories shifted inside him like a child that stirs and shifts and rolls over in its sleep. He froze still as he could, every sense straining. 'Meya?' he whispered. 'Meya, are you there?'

'Keep up!' hissed Gulu, flashing a glance over his shoulder. 'You have to keep up!'

Bat ignored him and just stood.

'Meya?' he whispered again, this time a bit louder.

Gulu swivelled and fixed him with a ferocious stare.

Bat let the sack of flour he was carrying slip. His eyes were darting about him. The elephants had come. They were watching him. They knew he was there. But where? He searched frantically. The forest was so thick.

'Keep up!' a voice hissed in his ear. It was Gulu. He had come back. 'Keep up! If you don't they will kill you.' He shook Bat roughly by the wrist. There was a look of complete desperation in his face. 'They will kill you . . . there will be no second chance . . . and then' – Gulu's voice dropped down to a barely audible murmur – 'and then I'll have no one,' he whispered. 'I will have no one at all.'

Bat swept one last desperate look around the trees; the shadows held their secrets. Nothing stirred. Perhaps he had only imagined it. Perhaps it had all been a dream whipped up by his hopes. He willed with every fibre in his body to see them . . . but no lumbering shape disturbed the eerie stillness. No branch gave a rustle. No great beast breathed out. Shouldering his load, Bat set his weary step back to the slope. He was carrying a sack of millet flour. There were bottles hidden inside it. The Goat had found the palm wine that had been hidden in the thatch. It was heavy; so heavy. The nape of Bat's neck burned.

'There is hope,' he whispered, as he pushed himself forward. 'You have to hope, Gulu. You have to,' he said.

The boy did not turn, but still Bat heard the words that fell from his mouth, dry as the whisper of leaves in a drought.

'I can't,' he murmured. 'I can't hope any more. I have done such things . . . I have done things that no one could forgive me for.'

## CHAPTER TWENTY-ONE

A command from Lobo rang around the camp. The children scrambled instantly to their feet. Leaving whatever they had been doing, they ran for the middle of the compound and formed up into lines, just as they had been trained. A few moments later two strangers entered the camp.

The commander jumped to attention. Lobo stood beside him, equally tense. Bat waited obediently, trying not to shuffle or twitch, trying not to do anything that would single him out from the ranks. One of the strangers was tall, very tall. He wore a camouflage jacket that was belted round the middle and a pair of matching trousers. The lenses in his glasses reflected like mirrors. The other, bare-chested, carried a live animal slung over his back: an antelope, so young that its horns must still have been velvet. He threw it to the ground.

Its shanks were bound tightly with a length of wire flex. It stared helplessly up at its tormentors. The man in the camouflage jacket delivered a casual passing kick. It gave a desperate wriggle. The man turned and smiled. The slit was thin as a razor cut. Three scars marked his forehead.

Bat's heart missed a beat. He knew this dark frown. He had seen it before; and with a sudden jolt of horror he remembered from where. This was the man who all those years ago had been out on the savannah, the man who had slaughtered Meya's mother and hacked off her tusks. He could see him even now, bending over the broken chainsaw, cursing the faltering engine and his frightened companions. For a few panic-stricken moments, Bat feared that he might be recognized back. A mirrored stare swept the ranks. The boy shrank. The fright was spilling from his face. But the man just drew on a cigarette and, with a nod to the commander, turned away.

The harsh smell of tobacco wafted across the lines of waiting children. Nobody moved. The man exchanged a few muttered words with Lobo but, when he then beckoned, it wasn't to Bat.

It was a girl who walked out. She must have been about the same age as Muka and, like her, she was tall, slim and supple. But the resemblance ended there. Where Muka's eyes were still lit by a fierce inner life, this girl looked defeated. A smile was pulled, as if by some mechanical contraption, from her lips. It seemed to work quite separately from the rest of her face. The man with the scars took a necklace from his pocket and, leaning forward, fastened it around her neck. The two spoke, but none of the children could hear what they were saying. Bat thought of his grandmother: 'The neck wears jewellery while the heart wears troubles,' she would say. The man crossed the compound, the girl following behind him, and they disappeared one after the other into a far hut.

It was much later in the afternoon that Bat was called. Lobo came to fetch him.

'The Leopard wants to see you. You're to come with me. There's nothing to be frightened of,' he encouraged. There was a mixture of excitement and pride on his face, as if the boy whom he now led across the compound was in some way his possession. He laid a hand on Bat's shoulder like a mark of ownership.

The man they called the Leopard was sitting sprawled in a chair under a rickety bamboo-and-palm-leaf construction, his legs resting on the heels of a pair of heavy black leather boots. Their criss-cross of laces reached almost to the knees. His skin glistened like the barrel of a well-oiled rifle. Bat could smell its sharp tang. He looked into the man's eyes. Now that he had taken off his glasses, he could see they were dark as stagnant pools. Bat lowered his lashes. Even the girl who was now crouching at his feet smoking dagga seemed not to want to look. Her eyes were remote. She was drifting away on the wisps of her smoke. The commander was lounging nearby, a half-finished bottle of palm wine beside him. The baby antelope was roasting, a charred silhouette on a spit. Its four legs stuck out, stark as a cry for help.

'This is the boy, sir,' declared Lobo. 'This is the elephant boy I told you about.'

'Ahh. So you're the one they call Bat.' Slowly he looked him up and down. Bat fought to keep his face blank. He remembered that voice, harsh as the saw of a serrated blade against bone.

'And you can speak to the elephants?'

'Yes, sir! He can, sir!'

'Let the boy talk for himself!' the man snapped.

'Yes, sir.'

Normally Lobo would have been slouching in one of the two chairs. Now he stood nervously aside, casting his eyes about as if worried, but all the time smiling as if he felt at ease. The other visiting stranger, the one who had carried the antelope, also loitered watchfully.

'So, Bat.' The Leopard drew the boy towards him. 'I've heard a lot about you.'

Bat felt an undefined fear rising up within him. His mouth was starting to feel all fuzzy round the edges. He clamped his lips tight so that they would not shake.

The Leopard picked up the bottle and took a long draught. 'So you like your new life as a soldier?' The voice was perfectly level and yet it flashed menace, sharp as the blade of a hidden knife.

Bat nodded. He knew what was expected.

'Good. Well, my commander says you've done well. He tells me you are ready to work.'

The commander beside him gave a grunt of agreement.

Bat just looked ahead. He was fighting to keep his gaze steady; to stop it from skidding all over the place.

'Our war isn't a cheap one,' the Leopard continued. 'We need weapons and ammunition to keep you all safe.' The word safe, on his lips, sounded almost like a threat. 'We have to feed you,' he said. 'And buy fuel. A jeep drinks more than a thirsty cow. And mine needs repairing . . . get that boy Gulu to take a look at it,' he added as an afterthought to the commander. 'There's a clank in its engine. Get him to put it right.

'We have to buy things.' The Leopard came back to his point. 'And our country has riches. They're there for the taking.' He paused and gave a dry laugh. 'They're there for the taking, if you know how to get them.'

Putting a cigarette to his lips, he flicked at the wheel of a lighter with his thumb. The flame leaped and flickered and then steadied. A wristwatch flashed in the light. The black eyes prowled Bat's face. 'Do you know what I'm talking about, boy?' asked the Leopard as he slowly breathed in. Then he gave a nod. 'I think you know what I'm talking about. I'm talking about ivory. I'm talking about the ivory of the elephants.'

Exhaling a long stream of smoke, he glanced at the girl as she squatted on the ground beside him. She wasn't even listening. Her eyes were unfocused. But the necklace he had given her, fastening it like a collar around her slender neck, gleamed in the sunlight. It was pale as bleached bone against the blackness of her skin.

The sun was beating down on the compound. Bat felt the top of his head turning soft as the heat worked into his brain, unloosening its coils. His thoughts were starting to swim. A vision shimmered through his mind. He remembered the last time he had seen the elephants:

the herd ambling off through the silvery moonlight, swaying across the great open spaces of the world, swinging their trunks as if moving to some unheard rhythm, bearing their great tusks before them like precious gifts for the gods. For a moment he was there with them, wandering along behind them.

'You will take us to the elephants.' The command struck him hard as a stone.

'Take you to them?' Bat stuttered. Now everything inside him was dissolving. His knees were giving way under him. He was trembling violently. His throat was so tight he couldn't breathe. 'I don't think I can . . . sir.'

He watched the eyes harden. Two hands reached out. They clamped Bat round the wrists. He was standing between the man's knees now. His palms were pressed down upon muscular thighs. Bat could feel the hard sinews beneath the cloth.

'They're there in the forest. We know it. Their tracks have been seen. But we need you to find them for us.' A pair of thin lips was pulled back from a row of yellowing teeth. 'Do you understand me? That is your job. Why else do you think we would have gone to so much trouble to get you?' The man gave a laugh like a bark. 'And there's no need to worry about trouble from the rangers,' he added, glancing at the man who had accompanied him to the camp. 'George here, he's a ranger. He'll make sure his friends don't come visiting.' The man shifted his weight and grinned nervously, but the Leopard had already turned away.

Bat tried to steady his mind. So now, at last, he knew why it was that he had been captured. Lobo had told them about the elephants. He shot a bewildered glance at the boy, but Lobo had already slid his eyes well out of reach. Hands deep in his pockets, he was staring down at his boots.

Bat wanted to run. He wanted to run and to run regardless of what they would do to him. He didn't care if that meant a bullet in the back. How could he do what they asked him? How could he betray Meya and the elephants? But then, what about Muka? He couldn't betray her either. He needed a firm answer but his mind was a swamp: thoughts emerged and then sank, sucked down into its depths. He shut his eyes for a moment. The inside of their lids burned hot red. He listened to the *sit sit sit* of the Leopard's wristwatch. If he could just have more time he might come up with something. But time was now moving in seconds, and it was quickly running out.

When he opened his eyes again, the black stare was waiting, its pupils like pebbles that are flung into polluted depths. Bat braced every muscle in his body. Then he nodded his assent.

The ranger gave a low grunt of satisfaction. Lobo shifted uneasily, a look of relief on his face. But Bat didn't notice. He was thinking only of Meya. Where was she now? he wondered. Was she no longer safe? A sense of her presence passed over his mind like a shadow. Normally at this time of year the herd would be grazing by the river, but the short rains had failed. The savannah would be parched and the long rains were now late. The elephants would have retreated deep into the forests. They would have followed ancient paths to their secret drinking pools. He imagined the cows standing in the dappled sunlight, their calves tumbling and playing, squirting bright rainbows of water. Was it possible that it had been them he had passed in the forest; that it had been his herd? He shook his head quickly to dislodge the gnawing fear.

The Leopard slackened his grip. The boy was no longer the focus of his attention. He was talking to the ranger. 'It'll be simple,' the man was saying. 'We'll work as a gang. The boy scouts them out . . . he gets their trust . . . that's the most difficult bit. I make sure that my colleagues are nowhere about. Then we circle the animals . . .'

Bat's mind was a blur. He watched a girl on the far side of the camp cleaning her rifle. She was singing a song to herself as she rubbed it with an oily rag. *It's funny*, he thought, *how life just goes on regardless*. He looked back at the ranger. He was still talking. He studied the movements of his tongue, teeth and lips. They worked with a curious precision . . . like some insect, he thought. But his thoughts were swirling too fast to take in what he was saying.

A plate of charred antelope meat was brought. The Leopard ate fast and swiftly. The juices ran down his chin as he chewed. They left bloody streaks. He didn't wipe them away. He just went on eating until at last, with a belch, he gave a satisfied nod.

'And you're confident?' he asked, turning suddenly to Lobo.

'Yes, sir.' The boy gave a sharp salute.

'Good.' The commander smiled thinly and, stretching

for a bottle under his chair, took a long draught before passing it to Lobo. The boy's face spread in a smile as he tipped it to his lips. 'Oh yes, I'm confident,' he said as he swallowed. 'And I know about the elephants too.' He gave a low laugh. 'I've even ridden one . . . once . . . it was . . .'

The commander frowned sceptically as Lobo fell silent and straightened his face quickly. He took another pull at the bottle as if to wash his boast away. 'I'm confident all right,' he muttered.

'You'd better be,' the Leopard snarled. 'Now I'm tired. I'm turning in.' He rose with a slow feline ease. 'Well done, boy,' he growled at Bat. 'You've shaped up well.' He laid a hand on the boy's head, gave his hair a brief rub. 'You will be all right . . . as long as you do as you're told. If you don't . . . well, that girl Muka, the one I've been telling Lobo here he can't touch . . . well, let's just say her life won't much be worth living,' he said, and he smiled. It was a terrible smile. The muscles moved over its void like bright water over a crocodile's back.

## CHAPTER TWENTY-TWO

Bat couldn't sleep that night. His head was churning with questions. In the morning, he stared about hopelessly at the encircling trees. They rose up like the stockade that a nomad weaves for his cattle: a spiny barrier of branches and creepers and great brindled trunks. The camp was a prison and, as if to prove it, a sentry slipped at that moment out of the shadows and began to pace back and forth. He had orders to shoot anyone who tried to come in – or get out. He would pull on the trigger without so much as a second thought; and besides, even if he did manage to escape, Bat thought, what then? The jungle was vast. He didn't know where he was. He didn't even know what country he was in.

Defeated, he stared up into a scrap of sky. For so long he had managed to hold everything together. He had struggled on like a market woman labouring under her load: chin lifted, eyes fixed only on the path ahead. But now the load had slipped. He felt as if he had been turned upside down, and everything that he had thought to be fixed firmly inside him had come tumbling out. He stared at the ground as if the pieces of his life lay strewn all about him. He didn't think he knew how to fit them back together again.

He was tired and hungry and utterly empty. He slumped down against the banana palm and stared bleakly across the compound. An ant crawled up his shin but he didn't bother to slap it. A lizard slid out from behind a stone. If it didn't slide back again quickly it would get put in a stew, he thought. He watched it seize a fly and toss back its head. Translucent wings glinted on either side of its grin before disappearing into the crunching jaws.

From the far side of the clearing Muka was watching him. Her brow was knitted in confusion. Normally he would have flashed back a reassuring glance but now he just dropped his head. What was she looking for? he thought miserably. What did she expect? He could not help her. He could only bring her harm. So why was she looking at him as if he had an answer. Why didn't she just give up on him? He had given up on himself.

All day he avoided her. He chopped wood for the cook-fire with little La. He made a good companion, Bat thought: he didn't ask any questions. He didn't speak.

In the evening Gulu wandered over. He had been out all day working on the Leopard's jeep. His shirt, face and hands were covered with grease.

'What's wrong?' he asked softly.

Bat turned away. 'Nothing,' he answered. He meant it. Without hope there is nothing, he thought. Gulu knew that; the army had taught him . . . and now Bat belonged to the army as surely as Gulu did. Gulu was a part of it because he was a mechanic; Bat they wanted because he could lead them to elephants.

Again that night he couldn't sleep. As soon as he closed his eyes he would see the huge creatures: a long quiet line swaying softly through the trees, the light falling in dapples of shining on their skin. He was standing by the path. As each of them passed him, it fixed him with a look of sad reproach. He couldn't bear it. He forced his eyes open and stared emptily out into the black.

The next day, despite his tiredness, he threw himself into his drill. He ran, jumped and crawled with a furious energy. If anyone had tried to stop him, he would have attacked. He wanted to drive every thought of the elephants from his head. He could live only in the moment. What else was there left? And yet, still, at the fringes of his mind, the memories were lurking. Wherever he was hiding, they came creeping to find him; whenever he was resting, they came slinking up beside him and he would have to get up again. All day he fled.

In the evening, when he saw Gulu again crossing the compound towards him, he rose quickly to his feet and, for the first time since he had been brought to the camp, he dashed over to join in a football game. At least that way the boy couldn't nag him with questions, he thought, as he shoved through the throng. Gulu never played ball. It hurt his broken foot. Scuffling and tussling, zigzagging and darting, Bat ran so hard that for a while he managed even to dodge his own thoughts.

'Here, over here!' he shouted out to Lobo as the boy looked about for someone to take his pass. Bat scored a goal from the shot.

Lobo grinned. He put an arm round Bat's shoulder as they came off the pitch. 'Come with me,' he said. And Bat did as he said. Why not? he thought. Why not just accept things . . . obey orders . . . there was no alternative.

'You're good.' Lobo was flattering. 'Why didn't we know it before? You can be on my team. We're on the same side now. After all' – he smiled – 'we both come from the same village.' He drew Bat closer towards him and together they went inside Lobo's hut.

Pulling out a bottle, Lobo took a long gulp himself and then passed it over. Bat tipped it to his lips. It burned the back of his throat. He spluttered and coughed. Tears sprang to his eyes, but he took another sip, and then another, and then he sat down on a mat. The alcohol soaked through his mind like palm oil poured onto a piping hot yam.

He began to feel giddy. The walls were swirling about. He could hear his own voice talking, but it sounded a long way off. Raising a hand, he held it up in front of him. It looked like some peculiar creature. He wriggled the fingers about. They felt no more a part of him than some half-squashed creature still writhing. The whole world had receded to the end of a long tunnel. What did he care for those shadows that flickered against the far distant light? He kept on reaching for the bottle. He understood now why the soldiers drank. Lobo smiled and nodded. 'It puts fire in your belly,' he said, laughing.

Bat was violently sick on his way back to bed. Doubling over at the edge of the compound, he retched into the leaves. A guard watched him indifferently; the muzzle of his gun raised. Bat looked up at the trees. They were reeling and swaying; but beyond them he could see the face of a new moon. It was so very bright. It stared into his dizzy head. He shuddered. The gods were looking down. They had seen him. They knew what he had done. But then what did they care, he thought angrily, as he struggled back to his feet. What did they care about the lives of the children in that compound, all fighting and suffering and dying and giving up?

He stood swaying a moment as he planned his next move. Like a chameleon, he thought, weaving from side to side as if about to make some tremendous leap but in the end managing only a small forwards waddle. He pitched over. Suddenly, everything seemed tremendously funny. He convulsed in mad giggles. The noise fell about him like a clattering pot.

Gulu was waiting for him as he stumbled to his mat. He could see the boy's eyes glittering in the bright moonlight; but Bat didn't speak. He lowered himself unsteadily and stretched out. Everything was swirling around him. He scratched at his neck where a mosquito had bitten him. Another was wailing by his ear. He slapped at the air, hoping that he had killed it, then fell straight from the brink of consciousness into a deep, plumbless slumber. There were no dreams; only black. He woke just as abruptly in the thinning darkness before dawn. The dew was cold on his skin. He was shivering on the outside, but inside he burned hot. A headache pounded his skull. He rose unsteadily to his feet. The light sliced like spear grass. He was swaying as he stood in line at morning drill. He saw the commander watching him as he stumbled, noticing his slowness where the day before he had been swift.

Lobo was watching him too, and also Muka. Why was everyone staring at him? Bat felt suddenly irritable. He shrank back and tried to pretend that everything was normal but he could feel his stomach churning. The bile rose in his throat. He dropped his head in shame. And then, falling to his knees, he was vomiting again.

'The only cure is another drink,' persuaded Lobo when the day's work was done. He seemed almost gentle. 'It's awful the first time,' he cajoled. 'But it gets better after that.'

Bat followed him into his hut.

'You see, life in the army is not so bad,' Lobo told him. 'At least it's better than the village . . . and less boring,' he said. 'Who wants to spend all day digging holes for cassava? Why hack with a hoe when you can get what you need with a knife?' He laughed and clapped Bat so hard on the shoulder that the boy bit his tongue. 'Only joking,' he cried. 'But you've got to admit it. Life in the army does have something to offer. I mean, look at me – in the village people treated me like I didn't matter, but here I'm a sergeant already . . . I have respect, and soon I'll be promoted. The Diviner told me that. I've met him, you know.' Lobo puffed out his chest. 'The Diviner's not like you think. People in the villages blame everything bad on him . . . but he's not a bad person.' Lobo searched Bat's face for a sign of assent. 'He has powers, you know.' His voice dropped to a whisper. 'I saw him conjure up a rainbow in the middle of his camp. Some of the soldiers were frightened. They started to run . . . but not me. I'm not scared of the spirits.'

The boy took another long pull at the bottle and then, sliding his arm around Bat's shoulder, leaned close. 'You can meet the Diviner too. I can fix it,' he hissed. 'I can fix it, if you want, as soon as things get better . . . as soon as these troubles have passed. Right now everything is a bit difficult – it's the government soldiers.' Lobo spilled his confidences into Bat's ear. 'The government is—'

A shadow fell suddenly upon them. The Leopard was standing in the doorway. His head was so high that it brushed the palm-frond roof. Neither boy could read his face. The sun was behind him. But Lobo shrank from the scowl of fury in his voice. 'The child's drunk,' he growled. 'What the hell are you up to? I don't want a dithering fool. I need an alert tracker.'

Snatching his arm from Bat's shoulder, Lobo lumbered to his feet. 'He asked me to give it to him, sir. He said that he wanted—'

'Go!' the Leopard barked. 'This boy's got a job to do. I want him sharp as a dog, not lolling about like some savannah baboon.' He kicked out at Lobo with a booted foot and the boy, flat to the wall like a spider, slipped quickly past him and scuttled off.

The Leopard glowered at Bat. Then, picking up the bottle, he turned on his heel and strode off.

Bat didn't move. He didn't feel scared or worried or guilty or nervous. He didn't feel anything . . . and yet, to feel nothing, he mused blearily, was one of the strongest feelings that there is. He stared at the ground. Was this, he wondered, what it was like to be dead?

Across the compound, he could see the child soldiers gathering around the cook-fire; the older ones barging and jostling their way through to the front. They were craning to peer into the pot of simmering millet porridge which, now that every scrap of yesterday's antelope had been finished, the bones cracked for their marrow, the hide scraped for its fat, was all the children had to eat. But Bat didn't get up. He was beyond hunger now. He dropped his head to his knees and gazed dully at the ground between his feet. An ant was hauling a speck of food across its dusty expanses. He put out a finger and blocked its course. The ant changed direction and looped its way around him. Bat blocked it a second time. Once more the little creature turned. Again and again Bat set down his obstacle; again and again the ant resumed its course. It was such a tiny thing, the boy thought, and yet it had so much resolution. In a battle of wills it would always win. Somewhere behind him he could hear the noise of a radio. It fizzled as busily as the blankness that fizzled inside in his head.

*We are launching a new offensive.* The announcement from the radio snagged his attention.

*The rebel army is a parasite*, a deep voice was booming. Then the radio crackled and spat. Bat strained his ears now to hear the government broadcast, but only a few tattered fragments drifted across . . . *a troublesome jigger lodged under our skin . . . we will impale it . . . pull it out of our land. Our soldiers are*—

The transistor was abruptly switched off. A few

moments later the Leopard stormed out of his hut. There was a thunderous frown on his face. He called the commander over. Bat watched them as they conferred. The Leopard paced back and forth, back and forth, restless as a caged animal, his hands clasped behind him. The commander just stood, his jaw muscles gripped.

Suddenly the commander whipped round. 'What are you hanging around for?' he screamed at the children. 'We don't feed you here so that you can just laze about. This army is alert. It's strong. It's all-powerful! It will defeat those government hirelings. It will grind them into dust.'

His cries rang around the heads of the soldiers as they scrambled to attention. Then, swallowed up by the forest, they slowly faded and died, leaving nothing but a huddle of thin children standing bewildered in a clearing and a mood of anxiety hanging in the air.

# CHAPTER TWENTY-THREE

'Elephants! Elephants!'

It was the Goat who was shouting the next morning, arms waving in excitement as he arrived in the camp. He must have walked all through the night to get back at this hour. But the hungry children who, on seeing his arrival, had looked up from the breakfast fire and momentarily brightened, soon let their heads again fall. They were disappointed. For days they had been waiting for the return of his raiding squad. They had been dreaming of maize cobs and chickens and yam roots. But now here he was back from the forests empty-handed; carrying nothing with him but a piece of news.

Bat's heart gave a great jolt. It shook him out of his torpor. All the confusions created by drinking were suddenly cleared. His mind felt very sharp, very alert, very still. He rose quickly to his feet. Every nerve-end was trilling. Every muscle was steeled.

The Leopard, roused from his shelter on the far side of the clearing, was also now emerging. The commander, still barefoot, hurried along behind. Ears straining, Bat crept up as close as he dared.

'When we got near the village,' the Goat was saying, 'we found the government army. Soldiers were hanging off a jeep, thick as bats on fruit trees. They had automatic rifles and belts full of bullets . . . there were too many for us, so we ran. But we didn't take the normal path. We were worried they would follow . . . we didn't want to risk leading them back to the camp.'

The commander grunted his approval. But the Leopard remained silent, his thin lips clamped firmly shut.

'We followed the course of the dry river that runs down the ravine,' the boy was continuing, 'and it was then that we saw them . . . a whole herd . . . with vast tusks,' he said, stretching out his arms as far as they could reach. 'I could have shot one,' he boasted, brandishing his old bolt-action rifle, 'but I was worried that the government soldiers might hear it. I turned to check about me; and when I looked back, all the elephants had disappeared.'

'How far away?'

'Less than half a day's walk.'

The Leopard pivoted on the heel of his boot, only to find that Bat was already there. 'Get ready,' he barked, and strode back to his hut, turning only to snap a brisk order at Lobo. 'Give him some food!'

Bat hunched over a calabash of cold rice but he

couldn't eat. There was a knot in his stomach that took up all the room. The moment had come; the moment that he most dreaded. Only a few days earlier he had thought he had given up all hope, but all the while, he now realized, it had still been smouldering inside him, like an ember still glowing beneath the ashes of the fire. Why did people always tell you that hope was a good thing? he wondered. It wasn't. Gulu, all along, had been right. Hope was cruel: it was cruel as a fish hook. Just when you imagined you had finally got free of it, there it was, lodged inside you, yanking you back again.

He thought of the elephants; of those animals that for so many years had formed the horizon of his whole world. He imagined the great matriarch standing watch over them. He saw her deep hollowed cheekbones and her sagacious look. If only he too now had someone to guide him. If only he also had someone who could tell him what to do.

He looked up. Muka was hovering near him. There was a perplexed frown on her face, but when she saw his eyes lifting, she allowed a faint smile to flicker across her drawn features. It shone for a moment like a star between two parting clouds. Bat just dropped his head. He felt ashamed and confused.

'I don't understand, Bat,' he heard her murmur as she drew a few steps closer, pausing only when she was a few paces off. 'I don't understand what is happening. But whatever it is, I know you'll do what is right.'

Bat lifted his eyes helplessly. 'But I don't know,' he said sorrowfully. 'I don't know what's right. I don't know what's right and what's wrong any more.'

'But you will discover,' Muka whispered. 'You will find out when you face it. And I know that when the time comes you will find that you know too.'

Bat wanted to get up; he wanted so much to touch her, to take her hand in his own. He wanted to explain everything and hear her reassuring him. He wanted to hear her tell him that it could all be put right. But she was already leaving. He felt the air stirring as she brushed lightly by him; and then she was gone. A sob rose in his throat.

The next thing he knew, the Leopard was assembling a squad. Bat was trotting across the compound, he was falling into file. Lobo and the ranger were in line ahead of him, and behind him slipped four of the camp's most trusted child leaders: Bonyo, the locust; then the Thief and the Goat, then the boy called Kamlara because his temper was hot as a pepper, and last and most ruthless, the one nicknamed Kwet which meant 'brat'. All except Bat carried rifles slung over their shoulders. All had pangas and knives and ammunition belts. Bonyo and the Thief both also carried knapsacks, and Kwet and Kamlara had coiled ropes around their waists.

Bat didn't look behind him as they set off. He knew Muka would be watching. But what was the point of meeting her eye? It wouldn't be him any more she was watching. The village boy from Jambula had vanished long ago. Now Bat was a soldier. He was an instrument of the army. Like a melted-down hoe that is turned into a panga, he had been transformed into a weapon of war.

The Leopard took the lead as the forest closed around them. They were following a narrow trail. It was the very one that he and Muka had been forced along all those moons ago, Bat suddenly realized, as they jogged down a slope towards a stream. It was here, at the bottom, that he and Muka, still bound, had knelt to lap water. But what had been a pool was now no more than a parched fissure. Thin yellow weeds clawed their way across the cracked earth.

Eventually they reached a clearing where, just as Bat remembered from before, a jeep had been left beneath a covering of hastily hacked branches. The Leopard crossed to it quickly and, pulling a chainsaw from the back, slung it around his shoulder on a makeshift harness of rope.

'Let's go,' he growled.

This time it was the Goat who went first. He was leading them back to the elephants.

Scuttling across a wide track that cut straight through the forest, they headed into dense brush. They were climbing uphill now. Their faces were streaming with sweat. Flies clung to their foreheads, to their eyes, to their nostrils; they crawled up their necks and glued themselves to their mouths; but still they trudged on, hacking through thickets and pushing through the thorny underbrush, lifting their elbows to part hanging creepers and scrambling over fallen trunks. They were like machines, Bat thought, driven by the pump of their lungs and the crank of their muscles, by the tug of their sinews and the thud of their hearts. He listened to the sound of his breathing, but it seemed to come from another person who was walking beside him. An eerie quietness roared like a river in his head.

He prayed that the elephants had gone by the time they arrived. But the squad moved as swiftly and efficiently as a pack of wild dogs. It slipped through the shadows with barely a sound, and the sun had not even yet reached its noon zenith when they found themselves cresting a ridge. The slopes fell away below them into a dark gulley. The Goat raised a clenched fist. 'Down there,' he hissed.

The Leopard grunted and, pausing only to readjust his rope harness, gave a signal for his little posse to go on. They descended the slope in a long, slewing skid, their progress unbroken except once or twice when a dislodged rock rattled and they all froze in their tracks, ears straining for the sound of any answering motion, for any warning of other living creatures about.

When they were almost at the bottom they paused again. The Goat glanced briefly around. He had slipped and cut his elbow. His jacket was stained with drying blood. But he seemed not to notice. He was getting his bearings. With a sudden forward scoop of his arm he beckoned them, and once again they were travelling, this time following the line of a stream that crawled through a deep rocky fissure far below. And then, all at once, they were stepping into a small scrubby clearing and the Goat was un-shouldering his rifle; he was gripping the stock. His eyes were sweeping about him and the others were following suit. Weapons at the ready, they were scanning the trees, tuning their senses to every slip of a shadow, to every rustle in the bushes, to every crack of a branch . . . but nothing . . . the forest was quiet save for the endless unbroken scream of the cicadas. The jungle was drowsing in the sweltering noon heat.

But the Goat was right, Bat thought. There had been elephants there. He glanced at the Leopard. A marauding smile was creeping over his face. He too had noticed how the underbrush had been trampled, how the branches of the trees around had been snapped, and now he was dreaming of ivory . . . of the money it would bring him, of the guns it would buy.

Bat lowered himself to one knee. He knew that he had been brought along as a tracker. Now he simply did what they expected him to do. There was a pile of elephant dung among the leaves. He picked up a piece and broke it open. Forage was not good, even here in the forest, he noticed. He could see strips of undigested bark in the bolus and the jagged ends of torn twigs. But the ball was fibrous and dry. Beetles had already buried their way into the heart of it. The elephants must have left a while ago. He let the dung drop. The glossy insects spilled out onto the earth like black beads.

The Leopard was watching him carefully as he rose once more to his feet. His eyes were prowling his face. A sudden flood of bile rose into Bat's mouth. For a moment he feared he was going to be sick. He swallowed. It tasted as bitter as his thoughts. He looked around helplessly. The trees were reeling about him. What should he do next?

'Here!' It was Kwet who was calling, his voice urgent and low. He had found the onward tracks. It was inevitable, Bat thought. The elephants too would be following the line of the gully; they would be looking for a way to get down to the water, for a place to rest, drink and wash. He moved over to the spot at which Kwet was now pointing; saw the scuffmarks left behind by soft pads in the dust. They were pockmarked with drops of long-since dried morning dew.

Now the Leopard pushed him forward. It was Bat's moment to lead, and obediently, he moved on. The shadows were closing more thickly about them. The elephants, Bat thought, would see well in this dimming light. He followed the broken thread of their trail. At least they had been travelling swiftly, he noticed. They had descended this path at a fast swaying walk. He could tell by the side-to-side straddle of their tracks, and the way the ovals that were made by their hind pads had been planted in front of their more rounded fore-prints. But still, it was only a walk. Why hadn't they trotted? Why hadn't they hurried as fast as they could? Elephants could move at great speed when they wanted to. 'Streaking,' Bitek called it. Elephants will hang around in the same area for days, he had said, and then suddenly they'll go: moving without stopping along their secret corridors, and you won't see them again. They will vanish for months to some far-off feeding place. Was it possible the elephants would do that now? Was it possible they might be gone before the squad could catch up with them?

*Please make them not be here. Please make them not be here*, Bat prayed. Over and over he repeated the plea, but even as his lips stirred with his secret utterances, he seemed already to visualize them in his mind's eye up ahead. Soon the slender thread of water that ran downwards through its narrow fissure would seep outwards and broaden into a pool, and it would be there that he would find them, the cows indolently drowsing, swashing about lazily amid cooling currents while their freshly scrubbed calves scrambled playfully about. Bat shook his head rapidly to get rid of the picture. He had somehow to slow up his pace. Every moment that he could delay this posse of armed killers could be the moment that mattered most to the animals he loved. He began to let his steps drag. The barrel of a gun jabbed into the small of his back.

'Keep moving,' the Leopard growled. Bat could feel his breath burning the tender skin of his nape.

And now he saw that the elephants had slowed up too. The mark of the hind foot was behind that of the fore foot. There were faint S-shaped patterns where a trunk had dragged. The ground was getting damper. They were closer to the water. Bat felt his heart thumping as they reached a place where, if the rains had fallen, the stream would have spilled over and spread into a pool. In a patch of moist earth he spotted a footprint. Only the elevated edges were now dry. It couldn't have been left long ago. The elephants weren't far now. Bat turned away abruptly. He didn't want the Leopard to see his confusion. But the sound of the stream laughing, bubbling and chuckling as it pushed through hidden cavities, seemed to him now as mocking as the laughter of fate.

The gorge narrowed again. The stream vanished down a crevice. It taunted its pursuers with its echoing call. There were rocks underfoot now and the canopies were thinning. The tracks had all but disappeared. Only the occasional scuff mark or a scattering of dropped leaves, discoloured and drying, betrayed the recent passing of an elephant herd. Bat was careful not to point them out. Maybe he could tell the Leopard that he had lost the trail? He moved closer to the water course. Ahead there were falls. He knew it. He could hear the subtle change in the song of the flow.

A slab of grey rock soared up ahead of him. With a spring he was upon it, he was clambering up to its highest pinnacle. He was looking out over the forests that rose and fell endlessly around him. And then, suddenly, all at once he knew that at last he had found them. He could not see them: but he sensed them as surely as if he did. The air felt electric. The hairs prickled on his neck. They were there. They were there, far below him. He looked down, his head reeling. The water slid by through its deep chasm of rock. The falls lay just beyond. And below it were the elephants. That was where they would find them. It would only take a few minutes. They would steal up upon them in their world of ferns and wet mosses. They would trap them against the sheer cliffs of rock.

Bat felt the surge of his heartbeat. His pulse scudded and flew. He could almost hear the stutter of the gunshot in his head; the panicked screams of the youngsters as their mothers stumbled and fell dead. He imagined the water as slowly it ran red. He reached out for a branch. He had to steady himself. He had to regulate his breathing. He had to take stock. But there was nothing to cling to.

For a few moments he stood there, a frail silhouette against the splintering light. Eight sets of eyes were fixed upon him. Eight guns were loaded. Eight bullets were ready. He was trapped in a hinterland between this world and the next.

And then, suddenly, like an elephant that charges without any sign of warning, Bat knew precisely which was the right course to take. It was not a conscious decision. It was an act of pure instinct. He could no more have stopped it than he could have stopped the stream flowing, than he could have prevented the eagle that sailed through the skies far above him from slinging its slow lassoing loops around the world.

What mattered was something far more than just him and Muka; far more even than Meya. It was something that mattered to the whole of the world. What would life mean in a land without the elephants? How could a future without them be worth fighting for? These vast gentle creatures belonged to a place that lay beyond all passing struggles. They came from time immemorial. To betray them, he knew now, would be to betray everything.

With a sudden leap he launched himself from the edge of the rock. The world fell away below him. It was too far to jump. He could never cross the ravine. He was hanging suspended in the middle of nowhere, poised between rocks that opened their ragged jaws far below him and the reeling blue spaces of the sky far above. There was a ringing in his head. The whole universe was singing. He was hanging in space. And something like sheer exultation was surging right through him. Something like glory was shining from his face. He was alive with pure freedom. His spirit was flying loose.

And then he landed and sprawled, and his bare knees burst blood. He gasped for breath and his fingers scrabbled. He hauled himself slowly up a steep rock face and struggled to his feet.

Turning, he looked back across the chasm he had jumped. It was the gap he had opened between the elephants and their hunters, he thought, and he would have smiled with satisfaction had he not known that they would see him, that they would realize that he had deliberately made the leap to lead them off course. A gun on the far side of the gulf was trained directly on him. A dark scowl bridged the space. But he had faced death once already. It had lost its power over him. 'They've gone that way,' he shouted. 'I missed them. They must have crossed further up.'

Kwet and Kamlara rapidly unslung the ropes around their waists. With the efficiency of trained soldiers they hurled a line across the ravine. Bat caught it and fastened it, and the soldiers, pangas gripped between teeth and guns strapped to their backs, inched their way one by one across the chasm that fell away below them. The Leopard cast Bat a look of disbelief as he landed. The ranger was trembling. Lobo's furrowed brow was beaded with sweat. 'Madman,' muttered Kwet as, last in the file, he crossed over. He scratched at his louse-infested dreadlocks and grinned.

'Let's go!' Bat shouted. His cry rang around the rocks. He had meant it to. Surely the elephants would hear it . . . even over the falling water . . . they would hear it and be warned. Even now they would be slipping quickly away, vanishing like shadows into the underbrush. They would be safe for the time being. Despite bruises that were swelling into throbbing contusions, despite a sliced open kneecap around which the flies buzzed, Bat set off at a brisk trot. All that mattered now, he thought as he drove his battered body onwards, was that he should keep moving. All that mattered was that he should keep leading them away from the elephants.

He didn't look back. He feared meeting the eyes of the Leopard; he feared that his face might betray his lie. He could hear his fierce hard breath behind him. The chainsaw was heavy and it was starting to slow him up. He wouldn't take kindly to any so-called mistake. And then, all at once, Bat found himself once more on an elephant path. It was more than he could have hoped for. Now they would think that they were back on the elephants' tracks. He closed his eyes for a moment and thanked the gods for this gift.

The trail had not been used for some time. Bat could tell: the marks of smaller creatures blurred the elephants' old prints. But here and there he could still pick them out. Only a practised tracker could follow spoor this old, and even then it would be hard to know the right direction. Bat searched for the distinctive scuff marks that the hoofed toe made at the front, then began, deliberately as a village woman reravelling an unspooling cotton thread, to follow the trail backwards to the place from which it had begun. Now, every step they travelled was taking them further from the animals. Every step they were taking gave the elephants a better chance to escape.

The sun was lowering through the sky. Hanging vines clogged the path. Dry leaves masked any footprints. The leaves also hid deep holes. Lobo stumbled and fell. He let go a deep grunt. The Goat, half asleep on his feet, jerked his head up in fright. The ranger looked anxious. The Leopard gave a black scowl. 'How far, boy?' he breathed. He was thinking that at any moment they would come across the great animals, surprise them as they settled in some glade for the night.

Suddenly, the Leopard sprang forward. He held up a clenched fist. The squad froze. Silently, he pointed. A tatter of cloth had been left on a thorn. It was a sandy brown colour. And it came from the uniform of a government soldier. Each of them recognized it only too well. They glanced nervously about them. This was the sort of territory that their rebel army most favoured. It was the right sort of ground in which an ambush could be set. But now they knew that the government forces had been here too.

The Leopard shifted his grip on his rifle. Bat noticed the sweat-prints that his fingers left on the stock. His eyes raked the shadows. But there was nothing to be seen.

Step by stealthy step, the Leopard began to retreat. The squad which had set out that morning as predators had now, as the dusk gathered, become the prey instead. They were stealing back into the safety of the highest forests from where, looping about, Bat supposed they would creep back to the camp. But he was too exhausted even to feel relief. He just had to keep putting one foot down in the front of the other. He just had to keep struggling on. His knee was so swollen that every upward step pained him, his ribcage so bruised that every panting breath throbbed. And when finally the Leopard indicated that they would stop for the night, he fell instantly into a fitful sleep.

He dreamed of an elephant herd drifting through the forest. He dreamed that Meya was among them, that she was shambling towards him, reaching out with her trunk. He thought he could feel her touch, soft as a caress, upon his bruised cheek, but when he opened his eyes, it was only an insect crawling over him. He was shivering with cold and every bone in his body ached. The scream of the crickets was like a knife in his brain. And from the cover of the thicket under which he was hidden he could see a single red eye, like the eye of a crocodile, burning. It was the cigarette of the Leopard as he crouched amid the darkness and smoked.

By noon the next day, they were almost back at the camp. The Leopard didn't return with them. When they reached the Land Rover, he left with the ranger. 'I'll be back,' was all he said.

It was Lobo who was in charge of the exhausted little band that, a short while later, straggled into the forest clearing. They began to feel better once their bellies were full.

'Next time, Bat, eh?' said the Thief as he scraped up the last of the cassava porridge. 'We'll get them next time! Now we know where they are.'

Kwet laughed. He slapped Bat on the back. 'That jump! You're a madman. You deserve to be dead!' He pulled out a wad of dagga and started to smoke. 'You should have seen it!' he cried out. 'He was like a flying fox . . . like a bat. You are like a bat.' And he held his sides with laughter at his own joke.

Lobo sidled up. 'You're one of us now, boy,' he said, hunkering down beside him.

Bat nodded. But when he saw Muka passing, his eyes met hers clear and straight.

And yet all was not right in the camp. The commander was tense. He gritted his teeth when he learned that the Leopard had left. From then on he was restless and alert. He was waiting for something to happen. All night, the sentinels paced back and forth, back and forth.

But nothing: night passed into morning, morning into afternoon, afternoon into evening and then night again. There was no sign of anyone. The mood of strained waiting stretched out longer and longer. It started to feel like it would go on for ever, until suddenly, on the evening of the fourth day, it snapped.

# CHAPTER TWENTY-FOUR

The sky started to throb. What was happening? Bat's eyes scurried about. He leaped to his feet. Where was Muka? It was his only thought. A growing roar filled his ears. It was like the sound of a river as it rushes towards the rapids. The blood pounded his temples. All about him he could see children running, scattering like chickens when the shadow of a hawk sweeps the yard. They vanished into the trees. Where was she? The compound was all but deserted. And then, suddenly, he spotted her, darting bewildered across the open spaces, pausing befuddled in the middle of the clearing. He dashed towards her.

A strange creature was bearing down upon them from the skies. Its wings flashed in the sunlight like fast whirling knives. The tree-tops were surging and heaving, rolling and lashing. It was coming towards him.

The noise was deafening. Bat clutched Muka to him and stared, completely spellbound. It was as if a stone had been flung up and just stayed there, he thought. It couldn't be real. The tattered roofs of the palm huts started to flap and lift. Everything was vibrating. Muka could feel him shaking as she clung to his chest and then, suddenly, with a crash, they were flung down on earth. For a few moments they just sprawled there, too stupefied to move. 'Lie flat!' Gulu was screaming. He had flung his body across them. His grip burned Muka's wrist. The whirling dust was filling their mouth, throat and ears. 'It's a helicopter,' he was yelling. 'It's a helicopter. Keep down!'

And then it was over. The flying thing passed on. As its roar slowly faded, the other soldiers began to emerge. 'You're so lucky, so lucky,' Gulu was panting. 'You're so lucky,' he was repeating again and again. 'That was a helicopter. It could so easily have killed you. A helicopter sends bullets like clouds send down rain to the earth.'

Shakily they clambered back to their feet.

'We are leaving!' At an order from the commander, the whole camp sprang to life. Nobody spoke. The child leaders were efficient. They had done this before. They had lived so long in the army they had learned to fly without perching. Stuffing whatever food they could find into knapsacks, they shouldered their guns, strapped on knives and buckled ammunition belts. All prepared to go, they breathed deep and level, their hands clutching at stocks as they began to marshal the less practised soldiers. Everywhere, children were scurrying hither and thither in confusion.

'Carry as much ammunition as you can . . .' ordered the commander.

'But not too much,' barked Kwet, half emptying the pack of a frail young boy who was so heavily laden that he started to topple when he tried to stand up.

The Thief handed round strips of green cloth to be tied round their heads. 'If you see anyone without a band like this, then shoot,' he commanded. 'Shoot without even so much as a second thought.'

Like a machine that has been kicked into action, the children fell into files, as they had been taught.

'You are trained soldiers now!' The commander paced the lines, his slow bloodshot gaze searching each face in turn. 'You are ready to fight.' His heavy-booted tread passed between them. Bat's eyes met that dark bulging face without flinching. Gulu, tucked in behind him, stood tense. Muka was in the line next to theirs, in the squad of the child leader Kamlara. Last in her file was La, the little boy who would not speak. He had dashed back at the last minute to collect his bushbaby and now it was clinging to the edges of his pocket, uttering tiny high-pitched 'wheets' of confusion.

Lobo strode over and grabbed it. 'Do you want to get us all killed?' He flung the little creature down at his feet. It struggled up, hands spread imploringly. Lobo kicked it away. Even then La did not speak. Only Muka saw the tears that came rolling down his cheeks.

All morning the children were kept marching through the forest, stopping only for water when they came to a stream. They were tired and hungry. When they reached a thicket of wild sugar cane, one of the girls fell upon it but the Goat, spotting her, smacked her hard in the face. 'Are you stupid?' he hissed. 'Do you think the government soldiers can't follow that?' He kicked a spat mouthful of chewed fibres from the path while the girl watched, half stunned. The sugary juices dribbled between her parted lips.

The children pressed on. The helicopter could so easily have spotted their encampment. Even now, the government army was probably entering the clearing. Squads of trained soldiers would soon be following their tracks. The fear made them hurry. Sometimes they broke into a half-run. There was no sound but the swish of their knapsacks jogging against their backs. When the commander at the head of the line raised his clenched fist, they stopped. When he brought it down slowly, they would all squat on one heel, eyes scanning the spaces between shadowy tree-trunks. When he beckoned, they would run forward again.

Time surged and slowed and then picked up speed again. It carried them along on its waves. At one moment the children would feel so tired that they feared they could go on no further; at the next they would jog as if their journey had no end. They slid down steep slopes and scrambled rocky proclivities. At one point they crossed a broken-down bridge. It was made of nothing but a few hastily hacked branches. As he put his weight on them, Bat felt the whole disjoined structure sag. He looked down and felt his head spinning. The river in the gulley below had run completely dry.

By the evening, the child soldiers were so famished that the younger ones were beginning to flounder. They ate a handful of millet flour each and slept out on the ground. It was cold, so cold. They shivered and turned fretfully in their huddled heap. In the morning their clothes were soaked wet by dew.

The gradients steepened the next day. The children were moving higher and higher up into the mountains. But the pace was relentless. The bedraggled army marched endlessly on, its entire existence reduced to a simple blind obedience. The children's ragged clothes were stiff with sweat. Flies buzzed round the cuts where the thorns had raked their skin open. Their eyes ached with tiredness. Their heads throbbed in the heat.

On the second evening, just as dusk was falling, the girl they all knew as the Leopard's favourite collapsed all of a sudden and lay without moving. She had always seemed so strong, Muka thought, never speaking of her life before the army had abducted her, never spilling a tear or grasping at a forlorn hope. She had accepted her fate as impassively as she had accepted the necklace from the Leopard when he had reached out and fastened it round her. But now her solitary spirit had finally broken. She refused to go on.

'I can't make it,' she gasped. 'Just let me lie here.'

The commander nodded to Lobo, who fell back and jerked her roughly to her feet. He began to push her forward, a knife blade at her shoulders.

She blundered on for a while before stumbling to her knees and collapsing again. 'Leave me, leave me,' she murmured. Her plea was no more than a parched whisper. She crumpled down among the leaves and the darkness enclosed her.

Hauling her upright, the commander propped her against a tree. She stood there staring outwards with eyes too big for her skull. He stroked her face gently. For a moment it was almost as if he was soothing some poor trembling creature. For a moment Muka thought that he looked almost kind. Then a flood of dark blood spilled over his hand. The girl's head dropped and she slumped. The commander turned, wiped a blade and re-sheathed it in his belt. He spat on the ground. 'She was weak,' was all he said. 'She would have shown our enemies the way.'

He removed her gun and tossed it to Gulu. It was the first time the boy had been trusted with one since his failed escape. The army was reclaiming him. It was accepting him back as one of it's own. Gulu caught it. He clutched it. For a moment it felt like the hand of an old friend. And that was the moment he made his decision: not because he was thinking he had anything to gain from the future, nor because he was hoping he could recapture some long since lost past, but because suddenly he knew that he could not bear the present any longer. He turned. His eyes sought out Bat's and found them already waiting. Muka was standing stock still, a short way off. The boys caught the white flash of her glance amid the confusion. The other soldiers were milling about, bewildered, not sure what had happened. The child leaders had moved forward to remove the girl's body, as they had been trained.

For a split second the three children stood poised, bound together in a moment of horror; then, letting her gun fall, Muka sprang forward and seized Bat's outstretched hand in her own. His own gun also falling, he grabbed out for Gulu, already waiting, and, swept forward by a surge of shared courage, shared purpose, shared panic, the three of them plunged into the surrounding bush.

For a few precious moments it was only La who saw them. He watched them running away without speaking a word. Then the cry went up. It was the Thief who spotted them and Kwet who lifted his automatic. Spinning on his hips, he sent round after round juddering into the thickets. They ripped through the leaves and tore hunks of wood from the trunks. The spent cartridges sprayed up around him. Their shells gleamed in the dark. He paused to snap in a new magazine. When he looked up again, all he could see was the black. The escapees had vanished like divers into a deep pool. The surface was settling. Nobody knew if they would ever come up.

# CHAPTER TWENTY-FIVE

The three children dashed like panicked bush pigs, crashing through thickets and dodging round trunks. They heard the hard rattling stutter of the gun right behind them. Bullets sang in their ears like a swarm of disturbed wasps. They could see their glowing traces. At any moment they expected to feel that last fatal sting . . . they expected to fall . . . but until then they would keep running. Their fear lent them a new strength.

If the soldiers caught them, Gulu thought as he charged through the undergrowth, they would tear them limb from limb like a pack of wild dogs. He hurled himself onward, pushing blindly forward, slowing only slightly from time to time to check that his two friends were still following. Further and further into the darkness they fled, tripping and stumbling and picking themselves back up again, bruising bones against rocks and ripping gashes in flesh, until slowly the hooing and yapping of their pursuers began to fade; until they could hear nothing but the breaking of branches, the rustling of leaves as they parted and then swished shut behind them, the rasping of breath as it tore from their throats.

They were deep in the forest. The light of a rising moon silvered the high foliage, but down amid the dry undergrowth all was a shapeless black. Bat, Muka and Gulu kept floundering on, clambering over fallen tree-trunks and blundering through bushes, skidding and skewing their way down a breakneck slope until finally, almost at the bottom, they found themselves halting. They were standing upon a rocky brink. Below them they could hear water. A stream was flowing. Bat could see the thin thread of sparkling which laced round shadowy rocks.

One last downward scramble and the three children were beside it, splashing their burning faces and slaking their parched throats. Only then, when their stomachs were filled almost to bursting, did Bat turn to Muka. Only then did they seek out each other's feverish faces. They had managed . . . they had finally managed. They were free. For a few moments Bat crouched there looking at his two companions. He felt giddy with elation. They had escaped the army! Their lives had been set loose. They could go anywhere they wanted. They could go back home!

But how? Even as those first wild hopes of freedom eddied madly about, Bat felt the slow drag of a deadly undertow. How would they find their way back to Jambula?

'Move! We must keep moving!' It was Gulu who was urging. Despite his wounded foot, he was taking the lead. 'Hurry. We have to keep walking while we have the strength,' he was encouraging. He had lived as a rebel on the run for too long to think he would ever be safe.

By the time the faint light of dawn was beginning to leak through the foliage, shrinking the shadows and outlining dim shapes, the children had scrambled up another craggy slope and were picking a slow path through the forests ahead. The trees loomed up around them like a vast living fortress. Their steps were beginning to slow. Bat dragged himself wearily over a fallen trunk and waited for Muka. Ahead, Gulu was no more than a flickering shadow. What would they do without him as a guide? Bat wondered. He watched the shape of the boy dissolving into the gloom. Gripped with a sudden fear that the painfully thin Muka might not have the same strength, he urged the already faltering girl to keep up.

'What's that?'

They heard something moving in the half-light ahead of them and sank to their heels in an instant, like trained soldiers, their stares fixed ahead. Gulu raised his gun. His grip on the stock was steady. But it was only a bushbuck, its pelt dark with dew. With a bark of alarm it slipped back into the brush.

On and on they walked, crawling, scrambling and tearing their way through the undercover. As the sun climbed through the sky, the heat grew heavy as a blanket. The sweat prickled their skin. Flies buzzed round their faces, clinging to their eyelids and crawling around their lips. At first the children would blow and slap to get rid of them, but after a while, too weary to bother, they just let them sit. They were famished. When Gulu dug some white grubs from the pulp of a palm, they swallowed the damp morsels without even chewing, but still their bellies ached.

'Keep marching!' commanded Gulu every time they faltered; and so they did, following the contours of a mountain, walking and walking until the sun had fallen from its height. In the late afternoon they found a pool where they drank. It was stagnant. The water tasted oily and thick, but they lapped at it thirstily. Then, racked by terrible stomach cramps, they bent double with pain. Scuffing a shallow scrape for themselves under the bushes, they rested again for a bit. But the newfound freedom that just a few hours ago had filled them with elation was beginning to feel more like a trap. How would they ever get out of these forests? How would they ever discover in which direction their home lay? Bat held Muka's hand tight in his own as he lay in the underbrush. The evening darkness gathered rapidly about. Crawling things scuttled over him, but he was too tired to care.

'From now on we move only at night,' Gulu ordered. 'That way we're less likely to be spotted – by the government army or the rebel soldiers . . . and they're both just as dangerous to us right now.' He looked at Bat and Muka. It was up to him to take command now, he knew;

up to him to keep them safe. For a moment his mind flashed back to the times when he had stood at the head of some posse of abducted children, led them stumbling through the forests, too confused to do anything but obey. Then he had been delivering them back to his own commanders. Now he had to take the responsibility for himself. He shouldered his gun. At least he had that to help him, he thought. He wished the others had not cast theirs away.

They faltered on through a dark formlessness sprinkled faintly with moonlight, eating nothing but some figs which they shared with a colony of bats. Crashing like a tempest into the foliage, the flying creatures feasted among the high branches while the children had to make do with the fallen and half-rotted fruits. Their fingers groped at the pulp. However much they ran, they could not escape the feeling that someone was after them. It haunted their every step. At the creak of a tree in the wind they wheeled round in their tracks. Even the flicker of a moon shadow set their hearts thumping. Gulu, the seasoned soldier, constantly looked right and left. His watchfulness was unsettling. It made Muka feel more frightened than safe.

And then, suddenly, the trees stopped. They were at the edge of a wide track. A full moon glittered down on an unmade road that cut through the forest cover, raw as a new scar.

'It might lead us somewhere,' Bat murmured.

'Too dangerous,' Gulu answered.

'But it might lead to a village,' pleaded Muka.

274

Gulu shook his head. 'We're at risk in the open. Besides, it's just a logger's trail.'

Muka gazed at him helplessly. She didn't know how much strength she had left any more.

Gulu's brow furrowed. He glanced indecisively to his left and right. It was still dark. And at least they would travel faster without undergrowth to battle. At least if they followed the trail upwards they might cross more easily over the next hill. Maybe it would be all right for a bit, he thought. Just until the dawn. 'If you hear a sound, dive for cover,' he warned them and, eyes flickering warily, he took the first step out.

Just up the track a duiker froze for a second and then disappeared with a long stretching bound.

The children headed up the slope. They were travelling easily now. They felt their hopes quickening with the increase of their pace. The road cut sharp swags round the contours of a mountain. Sometimes they almost ran as it descended into a slight dip.

It can't have been many hours before dawn when they came to a fork.

'Which way?' asked Muka.

None of them knew.

'That one, maybe,' Bat suggested, glancing up at the stars where they floated in a thin strip of sky. 'It leads southwards and I think southwards may be the way back.'

Gulu wasn't so sure. 'That one slopes downwards and the plains are not safe.'

For a few moments longer they hovered indecisively, helplessly craning out into the black for a clue.

They had their backs turned to the three silent figures who were stealing towards them. And by the time they turned it was already too late.

'Run!' Gulu screamed.

They wheeled, bolting headlong downhill. A gun cracked behind them, but they were rounding a corner. They were swerving out of reach. They ran and they ran, their breath ripping from their throats. The rutted dirt cut their feet; the moonlight cast treacherous shadows that tripped them; but they raced blindly on.

An engine revved into life. A vehicle was coming. It wouldn't take long to catch up. They glanced right and left at the dense walls of trees. 'Round the next bend and then into the bush!' Gulu gasped.

They tore round a twist and found themselves entering a clearing. A logger's cabin stood ahead of them. Their pursuers would be arriving any moment, they thought as their eyes scudded frantically about. They could already see the headlights flashing through the leaves, but in a sudden swerve of brightness, Gulu spotted a gap under the hut's wooden floor and, grabbing Bat and Muka, he dragged them stumbling towards it. They dived headlong in.

## CHAPTER TWENTY-SIX

From where they were lying, bellies flat to the ground, the children couldn't see the jeep as it drew into the clearing, but they watched the beams of its headlights as they swept across the dry brush. The engine cut; the doors opened. They heard the passengers jump out. Something knocked against metal. It was a gun, Gulu thought. Every nerve, every muscle, every sinew was locked. He looked no more alive than a bundle of old sticks. Footsteps trod purposefully towards the cabin.

'They're in there. Start looking,' a voice barked.

The children felt their hearts jolt. They all knew it. It was the Leopard who was speaking. Face down in the earth, Bat could smell his own dread. He screwed his eyes tight but he couldn't escape the terror. He could see the scarred frown on that face.

'Find them!' came the order.

'Yes, sir.'

Bat recognized the second voice too. It belonged to the ranger: to the man from the elephant hunt. This was the person who took money to kill animals. He would think nothing of shooting children either, the boy thought. And now he was coming towards the cabin. The light of a torch bobbed about as he walked. Its beam swept its long, slow arcs across the clearing, casting about like a predator, nose to the ground for a scent. For a second it seemed to be shining straight into the cranny in which the children were hiding. Their breath turned solid in their throats; but they didn't dare swallow. Any sound at this point might have betrayed their hiding place. Muka watched a baboon spider scuttle out in front of her. It hunkered down on its haunches, silhouetted by the light. She let her eyelids fall shut. The earth smelled dry and musty. The dead leaves would crackle if she so much as flinched. The spider stretched out one leg and prodded tentatively at her cheek.

And then the torch moved and the children were plunged back into darkness. Above them, a board creaked. The searcher, unseeing, had stepped over the gap through which they had slid. He was climbing up to the cabin. The door scraped open. Footsteps struck upon boards. The light from the torch filtered down through the cracks.

'They must be here.' It was Lobo who was now speaking.

'We'll find them,' the ranger said.

Something was noisily kicked. They heard the flick of a lighter; they smelled cigarette smoke. 'There's nothing in here, sir,' came a shout. 'It's empty. Just a couple of old boxes.'

'Damn them!' The curse rang out across the clearing.

Two pairs of boots were clattering from the hut. They moved off, the beam of the torch bouncing, darting to and fro, prying into bushes and glancing off tree-trunks.

'They must be hiding in the bush, sir,' Lobo shouted. 'Shall we go after them?'

There was no answer, but the pursuers seemed to be moving ever further away. They were returning to the jeep. The children heard a door slamming. For the first time they began to dare believe they could hope.

'Hey, over here!' It was the ranger. 'Over here! Bring a torch. There's a gap under the hut.'

A fresh wave of fear swept hope away on its flood. The children lay motionless. It was as if somehow, if they kept still enough, they could stop this all happening, freeze this last precious moment until it lasted for ever. But they knew at the same time that their luck had run out. It was over. They were about to be discovered. They would be dragged from their hiding place, helpless as a litter of kittens. It was just as Gulu had first told him, Bat thought: once you had joined the army, there was no way out; you just came round in circles; you were caught in a trap. The noose was tightening about him. It closed round his future. He clamped his lips on the scream that now rose to his throat.

A beam of light slid towards them. They heard some-one grunting. It was Lobo who was looking. His torch cut through the darkness. It poked into the far corner and fiddled about in a pile of old leaves; then, sweeping across the middle, it came to rest upon Muka. Bat heard her stifled gasp. She stared frozen with terror into the blinding glare. Her lips moved to shape words but only silence came out of them. The cicadas shrieked louder and louder in the bush.

'What is it?' The cry of the Leopard rang out across the clearing.

There was no answer.

'What is it?' the cry came again.

'Nothing,' called Lobo.

'Nothing?'

'Nothing, sir.' Lobo's voice was flat.

The Leopard cursed. There was a rustling of movement. Footsteps retreated. The torchlight bounced about.

'We can't afford to waste time on them,' they heard the Leopard saying. 'Let's go!'

Slowly, ratchet by minute ratchet, the children let out their breath. What had happened? Were they safe now? Had Lobo seen them? He must have. So why had he lied to the commander? Was he playing some cruel trick? Or had he decided that he would not betray them? The thought fell like a burning spark into Bat's head. He felt a new hope inside him beginning to kindle. He strained the night for a clue. The door of the jeep creaked. They were leaving. Any moment now, the engine would roar into life.

'They'll be there.' A hard blunt voice stamped down on his hopes. It belonged to the ranger. 'They'll be there for sure,' it said. Bat reached out across the blackness for Muka. It might be the last time he ever touched her, he thought. The end was now so near. The torchlight was streaming back into the crawlspace. Beside him, he heard Gulu shift. He was edging forward on his elbows, holding his rifle. The barrel was trained straight out into the black. The beam of the torch came to rest directly upon him. He stared like a rat in a trap back into its glare.

There was a deafening crash and a sudden sharp cry. The torch bounced. Its light blinked once and went out. And then there was silence. It rang like the report of the gun in their ears, a strange quivering stillness that hummed and vibrated about them, rising and falling like the trilling of a million forest insects.

'Come out!'

The Leopard's cold order cut through the silence; but none of them moved.

'Come out now or we'll burn down the hut.'

Still the children lay there. The blackness around them was complete, but Bat could feel Muka trembling beside him. She was squeezing his hand so hard in her own that it hurt.

'Stay,' hissed Gulu. 'Stay where you are.' His voice was harsh as a threat. He was a soldier now. He knew how to deal with it. He had gone back to the army and he had been trained for this.

Inching his way to the edge of the crawlspace, he threw out his gun and then started to clamber out himself. With hands raised in the air, he walked across the clearing, coming to a halt only when he was standing directly in the head-beam of the jeep. He waited, a frail outline against its harsh light.

'And your friends?' the Leopard spat.

'They went that way,' Gulu said. 'My foot was too bad. They left me behind.' He must have pointed towards the forest because a torch beam leaped briefly in the direction of the bush.

'They left you?' The question was disbelieving. From under a peaked cap, a pair of sharp eyes prowled around Gulu's face.

'Guard him!' the Leopard ordered, darting a glance at Lobo.

In a few quick paces, he crossed to the hut. The dark shape of the ranger lay slumped by the entrance of the crawlspace. He prodded it casually with the toe of his boot. There was no movement. The man was dead. Calmly, he stooped to retrieve his dropped gun.

'You'll soon be wishing you'd died as quickly,' the Leopard spat. 'We'll be making a lesson of you,' he growled as, returning, he gave Gulu a kick that sent him crumpling without a cry to his knees. 'We'll cut you up into bits as big as a grasshopper.'

Then, raising his head, he turned his attention once more to the cabin. 'You two can come out from that hole now,' he said coolly.

Neither Bat nor Muka moved. Was he bluffing? Did he know they were there?

'I'm losing patience,' he snarled.

Still, the two children waited. They were shaking so hard they could hardly have got up if they had wanted to. A cigarette lighter flared. They smelled smoke. A bundle of smouldering grasses was carried over to the cabin.

'We'll fume you out like stuck porcupines.' The sneer curled through the dark. The first tongues of flames flickered out of the kindling. They started to lengthen and lap at the wood.

The smoke began to filter down into the crawlspace. Muka coughed and clamped a hand to her mouth. The dry leaves were curling, crackling in the heat. This time nothing could save them. The two terrified children crept out of the hole. And the Leopard was waiting. His eyes were no more than dark holes in his face.

# CHAPTER TWENTY-SEVEN

A blow on the back of the neck sent Bat staggering. He fell to the ground. It felt as if his skull had cracked. His thoughts were leaking like water from a broken clay pot. He lay completely still. He couldn't tell for how long. It felt like time had stopped. When he opened his eyes again he didn't know where he was. Had he fallen asleep beside a forest pool? The trees seemed to be floating upon mirroring depths. Where's Meya? he wondered blearily. Where was his little elephant?

Suddenly, he felt himself seized round the ankle. He was being dragged along, an arm twisted painfully underneath him, his head bumping and thumping over the hard ground. He dug his nails deep as he could into the earth; but there was nothing to catch hold of, nothing to keep him. Fistfuls of grasses tore away in his clutch. The whole world wheeled about him. Fire and sky spun in a whirl of dark and light, and suddenly everything that for so long he had kept locked up tight inside him was escaping. He had so much fright in him that he could no longer stop it coming out. 'Help!' he screamed at the top of his voice. The cry hardly sounded human. It spilled from his lungs like the shriek of an animal in a snare.

'Help!' The plea rang through the darkness. It echoed through the trees. 'Help! Help!' he yelled.

A boot thumped down on his back. There was a low dry laugh. 'There's no help here,' the Leopard growled.

And Bat was back in reality. His cries, swallowed up by the forest, slowly faded as his last struggles died in the Leopard's ruthless grip. A picture flashed onto his brain. He was watching the crickets that, as a herd-boy, he used to see among the grasses, flailing pathetically in clumps of poisonous foam, their serrated legs sawing ever more faintly and feebly until eventually they slowed to a final stop. It was strange how images popped into his mind at such inappropriate moments, he thought.

Yanked back to his feet now, he stood legs akimbo to try and control their shaking. He needed time to knit his nerves back together again. Muka was pushed over beside him. The tears ran down her cheeks but she made no attempt to hide them. They gathered on her eyelashes and dropped glittering down her cheeks. Gulu stared stonily. He looked as if he would never feel anything again.

The Leopard lounged back against the bonnet of the jeep. He gazed at his prisoners: three ragged children blinking blindly into the headlights, Lobo behind them, holding them at gunpoint. 'Well, well,' he said coolly. 'So here we all are again.' He lit a cigarette. Its tip glowed red as the eye of a demon in the night. He inhaled and then puffed the smoke back in their faces.

'Let's get going,' he said eventually. 'It'll soon be dawn.' He took a last glance at the body of the dead ranger. 'The jackals can have him,' he muttered. 'He's no good to us now.' And then he laughed. 'At least we have his jeep,' he said and, pivoting on the heel of his boot, he swung himself into the driving seat. 'Throw them into the back,' he commanded. Turning the key, he started the engine up.

'Move!' Lobo shouted. His eyes skidded from their faces. He found it far easier to keep his gun at their backs. Bat stumbled forward. His kneecaps cracked against metal as he was shoved into the back of the jeep. 'This is the last little trip you'll be making,' he heard the Leopard snarl.

The door slammed behind them. A lock was yanked into place. With a lurch, the vehicle was off, bumping down the track. The children clung tight to the roof struts as the incline suddenly steepened. The engine groaned with the effort; the wheels spun but couldn't grip. The commander swore loudly as he rammed down through the gears. Bat peered through the wire-meshed partition. The pale light of the dawn was creeping into the sky. He glanced back at his companions. Muka, head dropped between her shoulders, hung limp as she clenched her two fists round a roof bar, while Gulu, one foot braced against the wheel arch, was lost in a far

286

distance that lay deep within himself. They were almost at the end of their journey, Bat thought.

The Land Rover braked sharply to a halt. The windscreen turned dark. The next thing Bat knew, the vehicle was squealing and groaning and sliding backwards. The children were thrown against the tailgate in a bone-jagging heap.

They heard Lobo yelp as they jolted to another abrupt stop but they couldn't make sense of what was happening. Bat heard a furious scream. It sounded, he imagined for one moment, like an elephant. But how could it be? His mind was playing tricks. Then, through a hole in the smashed windscreen, he glimpsed for one fleeting moment a huge animal thundering towards them, trunk coiled and ears flapping, amid a cloud of red dust. It *was* an elephant, he realized in stunned amazement. Was he dreaming? Then the bonnet of the vehicle bore the full brunt of the charge. The jeep skidded backwards with a demented howl.

The next thing Bat knew, the entire vehicle was lifting. It was about to turn over. The children were hurled across the back. They landed in a stunned tangle. A bottle of alcohol had broken. Its giddy fumes filled the air.

Clawing at the mesh that partitioned off the cab, Gulu gazed up. A single great eye was looking down upon him. The monster was using the full weight of its head to flatten down the roof. He heard Lobo shrieking as the metal crumpled like paper. The cab's whole structure slewed. Letting go, Gulu slid down the tilted bed of the vehicle, hurling his body with all its force at the lock.

It was already damaged. The bent door was gaping. The catch snapped under the strain. The tail-gate clattered open, spilling the three children down the slopes of a mountain. They skidded and scrabbled. Gulu grabbed at a tree root and snatched out for Muka who, in her turn, stretched out a desperate hand for Bat.

For a moment they hung. The drop plummeted away below them. Then, little by little, spread-eagled against the incline, they scrambled their way back up. Plants came out in clumps where the soil was crumbling; rocks dislodged by their feet bounded away out of sight, but eventually they hauled themselves back over the lip where, scuttling for the safety of a nearby bush, they clung to each other in a terrified dazed heap.

Through the leaves of their hiding place they could see the avenging animal, Lobo squirming below it in the flattened cab. He was wriggling his way out of an open window. He collapsed in a tangle on the track. Blood was pouring from his head. Sitting up unsteadily, he glanced about, frowning and smiling simultaneously. Then, staggering to his feet, he started to lope off.

'Sergeant!' The Leopard roared from the cab.

Lobo glanced nervously back.

'Sergeant!' the scream came again. But Lobo ignored it. The Leopard was trapped. The steering wheel, rammed inwards, had pinned his slumped body. The arm that dangled through the open window looked broken. The barrel of an unreachable rifle sliced a dark line across the back of his neck.

The elephant drew back. The morning sun edged its way over the horizon and the first rays of light flared across the crushed jeep. The Leopard was squirming like a creature whose spine has been smashed. Bat saw the glitter of his watch as a sunbeam danced over it. But now it was counting down the last seconds of his life.

The elephant flared its great ears and, with a bellow of sheer rage, rolled up its trunk for a third and final charge. A huge bony brow smashed headlong into the mangled jeep. The vehicle rocked for a moment on the edge of the cliff. Then, with a grinding of metal, the Land Rover tipped over. It looked almost like a toy as it fell through the trees. It bounced off the rocks, glass spraying all around it, winking and glinting in the brightness of morning before vanishing away into the shadow far below.

A scream of animal triumph echoed through the forest. The children no longer dared look. At any moment the next attack could be launched on them. Shrinking back into the bush, they squatted on their haunches, heads between knee-bones, hands clasped behind necks. They steeled themselves: they didn't know for what.

The leaves around them were parting. Something brushed Bat's cheek. It felt warm and damp. Still he didn't move. There was a low rumbling growl. Bat's whole body trembled. It was as if a great wave was rising up inside him, surging right through his body, pushing him to his feet. He stumbled out. An elephant reared up like a rock-face before him. He could not have run even if he had meant to. *It just has to know it can trust us*, he thought. *It just has to know that we mean it no harm.* And he stood there, eyes screwed tight shut as he tried to muster his courage. Willing himself into calmness, he started to hum.

He heard the animal shifting. It leaned towards him. A current of warm air wafted across his face. He inhaled the heavy musk. It smelled so familiar . . . so very familiar. Tears bleared his eyesight as slowly he lifted his head.

'Meya?' he whispered. 'Meya, is that you?'

PART THREE

## CHAPTER TWENTY-EIGHT

How often Bat had dreamed of this magical moment: how often he had reached out in the darkness of the night thinking that his elephant was standing before him, only as he woke to find nothing but a vast emptiness. Could his dream this time be true?

He stretched out a hand. His fingertips brushed rough hide. Hundreds of wrinkles were criss-crossed about it. For a moment he traced them like lines on a map. A trunk reached tentatively towards him. An eye looked into his face. He could see his reflection: small as a fly trapped for ever in amber. It was Meya! He knew now. The certainty flooded him. It was Meya. And she had held him, held him there in her memory. She had come back for him. He felt so light-headed that he thought he would float.

Sobbing, he flung his arms around the animal. A trunk, strong and safe, curled about his back.

'Muka,' the boy cried, his voice choking with happiness. 'It's Meya! It's Meya! Muka! It's Meya! Our elephant's come back.'

With a cry of pure joy the girl ran towards the animal. She threw her arms in a circle around the broad trunk. A deep growl of greeting was rumbling through its body. It slowly unfurled until it filled the whole air and, for a while, as they clung to this great creature, the two children felt as if the entire world had stopped moving. They were enfolded in a moment of perfect happiness.

But where was Gulu? They both turned. Their friend had vanished completely. They looked about: but no trace. Could he have fallen? Their eyes darted to the precipice. Their two hearts skipped a beat.

And then, suddenly, Bat spotted him, shrinking back into the bushes, staring outwards with a mixture of terror and astonishment, unable to believe what his eyes were now telling him, unable to trust in what he thought he now saw. A few moments ago this animal had been a bellowing monster, madly attacking the men in the jeep. Now it stood there as peaceably as a tame cow. Was he dreaming? He shot a furtive glance over the edge of the cliff. The morning sun glinted on a wreckage of metal. It caught a broken mirror with a sudden blinding flash. So, it really *had* happened: the Leopard really was dead.

Gulu felt dazed. And now he could see Bat and Muka, who were pointing and laughing; laughing so hard that they doubled over and clutched at their ribs. All the terror and sadness and pain was pouring out of them, and the sound he was hearing was an over-spilling flood of unbridled merriment. And the longer Gulu just squatted there gaping, the louder and louder the bright clatter broke out, until even the dumbfounded boy found himself caught up by its currents. Shyly, he ventured a hesitant smile. It was the first time Bat had seen his face light up.

They could easily have stayed there for ever, explaining and talking and hugging each other in relief; but it was Meya the elephant who remembered that they were not out of danger, and now, with a low grumbling growl, she took the lead, setting off down the track at a hasty pace, kicking up clouds of red dust in her wake.

'Where's it going?' asked Gulu.

'She's not an "it", she's a she.' Muka smiled.

'Where's *she* going then?' Gulu asked. His eyes swept the landscape that fell away below them. The forests rolled away endlessly, an unbroken swell of green.

'I don't know,' said Bat as he turned to follow her. 'We have to trust her. Just let her lead.'

For a while they continued down the track until eventually, where it grew less steep, the elephant shoved her way straight through the dense undergrowth and down a slope.

'Where's she going?' cried Gulu a third time. The sisal leaves raked his skin. 'We can't follow her through this.'

'We just have to trust her,' Bat again assured him. 'Elephants know ancient ways. They have paths which their herds have trodden for centuries and Meya will know how to find them. And then . . .' He paused. And then what? He did not really know much more than

Gulu. He didn't know how Meya had found them. Was her herd in the forest? Would she take the children to them? Or was she alone? Had she heard Bat shouting for help in the clearing and come looking?

'Do you think she heard you screaming?' asked Muka as if reading his thoughts. 'Do you think she knew we were in danger? Has she come to take us back home?'

But Bat had no answers. He was as confused as she was. 'Elephants have powers far greater than we can ever know,' was all he could murmur. It was what Bitek the fisherman had always said.

The three ragged children pushed on. Spiny things scratched them. Branches sprang back and smacked them. Hanging vines blocked their paths. Sometimes they had to lie flat and wriggle under thickets that the elephant could just barge through. Sometimes they all had to scramble and climb until, suddenly, just as Bat had predicted, they found themselves standing upon a narrow track through the trees. It was easy to follow. The ground had been trampled to softness by hundreds of huge cushioned soles. This was the path they would now follow for days.

In the mornings the children were so weary that they could scarcely rise to their feet. Meya had to nudge them gently up from their beds, encouraging them onwards with her soft 'let's go' rumble. Washing their faces in dew, they would follow her, step by endless step. There was only one pace, and Meya set it with her ponderous stride. Bat walked behind her, and next in line was Muka, silent as a forest creature. Her once springy step had long since lost its bounce. Gulu limped always at the end of the file, fists clenched and eyes darting restlessly about him. He was trained as a soldier to keep constant watch.

They glided like ghosts through the silver-trunked caverns. High above them, the sun glittered through the foliage, catching the brilliance of butterflies as they fluttered and floated; it sparkled on spiders' webs and glinted across leaves; but where they were walking there was only green shade. Sometimes the path narrowed to a long gloomy tunnel. Occasionally, where some great tree had fallen, a dense tangle of smaller plants made a mad dash for the light. A few of the creepers had poisonous spines; they raised hot itching welts on the children's bare skin, but others were edible. Gulu would follow their stems down to sweet-tasting roots.

The boy knew how to find food. He knew that you could only catch grasshoppers in the morning when the dew was still damp. Later in the day, when their wings had dried, you could dash about wildly but only catch one or two. He would turn over stones and find crunchy black beetles and discover soft yellow seedlings in the shade of rotting trunks. On the first day he grubbed up a bed of wild yams, their pithy brown tubers the size of a baby's curled fist; but on the second he found nothing but the leaves of a bitter shrub. A trickle of sour juices leaked into their mouths as they chewed, but it allayed the nagging hunger that gnawed constantly in their guts.

On the third day, Gulu spotted a honey-bird mewing in the branches, calling to them anxiously before dashing off. It led them to a comb in the hollow of a tree.

It would have been far too high and the bees far too furious for the children to fetch, but Meya, driving her tusks deep down into the loam, rocked at the trunk until the tree was uprooted and then, ears flapping, she waded blithely in amongst the buzzing swarm. The honey dripped down the hands of the children as they feasted, and when, only a few hours later, Meya drove a troupe of baboons from an avocado bush, they ate their fill for what felt like the first time in months. They would have slept peacefully that night had it not been for the bitter complaints of the ousted troupe leader. His deep *boh boh boh* beat for hours in the dark like a drum. Once the noise might have frightened the children, but by now they had grown used to the sounds of the night, and when the dark was so thick that they couldn't see their hands even when they held them right up in front of them, they would lie there amid a wilderness of whoops, howls and grunts, picking out the snarls of the chimps and the screams of the hyraxes, the hoots of the owls or a civet cat's cough.

A gaggle of bushbabies crept down from the blackness to inspect the strange band of humans huddled below them. Wonderment shone in the dark globes of their eyes.

'What do you think the child soldiers are doing now?' asked Bat. He was thinking of the little boy La, who for so long had refused to speak except to his tiny pet. He was remembering the sound of his whispers in the night.

Muka read his thoughts. 'La will be so lonely,' she murmured, recalling the tears that had rolled down the boy's cheeks on the day they had left. The high-pitched 'wheet' of the abandoned bushbaby echoed in her head.

'And what about the others?' Bat said. 'What do you suppose they are doing now; now that the Leopard is dead? Do you think they're still out here, out in the forests? Do you think they are still following the commander through the trees?'

'And will Lobo have found them again?' Muka asked. She cast her eyes quickly about her, imagining him for a moment even now creeping up behind her in the black, hobbling and broken. 'I know he saw me that night,' she said. 'I know he saw me that night under that hut.'

'Then why didn't he say so?'

Muka shrugged. 'Maybe he was sorry?'

'Maybe he hoped to come back with us to Jambula,' ventured Bat.

Gulu shook his head. 'That boy belonged to the army.'

'But maybe Bat's right,' said Muka. 'Maybe he didn't want to be there any more.' They were both remembering the words of Bat's grandmother.

Bat nodded. 'Perhaps.'

But Gulu was unconvinced. 'Well, whatever he's doing, don't think that the army will have forgotten us,' he muttered. 'We're not safe yet. The rebels have camps all over the forest.' He glanced warily around him. They had camped among the trees at the top of a steep-sided gully. 'It's places like that down there that they like,' he said, 'with thick brush for an ambush and no chance of an exit. You will think it's deserted, but the next moment you'll be dead.'

Muka and Bat felt their hearts flip with fright.

'If they find us, they'll kill us.' Gulu pressed his point home. 'They always take their revenge.'

'So will none of the other soldiers ever find a way to escape?' Bat wondered. 'Will none of them ever find their way back home?'

For a long while Gulu was quiet. He drew his legs up to his chest-bone. His knees and elbows stuck out like the knots on a stick. 'Some will,' he eventually said. 'They will reach the point when they are ready to risk everything. Then they will run. The best time,' he murmured, 'is when you are out on a raid and crossing a road. The army only dares send its soldiers across one by one. It's dangerous out in the open. One by one each squad member dashes across. If you are among the first to the far side, that's your chance to vanish. You duck your head low and disappear in the scrub. Then you just have to run and keep running and keep praying that no one will catch you up.'

'And then what?' asked Bat.

'And then,' muttered Gulu, 'if you know your way back to your village you try to reach it. But you'll probably find that it's been abandoned. And then' – he drew in a deep breath – 'then you go to the town, you find an army barracks. You give yourself up.'

'But the government soldiers?' cried Muka.

'The government soldiers don't harm you,' said Gulu flatly. 'They want to encourage defectors. They will keep you for a while; you will stay in a camp. And then an announcement will be put out on the radio. Your name will be listed. They will say they have found you, that your family must come to fetch you. And if you are lucky they will. They will come to the market square; they will search the lines of ex-soldiers and find you.' He paused for a moment. 'They will recognize you by your face,' he eventually added. 'But they won't know who you are in your heart any more.'

'But whatever has happened, deep down it can't change you?' ventured Muka. 'You'll still know who you are, know that deep down you're the same?'

The boy didn't answer. He just stared into the black. The children couldn't see his face; but Bat knew the memories would be moving across it like the shadows of clouds sweeping over a rock.

What was it that had happened to Gulu? he wondered with a shudder. What had cut him so deeply that his very soul was scarred? He remembered the words that the boy had once whispered. 'I have done such things. I have done things that no one could forgive me for,' he had said.

Reaching out gently, Bat slid an arm around his friend. But Gulu gave no response, and a few moments later, pulling himself away, he lay down, his back like a wall turned against them. He clutched his knees close to his chest. As if he was locking them out . . . and himself in, Bat thought.

Gulu did not speak another word that night. But the next day at dawn he was the first to get up. 'We have to keep moving,' he urged as he roused them. 'We can't afford to slack. We have to keep going . . .'

He was more jumpy than normal that morning. His eyes were constantly darting. The bark of a jackal made him freeze in his tracks. The bustle of a bush pig sent him sprawling face downwards. Even the flick of a grasshopper was enough to draw him up short.

In the afternoon they found an orange tree. Its fruit was hard and green: so bitter it pulled grimaces from the children's lips. Only Meya could eat without wincing. She soon stripped the bush. A family of colobus monkeys crept down from the high canopies to see what was happening. They purred as they parted the branches with flickering paws.

'It's not safe; it's not safe here!' cried the agitated Gulu. The monkeys sprang back to the tree-tops, clicking their tongues. 'We must press on.' Gulu was looking wildly about.

'Can't we rest a little longer?' pleaded Muka. She was feeling so weak she was not sure how much more she could manage. She looked imploringly at Bat. He was weary too. Even Meya was flagging. The elephant should have been feeding throughout the mornings, not waking straight from a brief fretful sleep and moving instantly on.

Gulu glanced up at the monkeys, whose long rolling croaks were now resounding across the canopies. 'We can't stay,' he cried. 'Any wild thing out here will know where we are now. The warning of the monkeys will lead them straight to us.'

But it was not the forest animals that scared the boy, not the skulking leopard, its skin sliding like silk over sinew and muscle; not the poisonous scorpion or the swivelling snake: it was men.

Towards the evening of the fifth day, Meya came to

an abrupt halt. Spreading her ears, she lifted her trunk, probing the air for some unfamiliar scent. Suddenly Gulu froze. He too had just noticed the track that cut through the trees ahead of them. He too had just heard the sound of an approaching engine. He leaped forward and pushed his companions down flat.

'Why?' Muka whispered, when she had regained her winded breath. 'It might not be the army. Isn't it more likely to be someone who can help?'

'No one will help us,' Gulu hissed. 'They will probably kill us. They are sure to have guns. No one would be out here in the jungle without a weapon, and they will shoot a stranger rather than run the risk of trust.'

'But when they see we are just children?'

'Especially when they see that we're children,' Gulu snapped. 'No decent villager will ever trust a strange child: not now that they have learned what children are capable of. Now quiet!'

Muka huddled miserably down in the leaf mould. She felt so very tired. She listened to the noise of the engine as it gradually faded. It sounded to her like the ebbing of hope. She hauled herself upright, momentarily giddy. The sudden harsh sunburst of light on the track pierced her brain. She felt herself staggering. Then she was across, swallowed up by the forest gloom again.

For a short while the path plunged steeply downwards. They stumbled and slipped. Every muscle in Muka's body felt like it was tearing. But then they had to start climbing again, on and on until every pace started to feel to her like the last. Reaching the base of an

305

insurmountable cliff, they began to wind their way round. It was a slow out-of-the-way route.

At least the elephant paths were carefully graded, Bat thought. However slow the climb felt, it was never more than he could manage. But whenever he turned to check on Muka, she was flagging, and night had not yet fallen when even Gulu agreed that they should stop.

They were crouching under a bush of hard pear-shaped fruits. The seeds were so acid that they had to spit them out, but the fibrous flesh was good. And yet Muka was now almost too weary to care. 'We can't push her any further,' conceded Gula at last. 'Let's just stay here for the night'. He began to scrape a shallow hollow in the leaf mould for her to lie down. She was shivering as he settled her and, taking off his shirt, laid it tenderly over her. Despite her trembling she felt hot. Her skin burned to the touch.

As Bat took the first watch, he wondered how much longer the three of them would last out. Muka was fading. Her breath as she slept was no more than a faint rasp in her throat. Every knobble in Gulu's spine poked out through his skin. He twitched and flinched amid dreams that would not let his mind rest. If they didn't get somewhere soon, they would just die in the forest, Bat thought. He gazed dully around him with huge for-lorn eyes. A sense of despair settled over him like dust.

Suddenly he tensed. There was something there: a faint movement, somewhere among the trees. Instantly alert, he rose stealthily to his feet, every muscle steeled, every sinew strained taut. He darted a quick sideways glance at Meya. She was already awake and on guard, standing head tilted, ears spread. Together they waited. And then Bat saw them, emerging from the shadows: a line of magical creatures gliding silently through the trees. He stared, entranced.

Elephants! But not like any elephants that he had ever seen. They were the same as Meya and yet, at the same time, they were not like her at all. They were slighter, more delicate, with smaller ears and slender tusks that were tinged a faint pink. Bat's heart leaped in his throat. He remembered a story which Bitek had once told him. All elephants had originally belonged to the same family, the fisherman had said, but slowly this family had drifted apart. Driven from their homelands by humans, one group of elephants had taken refuge in the forests, moving deeper and deeper and never coming out, until gradually, over the centuries, they had grown apart from their savannah-dwelling cousins. Now they lived only among shadows, Bitek had said. They moved through the trees in their shy, graceful herds, singing songs to each other in musical harmony. People said that their strange humming could be heard with the soul.

Bat stood as if spellbound. Meya was listening too. She lifted her trunk in a tentative greeting, winding it round like she did when she was uncertain. But the creatures passed her like phantoms. They faded back into the shadows from which they had first come.

## CHAPTER TWENTY-NINE

A pair of hands parted the leaves. A face popped out between them. It peered straight at the children.

'There's someone there,' Gulu hissed. It was he who was now on watch. Seizing a branch, he brandished it like a weapon, but there was nothing there. He swivelled slowly about. The trees soared up around him like the stakes of a trap. The moonlight fell in bright shards through the foliage, sharp as the fear that flashed in his eyes. Meya, a dark mass amid the greater darkness around her, shifted. Her pale tusks gleamed.

'Get up. We must go.' Gulu shook Bat's shoulder, rousing the huddled boy roughly from his sleep.

He turned quickly to Muka. The girl's eyes were open but she barely stirred.

'Get up, Muka!'

She lifted her head. It seemed so very heavy; she let it

sink back onto her dusty pillow of leaves. She hadn't the strength to stir. Her breath had thinned to the finest of threads in her throat. It was fraying. At any moment she felt as if it might snap. Then she would no longer be tethered, she thought. She would be set free to wander without the tired weight of her body. She stared out into the black. She was already coming loose. Her mind was all fuzzy round the edges. She was dissolving away into the darkness of the night.

Putting an arm round her shoulder, Bat tried to lift her. She felt light as a bird flying free of his grasp. 'Leave her; let her sleep a while longer,' he told Gulu. 'She can't walk any further right now.'

'We can't wait,' the boy urged them. 'We must go. There's someone watching . . . someone waiting. I can't see them. But they're out there, I know.'

Bat glanced around quickly. 'It's the brightness of the moon that disturbed you,' he ventured; but when he looked at Meya he knew that she too had sensed something. She was shifting uncertainly, her foot lifted and swaying.

Just at that moment a figure stepped out in front of them. Bat felt his heart ricochet. He sprang backwards; saw Gulu spring forward at the same moment, fast as the shadow that leaps from a lantern's swinging light. There was a thump and a cry. Gulu vanished. He was down on the ground. A dark figure stood above him. It was a child. Bat's heart dropped and lay thudding at the bottom of his gut. The soldiers had found them; they had come to reclaim them. He dropped into a crouch and got ready to launch a last frantic attack, but just at that moment he noticed that the figure too was stooping, stretching out a hand to help his fallen friend; and it was not a child, but a man: a man no taller than a child, with short legs and a broad back and a string of animal teeth around his neck. They shone in the moonlight like the smile that now spread over his face.

Slowly it dawned upon Bat who this person might be. He was one of the little people who lived in the forest, one of the pygmies who his grandmother used to tell him about. 'They hunt for their food,' she had told him, 'and they sell medicines to traders.' He snatched at the hope. Maybe this man could help Muka now? Maybe he could make her well again? He glanced down at the girl. She was no more than a tiny huddled heap in the darkness, sweating and shivering beneath Gulu's tattered shirt.

'She's ill. She has a fever!' Bat cried. 'Can you help us? She has a fever. She will die without help.'

The little man looked at him quizzically. He didn't understand the language which Bat was speaking, but he seemed somehow to pick up on the sense of what he was saying because now he was turning, gazing gently down at the girl. As he watched him, Bat suddenly realized it was the first time he had seen kindness in the face of an adult since all those months ago when he had been snatched.

The little man jerked his head as if to say follow. They had to trust him, thought Bat. It was their only chance. He darted a look at the still-dubious Gulu, but it was Meya who persuaded him. Though she had edged softly into the deepest shadows, she was calm.

Hauling the limp Muka on to her feet, the two boys draped her arms round their shoulders and set off in the direction in which the pygmy led. He seemed not to notice what a burden she was, hanging all but insensible between them, half stumbling, half dragging, her head jerking and lolling. He moved along at a jog, humming to himself as he skimmed lightly through the trees, flickering through the shadows like some strange burly sprite; disappearing into the darkness and leaving only the trail of his song to guide them before suddenly darting back to check that they were still following.

Dawn had broken when they found themselves stepping into a slight clearing in which a circle of small domed dwellings had been built around a central barrier of brush. The sunlight filtered down through the forest canopy, catching the smoke as it spiralled from a big central fire. Around it a small group of people were squatting, warming themselves and sleepily blinking. They all turned to look at once: first briefly at the children, and then, much harder and longer, at the elephant.

The children, however, were thinking only of food. They could smell it. They could see it in front of them. Handful after handful the boys ate from a calabash of rice while Muka, propped up by the women who gathered chattering around her, swallowed weakly at a broth that was being dribbled down her throat. A draught of bitter liquid was poured into three little leaf cups and given to all of them. When Gulu shook his head, they just pressed it to his lips until he had drunk. And then, a short while later, and with a great deal of excitable argument, the children were led towards one of the strange domed huts.

It was made of nothing more substantial than a framework of bent saplings covered with leaves; but the three of them, guided towards three small beds, their stick frames bound by vine thongs, were ready to collapse. They lowered themselves onto mattresses of stretched goatskins. 'Are we safe now?' murmured Muka; but the boys had already fallen asleep.

All day and all through the next night the children remained in their makeshift cots, hearing only the never-ending sound of the forest; the rustling of a stream that flowed not too far off; the chattering of the pygmy people in whose village they were staying. The pygmies seemed to talk all the time, jabbering and laughing and arguing in voices that rose and fell like running water, ringing back and forth between the clustered huts. And as evening drew in and their banter got slower and drowsier, the children lay listening to the strange hollow wail of their music, the sound of their singing rising and falling and drifting slowly away through the endless spaces of night. Sometimes, when Bat woke, he thought he was still sleeping. He thought he was back in the army camp, dreaming of life in Jambula. His head was so confused. But then slowly, as his new reality seeped giddily into him, as he gazed up at the roof swirling hazily above, he would feel his whole body suffused by a sense of rest and relief.

It was dawn on the second day when Gulu finally rose and sat on the edge of his cot. Through the open doorway he could see the clearing jungle mists. He could hear people moving about.

'This is not our camp,' he said blearily.

Bat rose up on one elbow and smiled.

A woman came in. She wore nothing but a piece of bark cloth round her waist. Its end hung down, a long flap that brushed the ground behind her as she stirred up the fire which had been kindled the previous evening to warm them.

'Who is she?' cried Gulu as she disappeared with a grin.

Bat grinned back. 'Just one of the little people,' he said. His mind which for so long had felt muddled and bleary, was now suddenly clear. 'Just one of the pygmies who live in the forest. Village people often laugh at them,' he said. 'They say they are puny because they are so small. They call them monkeys and say that they even have tails. But the tails are just the cloths that they wrap round their waists; and though the villagers mock, my grandmother once told me, to the little people it is us who seem funny. They think we are too large. They say we are clumsy as buffalo as we go blundering through the bush.'

'They made the medicine which we gave to Meya when she was bitten by a mamba.' It was Muka who was now speaking. The boys both turned at once. She looked thin as a famished rat, but her fever appeared to have passed. Her limbs were no longer trembling. There was no sweat on her brow.

'My head has stopped throbbing,' She smiled as she too sat up on her cot.

313

A man entered. He was not the one who had led them through the forest; but he looked the same, the children thought. He had the same neat round head, wide-set eyes and broad flat nose; but the belt round his waist was elaborately braided and, though the other pygmies all seemed to wear caps made from banana leaves, he sported a hat made from a spotted cat-skin.

'Eat,' he said, handing them a piece of honeycomb.

The children gaped, astonished. He was speaking in their tongue.

'Eat!' he urged them. 'It's the best food in the forest.'

They didn't need telling twice. They stretched out their hands and ate greedily, the wax gluing their teeth.

Then the man held up a bowl of water. 'Drink,' he told them. 'This isn't like the water in the villages, which is dirty. Here in our forest you can drink from any stream.' And folding his hands over his chest, he watched them with satisfaction as they washed down the cloying mouthfuls of sweetness with great gulps from the calabash.

'My name is Yambabo,' the man said at last. 'It was my kinsman who found you in the forest. He had been following you for some time. But now you are welcome in our village, you and your elephant, because my people and the elephant have always shared a home.'

He squatted down on his haunches and stirred at the fire. 'In the days of our ancestors,' he said, 'my people and the elephant walked the forest paths together. It was the elephants who showed us how to live, who

314

opened the thick brush so that our plantations could flourish, who found water holes to drink from and made trails that led between them, who kept dangerous predators at a safe distance; and it is in honour of this ancient memory that we now welcome you and your she-elephant.'

'She's called Meya,' Bat said, struggling to remember the manners that his grandmother had taught him, to accord this man the respect that an elder of the village deserved. 'I saved her when she was a baby. Then she came to save us. Now she is taking us home.'

The man nodded. 'She will find the way. The elephants know this land. They know it even better than my people. They roam far beyond the forests in which we like to stay. They can find places to drink even when all the streams run dry. They remember where the fruit trees grow. And it's said that there are great caves hidden far in the mountains in which, at times of great hardship, they can always find safety. They say there are caverns so secret that no man has ever found them since those far-off days when our forebears followed the elephants' tracks. Yes, your elephant will know how to lead you back to your tribe. Meanwhile, stay with us until you and the animal are stronger. Besides, it's not safe to be wandering about in the forest. There are evil men with guns.'

The children looked at each other and then at him and then at each other again. No shared language was needed to understand the feelings of which their faces now spoke. They had been running alone through the wilderness for so long. They had been so tired, so desolate, so frightened, so sick. Now they had been found by these people and they were offering to care for them. Tears of gratitude rolled down Muka's cheeks.

The children stayed with the pygmies for several weeks. All day the men-folk would be away from the encampment. They left early in the morning with their nets, spears and bows, always singing a hunting song before they departed, clapping their hands and leaping extravagantly, imitating the animals which they hoped to kill. Then they would slip off into the shadows with long graceful steps. It was the only time they were quiet. When they were not hunting, they would be constantly prattling and laughing and singing. It warned away the animals, Yambabo told them: the leopards which lay in wait upon overhanging branches, the buffalo that would attack sooner than pause to think.

While the men were away the women would bathe and draw water; then, sitting outside their huts, their legs stretched straight out in front of them, they would cook: roasting green plantains in the hot ashes, stewing the roots and the creepers and the fluffy pink mushrooms which daily they went out into the forest to collect. The older children liked to hunt too. One day, as he was prowling the clearing, watching constantly about him as he always did, Gulu saw a boy who stood barely higher than his chest kill a starling with a slingshot from at least thirty paces. Even he, who had been handling a rifle since the age of eight, was impressed. But to the boy it felt as natural as it would have to a chameleon whipping out its long sticky tongue for a fly. How Gulu coveted that skill! He wanted to ask the child to teach him, but in his time in the army he had forgotten how to ask for anything – he had forgotten that there were people in the world who would give – and so, with a carefully manufactured look of indifference, he just studied him quietly through lowered eyelashes.

At night, the whole village sat round the fire and ate, all the families sharing the same dish and gossiping constantly, teasing and bantering and arguing and squabbling, until finally they had finished and it was time to sing.

'What do your songs mean?' Bat asked Yambabo one evening.

Yambabo looked up from the piece of wood he was whittling into a bow. Sweat ran in trickles down his polished skin, but he still wouldn't remove his little spotted fur cap. 'Our songs are very simple,' he said. 'They tell the forest that it is good. Normally everything goes well in our world; but sometimes at night, when we are sleeping, harm comes. Army ants invade the camp; leopards come in and steal a hunting dog; and now strange bands of people are seen prowling about. They have darkness in their eyes. And then we know that the forest is sleeping; that it is not looking after its children as it should. So what do we do? We wake it up; we wake it up by singing to it, because we want it to be happy when it awakes. Then everything will be well and good once again.'

Yambabo turned and made a comment to the others and they all looked up and smiled, and one of them pointed at Meya drowsing at the edges of the clearing and shouted out something which was obviously funny

317

because he broke into laughter and clutched his hands to his side. And the more he thought about it the funnier it seemed to become to him. Soon he was lying on the ground, squirming helplessly, tears pouring down his cheeks.

Bat and Muka didn't understand him; but they couldn't help giggling too. Only Gulu remained silent. Gulu, Bat noticed, would never join in, and though he would glance up warily when the pygmies called out to him, he would return to his brooding again as soon as they left him. Often he would whittle at a stick as he sat by the fire, and even when the little people looked directly at him, his eyes would stay fixed on his hands.

'What are you thinking about?' Bat asked him one evening.

'I try not to think,' Gulu said.

'But the longer you try not to think, the longer the days in which you have time not to think will start to feel,' Bat replied.

Gulu just shrugged.

A long pause fell over them.

'Tell us about your village,' Bat eventually coaxed.

'Tell us about your family,' Muka encouraged.

Gulu just turned away, drawing his thin legs up towards his shoulders, clasping and unclasping his constantly restless hands. He had never spoken to them of his life before the army. It remained a secret locked inside his head.

'He doesn't want to remember,' Muka said later when she and Bat were alone.

'But he has to,' Bat answered. 'Your memories are

what you are made of. How can you have a future if there is no past?

'If you want to go forward you must first go back,' he told Gulu the next evening as the three of them sat eating. 'Don't you want to go home? Don't you want to get back?'

The boy shook his head. His hands knotted and unknotted. 'I can never go back,' he whispered.

'But you must!' Muka urged him. 'You must go back. You must find your past life so that you can move on.'

Gulu looked down at the ground between his feet. 'My past is lost,' he murmured, 'and once you've lost your past, you'll never find your way forward into the future again.' For a long while he just stayed there, not moving, not speaking. Then he got up abruptly and wandered off into the night.

Then, one evening, late, long after the chattering had slowed, and the elders begun yawning, long after the pygmies had straggled back to their shelters and their last hurled taunts had faded into the night, Gulu began to speak. The children were crouched round the fire in their hut. The smoke was drowsy and thick, but through it Bat could see Gulu who, without even pausing to take a breath as people do at the start of a story, started talking. It was as if he was picking up on a tale that was already halfway through in his head.

'They called me Gulu,' he whispered, 'because that was the sound the stream made as it ran through our village. My mother wanted my life to flow as bright and clear. And it did. I used to make little cars out of twisted wires. I was the best in the village. I would even attach an old bicycle spoke so that you could stand up and still steer them. And my mother would sell them in the market. They fetched a good price. And sometimes I made their passengers too . . . little people sewn from cloth. I had my own special man that I always kept. He was a soldier. He wore a camouflage uniform and I painted a big smile on his face with charcoal because I hoped that one day I would be like him and drive a car like that. I wanted to be a soldier. But I never thought that dream would come true in the way it did.'

He faltered and swallowed, and started speaking again.

'We had all heard the rumours,' he said. 'But it wasn't until the refugees started passing through our village that we began to wonder if we should really believe them. Whole families would arrive. They had been walking for days. And we could tell they were frightened: the children would jump at the noise of a dog barking; the adults would drift off in the middle of a conversation. They couldn't stop worrying. It was something much more than just tiredness that was troubling them, but when they tried to tell us what this was, when they spoke about armies of children coming down from the forests, raiding their shambas and killing their cows, burning their houses and shooting anyone who argued, we just couldn't accept it. We didn't believe them. We tried to be kind to them. We would offer them food. We would tell them they could stay with us, but mostly they refused; they said that the army would eventually reach our village too.

'And it did.' Gulu's voice dropped even lower. He

clutched his hands around the bones of his shoulders and glanced out of the hut as if to check that no one was listening, but there was nothing outside.

'One day the soldiers arrived in broad daylight. They had knives, sticks and guns. The shots rang around the village and everyone scattered. I saw my neighbour racing back to his hut, only to find that his whole family had fled. Everyone was running; all in different directions. The children were crying as they looked for their parents. The mothers were wailing for the children they couldn't find. The goats were all bleating and dashing about. The chickens flew squawking up into the trees. I saw a man falling and his sister running towards him, putting her arms round him, begging him to get up; but he couldn't. There was blood pouring from his mouth.

'I saw a village elder: he was bent and his face was all wrinkled and he was hurrying, but the little boy who stood in front of him didn't care. He pushed him with a gun. I could see his legs were shaking. I had come from a village where you would never speak rudely to your elders, where the old people never needed to raise their voices above a whisper: they knew they would be heard, however quietly they spoke. I remember my mother flinging her arms around me to try to keep me safe; and my little sister was crying and tugging at her wrap. But then one of the soldiers came running over. He was only a child himself; but he grabbed at my little sister and held a knife to her throat. 'Give me the boy and I'll give you this girl back,' he said. He was laughing. I could see the excitement that was burning in his face; and I turned to my mother. I wanted her to look at me; but she was too frightened. Her eyes were flapping about. My little sister was crying, but silently now. The knife was pressing into her skin. And when I looked back at my mother, I saw water streaming down her ankles, spreading over the ground at her feet.

' "I'll go," I said, and I tugged myself loose. My mother did nothing to encourage me or to pull me back. She just stood.

'Nothing is very clear after that,' Gulu continued. 'All was confusion. All I can remember was shouting and rough hands shoving. I was trying so hard to do whatever they said. It felt like one of those nightmares when you can't open your eyes even though you are screaming. I was terrified of waking in a pool of my own blood. We were all huddled up under the meeting tree.

'I could hear my mother wailing across the village now. "Gulu, Gulu," she was crying, again and again. And it didn't sound like the gentle trickling of our stream any more. It was the sound of something that I have been trying to block out ever since.' Gulu paused. Knees hunched to his chin, he gazed silently out into the darkness. His face was blank as the night.

Muka tried to put an arm round his shoulder. But there was no response to her touch. Gulu remained fixed, fists clenched so hard that the cords on his neck sprang out. He stared out through the open doorway as if searching for something that he knew he could never find; something that lay far beyond the horizons of the other children, beyond any understanding that the pair of them might have.

Then he began speaking again in the same flat monotone.

'I don't know how long we were there, but suddenly I saw my father coming, though he couldn't see us, and he was heading towards the bridge. The youngest soldier in the squad ran to wait for him. We listened to the footsteps as my father crossed. My whole body was crying out to him. "Go back, go back," it was shouting. But he wouldn't. He knew something was happening. He was coming to help. But how could he? As soon as he arrived he was held at gunpoint.

'Until then, the squad leader had just been watching, leaning against a tree and smoking as if nothing mattered very much. Now he strolled across. 'You are against our cause,' he said to my father. My father shook his head. He looked utterly bewildered. "Do you have any last words?" asked the leader. My father didn't speak. His lips trembled but no sound came out. The leader smiled and shrugged. "Then, boy, since he hasn't got anything interesting to say you might as well do your first job."'

Gulu dropped his gaze, picked up a stick and poked at the low fire. A flurry of sparks flew glittering through the gathering silence. Shadows leaped and flickered like ghosts around the walls.

'And suddenly I realized he was talking to me,' Gulu said. 'I was being pushed out of the line. I was stumbling across the compound. They were putting a gun in my hands. I was staring down the length of its barrel. I had never held a gun in my life. The point was jerking about with every beat of my heart. My chest was so tight that I felt as if I was suffocating, but I couldn't release the pressure. Everybody was watching me. "Pull!" the leader said, "or it will be your mother and your sister and your grandmother too . . . if we can find her." They all laughed. But I didn't do anything. It was as if a storm was about to break in my head. And suddenly everything around me seemed to be falling away. I felt dizzy. I could see the leaves on the trees swaying but I couldn't feel the wind.

'My father tried to look me in the eye. He might even have tried to smile at me, but his smile was no more than a grimace of fear. He held out both hands, palms upward. I could see the beads of sweat bursting open on his brow. I watched them streaming down his face. He was speaking, he was saying something over and over, but I couldn't hear the words that came out of his mouth. I couldn't understand anything. I was far beyond that. And it came almost as a surprise to feel the kick of the gun, to see the answering jerk of his body, to look at the corpse as it rolled over in the dirt. I looked down. And I felt nothing. All I could feel was the arms of the leader circling around me. "You are one of us now. You are our brother," he was saying.

'They left the body like a rat that has had its neck broken. I only turned back to look once. It was as we were leaving. The huts were all blazing. But my mother was kneeling, she was bending over the body, she was cradling it as gently as if it was still living, as if it still meant something even though it was dead and meant nothing any more. And I knew at that moment that my whole world had changed; that I could never go

324

back. I understood at that moment that it was not that there was no right or no wrong any more: it was just that there was no right.

'From then on I lived with the army. They had made sure that I would. That's what they do to children. They make sure that their villages won't take them back. From then on the forests were my home, my squad was my family, my gun was my protector and my law was "kill or be killed". And I just kept moving onwards. It was all I could do. At least it stopped me from thinking. We just marched and pitched camp, and then marched on again. Surviving through the day was my only goal. If I found fresh food or water I felt happy, but it was only ever for a while and so it didn't seem to matter and in the end it seemed easier just to stay always sad. It's not hard to give up hope when there is no hope left at all. Once you know for sure that you can never be forgiven, then there is nothing to worry about any more.'

Gulu stopped speaking as suddenly as he had begun. He was completely drained. He lay down to sleep. Bat looked at him as he huddled on his little wooden cot, his knees drawn up to his breastbone, his fists tightly curled.

## CHAPTER THIRTY

It might have been two weeks later, it might have been three – they had lost all sense of time passing – that the children found themselves standing on a high mountain ridge gazing out over expanses of unbroken forest.

'Keep close to that river,' Yambabo was saying, pointing out the long snaking line of a watercourse far below them. It scoured its slow way through distant dusty flatlands, vanishing into the heat haze of the furthest horizon. The empty sky sang in the heat of the noon. This was not the life-giving savannah that he had grown up with, Bat thought as he squinted; this was the merciless Africa, the vast waterless land. He felt the first stirrings of fear in his gut.

Yambabo noticed. 'A man could walk for all time across that desert and never get anywhere,' he said. 'Why don't you wait for the rains to come? Why not return to the forest with us?'

The children glanced at each other uncertainly.

'There's a drought,' Yambabo urged them. 'The rains will not fall. The animals are all dying. In the villages, the pigs are frying in their own fat.'

It was Gulu who gave a firm shake of his head. A few days ago the pygmies had returned from a hunting trip with tales of huge strangers: men with black boots and guns dragging lines of ragged children with ropes around their legs. The children had looked almost starving, they said. They were stumbling and bleeding, but the men with the guns kept driving them on.

Gulu knew then that their hiding place was no longer safe. These were government soldiers the pygmies had seen. They were rounding up the rebel army, capturing the children. 'They will not be kind to those they have had to come out and capture,' he said. 'They will make an example of them. If they find us, they will kill us. They will kill us or worse.'

'But look!' Bat now cried, staring out helplessly over the emptiness that unfurled far beneath them.

'It's safer than the trees,' Gulu said. 'The forest is a trap.'

Yambabo spread his hands. He was surrendering responsibility. He had done all that he could. 'Then, if you must leave, listen carefully,' he said. 'After a few days, the river leads to a lake. There you can drink, find fresh grazing for your elephant. And from then on it is the elephant who will know where to go.'

'How many days will it take?' wondered Muka.

Yambabo just shook his head. 'I've never been so far. I'm a child of the forest. I don't leave it. I would be frightened of that.'

He was frightened now and when, that evening, they reached the ragged scrublands which lay at the thinning fringes of the trees, neither he nor his cousin who had accompanied him on this journey slept. All night, they perched on a pair of stones staring out into space, only rising every now and then to stalk about restlessly, shaking their heads. 'I'm trying to remember a tune to sing,' Yambabo told the children, 'but now no tune will come into my head.'

Even as they were about to say their farewells, he made one last attempt to convince the children they were making the wrong choice. 'The pygmies are decamping deeper into the forest,' he said. 'We are going to places that no one except us little people has ever found. There, even when the sun has risen, there will still be darkness around you. And when it is the darkness of the forest it is good, because we are the children of the forest and have no need to fear it. But out there,' he said, nodding in the direction towards which they would be going, 'is darkness of a more dangerous sort.'

Bat felt his heart gaining a sudden rapid momentum. He put his arm round Muka, felt her shrink in to his side. But Gulu stood firm.

'Don't worry about us,' he said. 'We will find a way. We have all the food you gave us.' He nodded at three little baskets of berries and mushrooms and salt meat that the pygmies had gathered for them. They were to be carried on the back with a thin string of bark slung around the brow to secure them. When Muka had at first tried to lift one onto her head, the pygmies had all giggled. Every low-hanging branch in the forest would have knocked it off, they had said. But Yambabo was not smiling now.

'Make sure that the water bottles are completely full,' he told them, leading them downwards towards a small stream. The water should have flowed fast and sparkling at this time of year, but it had shrunk to a sludgy brown trickle in the drought. They dipped in their little goat-skin bags, turn by turn. Then Meya stood, long after the others had finished, drinking and drinking until it seemed as if the whole stream would be sucked up.

Muka popped one of the little leaf hats that the pygmies had given them onto her head and peeped shyly out from under its green brim. 'Do I look like one of the forest people now?' she giggled.

But Yambabo didn't respond. 'You must lead them,' he was saying to Gulu. 'You know how to survive. Remember that a bolus of dried elephant dung will keep embers smouldering if you pack it up properly in a banana leaf. Then you can coax it back to life whenever you want.' He gazed bleakly out towards the horizon. The first light of the sun stained a long line of clouds red.

'May the gods of the ancestors go with you!'

He lifted his hand as he gave his parting words. He looked deep into Meya's eyes as if he was telling her something, and then he stood there and watched without waving as they turned.

When they looked back to give him a last sign, it was as if he and his cousin had already forgotten them.

They were standing in the stream, their skin gleaming in the low rays of the sun, giggling and talking as they splashed one another. They scooped up the water and let it pour down their bodies. It was as if they were washing every last trace of a world that was not theirs from their skin.

## CHAPTER THIRTY-ONE

For days the children walked. They would be up before dawn. They needed to get going before the sun rose. It did not come up gradually: it burst over the horizon, a glaring red ball, kindling the dry scrub and singeing the thorn trees. The hornbills that roosted among their bare branches looked gnarled as old bones that have been charred by the fire. They ruffled their feathers and squawked at the elephant as she passed.

The heat mounted fast, and with it came a dry wind that kicked up the dust. It whirled about the children in rough gritty eddies, clogging their breathing and chafing their skin. At their feet, the dead grasses had been gnawed right down to the nub. Herds of scattered grazers still tugged at the roots. But they couldn't find enough food. The once butterball-fat zebra were gaunt and lethargic. Wildebeest stood like boulders draped with moth-eaten rugs. Even the buffalo, normally so formidable, had grown too listless to do much more than shuffle. When Meya brushed right by one, shoulder grazing against horn tip, it barely even bothered to lift its blunt muzzle.

The children followed the river, as Yambabo had told them. At this time of year its flow should have been swift, spilling over the banks into emerald marshes. Now, there were only a few stagnating pools left, thick with mosquito larvae and the droppings of parched drinkers. The children had to fill up their water-skins from this slimy soup.

'It's better than nothing,' Gulu said when on the first day he noticed Muka shrinking. He seemed possessed by a new determination. 'Drink as much as you can. I don't want you flagging. I will get you back home, if it's the last thing I do.'

Muka grimaced as she took a great gulp. 'I will drink.' She took a second long draught. 'But it won't be the last thing you do.' She sucked at a third palm-full. 'You will come to live with us in Jambula,' she said, eyeing him from over the rims of cupped hands. 'You will find a new home.'

A smile hovered tremulously upon Gulu's lips. The despair that for so long had held him tight in its grip was beginning, little by little, to release its cruel fingers. 'Will you want me?' he murmured.

Bat sprang instantly towards him. He threw his arms about him. 'Always!' he shouted, almost knocking the boy flat.

For the rest of that morning the children were full

of plans as they trudged along. They talked of Jambula and the people who lived there, of Bat's grandmother and Fat Rosa and the headman and Marula and Bitek the fisherman and old Kaaka who could summon spirits up; they talked of the crops and the goats and the chickens and the cattle and, though Bat flinched deep inside when he remembered Kila, he ran through their names in his head one by one.

'Imagine their faces when they see us returning with Meya!' cried Muka. It was the first time since their escape that they had dared conjure such hopes.

But as noon drew nearer, as the sun clumped up the dome of the sky and the wind dropped and their shadows shrank to specks, they gradually fell silent.

The heat beat down on the dry earth, and then beat back up again. The skeletal thorns could offer no respite. Sweat ran down their faces; it dripped off their eyelashes and coursed down their cheeks. Meya fanned her ears constantly. She creaked as she walked, like a dry tree in the heat.

In the afternoons, when it was finally unbearable to go even a step further, they would descend to the dried river, Meya kneeling to lower herself down the crumbling bank.

'Be careful,' Muka warned the first day as they hopped across the cracked bed, jumping from one sun-bleached stone to the next as they looked for the last murky pools from which they could drink. 'Crocodiles lurk in places like this.' Like all village girls who have to go and fetch water, she feared more than anything these fierce scaly monsters that, even as they winked and pretended to slumber, would surge up to grab you between savage jaws. They didn't eat you straight away, the women always said. Instead, rolling you round and round in a whirlpool of coils, they drowned you before lodging your body in one of their muddy larders. They would then pick at your corpse like a kola-nut snack.

But the children had to risk going right to the brink. They needed the water and the grazing was often a little better on the far side of the river too. While the children ate food from their little woven baskets, Meya would pick at whatever sparse forage she could find. Twirling her trunk around the dry brittle stems, she kicked with her foot at the base of the clods, dislodging clouds of dust. Then, placing the strands in her mouth, she began slowly chewing while the whole laborious process of twirling and kicking was started over again.

When there was no grass, she had to tusk the ground for roots, stabbing the soil with short, hard prods; or stretch for the high acacia branches which most foragers couldn't reach. Their long thorny twigs had to be carefully manoeuvred, but the bark, which she peeled off in strips and then folded, was easier to manage.

But still, by the time they reached the fourth day of their journey, her belly was growling with hunger. Bat thought of the days when he would place a whole pineapple in her mouth; watch her as she crushed out the ecstatic rush of juice. He dreamed of the spreading jambula tree in his village, of the bitter-sweet freshness of its ripe fallen plums, of the soft throaty cooing of a dove in its shade; but now none of them spoke of it. They were beginning to feel the folly of their first excited hopes.

Meya longed for better times too. She was growing thin again. Her hide was beginning to sag and her back, where the ridge of her spine rose in a line of hard knobbles, was burned raw by the sun. The claws of the ox-peckers felt like sharp licks of flame. Sometimes she would pause, rumbling out a long low alarm call to her family, but the earth was too compacted to carry the vibrations. Occasionally she would trumpet through a lifted trunk, then listen for an answer, eyes downcast and ears spread. But she never got a response. The insects shrilled out their long strands of sound in the relentless noonday heat.

When the day was at its most harsh, the little band of travellers would fall asleep in whatever sparse shade they could find. But it never seemed long before they awoke, their lips parched, their tongues puffy. Sometimes wild dogs would be watching them with glittering eyes.

Not until the sun had begun its slow downward journey would the posse move on again. The air felt close as an oven. The dry grass would crackle and the ground burned their feet. Their soles began to bleed. Meya's steady lumber grew slower and slower. She breathed in short puffs that blew dust from the ground.

Then, in the late afternoon, the wind would get up again, sending storms of dust crashing across the open plains. They coated every branch of the swaying acacias, filmed every last surviving leaf of every scattered bush with red. Dust filled the children's nostrils and choked their parched throats. They tried not to drink from their water-bottles too often but, on the fifth day, Bat, in a fit of sudden desperation, drained his in one go. The water sloshed about in his belly as he walked; but his thirst was not abated. 'If anything it feels worse,' he moaned.

'Never drink too quickly,' Gulu warned him sternly. 'It just blows up your stomach without slaking your thirst. Just take a small gulp and rinse it round and round your mouth. Let it soak off the dried slime before you start, tiny bit by tiny bit, to let it trickle down your throat.'

But later that afternoon they found some tamarind beans still hanging. They were far too high for the children's clawing fingertips to reach; too high even for Meya's stretching trunk. Placing her tusks either side of the tree, bracing her great baggy legs and heaving her whole body slowly back and forth, she managed to shake it so hard that its last scattering of pods fell. Inside the hard twisted shell, the little dry beans were wrinkled and brown.

'Suck them,' Gulu said, 'and they will slowly grow softer.' The others did as he said and a welcome mouth-watering sourness began to leak out.

Wearily they plodded onwards, eyes slitted against the dust. Meya was hearing and smelling rather than seeing her way forward now. She moved with a sense of slow purpose and direction, her trunk raised in the air, sniffing the wind. The children barely spoke. They were far too thirsty. Their breath wheezed from their throats in short shallow gasps. Sometimes they would pass a dead animal lying stretched in the dirt, a zebra or antelope that had finally given up the ghost, staring up at the sky from which the water that they had longed for so desperately had never come.

'Keep going,' Gulu would encourage. 'The lake can't be too far away. There we can rest, find fresh pasture for Meya.' But though Bat and Muka would marshal their energies and, adjusting the thongs of their baskets, try to quicken their pace, it was Gulu himself who was now always lagging. His lame foot was dragging and he was troubled by a harsh cough which, when it started, would send him into chest-racking spasms. Sometimes, when he had finished, there would be blood on his lips. 'I'm all right,' he would say. 'I can go on all right.' But still Bat decided to empty out Gulu's basket so that he could carry its contents himself.

Only at sunset, would the wind finally drop. The land would smoulder in the fading red light. The children's thin shadows would lengthen upon the baked earth. Nightjars would sweep by on soft wings, scooping up flying insects. The cooling darkness would steal across the plains. The fireflies would flicker on and off in their branches. It was as if days and nights were passing in mere moments. But then time didn't mean very much any more, thought Bat. There was only ever the present, only the endless slow rhythm of their onward plodding feet.

When the moon rose vast and eerie over the desert, the whole world seemed to glow hard and brittle in its glare. Things that in the day had looked perfectly ordinary now seemed menacing presences. The tall fleshy clusters of the candelabra-like cactuses reared up in the darkness like great citadels. The children kept well away. Just to touch the white sap of these plants left a burn on the skin. Their poison would kill any animal

338

that tried to feed. And yet, sometimes, thought Muka, these lone plants seemed the only living presences to stalk the dead lands around them. Beyond was nothing but the night sky. It wept shooting stars.

Before sleeping, the children always kindled a fire from the smouldering dung that Yambabo had taught them to wrap in a leaf. Blowing on it gently, they ruffled up twists of smoke which burst into flame as dried leaves and scraps of tinder caught. Then they cooked. There was no shortage of meat, and even as the supplies in their little baskets grew lighter and lighter, Gulu cut more from the carcasses of the famine-stricken animals that they found on their path. Then, clearing sharp stones and twigs from the ground, they would dig a shallow hollow with their heels for their hips, scrape up a little heap of sand for a pillow and lie down. It was cold at night. After burning all day, they would begin to shiver. Even when they huddled together, they could never get warm. They would stare up at the sky. The stars were so far away and yet often, amid the vast expanses of the desert, they seemed to the children their closest companions.

'Maybe it might rain tomorrow,' Muka would look up and say every night. But it never did.

## CHAPTER THIRTY-TWO

As each day passed, the little posse grew weaker. The days seemed to grow hotter; the nights starker and more cold. The children's parched lips were cracked. Their joints ached all the time. Their ribs stuck out like bars on their chests. They had finished all the cassava that the pygmies had given them; eaten the nuts and the mushrooms and berries. They longed for something other than meat. But it was Meya who was starving. She looked like a spectre. All her great bulk of muscle had fallen away. Her shoulder-bones jutted and her hips jagged out through skin that hung draped in slack folds. Desperately she foraged, tusking for grass roots and devouring bitter scrub. Once she found a hidden cache of buried tubers that not only sustained her but helped take the edge off her terrible thirst.

It was the thirst that tormented them. They felt as if

they would choke on their own swollen tongues. By the sixth day of their journey, the riverbed was all but dry. The few pools that remained were no more than damp sludge. Meya swung her trunk, sniffing and snorting for water, smelling its delicious freshness far beneath the hot sand. She sunk in her tusks and began gouging, deeper and deeper. A trickle of liquid seeped into the hole. It took several minutes for even a small calabash to fill. It was thick with silt. But still they drank. And when the children had filled up their goatskins, Meya stayed there, sucking it up mouthful by tiny mouthful with the tip of her trunk. When they finally left, a cheetah slunk swiftly down after them, ears flattened, sleek body hugging low to the ground. Twitching her tail from side to side, she frantically lapped. An impala looked on. Its saffron shiny coat had dulled to a matt brown.

'A man could walk for ever across that desert and never get anywhere.' The words of Yambabo beat like a drum in the children's heads. They imagined the pygmies flitting through their shaded forests.

'Should we turn back?' Muka whispered. 'Should we turn back now while we still can?'

Bat shook his head. 'The lake can't be far away. It can't be so far to go now. And once we have rested, once Meya has fed . . .' His voice trailed away as he clutched at the girl's fragile hand. Together they glanced at Gulu. They wanted reassurance.

'There's no way back now; we can only go onwards,' he whispered.

Then, two days later, just as Bat had predicted, they saw water. It was Bat who first spotted it, shimmering in the distance; a sheet of glittering light. He tried to cry out, but his dry voice cracked. Instead he just pointed. They stopped in their tracks and stared. There it was, sparkling ahead of them: an oasis of life. Even Gulu, whose hacking cough bent him double, clenched his fists tighter and looked upwards with something like eagerness. 'Not far now, Meya!' Bat encouraged as he patted the elephant. For the first time in days they felt hopeful as they pitched their camp. They didn't even shiver when they heard the far-off roaring of lions: less a sound than the pulse of a rumbling vibration, filling the night air with its low resonance.

They got up earlier than usual the next morning and set off. There would be time to rest later. They drank more than was normal from their water-skins. 'Not long now, Meya,' Bat whispered. But the elephant didn't seem to share in their optimism. Her lumbering steps left a trail of scuffmarks in the dust to which Gulu, now lagging with his bad foot, contributed his own pattern of strange wandering strokes. It was nothing but hope that hauled him along behind the companions who, eyes fixed ahead of them, quickened their paces. They could all but taste the water's freshness as it poured down their throats.

Not *so* much further, they thought with growing desperation as the sun slowly crawled to its glowering midday heights. They inched their way onwards as it lowered itself down the far side of the sky. The lake shimmered just ahead now. 'Not so very much further,' Bat whispered as, tipping his goatskin, he drained it and pushed himself into a last run. Muka watched his frail figure slowly drawing away from her. She quickened her own pace, and for a few moments both of them were floundering, one after the other, the sand scuffing up in bursts of sparkling from their feet, until, almost as suddenly as they had begun running, they both slowed down again to a bewildered stop. They squinted desperately ahead. Surely what they were now seeing could not be right. Befuddled and frantic, they rubbed at their eyes. But a dreadful sense of reality was beginning to take hold. It was not water but a mirage of water that lay spread out ahead of them. The lake had been turned into a dustbowl by drought.

Blinking, the children picked out the shapes of huddled grazers, of wildebeest, zebra, giraffe and gazelle. Their shadowy outlines wavered in the heat as they stood gazing out over the emptiness as if collectively dazzled. The sun glittered and danced over the expanses of dried silt. The silence was eerie. It was the silence of utter despair. There was not a word in the children's mouths as, with failing steps, they walked onwards into awful truth.

Families of baboons, lean and squalid, were strung out along the banks of the empty lake, a mother with her dead baby still clutched to her belly. A skeletal impala took a high twitching step. A buffalo lay down, defeated, and groaned. A long string of mucus was dangling from its snout. It swayed as slowly it shook its cumbersome head. Spots of blood flecked its muzzle and its eyes were half closed. The vultures swarmed everywhere. They perched in the boughs of the twisted acacias, necks arched, wings outstretched, waiting to drop down upon their next feast. A zebra had barely drawn its last breath when they descended and started looting the gore, hissing and jostling and flapping and crawling, before the approach of a big cat sent them beating back up, like black angels, gobbets of flesh dangling from their greedy beaks.

Only the predators looked sleek in this dreadful place. The lions, so bloated that their stomachs brushed the ground, collapsed, moaning low songs. The dry wind brushed through their manes. Even the cheetahs were torpid, draped supine over branches from which the deserted nests of the weaver birds dangled, swaying and twisting and scattering dried twigs. Below, the hyenas skulked, sated. The children stared, appalled. The reek of death filled their nostrils, so thick they could taste it. It stickied their breathing and clung to the backs of their throats. They gazed at the flies that were scrambling over everything. The whole grisly scene was alive with their hum.

Water had been there until recently, Gulu noticed; perhaps until only a few days ago. There was a frill of wilted grass around a patch of damp soil. A vicious baboon guarded it, yellow fangs bared, but when Meya raised her trunk it shuffled reluctantly aside, grunting in fury and slapping the ground with its fists. Smashing through the crust, Meya found a soft ooze. She lowered herself to her knees, rocking slowly back and forth, coating her burned skin with a thick paste of mud. Bat could smell the stench of rotting catfish. An antelope crept a step closer, hoping that there might be water. But it was no good.

Images of the past rose up like mad hallucinations in Bat's head. He thought of the days when Meya had bathed near the village, descending the banks in a splashing avalanche, setting the geese flurrying in clouds of indignant honking; the flamingo flocks scattering like wisps of sunset. The hippos would sigh gratefully as they sank into the papyrus; but now all he could see were the arches of their stripped bones. It was as if he was standing in a world that had been drained.

# CHAPTER THIRTY-THREE

Bat felt like a drowning man swept away by the currents. It was strange, he thought, as he plodded wearily on, to feel as if you were drowning when the whole world was dry, when all you could dream about was the coolness of water, when all you could think about was its taste on your tongue. But he no longer felt as if his fate belonged to him. His life lay in the hands of the land that he crossed. The desert could do with them whatever it liked.

He walked on, because he could think of no reason to stop. Nature had been filed right down to the bone in this place. It was unforgiving as rock. The dead scrub was black. Above it the burning air quivered and shone. The scream of the insects was like the dazzle of the sun. Mirages glittered and bullied. Sometimes he would see familiar shapes among them, the low huts of his village squatting on the skyline, the silhouette of his grand-mother coming to meet him; but he never held out his hands to greet her. He knew that it was only the sun's cruel trick. The air was alive. It flickered like a flame over the face of the earth, shining and waving like a sheet of running water, dancing and mirroring and duping and doubling, conjuring up fantasies and then dissolving them again.

The children's pace grew steadily slower and slower. The marks of their footsteps were more and more falter-ing. Gulu's bad foot dragged a juddering line in the dust. 'You have to keep going,' Bat whispered. He couldn't speak any louder. His tongue, when he tried, stuck to the roof of his mouth. It felt fat as a puff adder lodged in a dry cranny. 'If we stop we will die,' he breathed.

The landscape started to undulate now: an endless succession of ridges, each rising slightly higher than the last. This might be the final climb, they would think as they laboured; there might be water on the far side. They would inch towards the summit in a growing delir-ium of anticipation, but from the top they would see yet another barren horizon, the low clouds straggling above it like a broken promise.

Each time the disappointment was almost too much to bear. 'Please!' Bat would whisper inside his head. 'Please!' All his hopes had shrunk to this one imploring word. It fell like a raindrop in the dust of his thoughts.

Lumbering up each long slope, they half slid, half tumbled down the far side. Their breath burned in their throats. Their skin baked and shrivelled. The blood throbbed in their skulls. Soon it became the

347

only sound they could hear. They passed the wreckages of animals that had died on their journeys. A vulture dragged a limp snake along in its talons. It scuffed away the marks of their footprints and buried their scent. It was as though death was eradicating their very traces, Bat thought.

Meya walked as if she had fallen into a trance. There was nothing about this land that felt familiar to her now. She didn't know where she was. In the great thunderhead of her brow, there were no memories at all. She just continued southwards, the heat of the falling sun the only sign of her direction. The flies scabbed her raw flesh; but when she paused to spray dust it was all scattered by the wind. The flies rose and dropped back in a thick buzzing clot.

One day they found a small fetid pool in a rock and they shared it, and towards the end of the next day they came across a baobab. Meya could smell the hot wisps of water and paused, and Muka, standing on Bat's shoulders, hauled herself up into its branches. A monitor lizard, busy raiding an abandoned bird's nest, sprang through the air and fell hissing, its yellow belly flashing before it landed, splayfooted, and scuttled furiously off. A drowned bat floated in the slime that scummed over a deep hollow in the trunk, but still the desperate children drank and afterwards, lifting her trunk, Meya drained the reservoir dry. It was only a fraction of what she needed but it was just enough.

The ground was growing stonier now. It gleamed a poisonous mauve-blue in the low evening light. That night, when the children stopped, it was as if their soles had been sliced with the blade of a knife. They tried to separate the grit from the flesh but they couldn't. Without the heat to anaesthetize it, the pain was almost unbearable and it kept them from sleep. The following morning Gulu could hardly move. His lame foot wept yellow pus and, despite the chillness of dawn, his face burned to the touch. He put his cold hands to his cheeks to try to warm them, then bent over double, shaken by racking coughs. When he tried to rise, his thin legs folded under him and he collapsed back into the little hollow he had dug. Muka and Bat did their best to lift him. Holding him under the arms, they began dragging him along. But it was no good. They did not have the strength.

'Leave me,' whispered Gulu. 'I'm a hindrance now, not a help. I can't walk. Go on without me. Let Meya lead you.'

Muka shook her head. 'You must come,' she said. 'We won't go without you. We're going to take you with us.'

'You must come,' Bat echoed. His voice was a creak in his throat. 'You have to keep going. It can't be far now.'

Gulu barely responded. He couldn't see that future which, for a few bright moments, he had glimpsed. He was slipping back into the shadowy world of his past. Bat could see the despair brooding beyond falling eyelids. However far the boy travelled, however much distance he covered, Bat thought, he would never manage to leave his dark memories behind. They would rise back up within him with the rising of every sun.

'When I was a child, I thought that the dawn was beautiful,' Gulu murmured, as the first red light of the sun

349

stained the far-off horizon. 'Now I just think of blood. It's too late for me now. Just leave me here.'

The two children stepped back uncertainly. They didn't know what to do. They searched his eyes for an answer, but no answer came. And then, in what felt like a moment suspended in magic, Meya moved slowly forward. Stretching out her trunk, she lifted the boy's fragile body as tenderly as a mother, weary after her day in the shamba, lifts her sleeping baby. She placed him onto her back. He slumped over her neck, and then slowly she moved forward: the great African elephant that remains always untameable and the broken human child.

They were moving into a land of huge multi-spurred termite mounds now. Dried vegetation was beginning to crackle underfoot and in the far distance they could see a single ridge rising. Somewhere over its horizon, they prayed, their home lay.

Flat clouds drifted above. For days the children had stared at them, willing them to gather, to muster their forces and swell; but with the rising of the sun they had always been routed. In tatters and straggles they had faltered and dispersed. But now, as the children watched them, the clouds rolled and tumbled. They were massing their strength against the sun's onslaught. That evening Bat heard a Kori bustard calling.

'It means rain,' he whispered. 'It means rain, Gulu,' he repeated, clutching at the boy as he balanced on the elephant above. 'When herdsmen hear the bustard, they start out for their pastures. The rain isn't far off.'

Gulu didn't respond.

The next day they followed the tracks of an ostrich. It

was almost as though its claw-prints were towing them along. And even though the prints ended in a bloody scuffle, the pads of a lioness blotting out the bird's splayed marks, the strewn feathers stirred in a wind that for the first time felt soft.

Ahead of them reared the slope of a sudden steep incline. Bat braced himself for the gruelling ascent. Wearily he climbed, Muka struggling behind him, one dragging foot planted in front of the next. The dusty air scoured their lungs. Meya's breath came painfully in stertorous grunts. Gulu clung to her neck, but he didn't look up.

And then they were at the top, standing on the brink of a vast windswept ledge. The cliffs fell all but sheer to the bottom far below them. But the children gazed over the grasslands that rolled away ahead: a dizzying vastness that reached to the furthermost rim of the world. This was the savannah, Bat thought. His heart thumped as he reached out for Muka. They were standing on the escarpment. These were the rocks that for so long had formed the horizon of their lives. Somewhere down below them lay the place they called home.

'Look, Gulu! Look!' he cried, his voice cracked by the tears which his body was too dry to send. The little boy raised his head weakly. He felt his burning face cooled by the draughts from Meya's great flapping ears. But his dark eyes were glazed and his grasp was so weak that, when the elephant moved, Bat and Muka now had to walk either side of her, holding his dangling legs so that he would not slip.

For a while they followed the line of the cliff edge.

Bat remembered the words of the fisherman Bitek: sometimes the elephants would be away for as long as three years, he had said, travelling secret paths that led over the escarpment. Was Meya searching for one of these ancient ways now? Did she know a track home? He felt something change place somewhere deep inside him. It was the groundswell of despair giving way to a fresh surge of hope.

Then, suddenly, Meya was branching off, stumbling down a ravine that looked utterly impassable. She eased herself through a gap between two massive boulders. Gulu slid down her neck. He was clutching at her ears. But the elephant was unstoppable. She picked her way purposefully onwards down a dried watercourse, pushing through tangles of dead vegetation, forging a path so obscure that no one, Bat thought, could possibly ever have tried it. He tucked himself close in behind her. There was nothing that he and Muka could do now but trust.

Inch by skidding inch, Meya continued her descent. Probing at uncertain stones with her trunk, grasping at dried roots and testing loose stones, she transferred her great bulk from one treacherous foothold to the next. The rays of a lowering sun beat against the cliff, frying them like ants on a griddle of hot rock. How much longer could this go on? Bat wondered. How much longer before they slipped?

Just at that moment, Meya stopped. Reaching behind her, she twined her trunk around Gulu and, lifting him gently, laid him down on the ground. Then she knelt on her hind legs to lower herself over a rocky lip. For a few heart-stopping seconds Bat was sure she would fall. But no . . . she was safe . . . she stood waiting below. Muka scrambled down next, hanging from the ledge by her hands before she let herself drop. Then Bat passed Gulu down into her outstretched arms. It was easy. He weighed little more than a bundle of dry kindling. He groaned as she grasped him and then doubled up in a fit of frame-racking coughs. Bat and Muka bent over, putting their arms round his back to support him. His shoulder-blades felt sharp as wings.

It was only when they stood up again that they saw for the first time that they had reached a wide plateau: a magical platform poised midway between earth and sky. A huge cave was cut into the wall of the rock behind them. Meya had already entered. Picking Gulu up, they followed the elephant in. It was cool inside; blissfully cool: like plunging your face into a calabash of cold water. And somewhere far at the back they could hear a faint trickling. They blundered into the darkness. Meya was already there, sucking and sucking, as if she could never stop.

It was only the thinnest of runnels, Bat realized as he stretched his fingertips towards it; but it was fresh and clean, springing straight from some repository hidden deep in the rock. Scooping handful after handful, he and Muka drank desperately. Then they returned for Gulu, pouring cupped palms of water into his blistered gape. They moistened his face and bathed his burning temples. They splashed his hot limbs and cleaned the pus from his foot. And then they returned to drinking themselves.

Outside, where a waterfall would have plunged downwards in the rainy season, they saw whiskery grasses still growing about the fringes of the rocks. Meya was wrenching them up in swift eager mouthfuls, the first scraps of fresh fodder she had tasted for many days. Hank after hank, she swept it into her mouth. Her gut whined and groaned. Bat pulled out the last of the salt meat that the pygmies had given them, and he and Muka ate too, but Gulu waved it away.

'Take it.' Muka bent over him, gently encouraging. But Gulu couldn't see them. The cave was so dark, and yet the light in his head was too bright. He was shivering, but his brain was boiling. 'Let me rest,' he sighed and he lay down to sleep on a bed of dried leaves.

They left him and went out. A bush of marula plums grew nearby. The fruit had all fallen and fermented, but with cries of delight the children gathered it up in damp handfuls, cramming it eagerly between parted lips. Streams of sticky sourness flowed down their chins, running down wrists and forearms, dripping from elbows and splashing onto feet. Meya feasted beside them, her eyes closed in sheer relish, as she mashed at vast mouthfuls of pulp. But when Muka carried some into the cave for Gulu, when she shook him to rouse him, he just lay without lifting his head.

'I can't eat now,' he murmured, and his eyes closed again.

With one hand behind his thin neck, she lifted him, squeezing the acid succulents between parted lips. 'They will help you sleep better,' she pleaded. The juices ran down Gulu's throat and the boy swallowed weakly. Then he lapsed once again into a fit of violent coughs. Muka could feel his skin burning. His whole body was trembling. She wanted to hold him against her; she wanted to promise that it would all be all right; but, the spasm now over, the boy's eyes were once again closing. Gently she laid his head back down again and Gulu, turning on one side, folded himself inwards, drawing knees up to elbows, and lay without stirring. His fists were clenched tight as a pleader's before his parted mouth.

The fermenting plums were making them all feel faintly giddy. Even the elephant was blinking and swaying. They looked dizzily about. Hastily, Bat set to work in the cave, coaxing a fire from the embers that he carried. Kneeling, he blew at the sparks, fanning the flame gently, feeding it fragments of dry tinder until it finally leaped up. Shadows flickered over the walls of rock. A flock of bats scudded outwards into the twilight and, following them, the children sat at the rocky mouth, watching the sun as it slipped below the far horizon, the gathering clouds flaming bright vermilion and gold. The first stars began to appear. Soon the heavens would be studded with millions upon millions, packed sharp and close as a porcupine's quills.

Meya's tusks glinted silver in the moon's rising light. The children gazed up at her. But neither of them would have dared at that moment to have reached out and touched her. She seemed somehow transformed, somehow magical, they both thought. It was as if she had been invested with some power that lay far beyond them; as if she was part of a lost world that they would never reach. Quietly she stood there, silhouetted against

355

the great darkness, a vast looming presence as ancient as the prehistoric rocks.

Only when it was dark did they turn back to go into the cave. Gulu was calling. 'Look! Look!' he was crying. He was stretching his arms out and pointing. His black eyes were glittering. Bat and Muka peered through a darkness that was hazed with drifting smoke. And it was then that they saw it: a great elephant appearing, a huge shadowy form painted onto the surface of the rock. A tiny calf peeped out from under her belly, and nearby a man with an armful of firewood had been drawn, and a mother carrying the bundle of a baby on her back.

The children stared transfixed. This was the cave that the pygmies had told them about, the secret haven that only the elephants now knew. This was a place that went back to a time before history, to the days when man and elephant had walked side by side. Bat felt a chill at the back of his neck, as if some hidden presence was blowing upon him softly. But Meya merely lumbered over to lick at a rock. There were minerals here too for the elephants.

They slept deeply that night. Meya made a bed of mulch at the rear. Sighing and grunting she shifted until finally she settled, leaning her rump against the cave wall, while the children curled up nearby round the warm fire. It must have been somewhere near the middle of the night when they woke. The embers had faded to a rich orange glow and Gulu was calling out, as he so often did in his sleep.

'I'm sorry, I'm sorry,' he cried in the blackness. But this time he was not dreaming; he was sitting up. His thin legs were folded into arms of stretched sinew. The knobbled blades of his shoulders stuck out from his back. 'I'm sorry, so sorry,' he called to the night. The tears that, until then, he had always kept locked up in his head now flowed down his face. His sorrow and grief were pouring out in a flood. And, as if the dark world was lying there and waiting and listening, a long rumble of thunder rolled answering back. Great bolts of lightning broke open the skies. They lit up the cave with their eerie blue light, flashing over the carvings until they flickered with a mystical life.

When the children woke again at dawn, Gulu was sleeping. They could see his pulse flickering, a faint beat in his temple, but he looked calmer, more peaceful. His fear had passed. His face was still hot but his brow was smooth and clear and a smile drifted over his wide face as he woke. He looked like a little child again, Bat thought. When Muka put her arm around him, he did not shrug her off. He let her support him, while she lifted a palm full of water to his lips. 'This is a lovely home,' he whispered. 'I would like to stay here for ever.' And he looked at the carvings on the rocky walls. 'Did the wild elephant really carry me?' he asked in a voice full of wonder.

It was extraordinary how quickly the clouds appeared, as if conjured out of nowhere. One moment they had been streaking the rim of the horizon; the next, blown by the gusts of sudden fierce wind, they were massing and swelling and racing out across the sky. A little after noon, the wind dropped abruptly. The air thickened.

357

Then the whole world turned black. Bat waited in silence. The quietness was eerie. He could hear nothing but the piping of a plaintive hornbill. Everything seemed frozen, all motion suspended, as if every living creature was holding its breath. Then, suddenly, the silence broke with a great earth-shaking crash. Thunder rolled through the trees, echoing off the escarpment, rumbling back outwards in waves over the plain's dry expanse. Lightning flashed and hissed. Bat, crouching by the entrance of the cave, could almost taste it, sour as a piece of tarnished metal in his mouth.

A splat fell on his skin. It was a raindrop: and then another and another and yet another fell; plopping fat to the ground and pitting the dust. A few moments later, Bat heard a loud rattling. And then a sheet of rain swept across the mouth of the cave. It lashed down in ropes as thick as his fingers, crashing and beating upon the undergrowth. Where a minute ago there had been a dried watercourse, a surging torrent now raced, rushing between rocks as it tore its mad pathway, rearing and plunging as it hurled towards the great drop. It fell sheer down the cliff face, flinging out a cloud of spray.

Bat, Muka and Meya ran out into the storm, laughing and trumpeting in their wild delight. They gazed up, exhilarated, into the skies, their shouts and their squeals ringing out from the rocks. The water clung to their eyelashes and streamed down their cheeks, dribbling from elbows and tails and ear tips. They lay down and rolled in it and stood up covered in mud. Then they flung out their limbs and let it wash them again. At last, at long last, the rains had arrived.

The storm eventually passed. The downpour grew steadier, the rain slowly thinned. Patches of blue started appearing in the clouds. Sunlight flashed and sparkled. It glinted off stones and dripped from wet trees. Below, the parched plains sucked in the lying flood. Steam rose like a mist as the land gave up its stored heat. A lone rainbird called, its notes falling like water, and the children stood, heads cocked and listening. Their faces were almost broken in two by their smiles. 'We look like a pair of wet chickens,' Muka laughed. Bat gave a loud squawk. A glimmering rainbow leaped across the sky. It spanned its great dome, shining as brightly as if it had been painted on.

Then they heard Gulu calling, and they both ran in. He was lying on his back, staring up at the walls. 'Am I home?' he cried out to them. 'I am home,' he said. 'I can hear my stream. I can hear my stream calling me. "Gulu," it's saying. "Gulu . . . Gulu," as it runs down the rocks.'

Muka knelt over him. She damped his brow with fresh water. She could feel it still burning, but his hand in her own was chill. 'Mama?' he muttered. 'Mama, is that you?'

'Gulu, it's me, Muka. It's Muka,' she cried.

'Mama,' he answered and he tried to sit up. He was whispering. Both children leaned closer to hear what he said. But his words were like lizards on the walls of a hut. He couldn't catch them. They kept slipping back into the crevices of his thoughts. He stared at the carvings as if transfixed. Then he turned his head sideways and gazed slowly at Meya. His lips were framing lost syllables.

The elephant reached out for him with a slow gentle trunk. She laid it upon him like a father lays his blessing on a son. There was a look of infinite understanding in her eyes. But Gulu's own eyes were withdrawing. He was vanishing, sinking further and further away into his own world of thoughts. His last breath was fading. Bat slid a hand inside the boy's shirt. He thought he could still feel the flutter of a heartbeat, but it was only the blood beating in his fingertips. Gulu's own hands, always clutched into a fist, had slowly uncurled. They lay open amid the leaves. It was as if, at long last, he had finally managed to let something go.

The rain dripped steadily from the mouth of the cave, falling and landing in a pool of lying water. Droplets leaped out from the surface where they struck. They jumped up and down like soldiers marking time on the spot.

# CHAPTER THIRTY-FOUR

All that day the children remained high on their hidden plateau. They were mourning the life of the friend they had lost.

'Without him we would never have made it,' Bat whispered. 'Without him I don't think I could have survived the camp.' Tears streamed down his face as he remembered how they had shared not just a blanket together, but the comfort of each other's closeness on those long cold army nights. 'He could have come home with us,' he sobbed. 'He could have lived as our brother.'

'He saved us,' Muka murmured. 'Without him we would never have found a way out. And he was prepared to give his life for us,' she whispered as, bathing his body in their tribal ritual of cleansing, she thought back to that moment when he had left them behind in the crawlspace, ready to face the wrath of the Leopard alone rather than give up his two hidden friends.

Together the two children drank water beside Gulu's dead body as a sign that, as his clans-people, they shouldered their part in his life. Muka drew the line around his body, which would have to serve as a fence around his grave. Bat cut a stick for the spear which, in their traditional ceremony of forgiveness, would have been solemnly broken as a symbol that all violence had been finally renounced.

Meya waited quietly until all their rites were over. Only then did she approach, lifting one of Gulu's fallen hands and then laying it back down softly, brushing the lifeless body with the tip of her trunk. Then, gently, she covered it with a coffin of branches, as elephants often did in their own ceremonies for the dead.

'This place felt like his home,' Muka murmured. 'It was here for the first time that I ever saw him find peace. His spirit will be happy to return to this place.'

All day the three travellers rested and stood guard over Gulu. Sometimes Bat and Muka spoke of their memories, sometimes they sobbed or smiled. More often they just sat in meditative silence, listening to the birds as they chirruped and rustled, the rush of the river as it spouted over the rocks. Clouds of white butterflies fluttered over the bushes. An iguana hoarded its trove of sunlight. Muka watched a small dark snake sliding like an arrow through the undergrowth. Slipping into the water, it glimmered like a living rainbow.

From the lip of the escarpment, the children could clearly see the course of the river, a silvery vein of new

362

life winding out across the earth. A fresh tinge of green was already covering the ground and amid it they could see the scattered dots of distant grazers. They were all feeding eagerly for the first time in several months.

Soon they would be down there in that world, the children thought. And the next day, bowing their heads in a last sorrowful farewell to Gulu, they set off. Neither of them could see a way to get down that great cliff. But Meya, in the lead, didn't pause. Barely waiting to check that the scrabbling children could keep up with her, she forged her steady path back up onto the escarpment's lip. She seemed in a great hurry now. She strode along, scenting urgently, ears flared and trunk stretched.

Huge clumps of scrub had slipped away down the cliff in the rain. They left raw fan-shaped smears on the face of the rock. How would they ever get down there? Bat wondered. It looked completely impossible. But Meya was more confident. She pushed on ahead, continuing without pausing for what felt a long while before suddenly plunging down the slopes of a ravine so steep that the children had to clutch at exposed roots to stop themselves from sliding.

At the bottom the path levelled and grew suddenly easy again. Meya ate hungrily as she walked, snapping at boughs and cramming their bursting foliage into her mouth. The children gazed around them in delight at so much green. The smell of wet leaf mould filled the air, and sometimes they found themselves moving through patches of sticky sweet fragrance. Opening blossoms draped the damp air with their scent. Doves gurgled. It sounded like water pouring from a narrow-necked jar,

Muka thought. A troupe of black-and-white monkeys bounded through the trees overhead, their feathery tails flowing in the wind of their flight. Once they saw a leopard slipping low through the trees, a newly caught bird still flapping feebly in its mouth. It gave a muffled grunt of alarm and the children heard the high answering miaow of a kitten hidden somewhere not far off. They hurried on by as fast as they could.

It was only on the evening of the second day that Meya slackened her urgent pace. She stopped in a wide forest clearing to feed, stuffing in grasses which, releasing their rich juices, sent dribbles of green running down her bristly chin. Swathe after swathe she greedily plucked. And then, suddenly, she stopped. Bat and Muka saw her tense. The whites of her eyes rolled as she lifted her head and, raising her trunk, let its load of stems fall. Her pale tusks gleamed in the low evening light. She uttered a piercing squeal.

For several minutes the children heard nothing. They waited, hearts pounding, and then came the first sound of movement far off in the trees. They strained their ears: it was a low scuffing noise, almost as if something heavy was being dragged through the brush. Bat recognized it instantly. A dizzy rush of excitement flooded his brain. He closed his eyes for a moment, and when he opened them again a great shadowy form was emerging from the shadows. It loomed up before them. Bat's blood raced. Clutching at Muka, he drew her slowly backwards towards the edge of the clearing. This was the matriarch. This was the leader of Meya's herd.

The huge animal paused for a moment. A loud,

high-pitched rumble rolled out. It was a sound that produced an instant reaction in Meya. The two elephants were moving rapidly towards one other. When they were only a short way apart, they broke into a run, coming together in a turmoil of flapping ears and shrill screaming; of jubilant trumpeting and loud clicking tusks. And then they lifted their heads together and, twining their trunks, rumbled so deeply that it rolled through the trees like the breaking of a storm. Only then did the rest of the herd emerge, spinning and backing in their wild excitement, trampling the clearing and breaking down bushes, rubbing and leaning upon their lost friend. They slipped their trunks into her grass-stained mouth. Muka, who had never before witnessed this exuberant greeting ceremony, stared round-eyed with amazement. Tears of sheer happiness coursed down Bat's cheeks.

Only after several minutes did the elephants settle. The cows slowly calmed and began to feed. They were thin, Bat noticed: very thin. Their skin hung from gaunt bodies in deep leathery folds, and the little calves that now crept curiously out from their mother's legs were as wrinkled and wobbly as a litter of new-born dogs.

That night, Bat and Muka moved amid a forest of huge feet, and when the whole family lay down, one by one, on their sides, they too slept. Curled up amid the sound of the elephants' deep rhythmic breathing, they felt as if some great canopy had been stretched out above them, protecting them from the night with its slow puffing breaths.

In the morning the children rose with the dew wet on their skins. The elephants were ready to leave. The matriarch rumbled as she shambled towards the edge of the clearing. She wanted to lead her herd back to the plains; to take them to the river where the grasses would be sprouting and the leaves lushly unfurling.

Meya lingered uncertainly while Muka stroked her rough flank. She was humming a low song. But Bat could not speak. His heart was bursting. He knew that without the elephant beside them they would have been lost. His feelings welled up so thickly that he thought he would choke.

Meya stared into his face with her deep guileless eyes and Bat, blinking away the tears that swam blearily before him, stared back into depths of that infinitely trusting look. With the flat of his palm, he softly stroked her trunk.

At the edge of the clearing, the matriarch was rumbling, flapping her ears and swinging her foot.

'Go on, Meya, my little one,' he whispered as he pushed her. It was not like his first parting. He knew now that he had never lost her. And slowly Meya turned and, with her long graceful lumber, strolled off. She looked back only once, at the fringes of the forest. A low vibrating rumble rolled out across the air. The two children waved.

'Thank you, Meya, thank you. Thank you!' they called.

She lifted her trunk in a last farewell; then melted back silently into the trees with her herd.

# CHAPTER THIRTY-FIVE

Bat started to recognize trees and rocks. They were nearly home. *Not long now*, he kept thinking, and each time a surge of excitement would rush through his head. He thought of his grandmother. His pulse would flicker and skip. And then his worries would steady it. What if she wasn't there? What if the child army had raided the village? What if she was dead? Then his head would fall silent as a pen of goats after nightfall. He would try to focus on nothing except the movement of his feet. The red soil of the jungle was giving way to a paler sticky mud. It dragged at their steps.

And then, suddenly, turning a corner they came upon the honey-gatherer, his broad-face fogged by the smoke that puffed up in clouds from the fat roll of leaves that he held between his lips. When he saw the children coming, he drew it from his mouth and wiped the sweat from his brow.

'Will you help me to carry this back to the village?' He nodded over his shoulder at the comb that was slung dripping from his back. It was as if they had never been away, Bat thought. Perhaps he didn't recognize them?

'I'm looking forward to a plate of your grandmother's groundnut stew,' he said.

The hearts of both children leaped.

And then they were leaving the shade of the forest, walking down the dirt track that wound southwards, away from the escarpment. The ground that for so long had baked in the sun had now been turned to red clay. It squeezed through their toes and made them laugh as they slipped. There was a strong smell of wet earth and new grass on the wind. A flock of tiny red birds alighted, all twittering, and Bat heard the familiar call of the francolin. Crickets were chirruping from the unfurling bushes and a carpet of pink flowers unrolled across the plains. In the distance they could see the smoke of the village, the roofs of the huts squatting low to the earth.

A herd of cattle, thin as grasshoppers, foraged not far away, and Bat, hearing a familiar whistle, saw a little boy leap up. He stopped abruptly and stared as he saw the group approaching, and then, as they drew closer, ran bounding towards them, dancing and capering, his face split wide in a grin. It was Bim. The cattle, suddenly recognizing the figure of their old herder, were now trotting obediently in the direction of Bat, but

Bim dashed off. He ran for the village, arms waving and whistling as hard as his breathing would let him.

Bat wanted to drop his basket of honeycomb and start to run too; but the honey-gatherer was sauntering along calmly ahead of him, almost as if he did not know the meaning of haste. Bat recognized the way the wind fell on his face now. It was the feeling of home. He grinned at Muka. His thoughts were racing. Every step he took felt as if it was releasing him. He could hear the sound of the pounding cassava pestles now, see the women who were gathering at the end of the track, jostling and shouting and pointing as they started towards him, their children tagging behind them and tugging at the hems of their wraps. He recognized the bright turban of Marula, the legless woman, carried high on the back of one of her strong sons. He heard the loud ringing laugh of Fat Rosa . . . and was that Bitek the fisherman who was pushing his way to the front? Bat's heart was bursting open like a blooming hibiscus.

And then, there, in a space that was opening between them, was the figure of his grandmother. Hitching up her wrap with one hand, she was raising the other to her brow and squinting. Dropping his basket, Bat grabbed at Muka's hand and the pair tore down the track, arms flailing, feet slipping, eyes shining with light. She did not call out to them; but amid the hush of the watchers, her silence struck sparks that were bright as pure joy. Her old face shone with new light. The children fell into her embrace. They filled up their lungs with her dry wood-smoke smell. They clutched

369

tightly around each other as they laid their heads on her heart.

Far, far above, in the last fading dazzle of the dying sun, an eagle screamed. Its cry rang out like a peal of laughter that made a ring around the world.

# EPILOGUE

No one knew what had happened to Lobo. Some said he had been shot by the government soldiers sent into the forests to rout the child army; others whispered that he was still out there, wandering lost in the trees. A goat herder swore that he had met someone whose uncle had seen him mending bicycles in the town; but another man who seemed to be equally sure said that he had become a corporal and was living in the land across the mountains. A nomadic tribesman had met him at a border post, he said; he had even mentioned the viper scar.

All the villagers knew was that Lobo had vanished from Jambula as surely as the smoke from the medicine woman's fire. 'He will never come back now,' his mother had told them and, following their tribal custom, she had laid four large stones outside the door of her hut.

They marked the site where his body would have been laid had it ever come back.

But then one day a stranger was seen approaching the village: a wavering outline upon the horizon inching closer and closer, his broad frame supported by a stick. It was Lobo returning, limping like a lost spirit through the lands where he had once lived. He had been in prison, he said. He had been starved and beaten and his leg had been broken, and now he had come back because he had nowhere else to go.

Bat had a hut of his own in the village by then. It was close to his grandmother's. The same blue and yellow flowers spilled from the old paint tins that had been nailed to the lintels and he was sitting beneath them when the news reached him.

'Lobo! Lobo is back!' It was one of Fat Rosa's grand-sons who came running to tell him. Even in the soft warmth of a low evening sun, Bat felt himself shiver. For a long while he said nothing. He just sat. Behind him, through the doorway, he could hear someone singing. He listened to the low gentle hum of the voice and, so faint he could barely even hear it, the small snuffling murmurs of his newborn baby son.

He dropped his head in his hands. His heart flooded with anger. He folded his fists as dark memories rose up around him. They bumped about in his mind like black flies around a wound. They filled the air with their buzz.

'Let them go.' It was his grandmother who was now standing before him. 'Throw your heart out in front of you and then run ahead to catch it,' she said.

Several more minutes passed. Bat's grandmother waited until finally he looked up. She laid her old wrinkled hand on his head. 'When two elephants fight, it's the grass that suffers,' she told him. 'Lobo was cruel. But he had had cruelty shown to him. Now he is broken. Let him find a better way to mend.'

That evening a young couple left the village. Side by side, they kept pace as they went down the track. He was tall, lithe and strong with a quick, agile gait. She had a spring in her step, like the bounce of a ball, which set her braids swinging. The tassels of her wrap fluttered out behind as she walked. A little snuffling bundle was slung on her back.

When they got to the river, they both sat down and waited. A herd of elephants was grazing in the distant brush and one of them, spotting the two people watching, looked up and ambled across. The couple stood up at once, and the woman, unfastening the blanket that was knotted around her shoulders, gathered a tiny kicking baby into her arms. She held it out to the animal and hummed a low song.

For a few moments the elephant just blinked. Then, reaching out gently, trunk tip to naked tummy, she blew softly until the child chuckled and squirmed and stretched out chubby hands to clutch. The elephant seemed delighted and shook her great head.

Suddenly, she turned, but even as she shambled away she was watching, as if checking that the couple were not thinking of leaving. She slipped into the brush. The young mother, talking softly to her husband and smiling, bundled her baby back up into its blanket and, wiping the dampness of the elephant's touch from its skin with one corner, knotted it firmly again round her back.

A short while later the elephant returned. This time she was not alone. A tiny crumpled creature was tripping along at her feet, peeping out coyly from behind the barricade of her legs. Its trunk bobbed up and down like a piece of elastic. Its ears were snug as two cabbage leaves folded round its head.

And the faces of the young man and his wife spread in a pair of broad smiles. Each reached out for the other, their hands joining together in a movement that linked their shared memories and carried them both back to their own childhoods. But neither drew closer to the tiny wild creature. The other elephants paused in their grazing to look, shifting and snorting and warily shuffling. The man scanned them watchfully with a herdsman's keen eye. The old matriarch that he had known as a child was no longer with them. It was the mother of the tiny creature who now, turning slowly away from him, swung her leg to and fro and gave the soft 'let's go' call. She ambled away, the herd gathering behind her, drawing the stumbling newborn into its protective heart. It was she who took the lead as they drifted away into the fading light.

Bat and Muka watched the elephants go, retreating across the vast spaces of the endless savannah as if they had some appointment to keep with the end of the world.

# AFTERWORD

This story is a fiction, but it finds its roots in fact. In 1986, a Ugandan warlord named Joseph Kony launched a rebellion against his country's government. But what began as a fight for the rights of the Acholi tribe, soon escalated into a brutal guerrilla war. For more than twenty years, Kony rampaged through Northern Uganda, turning on his own people, accusing them of betraying him, of sinning against God. His rebel army – The Lord's Resistance Army – has been responsible for the kidnapping of thousands of children. Thousands of young boys and girls, just like Bat and Muka, have been captured and forced to fight. Their parents have been driven from their farms and murdered. Their villages have been burned. The stories of Bat and Muka and the people they meet are based on written testimonies of these children, and on interviews which I did with them in Northern Uganda.

Although Kony, at the time of writing, has still not been caught, his Lord's Resistance Army has at last been driven out of Northern Uganda. Families are returning to the farms which for so many years they had been forced to abandon. They are picking up the pieces of their broken lives. There are many charities which try to help them. They work on the rehabilitation of the former child soldiers and on the rebuilding of their rural communities. One of them is Send-A-Cow Uganda, a non-governmental organisation. If you are interested in reading more about it, or in trying to help, you can look up their website: www.sendacowuganda.org

The African elephant is also entering a time of extreme peril. These magnificent creatures are being pushed to extinction, by the poachers who slaughter them mercilessly for their ivory, and by the loss of their habitats, as they are increasingly forced to compete with humans for territories that were once theirs alone. Great beasts like Meya could have completely disappeared from this planet in your lifetime if something does not change. There are several conservation charities which work to prevent this. Among them is Tusk, which runs field projects right across Africa. These work not only to protect endangered species such as the elephant, but also to encourage sustainable development and education among the rural communities who live alongside them. If you want to know more about Tusk or would like to support it then you can look up its website: www.tusk.org

# ACKNOWLEDGEMENTS

I would like to thank my agent Georgina Capel and Rachel Conway of Capel Land for their winning combination of ebullience and measured advice; inspirational publisher David Fickling and his assistant Matilda Johnson; Hannah Featherstone and Lauren Bennett at Random House and Bella Pearson, my editor, who turned the book around with her invaluable expertise.

I am hugely grateful to my first readers: Alex Gilbert who marked the manuscript as diligently as any school English teacher; Xavier and Jude Woodcock who nagged their mother to read another chapter every night; and Ellie Miles, my god-daughter, who was so percipient.

I would also like to thank Josh Nickerson and Jess Denyer for practising being parents while I was away in Africa; Alfie Nickerson for giving me more than just my opening line and Ella Nickerson for being such a loveable step daughter.

Thank you to my father and mother, my sisters Anna and Tid and my brother Ben for their unflagging support and for putting up with so many elephant conversations. Alice Miles was, as always, an inspiration – but this time quite literally. Catherine Goodman, Noj and Katy Barker, Jamie and Ann Nickerson and their daughters Daisy and Flo, Clare Conville, Emily Patrick and Michael Perry, Jessica Berens, Adam and Katie Hilton, and Louise Starling are just a few of the people who have offered me refuge and help. I am particularly grateful to Tom Blofeld, a fellow children's author and his wife Leslie Felperin who gave me, when I most needed it, a home from home. And I am also indebted to Annie Blunt without whom I am not sure I would ever have managed the last hurdles.

Thank you, Aggrey Nshekanabo from Send-A-Cow in Uganda. More than just a guide and translator, you gave me so many insights into your culture.

I would like to acknowledge works that I drew on for details of elephant behaviour, among them Ian Douglas Hamilton's *Among the Elephants*; Daphne Sheldrick's *The Orphans of Tsavo*, Martin Meredith's *The African Elephant: A Biography*, Cynthia Moss's *Elephant Memories* and Rachel Payne's *Silent Thunder*.

And lastly, thank you to Bear and Flea for keeping me company during the writing.

# ABOUT THE AUTHOR

Rachel grew up in the country with her sisters and brother and a menagerie of animals which became her main companions.

She would work on the farm as a school child, and learned how to shepherd and work dogs in the Outer Hebrides. When she finished school she travelled to the Falkland Islands as a shepherd and had been there almost a year when the islands were invaded. Rachel, who at the time was taking a brief holiday in South America, couldn't go back. Instead, she moved on to Peru and found a job in the high Andes, working on an agricultural project with the indigenous people. She learned to speak Spanish and Quechua.

Rachel went to the University of Edinburgh to study Zoology but changed to read English Literature which she had always loved. In the Easter holidays she continued to shepherd in Cumbria to earn money. She spent two summer vacations in El Salvador, working in a camp for displaced people during the civil war. She drew on this experience – particularly the way war affects the lives of children – for this book.

After university, Rachel went to live in the Amazon rainforest – in a very remote area, 120km walk from the nearest village. She lived with a family of rubber tappers and learned to speak Portuguese. She was there for almost two years. She draws on her memories of this too for her children's story.

Returning to England, Rachel studied for a PhD on

modern and contemporary British poetry. She continued to travel from time to time, and most importantly to Africa, where she was introduced to the animals and way of life on the savannah by Tony Fitzpatrick. Tony had lived for many years with Joy and George Adamson on their "Born Free" camp and now looks after a wildlife reserve on the Kenyan/Tanzanian borders. Many of the details of bush life in *The Child's Elephant* come from this time. But they also come from a trip to Uganda.

After completing her PhD, Rachel joined *The Times*: first on the books pages, then as an obituarist and then as a leader writer, before, turning a long-standing interest in painting into a profession, she stepped into her current role as the art critic ten years ago.

It was as a leader writer that Rachel first found herself learning about Joseph Kony and his Lord's Resistance Army in Uganda. She recently travelled there, under the auspices of the charity Send-A-Cow, to interview former child soldiers about their experiences. And it is against the backdrop of this country and its conflict that her book *The Child's Elephant* is set.

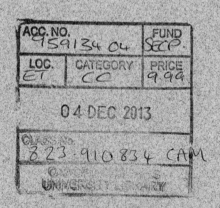